Steph Mullin is a creative director and Nicole Mabry works in the photography department for a television network. They met as co-workers in New York City in 2012, discovering a shared passion for writing and true crime. After Steph relocated to Charlotte, North Carolina in 2018, they continued to collaborate creatively. Separated by five states, they spend countless hours scheming via FaceTime and editing each other's typos in real time on Google Docs.

Nicole lives in Queens, New York, and is also the author of *Past This Point*, an award-winning apocalyptic women's fiction novel. *The Family Tree* is the duo's first crime novel.

THE FAMILY TREE

STEPH MULLIN &
NICOLE MABRY

avon.

Published by AVON
A division of HarperCollins*Publishers* Ltd
1 London Bridge Street
London SE1 9GF

www.harpercollins.co.uk

HarperCollins*Publishers*
1st Floor, Watermarque Building, Ringsend Road
Dublin 4, Ireland

A Paperback Original 2021

2

First published in Great Britain by HarperCollins*Publishers* 2021

A catalogue copy of this book is available from the British Library.

ISBN: 978-0-00-846124-9

Typeset in Sabon LT Std by Palimpsest Book Production Limited,
Falkirk, Stirlingshire
Printed and bound in UK by CPI Group (UK) Ltd, Croydon CR0 4YY

MIX
Paper from
responsible sources
FSC www.fsc.org FSC™ C007454

From Steph:
For my parents, Ann and Dave
And my husband, Danny

From Nicole:
For Mom and Dad

PROLOGUE

THE DAILY GAZETTE

Monday, April 2nd, 2012

THE TRI-STATE KILLER STRIKES AGAIN

The bodies of two Syracuse University women were found on Saturday, March 31st. They were discovered by bartender, Louis Castille, as he was disposing of the trash at the end of his shift. Castille noticed two large plastic storage containers that were sealed with duct tape, sitting next to the garbage bins in the secluded alley behind his bar. Castille called the police after opening one container and finding a body inside, which was later identified as Elizabeth Benton.

'It was terrible,' said Castille, still visibly shaken by his discovery. 'She was folded over at the waist like she was kneeling in the bin, her hair was hanging forward and blocking her face, but the smell hit me as soon as the lid was removed.'

1

The second container held the body of Kelly Davidson, Benton's roommate. The women were reported missing a little over nine months ago after they failed to show up for classes and work. After a thorough search of the small two-bedroom home the women were renting near campus, police found evidence indicating the perpetrator had broken in through a window at the back of the house, entering through the kitchen. What the police didn't find, however, were signs of a struggle, suggesting the women may have been asleep or otherwise taken by surprise during the attack.

The two deaths are believed to be the twenty-second and twenty-third victims attributed to The Tri-State Killer. To date, eleven pairs of bodies have been discovered in sealed containers across the Tri-State area. Benton and Davidson's bodies were in the early stages of decomposition, suggesting they had been killed not long before their bodies were discarded in the alley.

The Tri-State Killer is known for abducting and murdering young women in pairs, however the first killing attributed to him back in 1974, was a single victim. The body of Linda Lavelle, found dumped in the woods on a pile of assembled rocks, was connected to the subsequent double murders by the numbers penned on to each victim's forehead, including Lavelle. A statement from law enforcement noted, 'Most likely, the first murder was an unplanned victim of opportunity. This sloppiness is why our only evidence, a partial DNA sample, is from the first victim. He's been honing his craft, his method of kidnapping and murdering for almost forty years, which makes him extremely dangerous.'

A pair of victims has been found every two years since 1992, marking a distinct cyclical pattern to the killings. Other than the single DNA sample, law enforcement also has grainy CCTV camera footage from 1992 of the killer leaving a set of bins behind a restaurant, as well as a rough sketch from a botched kidnapping attempt in 1999. Both give nothing more than a general description of the killer, as he was skilled at keeping his face hidden during both sightings.

Police are cautioning women in the Tri-State Area to be on the look-out for suspicious behavior and only travel in groups of three or more, as well as to be cautious of opening their doors to strangers in the evening, and to keep doors and windows properly locked.

His fingers gripped the edge of the newspaper so tightly that it wrinkled, causing creases to ripple through the text. At the bottom of the article was the pathetic excuse for a police sketch that really didn't look anything like him except for the baseball cap. The guy in the dark, grainy image from the video footage could be anyone at all – it was almost comical, really. He laid the paper down on the scarred wooden table and sat back. They had missed several details. A sharp smile stretched across his face, lingering as he reflected on how he had outsmarted the police for so many years. While it was a mistake that he hadn't been aware of the security camera in the alley where he'd discarded numbers two and three, and he'd miscalculated the time the second roommate was arriving home that one fateful night in 1999, causing him to scramble out the back door, the fallout from both had been minimal. After forty years of carrying out his mission, they only had his approximate height and eye and hair color. He'd been savvy enough to adjust his process after that girl, Sara, had changed her routine. The solution was ingenious. It lured these women into unknowingly allowing him full access into their lives. And the police were still no closer to finding him, the imbeciles. He was not worried.

The sunlight filtered through the window above the sink, lighting up the small kitchen with its outdated appliances and broken cabinet knobs. The ancient refrigerator hummed loudly, most likely needing a new evaporator fan. He really should put some effort into fixing up the cabin, but he was getting older and even though he kept himself in good shape, the arthritis in his joints sometimes made home repairs a struggle. He preferred to save his strength for the girls. The cabin had been outfitted well for hunting and fishing, and the tiled cleaning and gutting room had certainly come in handy. But for his purposes, he'd needed other things added and adjusted. All the work he'd done in the beginning had been for function, not vanity. The appliances still worked fine, and he'd already replaced the roof when it'd been damaged by a storm a few years back. He felt lucky that in all these years the only repairs needed were the roof and the occasional broken floorboard, things he could manage on his own. If the plumbing had failed he would have been in a bind. The last thing he wanted was to bring a repair guy into his special place.

Clenching his fist, the heat rose to his cheeks as he

reread the article calling his first murder sloppy. The police didn't even use DNA evidence back then so how could he have known to be more careful? That didn't make him sloppy. He'd wiped off his fingerprints, hadn't he? All those other killers had been caught by stupid mistakes, mistakes he'd never make, and they had the audacity to call *him* sloppy? He slammed his fist down onto the table, causing his glass to tip over and crash down to the floor, shattering as it sent small slivers of glass in every direction.

A scream erupted behind him. Then another. As the screaming went on he rose from his chair and walked over to the door. He would give them a chance to stop on their own. No one would ever call him unreasonable. When the screaming continued, he pulled out the keys and unlocked the door. He gripped the handle and slowly turned. All noise stopped immediately. Satisfied, he released the knob and rubbed his hand up and down the door, savoring the grooves in the wood under his fingertips.

CHAPTER 1

'Liz, you better not have looked without me!' Andie shouted as she slammed the front door behind her, clicking the deadbolt to the locked position and throwing her keys into the bowl on the small entry table with a light *clink*.

She dropped her purse on the fifties style oval dining table that I had begrudgingly helped her drag up the stairs after she'd found it at the Brooklyn Flea. Andie had called it a 'steal' at $100, bragging about bartering it down from the original $200 price tag. I had noted the scratched legs and scuffs across the top but remained silent since Andie seemed to love it so much. The next day I contributed three chairs I'd found at a local furniture store, whose colors picked up the flecks in the tabletop. They elevated the vintage table and I had to admit, it had grown on me.

I rolled my eyes. 'Of course I didn't. I just called you five minutes ago to tell you the results were in and your very explicit threats were enough incentive to wait.'

I loved my cousin Andie and was closest to her out of

everyone in our large, loud extended family. Really, we were more like sisters than cousins and being only a year apart in age meant we did everything together growing up. Her quippy, vibrant attitude was always just what I needed to make me laugh or stop me from teetering over into what Andie referred to as my 'default serious mode.' She frequently made fun of my more responsible nature but also appreciated the way it helped keep her out of trouble. We butted heads at times but always balanced each other well. It just made sense that when we left our respective homes in New Jersey to cross over into the bustling work hive of New York City, we would be roommates to share both the memories and the expensive rent.

We'd been lucky to find a unique two-bedroom in a Greenpoint townhouse with tons of natural light that we could actually afford, something we hadn't thought was possible. While our side street was a bit rundown with boarded-up buildings scattered along the block, construction in the surrounding areas suggested improvement in the future. The townhouse was next to Belly of the Beast, a beasts of the world themed bar with a large outdoor patio. Previous tenants had complained about the noise that went on until the early hours of the morning, making it difficult for the owners to find renters, even after they'd updated the appliances and had the hardwood floors refinished. There were only three apartments in the building: the second floor occupied by a woman in her seventies who was hard of hearing, and the third-floor unit belonged to Mickey, the lead bartender at The Beast. The ground floor apartment had sat empty for over a month, a rarity in New York real estate, causing the owners to lower the price. While we had initially been avoiding ground floor units due to safety concerns, we couldn't believe the amount of space and amenities for the price. Both me and Andie slept like the dead, so when the owners nervously mentioned the issue with the noise keeping other tenants away, we'd felt like we'd hit the jackpot and signed the lease right away, pushing down any concerns and relishing the excitement over our first home.

Andie kicked off her clunky but comfy clogs and stripped shamelessly out of her green-blue scrubs as she crossed the living room before grabbing her cotton robe from a hook just inside her bedroom door. She wrapped it around herself and plopped down next to me on our blue and white striped Ikea couch, rippling the cushions and reaching for my laptop with gusto.

'Well it was me who gifted you the 23andMe kit for your birthday after all, my sweet baby cousin. Of course I want to see your results.'

'First of all,' I said, snatching the computer from Andie's reach, 'I really wish you would shower after work before getting so cozy next to me on the couch.' Andie rolled her eyes but gestured wildly at her robe. I'd yelled at her before for sitting down in her scrubs when she got home from the hospital, and apparently she thought this was a big improvement. I shivered at the idea of all the potential germs that could be clinging to her after one of her shifts. Sighing, trying to shake away those thoughts, I continued. 'And second of all, turning 27 means I'm far from being your baby anything.'

'Okay, okay,' Andie said, giving me a playful shove. 'Pull it up already!'

'Why are you so invested? You did your own last month, I'm sure my results won't be that different,' I replied as I typed my email and password into the 23andMe homepage.

'I mean we'll definitely have some similar results from our dads' Italian heritage,' Andie said as she reached forward and grabbed my glass of red wine, taking a swig.

'You could get your own glass you know; the bottle is on the kitchen counter like five feet away. Our apartment isn't *that* big.'

Andie ignored me, 'But it'll be fun to see what comes up from your mom's side.'

'Oh, you mean Italian, Italian, and some more Italian? I feel like these will be the least diverse results of all time,' I said, laughing, mimicking the large hand gestures as I spoke that were so common when anyone in my house was talking.

Andie laughed. 'It's 2019, Lizzie, get with the times. Everyone is checking their DNA these days and who knows, maybe you'll have some mixed heritage from way far back that you didn't know about. Plus, we know how much you need to know *everything, all the time*. I thought this would be right up your alley.'

'Hey, I can't help it if I have an inquisitive mind,' I said with a smirk. Andie rolled her eyes dramatically. 'But okay, I concede. It's a cool gift, alright? Let's just look at it,' I said as I clicked 'Sign In'. I could feel that familiar tingle of excitement I always got when I was on the verge of learning new information. 'Okay, so now what?'

'Click there,' Andie said, pointing to the Ancestry icon under 'Quick Links' on the left side of the page. I obeyed and a new page loaded showing a colorful wheel and a few geographical regions. 'Well that's weird.'

'What?' I asked, leaning forward to inspect the screen closer.

'I don't think those are the same as my main regions. Maybe your mom's genes influenced you more than your dad's. Click "View your ancestry composition" so we can get a more detailed breakdown,' Andie instructed.

I obliged and a new screen showing a list of what percentage of each region made up my complete DNA profile appeared on the page. 'That's interesting,' I said as my eyes scanned the information. 'It's saying my relatives are mainly from Mexico and Northwestern Europe. How is Italy not in the top two? What did yours say?'

'Predominately Southern European, with lots of Italy and Spain or Portugal.' She hesitated for a moment, her normally lively eyes looking a little anxious. 'Click the "Family and Friends" thing at the top and let's look at your relatives list so we can compare our results,' Andie said after a long pause.

'Okay, let's see . . .' I said, glancing at her out of the corner of my eye, not sure why she was fidgeting all of a sudden. I navigated to the screen showing my complete list of relatives in the 23andMe customer database. 'Where are you?' I said, scrolling down the first page of results. I didn't recognize any of the names listed. Andrea Catalano was nowhere to be seen. 'We have the same last name, how are you not on my list?'

'Yeah, this is crazy,' Andie replied, a look of confusion and worry etched deep into her warm brown eyes.

'I'm calling my mom,' I said as face recognition unlocked my iPhone. 'Clearly something weird is going on here.'

'Yeah, good idea,' Andie said as I quickly typed out a message asking my mom if she had time to talk. In typical loving-but-overbearing mother fashion, my phone immediately started ringing in my hand.

11

'Hey Mom,' I said as I answered the FaceTime call.

'Hi sweetie, how's everything going? Did you see that article I sent you yesterday about that new dating app everyone's using that matches you with friends of friends of friends? Maybe you should give it a try? You know I worry about you girls being all alone in that apartment. I know Andie has her boyfriend, but it would be nice if—'

'Yes, Mother, I saw it,' I interrupted with an exaggerated sigh, cutting her off before she really got going.

Ever since I'd dumped my last boyfriend Evan for cheating on me three months ago, my mom had nagged me about dating and her desire for grandchildren every chance she got. I'd caught Evan cheating with a coworker of his and that was the end of that. I didn't even cry when he tried to explain that he'd fallen in love with this other woman and that he hadn't meant to hurt me. Instead, I'd smashed his phone under my foot and stormed out. I'd told my mom countless times that I wasn't ready to date yet, that I needed more time, but Catalanos had a history of marrying young and my mom was anxious to become a grandma. I hadn't told her about the couple of dates I'd gone on in the last month for fear of her getting too excited about dates that would probably go nowhere. I had found something fundamentally wrong with each of them: too clingy, too messy, too boring. No matter how much my mom wanted me to be in a relationship, after dipping my toe in the dating waters I knew I just wasn't able to let anyone in yet. Keeping the dates from her had been nagging at me, as that was so out of character for our relationship, but I couldn't bear the full court press after each failed date. I would fill her in eventually.

12

'Hey Aunt Carmela!' Andie called out, leaning into the frame, almost pushing me out of it.

'Oh, hi Andrea. What are you two up to this evening?' My mom's enthusiastic smile radiated on the screen, and I was thankful for the change in topic away from my struggling love life.

'I'm not sure if I told you, but Andie gave me a DNA ancestry test kit for my birthday after we got back from the party at Gram's, and I just got my results in,' I said, trying to take the frame back over from where Andie had squeezed in.

'Oh, really? A DNA kit?' I noticed a twitch in my mom's smile as it fell. The color drained from her normally rosy cheeks.

'Yeah,' I hesitated, nervous by my mom's reaction. 'It tells you, based on percentages, what regions your ancestors came from and connects you with other family that have done the same kit. But it's weird, Mom.' Now, my mom was definitely fidgeting, her eyes darting out of the frame. And was I crazy or did I see the glint of a tear on her lashes? Maybe it was just the lighting, I rationalized, but then a crazy thought popped into my head. *Did my mom have an affair? Is my dad not really my dad?* A wave of fear swelled inside me but I quickly tried to tamp it down. 'Andie isn't showing up on my relatives list even though she did a kit too and our geographic regions are totally different. Is there something you have to tell me? Why wouldn't Andie and I be related?'

'Gary!' my mom called out over her shoulder.

'Mom, what's going on?'

'Gary!' she shouted out again instead of answering me. 'Can you come in here for a minute? I'm on FaceTime with Elizabeth.'

13

'What's our little Lizard up to tonight?' My dad said in his usual *I'm so funny* voice as he descended down the stairs and came into the frame.

'She did one of those DNA kits, Gary,' she told him, looking somber.

'Oh,' he said as the smile dropped from his face, sitting down next to her. He looked anxious, not an emotion I was used to seeing from my charming, goofy dad. He averted his eyes and looked at my mom. 'Well, we knew this day would come eventually.'

'Can someone please tell me what's going on?' I demanded, sharing a confused glance with Andie who was watching with rapt attention.

'Oh, Lizzie,' my mom said, a wobble in the video as she readjusted her grip on her own phone. 'There's something we have to tell you.' My dad nodded.

'Well, what is it?' I asked, on the edge of the couch cushion. My dad put his arm around my mom's shoulders before answering.

'We've debated telling you this for years, Lizzie, but the timing just never seemed right. You're always going to be our little girl and we just wanted to protect you. We didn't want to see you hurt or confused.'

'Dad, you're scaring me. Just tell me what's going on.' I could feel anxiety filling up my chest like an inflating balloon, ready to burst from the tension.

After a shared look, my mom finally said quietly and gently, 'You're adopted, sweetie.'

'What?!' I exclaimed in surprise. I looked at Andie, sitting next to me in stunned silence. She was staring at the screen, eyes wide and mouth agape. I had been mentally preparing for them to drop a horrible bomb on

14

me about my dad, but to not be related to either of them? I couldn't believe it.

'We adopted you as a baby. You came home with us from the hospital only a few days after you were born, so you see, you've always been ours. We've never thought of you as adopted. We'd waited years to be blessed with a baby after we couldn't conceive and you answered our prayers.' My mom was openly crying now, Dad hugging her close to his body.

'Adopted?' I whispered in disbelief. My world, everything I knew about myself and my identity, seemed to be crumbling around me. It couldn't be true. 'How could you keep this from me? My whole life?' My parents, the people who'd shaped who I was today, were not really my parents. Everything I knew about myself was a lie. Large, hot tears burned paths down my cheeks, crossing over my quivering lips. I felt Andie place an arm around my shoulders and squeeze.

'Oh, Lizzie,' my dad said. 'You came from a tough background, kiddo. Your birth mother was young and troubled. She gave birth when she was in prison for drug charges, and we didn't want you to think less of yourself or where you came from. We just wanted to protect you. We've always felt you are truly our daughter, regardless of who your biological parents are.' His voice was begging for forgiveness and understanding but I could barely look either of them in the eyes.

'I had a right to know!' I shouted, upset and lost in a spiral of confusing emotions racing around my brain. I dropped the phone, jumping up from the couch and pacing the room. Absentmindedly, I swiped at the tears and snot that were streaming down my face. Andie scrambled to pick up the phone, but for the first time in my life, she was speechless.

'Please sit down, Lizzie, so we can explain,' my dad said. 'We're so sorry we didn't tell you sooner.'

After a long pause, I circled back to the couch and sat down. I took the phone back from Andie and tried to compose my thoughts.

'Does the whole family know?'

My mom looked at my dad and then said, 'No, not everyone. Your aunts and uncles do, and of course your grandparents. They knew how much we wanted a baby and supported our decision to adopt, but they've kept it to themselves by our request. Your cousins don't know.'

I felt like my heart had been shattered into a million pieces. My entire life a good portion of my family had known the truth about me while I had no clue. I glanced at Andie's worried face, grateful that at least she hadn't lied to me all these years.

I took a deep breath and exhaled, trying to calm my anger. 'What happened to her? My biological mother? And what about my father?' I had so many questions, I needed to know it all.

'We don't know anything else,' my mom responded, wiping the tears from her own eyes. 'It was a closed adoption; she didn't want anyone to contact her once she gave you up. All we know is she went to prison in New York on drug charges and the agency didn't have any information on who the father was. We just wanted to protect you, Elizabeth,' my mom said, pleading in her voice. 'We love you so much.'

There was a long, awkward silence. I sniffled, wiping the tears falling from my eyes. My parents shared a troubled look. My dad whispered under his breath, 'I

16

knew we shouldn't have waited so long to tell her. I didn't want her to find out like this.' He rubbed his chin, eyes full of uncertainty.

I never thought my parents would have been capable of keeping anything from me, let alone something of this magnitude. We'd always been so close, calling ourselves The Three Amigos, sharing every gory detail of our lives with one another. I'd even told my mom the first time I had sex. My friends had thought I was crazy, but I hadn't been able to imagine not sharing something so important with my mom, my best friend. How could my parents have kept this from me? My whole, big, loving Italian family that encompassed so much of my identity and was all I'd ever known, was all a lie.

'Are you still coming to family dinner on Sunday?' my mom asked hopefully. 'I know this is a lot to take in but you're still our baby. We should talk more about this in person.'

'I don't know, Mom,' I said at last. My head was spinning, my heart racing. The phone was hard to grip, my palms were so clammy. I felt nauseated, like when you start to feel hungover from a big day of drinking before you even fall asleep. 'This is . . . a lot,' I finally mustered.

'Please don't pull away from us. I know we should have been more upfront with you, but we're still your family and we want to help you through this,' my mom replied.

'I need time to think, okay? I'll talk to you guys later. I just need some space to figure things out.'

My mom looked sad and worried as she glanced at my dad. They nodded. 'Okay, Lizzie,' he conceded. 'But we're here for you, for anything you need.'

I nodded and with an abrupt wave at the screen, hung up. I threw the phone down on the couch next to me and rubbed my eyes. When I looked up, Andie's face was inches from mine, mouth hanging open, eyes wide in complete shock. 'Wow,' was all she said as she opened her arms to pull me into a hug.

Tears poured freely down my cheeks as I leaned my head onto her shoulder. 'This is insane, Andie. I don't know anything about my family or myself anymore. I went from having like forty close relatives to zero. Who am I? Where did I come from?'

'First of all,' she said after a long moment, pulling back just enough to look at me. 'I'm always your family no matter what. And second, you have a whole list of potential relatives right there at your fingertips.' She gestured at the laptop on the table. 'Thanks to an extremely generous gift from your amazing and beautiful cousin, which should not be thought less of just because it imploded your whole world.'

I laughed despite myself. 'Shut up, Andie,' and wiped my tears on the back of my hand.

Andie laughed and said, 'But in all seriousness, you can click into the relatives you have the highest percentage DNA match with and send them a message. Maybe some of them will get back to you and be able to tell you more about your bio-family.'

'Really?' I said, sniffling again.

'Yeah, here, let me show you.'

VICTIM 1

Linda Lavelle

1974

CHAPTER 2

He watched as she placed her hand on the guy's chest, laughing at some lame joke he'd made. The two kissed for a moment before the girl pulled away. The guy tried to draw her back in but she pushed harder and took a step back. She buttoned up her leather patchwork trench coat and tied the belt around her waist. Flicking her long blonde feathered hair over her shoulder, she exhaled loudly.

'John, I have a boyfriend. I can't just go making out with every guy I meet. He's the really big, jealous type, so you better watch out.' She giggled.

'So, where's your boyfriend now?' John looked around. 'Funny, but I don't see him anywhere.'

She laughed again. 'He's in his dorm room studying. Look, you're really sweet but I have to go. I don't want my friends to leave without me. They're my ride to the party.'

John protested and tried to pull her back but she slowly strutted away with a playful smile and a wave.

John conceded defeat. 'Okay okay, be like that, then.

Check ya later,' he said as he turned to walk in the opposite direction.

The man who had been watching the disgusting display followed in her wake. When she got to the empty parking lot, she looked around and groaned.

'Dammit,' she said, stomping her brown leather heeled boot. She glanced to her left and spotted a payphone.

The man walked toward his car as if he were there organically. When he crossed her path he said, 'Hi there, are you okay?'

Her steps faltered and she said, 'Yeah, my friends already left so I'm gonna call a cab.' She pointed to the phone booth still several yards away.

'A cab? That'll take at least thirty minutes to show up. I can give you a ride, if you want. Where are you going?'

She hesitated. 'Oh, thanks, but that's okay. I can wait for a cab.'

She took a few more steps toward the phone booth but he persisted. 'With the game just ending it could take even longer and my car's right there,' he said, pointing to his car parked by the streetlamp. 'I can drop you off wherever you need to go on my way. I'm just heading back to Albany. I really don't mind.'

The man was wearing a University Football t-shirt and had a cute smile. Not the kind of guy she'd go out with but he seemed nice enough. She was anxious to get to the party and furious at her friends for leaving her. At the same time, it was kind of her own fault for lingering with John. While he was definitely a stone-cold fox, she had no intentions of sleeping with another guy. She hadn't lied about her boyfriend being jealous. Glancing back at the payphone, she realized the man was right.

She'd waited before for cabs that took forever and sometimes never came at all.

The man smiled at her again and leaned forward, 'Come
on, a girl like you shouldn't have to wait around in a
deserted parking lot for a ride. You're too pretty to be
kept waiting,' he said, winking at her.

She smiled and looked the man up and down. He
seemed harmless enough. Certainly better than that guy
Eddie in the battered station wagon who'd picked up
her and her best friend, Shannon, last week when they'd
hitchhiked to the Three Dog Night concert. He'd creeped
Linda out but no one else had been willing to pull over,
so they'd reluctantly gotten in the car for fear of being
late to the concert.

She bit her lip, glanced at the man's pristine Camaro
and then back at him. After weighing her options, she
said, 'Okay thanks, if it's not a problem. I really appreciate it. I'm not going far, just a short drive down to
Genesee Street. It's pretty close to the freeway so it
shouldn't take you out of your way too much.'

'Not a problem at all,' the man said as he loaded his
duffel bag into the back seat. Linda noticed the muscles
in his arms and back bulging with each movement.
He was in good shape. If he were a bit more attractive,
she might have been interested. But his face was too
wide, his nose too large and his skin showed the remnants
of bad teenage acne. After a slight moment of hesitation,
she got into the passenger seat and waited for him to
come around and start the car.

She reached her hand across and said, 'I'm Linda.
Thanks again, you're a real life-saver.'

They shook hands and he smiled at her but didn't offer
his name in return. He turned on the radio and Elton

John's *The Bitch Is Back* blared through the speakers. 'I love this song,' she said, shimmying her shoulders back and forth. The man watched her move out of the corner of his eye as he drove out of the parking lot. 'You go to school at U of A?'

'Yeah, U of A,' he said, nodding his head as he clicked on the blinker and turned left. He glanced at her, then quickly averted his eyes. *Guess he's not a big talker,* she thought. *He'd seemed much chattier before we got in the car.* Determined to fill the silence and make the ride less awkward, Linda rambled on about going to school at Syracuse, shooting him smiles and laughing as she recounted stories of her and her friends.

'You probably drive all the men wild, don't you?' he interrupted, glancing sideways at her for a brief moment.

She playfully swatted his arm, her hand lingering on his bicep for a few seconds. He stared down at her hand, then turned his eyes back to the road. Linda, distracted by the story she was telling him and the song pumping through the speakers, didn't notice that he'd turned down the wrong street. Finally, the song ended and The Eagles' *Already Gone* came on. She frowned and turned the volume down.

'Not a fan of that song. Reminds me of my ex-boyfriend, Ted.' She looked around, squinting into the darkness outside, and said, 'Hey, I think you might have taken a wrong turn. Genesee is back that way.' She hooked her thumb toward the rear window. He slowed the car and pulled over to the side of the road. She looked at him and laughed nervously. 'What are you doing?'

He slid his arm around her shoulders along the back of the seat and leaned closer. 'You're real pretty.'

She laughed again nervously and leaned away toward

her window, trying to put distance between them. 'Thanks, but look, I have a boyfriend. You're really nice but I just can't, I'm sorry. You understand, right?' She smiled and blinked her eyes a few times.

'I saw you kissing John after the game. Seems like having a boyfriend doesn't stop you.'

'How do you know his name? Were you watching us?' her voice wavered and her smile slowly fell. He leaned in and tried to kiss her, but she turned her head and put her hands on his chest, pushing him away. 'John was a mistake. I shouldn't have done that. I'm really not that kind of girl.' She tried to smile again but the fear in her eyes was evident. 'You're just . . . not my type, okay? I'm sorry. I really am.'

His face hardened. 'Not your type? So, you just go around flirting with guys and leading them on?'

'No, I didn't flirt with you, this is all a big misunderstanding. I was just being nice because you offered to drive me to the party. Look, I'll just walk from here. Thanks for the ride,' she said, her fingers pulling up the lock on the door.

His breath came quicker and he could feel the telltale heat rise to his ears. His heart was beating so fast that his hands shook. *How dare she reject him!* Just as she reached for the door handle, he retracted his extended arm until his hand was hovering behind her head. The urge overcame him. He grabbed a fistful of hair.

'Ouch! Wait a minute . . .' she yelled.

He slammed her forehead into the dashboard. Linda screamed and started crying, begging him to let her go. He pulled her head back and slammed it forward again before letting her limp body lean back against the seat. Blood covered a round wound on her forehead. As her head lolled to the side, a trickle of blood slid down between her eyes. He quickly made a U-turn and headed back to the highway. She was quiet now. Just as she should be.

CHAPTER 3

I gripped my bottle of hard cider and gave an audible sigh. 'It's been two weeks. I can't believe none of the people I messaged on 23andMe have replied.'

Andie moved her hand from where it rested on her boyfriend, Travis's, leg to reach over and give my hand a reassuring squeeze. 'I know it's frustrating, girl, but I'm sure people don't see their messages right away. Maybe they don't have email notifications set up or just don't pop in there very often after getting their initial results. It doesn't mean you won't ever hear back.'

'I know,' I said, taking a long sip. 'I'm just getting impatient. I want to know more about my family right now.' I slammed my fist into the back of the couch on the last word. 'You know me,' I said, biting anxiously at my lip.

'Oh yeah, I know how much you hate not knowing things. Honestly, as shocked as I am that your parents kept this from you, I'm even more shocked that they were able to.'

I snorted through my frustration.

'What do you mean?' Travis asked.

'I know you haven't really experienced Lizzie's laser focus when she's on the hunt, but let's just put it this way, when she wants to find something out, there's no stopping her.'

'What can I say? It's what I do,' I replied smugly, patting myself on the back.

Turning back to me, Andie said, 'Yeah, yeah. Remember that time a pipe burst and flooded my house and I had to spend the night with you on Christmas Eve? Your dad made us watch the first three *Star Wars* movies, and then what happened that night, Liz?' Andie asked, squinting her eyes at me.

'Andie, I was thirteen.'

She leaned forward, playfully punching me in the upper arm. 'My point exactly. The sickness started early in this one,' she said in her best Darth Vader voice.

'Do, or do not. There is no try,' I replied in a mangled attempt at Yoda. As much as we'd groaned about my dad making us watch the originals, we'd actually loved them, even though we'd never admitted that to my dad.

Andie and I burst out laughing. 'Wait, what happened on Christmas Eve?' Travis interrupted.

When Andie caught her breath, she said, 'Oh, right. Well, Liz really wanted her own computer in her room to . . .' she pulled up her fingers to mime air quotes, '. . . do schoolwork.' She glanced at me with a sly smile. 'But what she *really* wanted was to secretly make a Myspace profile and keep tabs on everyone at school. Amirite?' I shrugged my shoulders, neither confirming nor denying the accusation. Andie rolled her eyes back to Travis. 'Anyway, she talked me into sneaking downstairs after her parents went to bed. She opened every single one of

28

her gifts looking for the computer and then rewrapped them so her parents wouldn't know. She couldn't even wait a few hours.' Andie laughed, shaking her head. 'She totally got away with it, too.'

Travis looked back at me. 'So, did you get the computer?'

I gave him a sly smile. 'Yep. And the world cracked open for me.' I spread my arms out wide before dropping them back in my lap. My smile fell as my current reality came rushing back. 'So, you can see why this is especially hard. I'm at this roadblock and I don't know how to get through it. How do I connect with my biological family if no one is responding?'

'Well, you could try doing some more kits. Maybe you have family who tested through different DNA companies and you can find more relatives that way? Could be worth a shot,' Andie said, before taking a swig of her own cider.

'Have you ever heard of GEDMatch?' Travis chimed in, stretching one long arm around Andie's shoulder as he looked across at me.

Andie and Travis had been dating for over a year and the three of us had become pretty close. Travis had proven himself worthy of infiltrating my and Andie's tight knit bond, graciously letting me be a third wheel on some of their dates once I became single.

'GEDMatch?' I asked. 'No, what's that?'

'I heard some people talking about it at my law firm recently,' Travis said. 'Apparently it's this website where you can upload your DNA profile and check for any matches across all ancestry platforms without actually doing every single company's kit. Other relatives would have to have uploaded to GEDMatch in order for them to show up in your results, but you might be able to track more of them down.'

29

'Wait, really?' I said, my heart beating faster. 'Andie, hand me my laptop, let's check it out.'

Andie grabbed my laptop off the wooden shelf under the coffee table and handed it to me. I quickly navigated to the GEDMatch homepage.

Hastily scanning the introductory page detailing how to use the website, I said out loud, 'Oh, amazing. There's a free version you can use. Why not, right?' I looked up at them, seeking affirmation.

'Absolutely. How do you do it?' Andie said, scooting further away from her boyfriend and closer to me. He gave an audible sigh, picking up his beer off the table and leaning back, but he didn't look bothered. I'd overheard a conversation between Travis and Andie one night where Andie had informed him that sometimes putting me before him was part of the package deal of dating her. I had felt bad at first, like I was intruding too much, but he had been kind about it and told Andie that she was worth it and it wasn't a big deal since he liked me anyway. The way he'd handled it in stride had gained him a lot of points in my book. I tried to be conscious of not putting myself between them, but in times like this, I was grateful he was letting me have Andie's full attention.

'I just need to download my raw DNA profile from 23andMe and then upload that to GEDMatch's website.'

'Seems easy enough,' Andie said, walking through the process with me. 'Trav, you're a genius,' she said with a big smile, gripping her fingers into his short beard as she kissed him. Used to their PDA, I ignored them and clicked 'yes' to approve the use of my data, as it said this was the only way I could get match results.

'Oh, look. This is interesting,' I said, pointing to the

next option, which I could tick to allow law enforcement to access my results.

Andie squinted at the screen. 'Didn't your dad say your bio-mom was in jail?'

'Yeah, that's the only thing my parents knew about her. She was young and went to jail in New York, they think on drug charges.'

'Maybe you should opt in?' Travis said, running a hand through his brown wavy hair. 'Can't hurt, right? I'm not sure how it works but if your mom has a record, maybe connecting with the police is another way to find stuff out about her.'

I considered what he was saying. 'I don't think any-thing bad could come of it, do you?' I looked to Andie for reassurance.

'Do it. You've been a relentlessly law-abiding citizen your whole damn life. I don't think you have anything to worry about. It's not like they're going to find your blood at a crime scene or something and nail you with a murder.'

'Yeah, you're probably right,' I laughed. I was always a little paranoid about living my life to the letter of the law, no matter how many times Andie tried to lure me into questionable adventures. It was impossible for them to link me to any type of crime. 'Okay, why not?' I clicked the box to opt in.

We stared at the screen, impatiently sipping our drinks in tense silence as the upload took its time completing. When it finished, the site said that it could take a few days for full matches to populate, so, closing my laptop, I leaned back into the couch and smiled.

'Thanks for the idea, Trav.'

'No problem,' he said, placing his bottle back down on the table. 'Okay, so what's the plan tonight, ladies?'

'I saw that Brooklyn Bridge Park is doing one of those outdoor movies tonight. Wanna grab snacks and go?' Andie said eagerly. She loved any excuse to sit outside with a bottle of rosé stashed in her purse.

'Ooh good idea, let's look up which movie's playing,' I said, popping the laptop screen back open.

'Sounds good to me,' Travis said. 'Oh, and you know what, Liz? I just had another thought. You should ask your parents which adoption agency they used. They can be pretty hard to get info out of for legal reasons, but now that you're an adult you may be able to reach out to them for information about your records.'

'I can't believe I didn't think of that,' I said, annoyed with myself about how obvious the idea was.

'Don't be too hard on yourself, Lizzie,' Andie said. 'He's got that whole, practical-lawyer-brain thing going on.' She laughed at the look on his face, unsure if it was an insult or a compliment. Andie liked to teeter on the edge of that distinction frequently.

'True,' I said with a distracted smile, crafting a text to my parents asking for the information, while Andie snatched the laptop from me to look for the movie details.

I'd been dodging my parents' calls since I got my results, sending them short text messages in response, not quite ready to face talking to them about all this yet. I felt a little sad, maybe even guilty, wondering how they were doing. I was sure this whole situation was hard for them too, and I was torn about whether I should work through my feelings with them or on my own. But I was still hurt by their deceit and I wasn't quite ready to let them back in. I needed this information though, so I hoped they felt bad enough that they would just give it to me without a fuss.

'Looks like the movie playing is a nice throwback, *Juno*.' Andie arched one eyebrow, 'Into it? Or is the whole adoption thing hitting a little too close to home?'

'Shut up, Andie,' I laughed, giving her a playful shove.

VICTIMS 2 & 3

Catherine Martin & Ruby Williams

1991

CHAPTER 4

Ruby heard the knock on the door as she teased her limp hair as high as she could in the hallway mirror. She sprayed Aqua Net liberally over the newly-formed waterfall bangs to cement them in place and dropped her brush on the small table underneath the mirror. Cathy, her roommate, was taking a shower, getting ready for the party at Omega Phi Delta. The research Ruby still had to do for her Comparative Politics paper nagged at the back of her mind, making her reconsider going tonight. Cathy's Art History major didn't take up as much of her free time as Ruby's Political Science major, and she had to admit, she was jealous of Cathy's schedule. But a record number of women were running for the United States Senate in the upcoming election and Ruby hoped to add her name to that list someday.

Ruby looked at the clock as she moved to answer the door. *Who would be stopping by at eight-thirty at night?* she thought. *And when am I going to have time to research this paper?* When she opened the door, a tall

37

man wearing dark blue pants, a button up shirt and a plain grey baseball cap greeted her holding a clipboard.

'Hello, sorry to disturb you, ma'am, but we've had reports of a gas smell in the neighborhood. We're checking valves to make sure there are no leaks. Do you mind if I check your stove, oven and water heater?'

'Oh, sure. I haven't smelled anything but it's an old building so it's possible. Come on in.'

As the man walked to the kitchen, he looked around their small apartment and then back at Ruby and smiled. He pulled out a device, hovering it over the stove and checking the gauge. Ruby walked over and inhaled. She smelled no trace of gas. She glanced at the man.

'Find anything?'

'Oh yeah, I found something that badly needs to be fixed.'

Ruby's eyebrows came together. 'Really? I don't smell anything,' she said, putting her nose closer to the stove.

'You don't smell that?' he said, sniffing deeply. 'Because I smell a whore.'

'What?' Her head snapped up towards the man just as the needle entered her arm.

Her eyes widened and before she could scream, he clasped his hand over her mouth. She clawed at his strong arms, her hands slipping helplessly off the fabric as she kicked her legs wildly. She tried jamming her finger in his eye but she was getting weaker, her limbs feeling sluggish and heavy, and he easily shrugged her hand away from his face like he was swatting an annoying fly. In a last-ditch effort she kicked her foot back against his knee. He grunted in pain and released her. She collapsed down to the floor, trying desperately to scream but all that came out were hoarse, weak pleas. Her eyes were still open, still seeing, still terrified, but her legs were no longer responding. The man crouched down and stared at her, his dark brown eyes boring into her own as if he were savoring her fear.

Ruby distantly registered the sound of the shower turning off and her tear-filled eyes darted to the hallway that led to the bathroom. She was getting drowsier and weaker with each passing second, darkness crawling into the corners of her vision as she struggled to stay conscious. The man swiftly darted away from the kitchen, ducking into an open room at the end of the hall. He flattened his body against the wall, another needle in his hand poised to strike from the shadows. Ruby tried again to yell a warning to Cathy but it came out as only a whisper. She heard Cathy open the bathroom door, heard her singing *Hold On* by Wilson Phillips as she walked down the hall to her bedroom: the room where the intruder lay in wait. Cathy came into view wearing her favorite fluffy pink bathrobe, rubbing her hair vigorously with a grey towel. When she caught sight of Ruby on the floor, she paused for a long second, confused. Before she could react, the man leaped forward and plunged the needle into her neck. She screamed but the man trapped her in his muscular arms and covered her mouth, muffling the sound just as he had with Ruby. Cathy thrashed, screaming through his fingers. Whatever he'd injected them with was taking longer on her. But finally her body relaxed and he watched with a smile as she slunk down to the floor. The two women looked at each other from the ground just ten feet apart. Tears were falling from Cathy's eyes.

CHAPTER 5

Sitting at my desk in my office in Midtown, I mumbled the words under my breath as I read through the fourth article of the morning on Saint Anthony's Feast, an Italian festival taking place in Boston over the upcoming weekend, making sure I had every fact checked before approving my post to Facebook. My boss had encouraged me to start posting about events that could revolve around a day or weekend trip so we could diversify and grow our audience. Working on the social media team at Sway, I got to attend a wide variety of events to feature on our site. Our followers relied on us for honest entertainment reviews, so I always made sure it would be worth their time and money.

After being raised in a loud, Italian family, picking Saint Anthony's Feast to focus on this month was a no-brainer for me. I'd dreamed of dancing along to the music in the street and tasting all the fresh mozzarella and pasta that I could get my hands on. Now that I knew I didn't have Italian blood coursing through my veins after all, I felt like a phony as I drummed-up hype on an event that looked different through the new lens of my true history.

Clicking through a few links on the last news article I was browsing, my eyes caught sight of a photo of two young women. It was paired with the headline, *BOSTON ROOMMATES DAVIS AND WILSON STILL MISSING NINE MONTHS LATER*.

That's so sad, I thought to myself as I took in their features. They looked similar in age to myself and Andie, living together just like us. *Hopefully they're found soon.* Although I knew after that much time had passed, the odds of a happy outcome went down drastically. I hoped they'd run away together and started a new life somewhere else, instead of the darker but more likely scenario. Just as I was ready to cave into temptation and click the news article to read more, feeling the all too familiar itch to know the details, I caught sight of the time and realized I had to get my post up ASAP. I quickly clicked back to Facebook and proofed my copy one last time.

Normally I would be eager to get ahead on research for future posts but it'd been hard to focus on work recently, as my thoughts constantly fell on the mystery of my biological family. A notification popped up on my screen, grabbing my attention from my mindless Instagram scrolling. *The adoption agency, finally!* I leaned forward on my seat, clicking the email and reading it quickly. My excitement turned to disappointment as I reached the end.

My mom had begrudgingly given me the name of the adoption agency after several rounds of 'You'll always be my mom no matter what I find.' But the first time I called, the agency turned out to be a dead end. Since it had been a closed adoption they couldn't legally give me any more information than I already had. My records were sealed and the chances of obtaining my original birth certificate were slim. They'd told me the adoption laws in New York City were some of the most restrictive in the country. I'd reached out to them repeatedly, by both phone and email, but kept getting the same result. I'd made one last effort, asking them to escalate my case to upper management, but it was clear that hadn't worked. My frustration mounted at all the roadblocks I kept hitting as I re-read the latest correspondence.

Ms Catalano,

As I mentioned to you on the phone during our last call, the only way we are able to release your original birth certificate is with a court order. This is usually only granted for medical purposes in life or death circumstances. I understand this is a difficult situation for you and your family and I am sorry I cannot be of more help. While we cannot assist you in your request, you may wish to look into the Adoption Information Registry. The Registry can share non-identifying information, like religion, general appearance, and occupation of biological parents who have adopted out their children. I hope this is of some help and comfort to you.

Best wishes,

Darla Kinney

I sighed, leaning back heavily in my seat. I had submitted my form into the Adoption Information Registry website after one of my previous conversations with the adoption agency, hoping to at least get a little more information on my biological parents. Unfortunately, the confirmation email said it could take up to six months. I knew it wasn't likely to help me much in finding my biological parents anyway, but I wanted to explore every avenue.

Not able to concentrate on work anymore after taking this hit on my search for answers, I logged off and grabbed my purse.

'Hey girls, I'm heading out, I'll see you tomorrow,' I said quickly to Lilli and Megan, the other two women on my team who sat next to me in our corner. They called out goodbyes as I hustled out the door, riding the elevator down and pushing into the wall of humidity outside. Ignoring the sweat building under my silk blouse, I jogged down the subway stairs and felt a wave of relief at the cooler gust of air as the train whooshed into the station just as I hit the platform.

After exiting the train in Greenpoint, I pulled my phone out and shot a text back to my boss who had sent me a question just when I'd lost service underground. I hit send and looked up as I reached my block, my eyes landing on a family of three walking in my direction. A very pregnant woman waddled uncomfortably behind a young girl in light blue denim overalls. She looked to be about three years old and was holding her dad's hand singing *Pop Goes the Weasel*. I smiled at the girl's energy as she skipped down the street, her golden blonde ringlets bouncing with each step. When they got closer, the girl slowed to a walk and turned to place her palm on her mom's belly.

'Mommy, did I come from inside there, too?'

My breath caught in my throat, my steps faltering. Mom and Dad shared a quick, amused glance before looking down lovingly at their daughter.

The dad crouched down and said, 'Yes, you did. Mommy kept you safe in her belly for nine months before we got to meet you. And now she's doing the same for your brother, Jordan.'

'Can I go in there and say hi to him? Pleeeeease, Daddy.'

Both parents laughed and I found myself smiling along with them. The dad straightened and the mom stroked her daughter's hair as they continued down the block. 'I'm sorry sweetie, but you have to be patient. He'll be coming any day now,' she said with a warm smile in my direction as they passed by me.

The child looked at me, smiled and waved her chubby little hand. I waved back and as they walked away, the child said, 'Mommy, why is that lady crying?'

Startled, I swiped at my cheek and my hand came away wet with tears. *What is wrong with me?* Shaking my head, I wiped away the rest with the sleeve of my shirt. My emotions were all over the place and, what was worse, I felt like I couldn't control them anymore. Taking a deep breath, I pulled out my keys and made my way into our building. As I slid the key into our front door, my iPhone dinged. Glancing at my email, I gasped when I saw I had a notification on 23andMe. I quickly opened the door and slammed it shut behind me. After jumping over the top of our low sofa and collapsing onto the cushions, I opened my laptop. The minute my messages loaded on the 23andMe page, I noticed it was a reply to one of the messages I'd sent over two weeks ago. I'd messaged about twenty of my closest matches, most predicting a first or second cousin relation. In my emails, I gave them my age for reference and said I'd been adopted out of New York City as a baby but only recently found out. I outlined what little information I had on my birth mother. Not one of them had replied until now. The message in my inbox was from a man named Cristian Dominio. I excitedly clicked on the message.

Dear Elizabeth,

I am sorry for the delay in responding. We've recently been dealing with a death in the family, so I haven't been online very much. Our match is coming up as either a first or second cousin, but I don't think that is possible. You see, I'm 65 years old. However, you mentioned your birth mother was incarcerated when she gave birth. My brother had a daughter who was in jail in New York City nearly 27 years ago, around the time when you would have been born. Given the information you provided and the fact that, from your photo, you do look a lot like Teresa, it seems likely that my niece was your birth mother. If so, we were never told she was pregnant, nor do I know if my brother was ever aware. He certainly never mentioned it to me or my wife. Teresa chose a rough path and for many years, she was estranged from the family. It would not shock me to learn that she had kept this from us. Feel free to reach out if you'd like to know more.

Sincerely,

Cristian

I stared at the email, reading it over and over, a tear escaping as I accepted this new gift of information. Teresa. My mother's name was Teresa. That little piece of knowledge made me happy in a way I didn't think was possible since this whole ordeal began. I swirled the name around my mouth, saying it out loud, enjoying the way it rolled off my tongue. *My biological mother is Teresa.* I smiled and a short laugh escaped. Having a name to attach to her made everything feel so real. If I connected with Cristian and they were no longer estranged, would he be able to put me in contact with her? Or at least give me some insight on how to track her down? And then another feeling seeped in, spreading through me like wildfire. Nerves. What little I knew about Teresa sounded so different from who I was. What if she was still a drug user? Or didn't want to get to know me at all? She'd opted for a closed adoption, after all. I wasn't sure if I could handle finding her, only to have her slam the door in my face. But I needed to see what my life would have looked like if she hadn't given me up.

A glass of wine was sorely needed as I mentally crafted my response. I hopped up and went to the fridge, the laughter and clinking glasses from the bar outside filtering through the thinly sealed windows like white noise, the soundtrack to my messy life. There was still at least one glass left of the sauvignon blanc Andie and I had shared last night while watching a movie, so I grabbed that from inside the refrigerator door. As I poured the wine, I thought about the email from Cristian. My grand uncle. I needed to know more about my mother and I still had no information about my father or any other living relatives. Settling into the couch, I pulled my computer close to me again. After taking a large gulp of wine, I set it down and hit the 'Reply' button on the page.

Dear Cristian,
Thank you so much for responding. I'm sorry for the loss your family experienced recently. I haven't had much luck connecting with relatives on this site

until your message hit my inbox. From everything you've told me, it does seem like Teresa was my biological mother, which I guess would make you my grand uncle. I can't tell you how much it means to know I resemble her. Since I found out I'm adopted, I've been feeling disconnected and lost. I noticed from your profile that you live in Connecticut. I'm wondering if you'd be willing to meet? I'd love to get to know you and hear more about my mother. If you know how to contact her, I would really appreciate the opportunity to speak with her as well. My job hours are flexible so I could drive up on a day that suits you. Let me know what you think.
Best,
Liz

My finger hovered over the 'Send' button. Before I could talk myself out of it, I squeezed my eyes shut and clicked. I sat back and imagined a thousand different scenarios. My uncle greeting me with open arms and a kiss on the cheek. My uncle replying no, he wasn't interested in meeting me, he had enough family. Me showing up and him opening the door, an awkward silence following that neither of us knew how to break. I was pulled from my slew of imaginary scenarios when Andie blew through the front door.

'Hey Cuz. Oh nice, are we drinking already?' Andie dropped her bag and keys right in the entryway. The air came alive in the room with Andie's energy. She swept the curtains over the dining room window apart, blanketing the room in a warm amber glow from the sunset.

'You bet I am, grab a glass and join me. Guess what?' I replied, unable to keep the smile off my face.

'That guy you went on a date with last week finally texted you?' Andie said with a big expectant smile as she walked through her open bedroom door.

'No, he definitely ghosted. Not that I really care, I have way more important things to focus on right now. This news is so much better. I got a reply on 23andMe!' I hollered into the other room.

'Oh my God! From who?' she said, breezing back into the living room while she pulled a white tank top over her head, sitting down next to me. She reached over and took a swig from my glass.

'Must you always drink my wine? Can't you get your own?'

Andie shrugged her shoulders. 'Yours tastes better,' she said with a mischievous wink. 'So. Tell me. Who replied?'

'I've got a grand uncle!' I said, throwing my arms open wide like I'd just told her I'd won the lottery.

'Grand uncle? Is that even a thing?' Andie said, her eyebrows arched high on her forehead.

I swatted her arm. 'Stop it. Yes, it's a thing. But you wanna hear what the real kick in the nuts is? He said my mother was estranged from the family, so I'm not sure if he even knows how to contact her. I'm trying to set up a meeting so I can find out more, but he did tell me her name: Teresa.'

Andie rubbed my arm in support. 'That's really great that you're finally getting some answers, Lizzie. I know this has been super hard for you.'

'Yeah, thanks. I hope he's willing to meet me. It just makes me so mad that Mom and Dad waited this long to tell me the truth. I feel like they stole a whole part of my life from me. Maybe I could have had a relationship with my bio-family all these years.'

'Okay, I know they should have told you long ago, but let's not get overly dramatic. You know they only kept it from you because they thought it was best.' I gave Andie a look and exhaled loudly. 'Okay, okay. But look at the bright side. You found a . . . what did you call him? A grand uncle? That's something. What did he say? Is he nearby?'

'He lives in Connecticut.'

'Oh my God, that's amazing! That's only a two-hour drive from here.'

'I know, right? I've offered to go there to make it easier for him, if he'll agree to meet me.'

'Ooh. If he says yes, I'll ask Travis if we can borrow his car and I'll go with you. Safety in numbers, baby.'

'What about work? I told him I could come any time since my schedule is so flexible and I can pretty much work anywhere from my phone.' Andie's schedule was erratic, sometimes changing weekly, and she was always the first person to volunteer to cover a shift if someone called out. She was serious about her job, even if she wasn't serious about anything else in her life. She wanted to head the radiology department one day so she said she had to start putting in the hours now to make that happen. 'Work hard, play hard', seemed to be her life motto.

'I've got some personal days saved up. There's no way I'm missing this and letting you go alone.' Andie threw her arm around my shoulders. 'Let's open another bottle. This is cause for celebration.'

I laughed because everything was cause for celebration where Andie was concerned. After we had donated blood last week, she'd exclaimed, 'that's over, let's celebrate', which led to us having dinner at our favorite

50

Argentinian restaurant, The Inkan, and indulging in the Ladies' Night drink specials, wobbling home at midnight. Andie's excitement was infectious, and she was right, this *was* cause for celebration: I'd found my biological family. I gave my cousin a sloppy kiss on the cheek and jumped up to grab another bottle.

VICTIMS 4 & 5

Julie Jenz & Linda Styles

1993

CHAPTER 6

Linda's head was pounding. She rolled over and tried to grab her forehead but her hands were stuck together; something tight and scratchy tugging on her wrists. She opened her eyes and saw Julie staring at her from just a few inches away. They were in a dark, confined space that didn't allow for much movement. The space was dimly lit but Linda couldn't tell where the light was coming from.

'Oh my God, you're awake,' Julie exclaimed in a hushed, urgent tone. A tear rolled down her flushed cheek.

'Where are we?' Linda asked, her voice hoarse. The black velvet choker around her throat was too tight, making it even harder to get the words out.

'I think we're in a trunk. Can't you feel us moving? The last thing I remember was a man knocking on our door from the gas company. We need to find a way out of here.' Her rapid thoughts and questions flew out of her mouth one after another, overwhelming Linda in her groggy state.

'A trunk? Like the trunk of a car?' Linda's head was

lost in a dense fog. 'Why are we in a trunk?' She was trying desperately to understand but her mind felt disconnected and distant from the reality around her, like the one time she'd done shrooms and woken up with a chunk of hours missing from her memory.

'Linda, that guy kidnapped us. He said there was a gas leak, so I let him in. I'm so sorry,' Julie sobbed. 'That's all I remember.'

Images crept into Linda's mind, spreading pieces of clarity that lifted the haze in slow motion. She'd been in her room, working on a last-minute presentation her boss had dropped in her lap earlier that day, when she'd heard the doorbell. She'd known Julie was in the living room watching TV, so she had let her answer it. A few minutes later she'd heard a thump and then silence. She'd called out Julie's name but it went unanswered. Goosebumps erupted on her arms, shivering at the memory. Her baby-doll dress offered little warmth but she was glad she'd at least thrown her favorite plaid flannel over it.

'Wait,' Linda's voice cracked. 'I remember now – I heard the doorbell and then a weird sound, but you didn't answer me when I called out, so I went to see what was going on and . . .' her bound hands flew to her mouth. 'Oh my God. You were on the ground.' Tears poured from Linda's eyes. 'I felt someone grab me from behind and a sharp pain in my neck. I think he injected me with something. I remember trying to fight him off but he was so much bigger than me and my arms and legs felt so weak.' She paused, taking a deep shuddering breath. 'I don't know what happened after that, I must have passed out.' The car rocked them from side to side as it hit a bump in the road. 'How long have we been in here?'

'I don't know,' Julie said, her eyes darting around the

small dark space. 'I think I woke up like a half hour ago, maybe? It's hard to tell. I tried to wake you, but couldn't . . . I was so scared you were—'

Julie was cut off by the surprise of an amber light intermittently filling the trunk as the turn signal clicked on. They felt the car changing direction as it turned and rumbled over an uneven surface.

'Where's he taking us?' Linda asked.

'It feels like we're on a dirt road or something.'

The car hit a large hole and the girls smashed into one another, both grunting out in pain as they smacked foreheads before being bounced up against the hood. They lay in a fearful silence as the bumpy terrain in the car's path continued to roll their bodies back and forth in the confined space for about twenty more long, torturous minutes.

'Julie, what are we going to do?' Linda finally whispered through her tears.

Julie was silent for a moment, then replied. 'Feel around and see if there's something we can use as a weapon. Or something that will release the trunk from inside. Maybe we can roll out and make a run for it.'

The women felt around their heads and then their feet as much as possible with their wrists bound, pushing their hands into the crevices of the small space. 'There's nothing in here, Julie,' Linda whispered frantically.

'You're closer to that tail light than me, can you kick it out with your foot? Then maybe we can signal someone nearby through the hole.'

Linda turned, pulling her leg back and slamming the toe of her brown leather Doc Martens into the amber light. It didn't budge. She tried three more times but she couldn't get enough strength behind her foot with the limited space available in the trunk. Linda rolled back over to face Julie and started crying.

Julie closed her eyes and then said, 'Okay. When he opens the trunk, let's both lunge up at him at the same time. He can't take both of us at once.'

Linda's hysteria took over and she started screaming 'Help!' over and over as loud as she could. The man turned the stereo on, blasting the volume to drown her out. It was a song she didn't recognize, but it sounded like Elton John, singing about a 'bitch' coming back. The car went up a slight incline and then suddenly stopped. The engine cut off, throwing them into a tense stillness that stunned them back into silence.

Julie grabbed Linda's arm. 'Be ready,' she whispered forcefully, trying to adjust her position. 'When he opens the trunk, punch him as hard as you can, okay?'

Linda was still crying. 'I don't know if I can do this.'

'You don't have a choice, Linda. Do you want to die? You can do this.'

They heard the man get out of the car, slam the door, and walk around to the back. The key went into the trunk and when the lid slowly opened, both Julie and Linda's bound fists launched into the air in his direction. But the man had anticipated it and stepped back out of their reach, swift and effortless. Their arms hit the trunk lid instead, bouncing it back roughly. Linda saw a red blanket flying toward them just before it settled over their bodies, covering their arms and faces. She scrambled to pull the blanket off when she felt a pinch in her leg.

Linda screamed, 'Don't touch me. Get off me. Help!'

Julie started screaming, too, hoping they could alert someone nearby. The man's deep laugh rang out.

'Please,' Julie begged through her sobs. 'Please, don't kill us. We won't tell anyone I swear, just let us go.'

Linda tried to reach for Julie but her limbs were heavy and unresponsive. Everything was moving slowly, as though she were wading through deep water. *He injected us again*, she thought just before she passed out.

CHAPTER 7

We were stuck in traffic on I-95 just past the New York/ Connecticut border. According to the GPS there was a car accident a mile ahead, causing us to inch forward, painstakingly slow. One of the things I loved most about Andie was her ability to turn an annoying situation into an enjoyable one. Her road trip playlist was blaring *Don't Stop Believing* through the speakers of Travis's Audi sedan he'd graciously offered up for the trip. Andie was dramatically singing the words at the top of her lungs, intermittently miming an imaginary microphone in my direction during the chorus. The windows were down as we crawled forward, letting in the warm end-of-summer air. Every time we passed a car, the passengers looked in our direction, some frantically rolling up their window with a frown, others joining in as Andie passed the imaginary mic across the span of the two cars in their direction. Andie could make anything fun but her energy became a hindrance when we were doing more serious tasks, like trying to pay bills or clean the apartment, both chores that Andie loathed.

'In one mile, take Exit 3, Arch Street,' said the British female voice on the GPS that Travis had chosen.

'Why is she British?' I asked Andie, turning the music down.

Andie rolled her eyes. 'Travis has a thing for British women. Well, let me clarify, he has a thing for British accents. Don't even get me started on the accents he asks me to imitate in bed.'

'Yeah, I'm good, no need to give me the gory details,' I groaned, putting my hand in the air to stop her from elaborating.

Andie leaned in closer. 'Sometimes he wants me to talk like I'm Helen Mirren. He has a thing for older women, too.' Andie said in a Helen Mirren-esque voice.

I frowned, trying to force the newly formed image out of my head. 'Stop. Now all I can think about is Travis getting a boner over Helen Mirren.'

Andie dissolved into a fit of laughter, leaning back into her seat.

'You're so lucky you have a job that allows you to take off at a moment's notice,' she said after she'd regained her composure. 'Margaret was kind of a B when I requested today off. Like, hello? I haven't taken a personal day since my birthday last year.'

'Did you tell her that?'

'I did, but I also included how she'd just taken two personal days to visit her daughter in Florida a month ago. She at least had the decency to admit I was right and stop fighting me on it. It's not my fault I'm the only reliable technologist she has on staff.'

I laughed at Andie's exasperation. I heard this diatribe from Andie at least once a month, and while she was 100 percent correct in her frustration because the other two X-ray techs were flaky and missed shifts that Andie had to cover, I knew Andie loved her job. She'd wanted to work in medicine since she was a kid. We'd often played 'doctor's appointment' where Andie would take my blood pressure, hold the plastic stethoscope to my chest and ask me to cough. But by far her favorite part was always the imaginary X-ray, where Andie would make a buzzing sound and describe what my insides looked like in graphic detail. It was much more interesting than my own childhood aspirations, when I acted like a reporter as I held a large spatula in her face like a microphone and asked hard-hitting questions about what she'd witnessed on the playground that day. My career path had evolved once I got into social media and events but Andie had always known exactly what she wanted, something I admired about her. Although, I hadn't given up on the idea of being a reporter just yet. My dream job still lingered in the back of my mind, the idea of chasing down stories to get to the truth still appealed to my researcher brain.

I exited the highway just after we passed the fender bender that had caused the lengthy delay. Now that we were within a few miles of my grand uncle's house, I felt my nerves start to jangle. I kept checking the fuel gauge, the speedometer and the GPS anxiously. I wasn't sure why Andie had agreed to let me drive.

'Well, I'm just glad you were able to come with me,' I said, rolling up the windows and fidgeting with the dial to turn on the air conditioning. I swiped the sweat off my brow, not wanting to be a clammy mess when I met my new grand aunt and uncle. 'I'm so nervous and not sure what to expect. I feel like I'm going to sweat through this shirt.'

'Are you kidding me? I would have quit my job before I'd miss this. That hospital needs me more than I need them, let's be honest. You're my cousin, Lizzie, I would never let you go meet this guy alone. We know basically nothing about him.'

I rolled my eyes. 'He's in his sixties and his wife will be there too. I'm not really worried about it being safe.' The British voice, that now sounded exactly like Helen Mirren, instructed us to take the next left. 'I'm just worried that it'll be awkward. And what if I don't like them or they don't like me? What if they're weird, or rude or . . .'

Andie turned the volume of the music down further and interrupted me, shifting in her seat to stare pointedly in my direction. 'Stop spinning out. I get it. It's a weird situation, I'll give you that. But I'm sure it'll be fine. He invited you up to meet him, didn't he? He obviously wants to meet you, too. And you're not alone, I got you if you need a buffer.'

'You have arrived at your destination,' came the voice from the GPS.

As I slowed the car, Andie followed my gaze out the front windshield. 'I think this is it. Check the address,' I said.

While Andie grabbed the slip of paper I'd written the address on and read the house and street numbers, I took in the details of the home in front of us. It was a white two-story house with black trim, a bright red door, and an attached garage. There was a cupola on the roof of the garage that seemed like it would make a good lookout spot. I suddenly wished I could climb up there and see the view of the neighborhood and its lush trees. Maybe I would one day, if everything went well.

Andie waved the paper in front of my face. 'Hello? Are you going to park? This is definitely it.'

I snapped back to reality, pulling the car into the empty driveway and exhaling a long breath. Andie grabbed my hand and squeezed. 'I'll be right by your side. If you want to leave, just blame it on me and say I have to get back for work or something.' I looked deep into Andie's eyes, trying to siphon off some of her bravado.

We exited the car and walked up the path that led us through an impressive lawn. Someone had taken great care to evenly mow the grass in distinctive lines and trim the bushes into elaborate shapes. On the right side was a beautiful rock garden that formed a sundial. There was a small wooden rake resting against a planter off to the side that was clearly used to move and shape the rocks that ranged in size from large boulders to tiny pebbles.

'Someone has a lot of time on their hands. Look at that thing. Laying out the different colored pebbles for the dial must have taken forever!'

'It's beautiful,' I replied, while Andie dragged me up to the front door. She knocked loudly and then pushed the doorbell.

'Andie! Give them a second to answer.'

Andie held her hands out and shrugged her shoulders. The sound of footsteps coming toward the door startled me. I gulped and pulled my shoulders back straight. I angled my head down slightly to each side, doing a quick smell test. Andie looked at me like I was a freak.

'What?' I said in a hushed voice, shrugging. 'I told you, I was nervous sweating.'

Andie laughed and I knocked my shoulder gently into hers, thankful that she was here with me, but quickly straightened up when the door opened. We were greeted by a tall older woman with impeccably styled light brown hair, sprayed into place so that not one strand moved when she did. She was wearing a floral dress with short sleeves that was buttoned up to her throat with a peter pan collar. A light blue apron dotted with spots of flour and the words, 'Kiss the Cook' in pink cursive letters covered the dress. Her makeup was immaculate with perfectly rosy cheeks and pink lipstick. She seemed to be plucked right out of a 1960s family drama.

She gasped and clasped her hands together. 'Oh, just look at you. I can tell right away you're a Dominio.'

I smiled uncomfortably and held out my hand. 'Hi, I'm Liz, and this is—'

The woman pulled me into a tight hug, cutting me off mid-sentence. I wasn't sure how to react. I came from a family of huggers, but I'd just met this woman. After several long seconds, I finally pulled away because it seemed like if I hadn't, we'd be locked in the embrace for hours. 'This is my cousin, Andie.'

'Andie?' the woman asked while shaking Andie's hand. Her forehead was scrunched up in confusion.

'Short for Andrea,' Andie replied, stifling an amused smile.

'Oh, that's a lovely name. Andrea,' she repeated. 'I'm Rosie.' She looked back at me with a big smile and grabbed my hand. 'Come on in.' I followed behind her and Andie mouthed the words, 'Is this lady for real?' behind Rosie's back. I gave her a stern look, telling her with my eyes to cut it out. 'Cris is going to be just thrilled to see you.'

We walked through the kitchen and into the dining room. Rosie motioned for us to sit at the long, polished oak table covered with full steamy bowls of rice and beans and a platter of enchiladas that made my mouth water. As we sat down, Rosie took a long moment to look at me. I shifted in my seat and plastered a smile on my face, hoping I didn't look too awkward.

'You just look so much like Teresa, it's uncanny. In certain places, like your eyes and nose. Your expressions, too.' I felt uncomfortable being sized up in this way and was unsure of what to say. I let Rosie watch me for another minute before she said, 'What can I get you girls to drink? We have coffee, tea, soda, juice, whatever you like. Cris!' She shouted in the direction of the stairs. 'They're here. Come on down.'

'Water is fine, thank you.'

'I'll take a soda. Do you have Pepsi?' Andie asked.

When Rosie turned toward the kitchen, I swatted my cousin's arm. Andie looked at me with wide eyes and whispered, 'What? She offered.'

'Is Coke okay?' Rosie answered over her shoulder as she filled a glass with filtered water from the front of the stainless steel refrigerator for me.

I shot daggers in Andie's direction. Andie hated Coke and was addicted to Pepsi, always refusing anything else. She sighed and her shoulders dropped. 'Yes, Coke is fine,' she replied, frowning at me.

I couldn't help but feel a little victorious, as I was in the Coke camp. We constantly argued about which was better and I smiled a little that my biological family seemed to have the same taste as me. I wondered what else me and my grand uncle would have in common.

I heard footsteps coming down the stairs and a man saying, 'Coming.'

I rose from my chair, my nerves mounting now that I

was so close to laying eyes on him for the first time. Andie stayed in her seat, staring intently at the scene unfolding in front of her like she was watching her own real-life soap opera. When Cris rounded the corner, I was face to face with him, just a few feet away. We both froze, taking in the other person. We had the same coloring, in eyes, skin and hair. Our eyes had the same almond shape and were framed by similar heavy eyebrows. Cris's were far bushier than mine but without my weekly grooming taming them into submission, I was pretty sure mine would be close to what I saw on him. I silently prayed that Andie didn't mock his eyebrows, the way she constantly called me out on mine. I hoped the smile on my face appeared kind and not forced. My breath was coming fast, overwhelmed by all the emotions rushing through me all at once. I struggled to think of something to say. But as we stood there taking the other in, I noticed he didn't say anything to me either. Maybe he was feeling just as overwhelmed as I was.

I wasn't sure how long we stared at one another before our mutual observation was interrupted by Rosie bringing the drinks to the table. 'Cris, come sit down, I made lunch. I'm sure we all have so much to talk about.'

Cris and I took seats across from one another while Rosie passed the platters and bowls around the table. Cris still hadn't spoken and I wondered if he was annoyed that I'd come. I almost felt like I was intruding. When Cris handed me the heavy enchilada platter, his arm muscles bulged under the dark green polo shirt he was wearing. Even though he was sixty-five with salt and pepper hair and a face full of wrinkles, he clearly kept himself in good physical shape. Andie eagerly piled her plate high with all the food, different to the Italian feasts we were used to, although definitely similarly large servings. When the food made its way back to Rosie she served up Cris first, and then herself. She took extra care in placing the food onto Cris's plate, making sure the enchiladas didn't touch the rice or beans. But when she served herself, the food was slapped onto her plate without the same precision, all the food merging into one dish. Just as Andie was about to take a bite, Rosie reached across the table to take her hand and Cris reached over for mine. Andie quickly set her fork back down on the table and uncomfortably both of us reached out our hands, and clasped each other's as well. Then we followed suit when Cris and Rosie bowed their heads. Cris began saying grace, Rosie nodding enthusiastically as he prayed. As I listened to Cris say words of thanks for the food in front of us, I thought about how different Rosie and Cris were. Rosie had been warm and open, eagerly showing her excitement at my visit, while Cris was withdrawn and hadn't said one word to me. I tried my best not to take it personally, but since I'd just met him, it was hard not to.

When we were done, Andie dropped the hands and said, 'Amen. Great prayer, Cris.'

I felt my cheeks warm as I picked up my fork. As much as I loved Andie, I knew she was a lot to take if you weren't used to her personality. Cris and Rosie both seemed slightly confused by her. They were handling it well, though, smiling and nodding at her comments. Andie had a big smile on her face as she dug into the chicken enchiladas with gusto, groaning loudly.

'Wow, Rosie, this is so delicious,' she said, a few pieces of rice falling out of her mouth.

Rosie beamed. 'Thank you dear, I made the tortillas

myself from Cris's grandmother's recipe. So that would be your great-great grandmother then, Elizabeth.' She wasted no time in steering the conversation back to the matter at hand. I shot a side glance at Cris, wondering if he'd join in at the mention of his grandmother, but still, he remained silent.

While Andie stuffed her face happily, I pushed the rice around my plate, the tension in the room suddenly killing my appetite. I looked at Rosie and Cris, who both smiled at me uncomfortably, and maybe a little expectantly, although I wasn't sure what I was supposed to say. Cris looked away first, but Rosie held my gaze. Andie glanced at the three of us after a few moments of silence had passed.

With a full mouth of tortilla and beans, Andie said, 'Well this is awkward.'

I glared at her. Andie's eyes widened, and she refocused on her food.

Rosie smiled tersely at Andie, then said, 'So, Elizabeth.'

I interrupted, 'You can call me Liz, or Lizzie.' I put my fork back down on the table, fidgeting with it where it sat next to my full plate.

'Okay, Liz, why don't you tell us a little about yourself?' Rosie said, picking up her own fork and cutting off a small piece of her enchilada, a long string of cheese still connected to the plate as she raised it to her mouth and took a bite. Cris followed suit. He cut into his enchilada with focused precision, sectioning the filled corn tortilla into exactly even portions, expertly slicing through the cheese so it didn't stretch to his mouth as it had for Rosie, before finally taking a bite.

I picked up my own fork again for something to do with my hands and said, 'I grew up in New Jersey. Big

Italian family. I went to school for Journalism and Mass Communications and now work at Sway Media as a Social Media Associate. Basically, I go to events and businesses and create social media posts exploring things people might be interested in. Andie and I live in Brooklyn.' I paused and took a sip of water.

'Well that sounds lovely. I'm sure you get to meet all kinds of people doing that. Are you married? Or do you have a boyfriend?'

Cris shot Rosie a look but she ignored it. I couldn't help but wonder if my relationship status mattered to him or if he was simply trying to chastise her for prying. 'No, I'm not married. I'm single right now. But Andie has a pretty serious boyfriend,' I answered.

'He's a lawyer,' Andie said, jabbing her fork in the air for effect. She loved to brag about her successful boyfriend, as though it said more about her than him.

Rosie looked at Andie and smiled politely. 'That's nice, Andrea.'

'I'd really love to know more about where I come from,' I interjected, pulling the attention away from Andie and finally saying what I'd been itching to say since we crossed their threshold. Politely waiting for the right moment to find out about my mom and other potential family members had been torturous. 'I'm hoping you guys can tell me about my mom and dad and any other family. Especially if you know how to contact my mom, it would really mean a lot to me to get to know her. And of course, I want to hear more about you two as well.'

My throat felt dry, so I took another quick sip of water before forcing myself to take a bite of the enchilada. The flavors were even better than I'd imagined. For a moment, I forgot I was too nervous to eat, and took another bite.

Rosie pointed her eyes at Cris, intimating that he should take the reins. Cris looked uncomfortable, setting his fork down and taking his time, wiping his mouth with a napkin. He seemed to be stalling.

'I'm sorry I didn't tell you over email, but it seemed like something that was better said in person.' Hearing him speak for the first time was a bit of a shock. His voice was deep, which fit his large stature, but it came across as more confident than what I'd expected from his awkward demeanor. 'Teresa passed away about four years ago. A drug overdose. I'm sorry that you never got to meet her.'

The fork slipped from my fingers and clattered onto the plate, splashing a bit of sauce onto the table. A lump formed in my throat. His words refused to sink in. My biological mother was dead. I missed meeting her by four years. I was too late. Mentally cursing my parents again for waiting so long to tell me the truth, I felt cold and rigid as I sat on the edge of my seat, staring at my plate without really seeing it. Andie reached over and put a hand on my arm. The gentle pressure of it brought me back to reality. I sniffled, straightening up. I quickly wiped up the splash of sauce when I noticed Cris staring at it and then straightened my fork. I tried to force back tears but they slipped down my cheeks anyway. I clasped my hands in my lap to stop them from trembling. *Why am I so upset? I didn't even know her,* I thought to myself in frustration. But then, I realized with a wave of sadness, it was because now I never would.

'Your mother was sweet,' Cris continued after clearing his throat. I was grateful he saved me from having to talk, giving me another moment to compose myself. Every time I swallowed a lump, another would form. 'Energetic

72

and outgoing. She loved animals so we used to let her volunteer in the vet office sometimes. Teresa was a good kid, popular at school and liked by everyone who met her.'

I frowned and wiped my tears. 'So then, what happened? If you don't mind me asking,' I added hastily, finally finding words.

Cris glanced out the sliding doors to the backyard and then focused on his plate of food, picking his fork back up. It looked tiny in his large hand. He took a bite and Rosie picked up the threads of the conversation.

'When she entered high school, she fell in with the wrong crowd. She started dating a boy your grandparents didn't approve of. He was a bad boy, so to speak. Your grandfather, Frank, used to say he had a wild hair up his ass.'

Andie snorted and I was finally able to give a small smile. Cris pursed his lips and looked sternly at Rosie.

She seemed properly chastened, averting her eyes from Cris's stare as she said, 'Sorry for the language.'

Cris flipped his fork over and over in his hand. I noticed that other than the initial mutual inspection we gave one another, he'd barely made eye contact with me even when we were speaking. He seemed uncomfortable and awkward, but then again, it was an awkward situation. I probably wasn't coming across as my best self either.

'Was that my father? Do you know his name?'

Cris looked in my direction but quickly averted his gaze again when his eyes met mine. 'I don't know for sure, but that's my guess. He's the only boy I ever heard of her dating. I never met him and sorry to say I can't remember what they called him, but Frank told me he had tattoos up and down his skinny, pale arms and was known to sell drugs. Frank really didn't like the boy. He had hoped she would find a man with the same Mexican values he'd raised her with and carry that way of life into the next generation. Even though Frank was from a blended family himself, it sounded like that boy was far from what he envisioned for his daughter. From the stories I heard and the path he led Teresa down, I can't say I blamed Frank. Once she started dating him things went south pretty quickly. Frank forbade Teresa from seeing him but you know how teenagers are. She was caught numerous times sneaking out to meet up with him. It was the first time she'd ever disobeyed her father and Frank didn't take that well. Her relationship with her family became . . . strained.'

Cris placed the fork back down next to his knife and spent the next few seconds lining them up perfectly next to one another. Rosie seemed uncomfortable with the silence. She folded and refolded her napkin, smiling at me intermittently.

Finally, she continued where Cris left off. 'Teresa was caught stealing a couple of times. Frank had some friends in law enforcement, so he was always able to get her off with probation. But she showed up to Thanksgiving one year high as a kite. She broke one of your grandmother's favorite vases when she lost her balance and didn't even apologize, just laughed about it. That was the last straw. Frank was furious and kicked her out. Two weeks later she was arrested for drug possession with intent to sell and Frank cut her off. We'd all been dealing with her drug use for a couple of years by that point and thought it best not to be in contact with her until she cleaned up her act, hoping she would pull herself together if we weren't enabling her. It ended up being longer than we anticipated.'

74

'So, she was estranged from the family, like you said in your email. For how long?' I asked, glancing at Cris. As usual, the only way I knew how to cope was to ask questions and get as much information as possible. He still didn't look me directly in the eyes.

'Yes, for almost sixteen years, we heard nothing from her.' After taking a bite and swallowing, Cris continued on, 'She called her mom a few times, asking for money. But Frank wouldn't allow it. Then Frank was diagnosed with prostate cancer back in 2013. While he was in the hospital, Gloria—' he paused and quickly looked at me, 'that's your grandmother, Frank's wife. Gloria called Teresa and convinced her to come see her father. It had quite an effect on her seeing her father like that, and it seemed like she was finally ready to get straightened out. Gloria helped Teresa get into rehab and for the next few years, she did very well. She got a job waitressing and was part of the family again. Until . . .' Cris looked out the sliding doors again.

Sensing his hesitation, Rosie interjected, 'Gloria died of a brain aneurysm rather suddenly. It was quite a blow. She had always been the picture of health and Teresa took it really hard. Gloria was the buffer between your mom and Frank, you see, and without her there, the two fought constantly. Teresa became depressed and stopped showing up for work.' Rosie paused, swallowing a few times. 'She just couldn't take the death of her mother. She fell off the wagon and overdosed a few weeks after that.'

The food in my mouth turned to dust as I listened to Rosie talk about the sad ending to my mother's life. I forced the rice down and took a drink. Rosie reached across the table and placed a hand over mine. It was quiet for several seconds as I absorbed everything. I could feel tears building on my lashes and fought to keep them from falling.

'What about my grandfather, Frank? Is he still around?' I asked quietly, fighting against the tight feeling in my throat.

Cris swallowed loudly and glanced at Rosie. He rose from the table, walked over to the glass doors and stared out into the backyard with his hands in his pockets.

Rosie watched him and then looked back at me. 'Frank recently passed away. He was the death in the family that Cris told you about when he first messaged you. Frank's cancer came back but they didn't catch it until it was too late. I'm so sorry, sweetheart. I wish you could have met him. He was such a character. Outgoing and funny. Frank never had a problem making friends, that's for sure.'

Another blow, another part of my family lost to me. I felt each loss like a punch to the gut. Mother, gone. Grandmother, gone. Grandfather, gone. My immediate biological family members were falling like dominoes. *How does a person deal with the death of so many family members at once? Family I hoped I'd just found were gone in an instant. Is it normal to grieve people I had never even met?*

Rosie continued, 'After seeing Frank's health deteriorate I convinced Cris to do the 23andMe kit. Now that they do genetic screening for things like prostate cancer and knowing Cris has it in his family history, not only Frank but also an uncle on his dad's side, I was worried about losing him. The whole thing terrified me so I hounded Cris until he finally relented. I thought it was best to check and be prepared. But thankfully, Cris does not have the gene. We were so relieved! And connecting with you has been such a nice bonus, Liz.'

I barely registered what Rosie was saying, my mind still whirling around my lost relatives, tears lingering on my lashes. No matter how many times I swallowed, the lump in my throat refused to go away.

Andie set her fork down rather loudly on her plate and said, 'So, tell us about you two. You mentioned a vet office?'

I gave Andie a grateful look. Cris turned and walked back to the table, sitting down and taking another bite of food.

'Oh us? We're about as boring as they come.' Rosie laughed. 'But yes, Cris has his own veterinary practice. I run the office, ordering products, scheduling and finances. That sort of thing. We never had kids, the doctors said it just wasn't in the cards.' She glanced nervously at Cris before continuing. He tensed at the overshare but said nothing. I gave her a smile tinged with a bit of sadness, thinking about how my parents had been in a similar situation. 'But with all our connections from the business,' Rosie continued, 'we usually have a foster animal or two running around here. We're in between them right now but they've always been like our children, keeping us busy, so we've been alright.'

'You foster animals?' I said, my tears drying up as I listened to Rosie tell us about their recent pets, like a dog who'd eaten Cris's favorite pair of shoes and a cat who'd peed all over the downstairs carpet, leading them to tear it up and put in hard wood floors. 'I love animals. We had cats growing up. My mom isn't a fan of dog drool and said she couldn't stand it if she had to vacuum up dog hair and eliminate that "wet dog" smell every time she had guests over,' I remembered with a laugh and Rosie nodded her head understandingly, smiling at me.

'So, there are no other Dominios? No other family I could get into contact with? What about my great-grandfather? Your dad? I know he'd be pretty old by now but is he still alive?' I persisted, looking at Cris.

Cris didn't say anything so Rosie covered for him again, 'Rodrigo died about fifteen years ago. Heart attack. But we like to say he died of a broken heart after Cris's mom passed.' She paused and reached across to squeeze my hand again, a sad smile on her face. 'They would have loved meeting you.'

After a pause, Cris interjected, 'As far as the Dominio side of the family goes, I had an uncle, and he had a son named Adam. Last time I saw them was when they came over for Frank's birthday, his thirteenth I think it was. My uncle died not long after that and since his wife had no family in the area, she and Adam moved away to the west coast.' Cris paused. 'I remember Frank not being happy that Adam came to his party and kept picking on him. But that was Frank, he was a joker and Adam always took his jabs too seriously. Those two never quite got along. We didn't keep in touch after they moved away.'

Hearing this, my hopes of finding more family were dashed. 'So, there's no one else?'

Cris shook his head. 'Frank's mom, Dorina, was an only child, so there's no family left on her side. After she passed away, our dad remarried my mother. Frank and I are half-brothers, you see.'

I scrunched my face in concentration. I hadn't realized Cris and Frank only shared the same father until now.

'You know what, I'm sure you'd like to see what your mother looked like, wouldn't you?' Rosie said, snapping her fingers and standing up from the table. She hurried

78

into the kitchen, taking something out of a drawer before hurrying back into the dining area.

'Oh wow, is this her?' I asked as Rosie handed me an old photograph.

My hand shook as I took in my mother's features, the chocolate brown curly hair, heart-shaped face and the beginnings of the thick Dominio brows. In the photo, my mother was young, not quite yet a teenager, but the similarities were striking. Teresa was standing next to a bench licking a melting ice cream cone, the joy on her face so palpable I felt myself smiling.

'You guys look so much alike,' Andie said, leaning over my shoulder to look at the photo. 'Same little button nose and everything.' Andie reached up with her pointer finger and booped me on the nose. I shooed her hand away. 'Not very tall though, huh?'

'Nah,' Cris said, leaning back in his chair. 'Even when she was fully grown, she was probably only about 5'2" or 5'3". Her personality sure was big, though.' He glanced off to the side and grimaced for a moment on these last words. *Did he disapprove of my mother's bold nature?* At the same time, I couldn't help thinking how different my mother and I seemed. Polar opposites really. I'd always been a bit reserved but had chalked that up to years of taking a backseat to Andie's loud gregariousness.

I smiled, thanking Rosie for sharing the photo and handing it back. Rosie looked at the photo with fondness before hustling back to the kitchen to fetch coffee.

While we sipped our coffee, Rosie did most of the talking. 'Your job sounds so interesting, Liz. Is that what you've always wanted to do?'

Shaking my head, I replied, 'No, I'm just getting started

in my career, so I'm hoping this job will be a stepping-stone. Ideally, I'd love to be a journalist or a reporter. Research is kind of my thing and one day I'd love to hunt down more important stories.'

'That's very ambitious of you,' Cris said, with a hint of a smile. For some reason, it was a relief that he seemed to approve of my career goals.

'Yeah, and she's really good at it, too,' Andie chimed in and I looked at her gratefully. With Cris's stand-offish demeanor I felt the need to impress him, to show him I was worthy, as ridiculous as that was considering I'd just met this man. But he reminded me of my tenth-grade English teacher, also a man of few words, who always made me feel as though I needed to prove myself. 'In high school,' Andie continued, 'she was on the school newspaper and broke a story about the President of the senior class stealing funds. It was quite the scandal. Our friends used to call her Nancy Drew.' I smiled at the old nickname.

'Oh, you like Nancy Drew?' Rosie asked, perking up.

'We were obsessed with the movie when we were kids. We watched it practically every weekend for a year,' I said, chuckling.

Rosie glanced at Cris and they shared a long look before he gave a quick, almost imperceptible nod. Rosie looked back at me and rose from her chair. 'I'll be right back.'

She ran up the stairs and I shared a confused glance with Andie. The three of us sat in an uncomfortable silence until Rosie padded back downstairs. When she rounded the corner, she handed me an old copy of the Nancy Drew book, *The Hidden Staircase*.

'Oh, wow, what's this from?' I asked, running my hands along the spine.

'Go on, open it,' Rosie smiled.

I opened the cover, the linen crackling with age. Two names were written on the inside, one neatly in pen and the other in childish writing. 'Was this my mom's?' I asked, with a big smile as I took it in.

Cris glanced at the book. 'Oh, yes, originally it belonged to your great-grandmother, Dorina. She read it often to Frank when he was a kid. They had a tense relationship because she was really hard on him, from what I understand, but the fact that he hung on to that book after she died, well, he must have wanted to keep a piece of her alive with him. He passed the book along to Teresa when she was little, and she loved it too.'

I traced my mother's name gently with my fingertips, Teresa Dominio, where it was written in crayon. 'I've always meant to read the books, but never got around to it.'

'You can have that if you want. I'm sure Teresa would have appreciated it getting passed down to her own child,' Rosie said.

'Really? Thank you so much, I would love that.' I looked at the other name inked inside above my mother's. Dorina Mattos, my great-grandmother.

I kept the book close to me on the table as we talked, glancing at it every so often, touched to have something personal of my mother's that traced all the way back to my great-grandmother. While Rosie poured coffee for us, I kept thinking about what a complicated family history my biological family had. Drug problems, tragic deaths, dysfunctional family dynamics, secret pregnancies. And somehow, I'd come from all of that. My adoptive family was easily three times the size of this one, and yet, the worst we'd encountered was my cousin Luca getting

81

kicked out of college for cheating on an exam. I'd noticed that Cris seemed to disapprove of my mother's path just as much as my grandfather Frank had. Perhaps that accounted for his cool demeanor toward me. I hoped I'd be able to show him how different from Teresa I was. When the sun finally dipped down and the crickets began to sing, we thanked them for lunch, and said we needed to get back as we both had work the next day. I'd learned so much from this visit, I needed some space to process everything.

At the door, Rosie gave both Andie and I a tight hug. When I turned toward Cris, I put out my hand, assuming a hug would be too personal for him at this point. He took my hand in both of his, holding it for a long second. In that moment, I felt an icy chip fall from Cris's shoulder as we let our hands fall. Andie and I walked to the car, but I stopped halfway down the path.

I turned to face Cris and Rosie, who were still watching us from the porch, and called out, 'I'm covering a beer festival in Port Chester next weekend for work. Maybe I can stop by again?'

Rosie smiled and said, 'Oh weekends aren't good for Cris. He and several other vets founded Pause for Paws. He goes around in the mobile vet station van and neuters pets for people who can't afford it, so he's gone most weekends doing that. But we'd love to see you again. Give us a call and we'll plan another date.'

'Look forward to seeing you again soon,' Cris called out.

I nodded and waved as we climbed into the car. When we drove away, I couldn't help but smile. 'They were nice.'

Andie was already scrolling through her playlist. 'Yeah they were. Just don't get into that neutering van. You want kids, right?' She glanced up at me and we burst into laughter.

VICTIMS 6 & 7

Nancy Downs & Casey Becker

1995

CHAPTER 8

The floor beneath Nancy's body was hard and cold. She shivered, wondering what was wrong with her bed. Her head was killing her. *Did I drink last night?* she thought through the confused haze. *Maybe I passed out on the floor?* It didn't make sense though, she'd never been one to drink that much. Her eyelids felt glued shut and she struggled to pry them open.

'Nancy. Nancy wake up!' she heard her roommate, Casey, whisper with urgency.

When she opened her eyes, all she saw was hair. She'd gotten 'The Rachel' cut just a month ago and still wasn't used to the new style. The layers were covering her eyes like a curtain. She blew hard and when her hair moved to the side, the light from the bare bulb hanging from the ceiling blinded her. Slowly she rose into a seated position and blinked until her vision adapted. The first thing that came into focus was Casey's dirty, tear-streaked face, which wobbled back and forth as Nancy's dizziness subsided. As she looked into Casey's terrified brown eyes, memories played out rapidly in Nancy's mind, like watching a movie in reverse. A pinch in her arm, the dark trunk of a car, another pinch in her neck and a large strong hand over her mouth, and finally, the man when she had answered the door. Her eyes popped open wider, the hairs rising on the back of her neck. She pulled her legs out in front of her and saw that both ankles were shackled together with thick rusty metal cuffs secured to a chain that attached to the wall behind her. She felt like she was on an episode of *The X-Files*, a mysterious man drugging and kidnapping them, taking them to some unknown room with cold cement floors. Except this wasn't *The X-Files*, and it wasn't a nightmare she could wake from.

'Oh my God Casey, where are we?' she screeched.

'Shhh!' Casey said forcefully. She glanced at the door and waited a second before turning back to Nancy. 'He's still here. I heard him moving around a little bit ago, behind that door. I don't want him to know we're awake.'

Nancy covered her mouth in an attempt to muffle her sobs. She looked around the room, taking in its minimal features. The women were shackled to opposite walls, facing one another. The cement floor had cracks running through it, the walls were wooden, and there was a single small window with bars over it near Nancy. It was just high enough to be out of reach. The wall with the window held a toilet and white pedestal sink. Both looked new, unstained, as if they had been added as an afterthought years after the place was built. Nancy's corner below the window held stacks of thin, cheap toilet paper and rough cotton towels that would surely rub their skin raw like a cloth version of sandpaper. There was also a medium-sized cardboard box containing beef jerky, granola bars and crackers.

'We must be in some kind of cabin,' Casey said as she rubbed vigorously at a dark oil stain on her yellow plaid skirt.

She must have gotten the stain in the trunk of the car on the ride over, Nancy thought. Casey had coveted that skirt for months at Hot Topic before she'd saved up enough money to buy it. She'd planned on wearing it to the big rally next week to impress Luke, a guy she'd been crushing on. Casey had been trying the outfit on when the man knocked on their door. While it was such a small thing in comparison to their much bigger problem at hand, Nancy knew Casey was probably devastated at the blemish on her beloved outfit.

'Remember the river we heard on the drive here? The last road we were on was bumpy and unpaved and we were on it for a while, so this place can't be on a main road.' Casey paused, straining her ears. 'Do you hear the crickets and rustling trees outside? I think he's driven us somewhere remote, like a forest or a farm.'

'What does he want from us?' Nancy asked, her voice shaking, afraid of the answer.

'I don't know. But we've seen his face, he didn't even bother trying to conceal it when he brought us in here. It's kind of a blur but when he heard me stirring, he came back in to check on us. I pretended to still be asleep, so he left the room after watching us for a few long minutes,' she shivered visibly at the memory. 'He didn't cover up what he looked like at all. That's not a good sign . . . the chances of him letting us go aren't looking very good.'

'I have to go to the bathroom,' Nancy said as she rose and wobbled her way over to the toilet. The chains coiled up around her ankles lengthened, making loud clinking sounds that made both of them cringe, while looking anxiously at the door. Luckily, it remained in place. She was just able to make it to the toilet and sit down with the chain stretched taut. He had measured it perfectly. When she turned to grab the toilet paper that was on the floor next to the toilet, she squinted and said, 'What's that?'

'What?'

'Right here, there's something scratched into the wood.' She pointed down to the bottom of the wall.

Nancy flushed the toilet and pulled up her pants while Casey crawled over to where she'd pointed, her chains scraping against the floor. Casey ran her fingers over the indentations. She followed the lines with her forefinger and then her head snapped in Nancy's direction.

'They're names. Look— There, it says "Catherine and Ruby," then underneath that . . .' Casey squinted and moved closer. '"Julie and Linda".'

Casey sat back on her heels, looking sadly at the names. Realization about what this meant dawned on Nancy and she began pacing back and forth, saying 'Oh God' over and over. She no longer noticed how much noise she was making, lost in the dark spiral of thoughts consuming her.

'We aren't the first.' Casey dragged her hands down her face and exhaled.

'Oh my God, Casey. Why did he take us? What's he gonna do?' she cried, tears flowing down her cheeks as she melted into a state of panic.

'Nancy, I need you to calm down. Come here.' Casey stood and pulled her friend into a hug. Both their chains were pulled as far as they could go and they were barely able to embrace one another. Nancy sniffed into Casey's fluffy black cropped sweater.

When they pulled away, Casey said, 'Let's see how far we can go with these shackles. We need to look for a way out of here.'

Each girl walked the length and width of the room as far as they were able to. They could both reach the wall with the toilet easily but their chains didn't allow them within two feet of the door. Suddenly they heard a key insert into the lock and Nancy rushed back over to Casey. The door creaked open slowly and the man's face came into view.

'Well look who's awake.' He had two blankets and pillows in his hands. 'This is my first peace offering. If you behave, then tomorrow you'll both get a mattress to sleep on.' He walked two steps forward and dropped the blankets and pillows on the ground near them. Casey and Nancy cowered away from him.

'What do you want?!' Casey screamed.

He gave a smile that didn't quite reach his cold, dark eyes. He didn't respond and instead, pulled two syringes out of his pocket and held them up. 'It's time to get you two clean.' He popped the top off one syringe and inched toward them. 'Don't worry, I've adjusted it. This time you shouldn't pass out.'

CHAPTER 9

Andie and I pulled out white cardboard boxes of rice and several larger containers of noodles and curry that I'd ordered for us from our favorite Thai place down the street, The Blooming Buddha.

'Thanks, dude. I'll Venmo you,' Andie said.

I smirked at her, 'Will you, though?'

'Yeah, probably not,' she replied with a mischievous laugh, biting into a spring roll.

'So, tell me, what were they like?' Travis asked excitedly after we opened all the takeout containers and dug in. 'I know I'm not in this family,' he glanced at Andie with a mouth half-full of noodles and winked, '*yet*. But the small details you gave me over the phone just aren't gonna cut it.'

'Yet?' Andie said, wiggling her eyebrows at him. Travis smiled but said nothing. 'Hey, it's not our fault you've been working late and haven't been able to come over until now.'

'Yeah, yeah, yeah. I've heard this complaint before. But you know I'm trying to make partner. Not gonna happen if I'm not working as much, if not more, than my coworkers. Don't you want me to make partner?' Travis said, looking at her pointedly.

'Uh, yeah,' Andie said dramatically, hoisting her fork in the air for effect. 'I plan on becoming accustomed to a lavish lifestyle. So, go earn that paper, Trav!' She laughed while Travis rolled his eyes. I took a bite of a spring roll while I waited for their banter to come to an end. It could be hard to get a word in once Andie got going. 'Anyway, you should have seen Liz's aunt. She was like someone straight out of *Leave It to Beaver*. Her hair was perfectly styled stiff, and she wore an apron over a flowered dress. She even wore some cute little vintage heels. It was adorable.'

'She was pretty proper,' I conceded, seizing on the opportunity to talk as Andie took a bite of her pad thai. 'But very sweet. I'm not sure what I was expecting but they were both welcoming and nice. My grand uncle is a little awkward, not as enthusiastic as my grand aunt, but he opened up a bit about where I come from. Their house is beautiful, you can tell they spend a lot of time upkeeping it. There's even an elaborate rock garden; it was so pretty and peaceful,' I said, a warmth spreading through me as I talked about my newfound family.

'What about your grand uncle? Did you look like him?'

Andie snorted and quickly covered her mouth after I gave her a withering stare. 'Sorry Liz. But it's hilarious that you both have those damned eyebrows. We've always wondered where you got those. Mystery solved,' Andie said, twirling her fork around a few inches from my face. I swatted at it as she dramatically darted it toward her plate to spear another bite of food.

In the following moment of silence as everyone chewed their food, my heartrate accelerated as I reflected on what Andie just said. My hand grew sweaty where it gripped my fork. I set it down, taking off my sweater as heat flushed to my cheeks. The rush of emotion came on fast and unexpected, like I'd been burying it deep, disguising it as excitement to search for my biological family. But now it was exploding to the surface.

'Is everything okay, Lizzie?' Andie asked, putting down her own fork and looking at me with concern. Travis stopped chewing.

'It's just . . .' I trailed off, trying to hold back the tears threatening to burst from my burning eyes. 'My whole life, everyone made comments that I looked like my mom and dad, that I looked like you,' I pointed at Andie, tears now escaping. 'It's all been just one big lie. They knew I wasn't related, that I had these features that no one else had,' I said with an emphatic gesture to my eyebrows. 'Yet, they piled on lie after lie to cover it up. How can I trust anything that was ever said to me?' I put my head down in my hands, the tears coming fast.

'Oh, Lizzie,' Andie said, moving closer and pulling me into a hug. 'Don't think of it like that. Your family loves you, they just wanted you to feel like you belonged.'

'How can you lie constantly to someone you love? How can you smile and say, "Yep she's got my eyes" when you know for a fact that isn't true? I just don't get it.'

'I guess they were trying to protect you? I know it was wrong, but it wasn't coming from a bad place. And hey, you do kind of look like me a little, you know. And your mom. Maybe it's like one of those things where if you spend so much time with someone you start to take

95

on their appearance? Like how dogs sometimes look like their owners?'

I laughed in spite of myself, feeling some of the tension ease from my chest. As I thought about what Andie said, the picture Rosie had painted of my bio-mom's drug problems and dysfunctional home life came to the surface. *How different would my life have been if Teresa hadn't given me up?* My parents had saved me from a potentially dangerous upbringing. I couldn't deny that they loved me deeply and had given me a wonderful life. I shook my head, trying to make sense of all the conflicting emotions battling in my brain. As I wiped the tears away, Andie gave me a cheeky grin and shook my shoulders gently.

'You're gonna be okay, kiddo,' she said with a wink, returning to her pad thai.

I took a deep breath, trying to steady myself, and picked my fork back up. 'Cris did have impressive eyebrows,' I said, trying to get Travis's concerned eyes off me and weave us back into the conversation. 'If I didn't have a standing weekly appointment at the threading salon around the corner, that's probably what mine would look like, too,' I said before shoveling a huge bite of fried rice into my mouth. 'Thank God for Mia,' I said after I swallowed, running my fingers self-consciously across one of my brows. My heart rate was slowly returning to normal and I pushed down the feeling of resentment that was still flowing through me.

Andie laughed, 'Yeah she's a wizard with those caterpillars. Maybe I should go see her, too.' I almost choked on my bite of rice, coughing and reaching for my water.

'What?' Andie said defensively.

'What would Mia even do for you? You basically paint

yours on,' I laughed, dodging the small piece of bok choy that Andie threw at me.

The tension from my meltdown seemed to dissipate into the universe. Having Andie around was good for that, she helped to keep things light.

'Was it weird seeing someone you've never met before who looked so much like you?' Travis asked, trying to bring the conversation back on topic.

'Well, besides the eyebrows and coloring, we didn't look that much alike. His nose is much larger than mine and his face is wider,' I said, pulling my hands up by my face to show how much larger his was than mine. 'But my aunt showed me a photo of my mother and I could see some resemblance in our faces which was pretty wild. My nose, the shape of my face, the same dark chocolate brown eyes. And she had these eyebrows too, of course, but not quite as extreme. Obviously, it's a dominant trait in the family. But she had this beautiful thick curly hair that I sadly didn't get. Mine looks like it tried to be curly and then got tired and gave up half-way.' Andie laughed and nodded her head in agreement. 'My uncle said my mother was on the short side, maybe 5'2" or 5'3". Since I'm 5'6", I wonder if my dad was taller. No one seems to know anything about him.'

Andie stopped chewing and narrowed her eyes at me. 'Man, you'll take any opportunity to throw those three inches you have on me in my face, won't you,' she said shaking her head.

I smirked at her while chomping on the fried rice, thinking about the photo of my mother holding a melting ice cream cone. That one glimpse had made her more real than anything else had, like all of a sudden, she was a part of me.

'It was a little strange seeing her, even though she was quite young in the photo. She was . . . I don't know, familiar?' I said, scrunching my face up. 'Like I'd known her my whole life, but at the same time, I didn't know her at all.' I took a deep breath and closed my eyes, rubbing them vigorously for a second before looking back up. 'Sorry, I'm not making much sense, am I?'

I felt confused and drained from trying to keep up with the extreme pendulum swings of emotion. I felt grateful to have been saved from the fate of my mother's life, but at the same time, I wondered if I could have changed her life for the better. Maybe keeping me would have sobered her up, made her realize she needed to change to take care of me. I guess I'd never know.

Andie reached over, placing a hand on my shoulder. 'It's natural that this would be a confusing time for you. Your whole life just cracked open.'

I was about to answer her when my phone rang. I didn't recognize the number, so I rejected the call. Probably a telemarketer or political call. Ever since I'd donated to a local politician's campaign, the calls came constantly.

Turning back to Travis and Andie, I said, 'Yeah, I feel like my life is a bunch of puzzle pieces right now and I'm not sure where any of them go. It's so disorienting. Sorry for my mini meltdown, it's all so hard to wrap my head around.'

'You don't have to apologize to us, Liz. That's why we're here. To help you put it all together, right Trav?' Andie said, looking at Travis.

Travis nodded his head enthusiastically. 'What's crazy to me is that you can't get a copy of your original birth certificate. I mean, I understand the ethics behind it, but that sucks for adoptees like you.'

Andie turned to me nodding, 'Totally. This major piece of who you are, that most people take for granted, is hidden from you like a dirty secret. It just doesn't seem fair.'

'Yeah,' I replied sadly.

'Did they tell you about any other family members?' Travis asked.

'Not really. My great-grandmother Dorina died quite young and was an only child, so that was a dead end. On the Dominio side, Cris only mentioned a cousin named Adam but they don't know how to contact him as they lost touch a long time ago.'

'He's one lead at least. Have you been able to track him down?'

'Not yet. If there's anything I excel at, we all know it's social media. But Adam Dominio wasn't on any of the usual sites when I did a search. Considering he'd be in his sixties or seventies now, I guess that's not shocking. I haven't had time to do a deeper dive yet.'

Before Travis could respond, my phone dinged, indicating the unknown caller had left a voicemail. I picked it up and turned up the volume. Before hitting play, I said, 'Wanna hear me get hit up for money? I swear,' I said, shaking my head, 'I only donated ten dollars to Anderson's campaign because she's amazing and I really want her to win, but it's like I've opened the floodgates. I get calls from unknown numbers asking for more money at least once a day.'

I hit play and an unfamiliar male voice rang out over speakerphone. 'Hello, Ms. Catalano. This is Special Agent Mark Hannigan. You recently uploaded your DNA to the GEDMatch database, and we'd like to speak with you about a potential familial connection to a case we're working. If you could call me back at this number, I'd greatly appreciate it.'

I scrunched my face up as I stared at the phone.

'Whoa, Special Agent? As in FBI?' Andie said, looking wide-eyed at Travis.

'Yeah, sounds like it,' Travis replied.

'Call him back!' Andie exclaimed, jumping up and down in her seated position on the couch.

I was dumbfounded and a sliver of nerves slunk down my spine. *What could the FBI want with me and my bio-family?* The hits on my identity just kept on coming. I glanced up at Travis and Andie. Andie's face was bright and excited.

'A familial match from my DNA? What, so like, I'm related to a criminal or something? Or do you think it's something to do with my mom? I mean, I did opt into that law enforcement feature because of her. And Cris and Rosie were a little vague about her troubles with law enforcement, other than the drug charge that put her away.'

'I don't know, Lizzie. Just call him back!'

Reluctantly, I hit the call back button and put the phone up to my ear. Andie grabbed it from my hand and pushed the speaker button. 'There's no way you are keeping this call private,' she whispered, scooching closer.

'Special Agent Mark Hannigan.'

'Uh, hi, this is Elizabeth Catalano, I think you just left me a voicemail.'

'Ms. Catalano, thank you for calling back so quickly. I wanted to see if you had time this week to meet up with me and my partner. We just have a few questions for you about your recent upload to GEDmatch that would be easier to go over in person.'

'What's this about? You said it's a case you're working on. Should I be worried?' I responded. I nervously tucked a loose strand of hair behind my ear.

'Oh no, no need for you to be concerned. A familial match for your DNA has been connected to a case we're working on. We just want to clarify a few things to assist in our investigation.'

'What's the case?'

'I'm sorry, I really can't say more at this point but our meeting shouldn't take long. Do you have time this week? My partner and I will come to you to make this as easy as possible.'

I paused, looking at Andie and Travis. They both nodded, Andie more excitedly than Travis. Quickly, I ran over my upcoming schedule in my head.

'Um, sure, how about Monday at 1 p.m.?' I rattled off my address, waving Andie away, who was frantically flapping her arms and miming words that I couldn't interpret. When I hung up, I looked at Andie. 'What?'

'I work on Monday. I want to be here when they come.' She crossed her arms over her chest and harrumphed.

'Oh, damn. I really don't want to meet them alone, but I have some events to cover this week so my schedule's a little crazy. Monday was the only day I could think to do it.' I bit my lip, debating calling Agent Hannigan back and trying to fit it in on a day Andie could join. 'Maybe I could try to move things around but with those events already being scheduled—'

'I can be here with you,' Travis interrupted.

Both of us looked at him. 'Really?' I asked.

Andie swatted his arm. 'Yeah, really? I was hoping she'd change the date.'

Travis frowned at Andie's petulance. I stifled a laugh

at his expression. Andie's impulsive and sometimes childish behavior was something he'd openly and frequently said he both loved and disliked about her. He said the thing that had immediately drawn him to Andie was what a complicated woman she was because it kept him on his toes.

He looked at me, ignoring Andie's pouting. 'I can take a long lunch. He said on the phone that it shouldn't take long. I've already wrapped up the paperwork on the Donnigal case, so barring any unforeseen issues, it shouldn't be a problem for me to get away.'

'Thanks Trav, you're a lifesaver. Plus, it might be nice to have a lawyer here. Who knows what they're going to ask me. I know I haven't done anything wrong, but I have no idea what I should or shouldn't say to someone from the FBI, or if I'll even understand everything.'

Andie pounded her fist on the back of the couch. 'I can't believe I'm going to miss actual FBI agents sitting in *my* apartment talking about an actual FBI case. Can you like, secretly call me and leave your phone up on speaker? I can mute my end.'

I laughed and pulled Andie into a hug. 'Girl, somehow I don't think the FBI would take too kindly to that if I got caught, but you know I'll give you a play by play when you get home.' I held her at arms' length. 'And hey, why don't I make Gram's lasagna that night as a consolation. We'll pig out and I'll tell you all the gory details. Deal?'

Andie's face morphed from sullen into a grin. 'Deal.'

Although a lingering sadness still lurked in the pit of my stomach about the upheaval of my world, Andie's contagious smile and obvious optimism that this would all turn out okay made me feel more at peace. For now, anyway. While I was both intrigued and nervous about meeting with the FBI, I was just a teensy bit grateful for the distraction the meeting offered.

Travis grabbed his phone and scrolled with a determined look on his face.

'What are you doing?' Andie asked.

'Just clearing my schedule so I can make it for that dinner, too. No way I'm missing Gram's lasagna,' Travis replied.

My phone buzzed again and I wondered who else could be calling. I wasn't expecting any work calls at this hour. I pulled my phone up and saw it was a FaceTime from Rosie's number. Excitedly, I answered the call. Cris and Rosie were huddled up together with a cute little black Labrador wedged in between them.

'Oh, so cute! Who's this?'

Rosie laughed when the dog licked her cheek. 'This is Lola, we just had to call and show you our new foster.'

Lola kept blocking the camera with her little nose as she sniffed it. I was melting. 'I don't know how anyone could pass up adopting her, I'm sure she'll be snapped up quickly,' I said as Andie and Travis peered around to get a view of the screen without coming into the frame. They gave me big smiles at the sight.

'We put her photo up today on the Pause for Paws site,' Cris said, ruffling her big floppy ears with his hand. 'We've already had a few applications. I'm sure we won't have her for very long.' Seeing Cris show such softness and affection toward Lola was in direct contrast with how I'd seen him interact with people so far, confirming my suspicions that underneath that awkward exterior was a man with a big heart.

Just as Rosie was about to say something, Lola jumped out of her arms and knocked over a nearby glass of water. Rosie tutted and rushed to the kitchen for paper towels. While she was gone, Cris and I looked at each other uncomfortably, not sure what to say without Rosie present.

Cris finally broke the silence. 'Oh, I forgot, I found something in Teresa's belongings that I think you'd like to have. Since we aren't sure when we'll see you next, I can drop it in the mail if you give me your address.'

A warmth filled my chest at the thought of having another personal belonging of my mother's. The Nancy Drew book had been a nice start but I yearned for more. I was also intrigued about what it was. I rattled off my address while Cris wrote it down on a scrap of paper which he then shoved into his shirt pocket.

'That's so thoughtful of you Cris, thank you.'

Cris looked away for a second and seemed to blush slightly. 'Yeah, well.'

Rosie came back into the room and mopped up the water while Lola jumped all over her, trying to lick her face. We chatted for a few minutes about their potty training efforts. Rosie recounted the story of Cris picking Lola up mid-pee to run her outside, ruining Cris's leather loafers in the process. But soon the dog's energy made it impossible to carry on a conversation. We said goodbye with promises to find a day soon for another visit. After hanging up a smile lingered on my face, grateful for the quick call that took the edge off the upcoming FBI visit. When I turned around, Andie was staring at me with one eyebrow cocked.

'One of these days you're gonna come home from Connecticut with a dog that we're gonna have to hide from the landlord, aren't you?' Andie said with a laugh.

'It's definitely a possibility,' I replied with a smile.

VICTIMS 8 & 9

Sasha Thomas & Rachel Wagner

1997

CHAPTER 10

The man had the needle in one hand and a small black device in the other. Sasha and Rachel stood in the center of the room clutching each other, whimpering.

'I'm going to inject you both with a mild sedative.' He held up the device and clicked the button. An electrical charge appeared between two prongs. 'If you're good, then you'll just get the injection. If not . . .' he clicked the button a few more times, '. . . you'll get the stun gun.' Sasha and Rachel said nothing. 'Go stand against your walls.'

Sasha began crying, 'No please. We'll be good. You don't have to inject us. We'll do whatever you say without it, we promise.'

The man inhaled deeply, his nostrils flaring, and closed his eyes like he was trying to calm his anger. 'Do not question me. Move to your walls. NOW!' he shouted.

The women jumped at his deep baritone growl. It reverberated through them, raising the hair on Rachel's arms and the back of her neck.

'Just go to your wall, Sasha. It'll be okay,' Rachel said,

backing away, but Sasha clung desperately to her shirt. Rachel gave Sasha a nod of encouragement in an attempt to calm her, pulling her shirt out of her friend's grip. Sasha's eyes were wide, her lips trembling. She gulped a few times but finally mirrored Rachel by backing up to her own wall. The man smiled at their obedient retreat.

'Turn around and face the wall.'

The girls hesitated, anxious about turning their back on the man and his unknown intentions.

'Now!' he bellowed.

They turned around quickly, their noses inches from the wall. Rachel whimpered, tears continuing to stream down her face. She squeezed her eyes shut tight, willing it to all be a nightmare that she would soon wake up from.

'Put your palms flat against the wall. Don't even think about trying anything stupid, or I'll be forced to punish you.'

The women assumed the position. He walked over to Rachel first. He pulled her shirt sleeve down from her wrist toward her shoulder, goosebumps popping to the surface of her skin at his touch. She flinched when the needle went roughly into her arm, like he couldn't wait another second to do it. He stared at the back of her head for a second, breathing in deeply, taking in her scent, then turned and walked toward Sasha. As he got closer, Sasha started crying again.

Rachel heard a scuffle and Sasha cry out, 'Get away from me!'

Rachel screamed, 'Sasha no, just do what he says!'

She turned her head and watched as the man lifted the stun gun and zapped Sasha in the side. Sasha screamed over its loud electric buzzing and doubled over, falling to the ground, her body jerking on the floor. Rachel sucked in a breath and closed her eyes again, afraid of what could come next.

The man leaned over Sasha's crumpled body and said, 'Would you like another?'

Sasha vigorously shook her head back and forth. He lifted her sleeve from where she lay, and this time he was successful in administering the sedative. He then pushed Sasha's upper body back against the wall roughly. When he turned around, his eyes landed on Rachel.

'Did I say you could look at me?' he growled. 'Face the wall.'

Rachel jumped and quickly snapped her gaze back to the wall. Out of the corner of her eye she saw him pull a small key out of his pocket and walk over to her. Bending down, he unlocked and removed the chain that connected her shackles to the wall. Her ankles were still connected by a small chain but she was no longer anchored in place. Rachel's vision wavered as a familiar dizziness set in, her limbs heavy and sluggish. He grabbed her by the scruff of the neck and shoved her face into the wall, her cheek pressed so firmly against it she tasted blood.

He put his mouth to her ear. 'I'm giving you a pass on that one but if you disobey me again, there *will* be punishment,' he spat out, droplets of his spit landing on her cheek.

He yanked her away from the wall and guided her from the room. She wanted to protest but her mouth wouldn't form the words. It felt like she was sleepwalking, just coherent enough to understand what was going on around her.

He pushed her out of the door and locked it behind

him, separating her from her now quiet friend. She glanced around the small rectangular kitchen with its round wooden dining table in the middle. The window above the sink swam before her eyes. She saw trees and sunlight swaying on the other side of the glass. A squirrel raced from one tree branch to the next. The kitchen counter and appliances seemed to be vibrating, humming loudly in her ears. She stared longingly at the window and then at the door that appeared to lead outside. Rachel was tempted to make a break for it, to pull herself out of his grasp and run toward freedom just like that squirrel. She knew it was futile, his grip on her was strong like she was his little rag doll to toss around and play with as he saw fit, so she shuffled forward alongside him. The man led her to the room next to the one they'd been kept in. When he flicked on the light, Rachel gasped. The whole room was tiled floor to ceiling and there was a drain in the center, like an oversized shower. *What's he planning on doing to me in here?* He pushed her further into the room, near the drain. The shackles and the drug induced haze fought against her movements, causing her to stumble, but she slowly regained her balance.

'Take off your clothes.'

Rachel turned and looked at him petrified. *Oh God, is he going to rape me?* she thought, as panic threatened to overwhelm her. She swallowed a few times before her shaky hands began unzipping her platform shoes. Next, she hesitantly removed her baggy jeans, afraid to disobey, afraid of the stun gun still clutched in his left hand. But with the shackles, she couldn't take her pants off. Standing exposed in her underwear, she looked at the man, pleading silently with him not to touch her. He grabbed a pair of scissors from a drawer along the wall and moved toward

112

her. She took a few steps back, shaking her head side to side. Her back hit the wall and her breathing became more rapid, desperate. He dropped to a crouched position. She flinched when his arm darted forward, the sound of tearing fabric echoing off the tiles as he cut her pants off.

'Now the shirt.'

She complied as if in slow motion, her limbs felt like lead, dropping down lifeless against her body after she pulled her shirt off. He threw her clothes into a trash bag, and then handed her a rose scented bar of soap and stepped back. He pulled a large hose that had been looped over a hook on the wall and turned the knob all the way to the left. He pointed the nozzle at her and blasted her with cold water. The frigid temperature sucked the air out of her lungs, the force so strong that she slipped and landed on the ground. A sharp pain exploded in her tailbone, traveling all the way up her spine. Goosebumps covered every inch of her skin. She screamed.

'Use the soap. You're a dirty whore, and whores need to be cleaned!' he screamed at her and then smiled. *He's enjoying this,* she thought. He was taking pleasure in her drugged compliance, the shock of the water causing her discomfort, and the imbalance of power he alone controlled.

She began scrubbing her skin vigorously, the cold water clearing a bit of the hazy stupor she felt trapped in. Anytime she slowed down he blasted her with the hose again and screamed at her. It lasted about twenty minutes before he deemed her clean enough. Her skin was bright pink and felt raw, her eyes red and irritated. She shivered uncontrollably, her teeth chattering. She'd never been this cold before and it felt like she would never get warm again. He grabbed a towel from a cabinet under the hose and threw it at her. Rachel quickly dried herself off. Then her captor walked toward her, ripped the towel from her trembling hand, and turned her around. She braced herself, clenching her jaw in anticipation of feeling him touch her exposed body, an impending assault that seemed inevitable. But it never came. Instead, he aggressively combed her short hair, yanking some out as he went. Rachel was crying and trembling. He pulled the comb away sharply, catching the top of her ear with the plastic teeth. She heard his footsteps retreating and turned around to see him rummaging in the cabinet again. She knew this may be her only opportunity to try and make a break for it while she wasn't tethered to the wall. But he was so large and muscular, and while she was feeling more alert from the water, she was still weak and slow from whatever drug he'd injected. She remained where she was, knowing she didn't really stand a chance. He pulled out a patterned dress, turning around and approaching her again.

'Raise your arms.'

She obeyed. He pulled the dress down over her extended arms and body and stepped back to admire his work, reaching out to smooth the wrinkles along the front of her stomach. She cringed, feeling sick at his touch.

'Button it up.'

Her trembling fingers began buttoning, which proved very difficult. It had small pearl buttons going all the way up the chest. There were so many, and they were so tiny, it was no easy feat in her drugged state.

'All the way,' he said when she stopped at the base of her throat.

Rachel raised her hands again and buttoned the last few so that the dress's collar went all the way up her neck and ended tightly under her chin, making it difficult to swallow. The dress looked like something from the fifties. It had long sleeves and the bottom hem fell near her ankles. When she was done, her arms dropped back to her sides and the man smiled.

'Very good, Number Eight. Let's go.'

'My name's Rachel.'

The man barked a short laugh. 'Not anymore.'

He led her back to her and Sasha's room, shoved her in and re-attached her ankle shackles to the wall. Then he went for Sasha who was still lying in a heap on the floor, tears streaming down her face. After he led Sasha out of the room, Rachel sat on the ground and listened as her friend was cleaned in the next room. She hoped Sasha wouldn't fight; it would only make things worse. They were at a disadvantage and for now, there was nothing they could do about it. She lay down facing the wall on the cement floor, her limbs still trembling from the cold as she wrapped herself in the lightweight, nearly useless, blanket covered with holes that he had given them. She was grateful that she'd cut her hair into an ultra-short bob last month. It would've taken hours for the long, thick locks she'd once had to dry in this frigid room, and Rachel was prone to getting colds.

Lying there, her teeth chattering uncontrollably, she noticed something on the wall and squinted, trying to make it out. Someone had made hatch marks, rows and rows of groupings of four lines with another line through them. She counted them up. 274 tallies. *Counting time*, she thought to herself as the realization hit. Rachel did the math and thought back to the list of names they'd already discovered etched into the wall. The previous women, who had to be the ones who'd etched these lines

115

into the wall, had been here around nine months. Her and Sasha had only been here one night so far, which meant they had a full nine months to either escape, or never set foot outside this cabin alive again. Her breath caught in her throat and tears streamed down her cheeks.

CHAPTER 11

By the time Monday rolled around, I couldn't decide which emotion was winning: anxiousness or curiosity. Andie was still at work but as promised, Travis came over to support me during my meeting with the FBI. I sat on the couch in silence next to him, watching the time tick by slowly on my phone. Absentmindedly, I picked at a loose thread on the couch cushion.

'It's going to be fine, Liz,' he said consolingly, giving my forearm a friendly squeeze.

I took a deep breath. 'I know, I know. It's just weird, right? Like what could my family possibly be connected to that the FBI would want to talk to me about? I know my mom broke some laws when she was young, but do you think there's another criminal in my family? Or maybe my mother did something way worse than a drug charge.' I bit my thumbnail, hoping that last comment was not the case.

'Don't jump to conclusions. There seem to be other options in your family tree, right?'

'Not really. At this point, there's only Adam and Cris on the Dominio side. I guess Adam could have children that I don't know about. Or it could be about someone on my father's side but I don't even know his name to investigate. Cris said he never met him and my grandfather only called him "that boy".'

I rubbed my eyes, feeling the prickling of a headache forming behind them. I noticed streaks of black eyeliner across my fingers as I pulled my hands away. *Damnit, now I probably look like a raccoon. Great.* Quickly bringing up the camera on my phone to assess the damage and wipe the smeared liner from under my eyes, I took another deep, steadying breath.

'I don't know how much help I'm even going to be since I've only met Cris at this point. My connection to my family tree is pretty sparse.'

'I don't know,' Travis said, slipping his own phone back into the interior pocket of his blazer. 'But if they ask anything that could get you into trouble, I'll step in. Don't worry Liz, I got your back, okay?'

'Thanks, Trav,' I replied, giving him a grateful smile.

I wasn't sure if we had ever been alone together without Andie around. Sometimes I worried that Travis and I were in a weird game of tug of war, vying for Andie's time and attention. I didn't want to come between them because I had to admit, Travis was a great match for Andie, who usually discarded men after only a few weeks of dating. None of them could ever keep up with her personality, until Travis. He had lasted way past the dreaded three week mark, and matched Andie barb for barb, making her happier than I had ever seen in her previous relationships. But today he was here on his own just to be a good friend to his girlfriend's cousin, and I deeply appreciated it. I hoped that one day I'd find a boyfriend as kind and generous as him.

The loud buzzer pulled me quickly out of my reverie. Leaping from the couch, I speed walked over to the front door. Travis rose and followed in my wake at a slower pace. Surely, as a lawyer, he was much more comfortable around law enforcement than I was. Come to think of it, I'd never even spoken to a police officer, let alone someone from the FBI. I figured they were the punctual type, as the clock ticked over to the exact time Hannigan said they would arrive just as I pressed the button to let them in. A minute later, there was a crisp, purposeful knock on the door. Taking a deep breath to calm myself, I gripped the doorknob and pulled, my heart pounding in my ears. *Why am I so nervous?* It wasn't like I'd personally broken any laws. But the anticipation of the conversation was making my palms sweat.

I came face to face with the two agents, one man and one woman, dressed alike in collared shirts with open tailored suit jackets and slacks. I envied how wrinkle free they appeared. These were two people who paid very close attention to detail, all the way from their impeccably styled hair and courteous smiles, down to the shine of their freshly polished shoes. I did a double take when my eyes fell upon the woman's black patent leather heels, the telltale Louboutin red bottoms peeking out from the sides.

'Hello, Elizabeth Catalano?'

My eyes snapped back up to the agents' faces. 'Yes, hi, you can call me Liz,' I said, reaching out a hand after trying to discreetly wipe the sweat on my jeans.

The man extended his arm first as if he was the one in charge, giving me a firm grip. He had blond hair that was longer on top, and icy blue eyes that still held a warmth despite their cool tones. There were creases along the corners of his eyes and mouth that suggested he had either laughed a lot or been thinking too hard. Probably the latter, I thought as I released his hand.

'Hi Liz, thanks for seeing us. I'm Special Agent Mark Hannigan and this is my partner, Special Agent Tamara Beck,' he gestured to his partner, who also extended a hand to me.

Beck was slightly shorter than Hannigan and had dark brown hair that was slicked back, ending in a neat low bun, not a single hair out of place. In stark contrast to the severe hairstyle, her face was soft and welcoming as she gave my hand a shake.

'Hi Liz, nice to meet you,' she said.

Her grip was not quite as firm as her counterpart's, her nails short and clean. I wondered if they ever played good cop bad cop, and if she would be the good cop. She was much less intimidating than Hannigan. They both looked to Travis, eyeing him up with curiosity.

'Oh, sorry, this is my friend, Travis,' I said, gesturing to him. He reached out his hand, assuming a professional persona that I had never seen from him before.

'Travis Baker,' he said, stiff but polite, shaking both of their hands in turn. 'I work with Sachs and Sullivan downtown.'

'Nice to meet you Travis,' said Hannigan. 'But I assure you, Liz, there's no need for legal counsel. We'd really just like to have a quick conversation.'

'Well that's a relief,' I said, smiling nervously. 'But really, he's just here for moral support. Why don't you come in and have a seat?' I stepped back and gestured them in the rest of the way toward the living room. 'Can I get you something to drink? Coffee? Water?'

'Oh no, that's alright,' said Beck. 'Just a few quick questions, it shouldn't take long. Nothing to be nervous about.' She was clearly good at reading people, trying to calm the anxiety she no doubt saw lingering on my face. I'd never been good at hiding my emotions.

I opened my arm toward the couch where they sat themselves on the edges of the cushions, not getting overly comfortable. Travis and I sat in two mismatched chairs across from them that I'd pulled around from other areas of the apartment. I spun my ring around on my finger, waiting for someone to break the silence.

'Okay, so let's just dive right in, shall we?' Hannigan said, giving me a smile.

'Yes, that would be great,' I responded. 'What is it that you want to talk to me about?'

'Yes, well, as you know, you opted-in to allow law enforcement access to your DNA results on GEDMatch when you loaded your profile to the website,' Hannigan explained. Beck folded her hands politely in her lap, watching my expression closely. I felt like I was being studied. 'Why don't you tell us a little bit about why you loaded your DNA and allowed it to be accessed in that manner?'

I cleared my throat, giving Travis a quick side glance. He nodded so I looked at Hannigan and explained. 'I recently did the 23andMe DNA ancestry kit and found out, because of its results, that I'm adopted,' I said. Their expressions remained neutral save for a quick shared glance. I assumed they were conditioned not to react to surprising information like the average person would but I was curious about what they were thinking. 'I wanted to find out more about my biological family, and when none of my matches from 23andMe responded to my messages, I decided to load it to GEDMatch to see if I could find any other family members who participated in different ancestry tests. The only thing I knew about my biological mother was that she was incarcerated in New York when she gave me up, so I thought I may find out more if I connected with the police in some way. To be honest, I wasn't really sure what opting into that would do.'

Hannigan and Beck both nodded politely, Hannigan taking out a small field notebook and pen from inside his jacket and flipping it open to take notes. He jotted down a quick line that I couldn't quite read upside down before turning his attention back to me. This time, Beck addressed me.

'Well, Liz, the reason we reached out to speak with you today is because, when you opted into that feature, we got a familial match to a DNA profile associated with a case that we are working on.'

'A familial match? What does that mean exactly?' I asked, hoping it didn't make me look stupid. I could guess but decided to risk asking a dumb question to make sure I understood every detail. Travis looked like he wanted to say something but stayed silent and watchful. Maybe I should have picked his brain more before they arrived.

Hannigan took the reins again. 'Basically, it means that DNA we've collected from a crime scene has enough markers in common with yours that we can conclude the suspect is related to you.'

'Oh my God,' I said, looking frantically at Travis.

Even though this was what I'd assumed it meant, having it confirmed that I might be related to a criminal on the FBI's radar made my stomach drop. Was I their link to a mysterious criminal hiding out there in the shadows?

If they were talking to me about my match, that meant they likely didn't know who their suspect was. I hated to admit it but part of me was intrigued to hear more. *What did my biological family get me involved in?*

'What crime is it?' I asked.

Hannigan and Beck shared a quick look. 'We can't go into too much detail at this time,' Hannigan continued. 'But we can tell you that we're looking into multiple homicides that cross state lines—'

'Wait,' I interrupted, my pulse racing. 'Multiple homicides. So, you're talking about a serial killer?' Travis leaned forward on his seat.

After a tense pause, Beck said, 'We just have a couple of questions we're hoping you can answer to help us in our investigation.'

'But are you saying Liz *is* related to a serial killer?' Travis persisted.

'I'm afraid we really can't get into specifics at this time,' Beck said. Hannigan made another note in his notebook. 'But can you please tell us if you've had contact with any male members of your biological family since completing the DNA analysis?'

Her determination to neither confirm nor deny my suspicion that they were investigating a serial killer case, made me pretty confident that my fears were founded. What else could multiple homicides mean? My heart thudded wildly in my chest, the pulsating sound in my ears was almost deafening. The small kernel of excitement I felt earlier gave way to complete panic. *Can I really be related to a monster?* This wasn't about a theft or some white-collar crime. They were talking about murder. And not just one murder. The level of danger I could potentially be walking into by searching out my biological family just multiplied exponentially. Pulling myself out of an oncoming downward mental spiral, I tried to refocus.

'I've only had contact with my grand uncle on my mother's side, and there's no way he could be involved in something like this. I've spent a little time with him and his wife and they've been so kind. From what I've gathered so far, the only other relatives on my mother's side have long since died or moved away. No one seems to know anything about my dad's side at this point. Is it possible there is some kind of mistake?'

Hannigan looked up from his notebook. 'Do you have your biological father's name?'

'No, I haven't connected with anyone from that side yet. Cris and Rosie, my grand uncle and his wife, didn't even know my mother, Teresa, had given birth until I contacted them. They knew Teresa had a boyfriend, but they never knew his name.'

Beck nodded and continued. 'Can you tell us about your grand uncle, Liz? And any other male relatives in the picture? That may help us decipher if anyone you know of is a candidate for our match.'

I shot Travis another nervous look but he gave me a nod, letting me know it was okay to continue. I took a deep breath. 'His name is Cristian Dominio. He lives in Connecticut with his wife Rosie, who is so sweet,' I added hastily, anxious to quell any concerns the agents may have about them. But suddenly I was doubting my first impressions. I really didn't know that much about them, even though they'd seemed harmless. Could it have been an act? 'He's my maternal grandfather, Frank's, half-brother. Same dad, different moms.' I squinted, concentrating, making sure I explained the relations properly. 'Actually, hold on. It may help if I write the names down for you.'

I looked around, about to stand up when Travis interjected, 'Oh, here, Liz, I got you,' and he quickly got up and grabbed his leather briefcase he'd brought with him from work. He handed me a yellow legal pad and a black felt tip pen.

'Thanks, Trav.' I pulled the lid off the pen and snapped it onto the back. Scooting closer to the coffee table and placing the legal pad down on top of it so that everyone could see, I leaned forward and started to write Cris's name, the ink flowing smoothly. *Wow,* I thought, looking at the pen appreciatively. *There's a high likelihood Travis is not getting this pen back.*

Underneath Cris, I wrote Frank next. 'The only other male relative Cris talked about in detail was Frank, my mother's father who I just mentioned, but he passed away before I met them.' I paused for a second, the pen hovering next to Frank's name and thinking back on my conversation with Cris. 'Cris also mentioned he had a cousin named Adam. But after Adam's father died, he and his mother moved away, so they lost track of them. Sorry, I'm not sure how helpful this is,' I said as I scribbled down Adam's name under Frank's.

'No need to apologize,' Beck said, smiling. 'You're doing great. Please, continue.'

I took a deep breath, looking down at the paltry list of three names, feeling like a failure for not having more to give them. Then I remembered another name I could add. 'There was also Frank and Cris's dad, Rodrigo, but he passed away a long time ago as well,' I said and wrote his name down. 'That's all that I know about the Dominio side.' I could feel my cheeks getting warmer, nervous about how little I knew.

Hannigan nodded, making a few notes in his notebook

but not skipping a beat. 'Would you mind if we hold on to that list for now? For reference?'

'Oh, um, sure,' I said, pushing the paper closer to him.

'Thank you. So, how well do you know your grand uncle, Cristian Dominio? Have you spent a lot of time with him?' Hannigan asked.

'I wouldn't say *a lot*,' I replied, now getting uncomfortable with answering questions about the only piece of real family I knew. 'I've met him in person once so far, and we've FaceTimed, but we're planning another visit. I really want to learn more about my biological family and Cris and his wife are all I have right now. I'm still getting to know them and they seem open to getting to know me too.' I paused, looking back and forth between the two agents. 'But there's no way you could really think it's him, right? I mean, he's married to the loveliest woman and he's a vet who rescues and cares for sick animals. There's no way someone with a heart like that could be a murderer. I've been to his house. He just doesn't seem like he could hurt a fly.'

'Did you say he's a veterinarian?' Beck said, giving a knowing look to her partner.

Their constant shared glances were making me suspect that there was something important they weren't telling me. Hannigan scribbled a note and then flipped the page quickly to reveal a blank one, hiding it from my prying eyes.

'Yeah, he has his own practice, has for years,' I said, sharing my own confused look with Travis as yet another look passed between the agents.

'Is that significant?' Travis asked, making eye contact with Hannigan. We both seemed to assume he was the one who decided how much information could be shared.

126

'We can't say more right now,' Hannigan said. He retrained his eyes on me. 'Would you be willing to let us access your 23andMe results? I know you said that you don't know anything about your father's side yet, but it's possible some of them are in your results as well. It would be a great help in identifying other potential matches if we can develop your family tree in more detail.'

I wrung my hands in my lap. What he meant was, it would help them identify other *suspects* in my family tree. I wasn't sure I wanted the FBI poking around into my biological family, searching for suspects. Though I didn't know these people, I would still be the one bringing the FBI to their doorstep. It felt like I was double-crossing them before I'd even met them. At the same time, if they were talking about an active serial killer, I wanted to help. If I let them access my family tree it could help catch a murderer. A chill ran up my spine at the thought of sharing DNA with someone capable of such horrible crimes.

Travis interrupted my thoughts. 'Liz, this is totally your decision. You don't have to give them your log in. But if it can help catch a killer, isn't it worth considering?' Travis's forehead crinkled as he looked at me, emphasizing his point. Hannigan and Beck smiled at Travis, clearly grateful that he was urging me to comply.

Nodding my head, I exhaled, looking down at my shoes that now seemed drab compared to those amazing, expensive Louboutins I'd envied on Beck's feet.

Looking back at Hannigan, I said. 'I'll give you my log in details on two conditions. If you find anything that disparages my biological family in any way, I'd like to know before the media finds out. I deserve the truth and don't want to find out secondhand along with the rest of the country.'

Hannigan looked at me thoughtfully. 'As this is an active investigation, we can only share limited information with you, otherwise it could jeopardize the case.'

'Do you want my log in information or not?' I said heatedly, not entirely sure where this newfound bravado was coming from.

I may have been testing the limits with the way I was addressing the FBI, but I was horrified by the idea that my family was wrapped up in this. I hardly knew which way was up or down anymore, and this was just more salt in the wound, more proof of how little I knew about where I came from. The agents looked at one another. I softened a little, not wanting to be too combative. I needed them to continue to share information with me and they were just doing their job.

'Look, all I'm asking for is a heads-up. Some advance warning so I don't find out from the news that someone in my family is a serial killer.' I splayed my hands out in front of me for emphasis.

Hannigan stared at me for a moment and then nodded his head. 'What's the second condition?'

'If you find any other family members that you clear as suspects, can you let me know? And maybe let them know I'd like to meet them? I haven't had much luck getting in contact with any other relatives and I'd like to learn more about where I came from.'

Hannigan gave me a small smile and nodded. Quickly reaching for the list of my known male family members on the table, I pulled it closer to me and wrote down my log in information on the corner of the page before pushing it back in his direction. I also wrote down my GEDMatch information, just in case that was helpful. It hadn't populated very many results at this point, but maybe they would see something that I hadn't. Hannigan tore the sheet of paper off the notepad and picked it up as he and Beck simultaneously stood. Travis and I jumped up, mirroring their movements.

'Thank you, Liz. Here's my card,' Hannigan extended a small, stiff business card in my direction. 'Please reach out if you think of anything that may be helpful. We'll be in touch if we have more questions as our investigation progresses.'

I felt rooted to the spot, staring at the business card in my hand, the inky black lettering etched into the crisp cream cardstock. They turned toward the door and my need for information took over, taking one last shot.

'Are you sure you can't tell me which case you're working on? I promise I won't tell anyone.'

Hannigan turned back around and gave me another small smile. 'Sorry Liz, not at this point.'

With my hopes dashed, I nodded and looked back down at the card in my hands, feeling overwhelmed by everything I had just heard.

'I'll show you two out,' Travis said, shaking their hands one last time and walking them to the door. I vaguely registered the click of the deadbolt turning as he locked the door behind them. When Travis came back into the room, I was standing exactly where he'd left me. 'Come on, Lizzie, sit down.'

'Did that really happen? Did they just tell me that I'm related to a serial killer?' I exclaimed, settling into the couch and ringing my hands together.

'Well, they certainly implied it. If the FBI is investigating multiple murders, that seems like all it could be. I'm so sorry Liz, this must be a lot to take in. Especially on top of finding out you're adopted.'

I barely heard Travis, my mind still whirling around the names I'd written down for them. 'There's no way Cris is a murderer. I know I haven't known him that long, and sure he's a bit awkward, but a murderer? Really? They just have to be wrong. DNA can be wrong sometimes, right?' I looked at Travis hopefully.

Travis sucked his teeth and pulled his head to the side, obviously not agreeing with my last statement. 'Well, it could be a match to another relative that you haven't met yet, or one that isn't in any of the ancestry databases. You only have part of your family tree at this point, there might be a hundred more distant relatives out there that could be the match. The chances of it being Cris seem small. I wouldn't write off your uncle just yet. But, be careful, okay Lizzie? They wouldn't talk to you if they didn't feel strongly that the familial match meant something. And their antennas clearly went up when you mentioned Cris is a vet.'

'Yeah, that was weird . . . I guess you're right.' I took a deep inhale, holding it for a long second before letting it escape with a loud puff. 'I'm going to give him the benefit of the doubt and keep getting to know him. I would hate to cut off the only family I've found if it turns out he's innocent, especially when they still have other people to look into.'

But I knew deep down I'd have to keep my guard up with Cris just in case. While Travis's logic was correct and the chances of Cris being a murderer were slim, it was still a possibility.

'Andie is going to be so mad she missed this,' he said, running a hand through his thick wavy hair, clearly trying to lighten the mood.

I chuckled, knowing he was right. I tossed Hannigan's

business card on the table, sitting down on the couch. Grabbing my laptop, I popped it open and pulled up a Google search.

'Getting back to work already?' Travis asked, his eyebrows raised.

'Oh no, not yet. I just want to take a look and see if I can find a list of active serial killers. Maybe narrow down the possibilities?' I replied, looking at Travis with a shrug.

'Good idea. I have a few minutes before I have to head back.'

After typing 'active serial killers' in the search bar, a number of results came up. As we scanned the page, I pointed to one list that seemed the most recent and clicked on it. I was able to cross many off the list by the fact that the murders were limited to one state, and from what the agents said, these murders were multi-state.

'Okay, looks like there's only a few active options that cross state lines. The Bus Stop Strangler, all the victims were women in their forties and were last seen exiting the bus at their usual stops near their homes. Bodies were found strangled with an extension cord, naked and bound in their bathtubs, and all the mirrors in the houses were covered.' I cringed, that horrible image trying to burrow its way into my brain. I quickly moved on to the next on the list. 'Then there's The Smiley Face Killer, a group of detectives came up with a theory that a number of young white men who were assumed to have accidentally drowned across the US, were actually the work of a serial killer or killers, because of smiley face graffiti discovered near where all the bodies were found. And they all had GHB in their systems. That one could be drug-related I guess, and we know my mom was connected to that world. The last victim was found in 2017.'

'Maybe,' Travis replied with a shrug. 'I've seen that one talked about a few times on the news, but no one can ever seem to agree whether they're all truly connected. Who else on the list has potential?'

'Well, then we have The Paradise Stalker, who kills women who vacation alone. Not only does he leave a "Wish you were here" postcard on the bed with a poem about why and how he chose the victim, but he also sends a matching copy of those postcards to the families of the victims.' An icy chill spread through me.

'That's so messed up,' Travis replied with a disgusted look on his face. 'Remind me never to let Andie go on one of her impulsive road trips without me ever again.'

'Yeah, I can't believe I haven't heard about that one. But damn, that is so creepy. I've never really been one to travel alone, not like Andie, but it's definitely off the table now. Looks like they've found bodies in Florida, California and Hawaii.'

'Are there any others it could be?'

'The only other one that's coming up as active is The Tri-State Killer. But there's a note that he's been dormant since 2012. Since then, no other bodies have been found that fit his method. I remember hearing about him on the news, but not for a long time. It's marked "dead or dormant" but still falls in the active category because he's never been caught. Probably not him since it seems like they were working on a killer who's still murdering, right?' I asked, turning toward Travis.

'It seemed like it, but I guess you never know. They didn't give us too many details.'

'Yeah, that's true. Ugh, I wonder who it is.'

After scanning the page one more time, I closed my laptop and leaned back onto the couch. Travis gave me a reassuring squeeze on the shoulder and said he needed to head back to work, eager to finish up in time to come back for dinner. Sitting alone in the apartment, I couldn't stop thinking about everything that had transpired. First, my parents had lied about who I was my whole life, shaking what I thought I knew about my identity to the core. And now, as I was trying to connect with my biological family, here came the FBI, poking holes in the weak balloon of hope that had swelled when I met my uncle. It just had to be someone I hadn't met yet. There was no way Cris was a serial killer.

Determined to sniff out any morsel of information, I decided it was time to do a deeper dive into Adam, the only other relative I knew of who was likely to still be alive. Since my previous attempts to find him on social media had failed, I put his name into a general Google search. I scrolled through two pages of articles and posts containing references to Adam Dominios who were all too young to be the Adam from my family tree, until I found what I was looking for. *Bingo!* An article from 2012 in a Boston newspaper about an explosion at a construction site that included Adam's name and photo. He was one of the injured workmen. Out of all the photos I'd found during this search, he was the only one it could possibly be, given how old Adam would have been in 2012. I know Cris had mentioned Adam moved away to the West Coast, but he must have moved back east at some point.

I checked the byline and found the journalist, Caroline Kraut's, contact email on the newspaper's website. If I was right and this was the correct Adam Dominio, I hoped the killer was him and not Cris. It was scary to be so closely related to a killer, but at least with Adam, I hadn't spent time getting to know him yet. While tracking him down could be dangerous, my only other option was waiting for the agents to give me more information. I knew I couldn't wait for that, and there was no guarantee how much they would even tell me. I sent Caroline an email letting her know which article I was interested in and asking her to call or email me as soon as she could. The article was seven years old but I mentally crossed my fingers that she would still have information from that story, and possibly help me track down Adam.

Sara Wolfe & Frankie Paige

1999

CHAPTER 12

Joey Ramone belted out about wanting to be sedated through the stereo speakers as Frankie walked into the living room to turn it down. The guy from the utility company went to the kitchen to check the stove. Frankie didn't smell any gas but there'd been a gas explosion in Newark a few weeks ago, so it was better to be safe than sorry. She turned the volume dial all the way to the left and took a swig from the Zima sitting next to the stereo. After setting it back down, she spun around and was startled to find the man standing right behind her.

'Um, did you need something?' She took a small step backwards, trying to put a more comfortable amount of space between them. She tugged her low slung bootcut jeans up. She'd noticed the man looking at her exposed belly below her crop top and it made her uncomfortable.

'Would you mind coming with me into the kitchen?' He gave her a charming smile. 'I just need you to turn on the oven for me while I check everything out. All these properties have such a variety of appliance models from different years and I want to make sure it's turned on properly for my final inspection.'

'Oh, okay. It's pretty simple to turn on actually,' Frankie said as she walked toward the kitchen, feeling him walking so close behind her that he was almost stepping on her heels.

She smelled coffee on his breath every time he exhaled. It was a standard oven knob, she wasn't sure why he needed her to do it, but the sooner he completed his inspection, the sooner she could set up plates and silverware for the food Sara was bringing home. Their favorite show, *Dharma and Greg*, would be on in a half hour. Sara was running a little late and Frankie hoped she wouldn't miss the beginning. Just before Frankie crossed through the doorway to the kitchen, she felt a sharp pinch in her neck. She swatted at the area like she would at a mosquito. She turned around to find the man standing there, a wicked smile on his face and a syringe in his hand.

'What the hell?' she yelled out, her hand now clasped tightly over the throbbing pinprick.

Her eyes grew wide, realizing what he'd done as her limbs became heavy and lethargic. Panic seeped into her bones. Relying on the trace of adrenaline surging through her from a primal urge to defend herself, she rammed her body into his despite him being twice her size. The two struggled for several seconds before he turned her around, pinned her arms down against her body and clenched one hand over her mouth to muffle her screams. She continued to flail and lash out but the world around her was swaying. It was like she was fighting through murky water, her arms and legs giving up on her one by one.

A jingle of keys from just outside the front door filtered through her cloudy but frantic thoughts. *Oh thank God! Sara!* The man paused for a millisecond at the sound and then began to drag her toward her bedroom down the small hallway. Frankie realized that rather than being able to save her, her roommate may actually be walking right into the danger, about to meet the same fate. She tried to scream to warn Sara but it came out muffled under his hand and she was weak. She pried her lips open under his grip and bit his finger as hard as she could muster. His hand immediately released her mouth, just as the front door flew open.

'I got Chinese. I know I'm late, but I hope you're hun— What the—?'

Frankie could just make out Sara's shape in the dim lighting from the solitary lamp next to the couch. Their porch light had been out for weeks, she had been meaning to replace the bulb.

'Sara, run!' she screamed with everything she had left in her, fighting to stay conscious.

Sara stood frozen in the doorway. The man stiffened, then dropped Frankie to the ground. Her body fell to the carpet in a heap, her head landing sideways in the direction of his retreating form. She watched as he ran to the back door and darted out into the night, her eyes level with his white athletic sneakers. Sara rushed over and rolled Frankie over onto her back, gently shaking her shoulders.

'Frankie! Frankie, are you okay? Stay with me, Frankie.'

She was barely holding on to consciousness. Sara's face swam above her as darkness crept into her vision. She vaguely registered Sara lunging for the phone near the kitchen and dialing 911, speaking frantically to them about an intruder and an assault as she made her way back to Frankie's side. Frankie closed her eyes and tried to remember what the man had looked like. She needed to tell them while it was still fresh in her mind. It was dark with the porch light out and only a lamp on in the living room, she hadn't really gotten a good look at his face. She'd been tired, flipping through a magazine while she waited for Sara and was anxious for him to leave. All she could find in the corners of her memory were vague impressions. He was tall, maybe 6'1", dark brown or maybe black hair peeking out from under a grey base-ball cap. Brown eyes, wide nose, thick eyebrows. She struggled to remember more, the shape of his face or the slant of his eyes, but she was fading fast and the images were slipping away like water leaking through her fingers. The image of the man disintegrated as whatever he'd injected her with took hold.

'Did you see him?' she whispered to Sara, trying desperately to hold on to reality. She wasn't sure if Sara even heard her.

'2975 Parkwood Lane. Yes, she's conscious, but just barely. No, no visible injuries,' she heard as if from far away.

'Injected,' Frankie forced out.

'She says she was injected with something.' Sara pulled the phone away from her mouth. 'They're on their way, Frankie. Hang in there.' She squeezed one of Frankie's hands tightly. After a pause Sara said, 'It was dark, I only got a quick look. He was tall, with dark hair, I think. He was wearing a baseball cap. He wore grey pants and a button up shirt.'

'Brown eyes,' Frankie said before her eyes closed again.

'Frankie says he's got brown eyes. Ten minutes? Will you stay on the phone with me until they get here?'

140

A cool night breeze blew in through the still open back door. Sara released Frankie's hand and jumped up, scurrying over and snapping it shut. She clicked the lock before rushing back to Frankie's side. Sara kept talking to Frankie but it was garbled, like she was talking to her from behind a thick pane of glass. Losing her last grip on consciousness, Frankie's final thought before she succumbed to the darkness was, *was that The Tri-State Killer?*

CHAPTER 13

I struggled to carry three heavy paper bags of groceries from Trader Joe's as I walked up the street to my building, the short handles digging into my forearms. After a long day at work, an intense craving for steak and a big fresh salad hit me, so I'd decided to splurge on organic vegetables and a nice rib eye at the market in addition to the usual weekly haul. A muffled ding sounded from my phone inside my purse as one of the bags started slipping. I placed all the bags on the ground and stretched my aching arms. Taking the opportunity to check my phone, I dug it out and clicked my email app. I let out a 'yip' when I saw the new email was from Caroline Kraut, the reporter I'd contacted in the hopes of finding Adam's employer. It had taken three emails and a bit of pestering to get her to look up the information from so long ago, but my tenacity had paid off. Caroline had emailed me the name of the company Adam had worked for, along with the phone number she had for them on file. It was a start.

With renewed energy, I picked the bags back up and

rushed up the steps into our building. On my way down the hallway, I quickly grabbed the mail from the small metal boxes lining the wall. After swinging our apartment door open, I spotted Andie sitting quietly in the living room, no TV on or Spotify playlist blasting through her laptop speakers. The calm silence was extremely out of character.

'Hey, cuz, guess what? That reporter Caroline finally emailed me—' Andie turned around and my smile immediately fell. She was visibly upset.

'I . . . I need to talk to you about something.'

I dropped the bags and mail on the kitchen counter and walked quickly to the couch, plopping down next to Andie. 'Okay, you're freaking me out. What's wrong? Did you have a fight with Travis or something?'

Andie shook her head. 'No, it's nothing like that.' She paused and looked at her hands. She was fiddling with a hair tie, looping it around her hand multiple times and then taking it off. I remained quiet, waiting for her to continue. I'd only seen Andie in this state once, when our grandpa had collapsed and been taken to the hospital. Finally, she looked up at me and there were tears in her eyes. 'You're gonna hate me, Lizzie.'

My entire body tensed. This wasn't about a hospitalized family member. A dry, metallic taste invaded my mouth and I swallowed a few times, trying to brace myself for yet another family truth bomb. 'Just tell me, Andie.'

Andie let out a deep breath. 'Okay. I think I might have known that you were adopted.'

I went into shock, my hands shaking. Not Andie, too.

'What? What do you mean that you *think* you knew? You either knew or you didn't. Which is it?' Another person I loved and trusted who had kept this from me. It couldn't be true.

'Just let me tell you the whole story, then you can yell at me.' Andie waited until I gritted my teeth and nodded. She took in a deep, shaky breath. 'Remember when I was eight years old and we moved to the McCadden Street house? Well, when I was helping Mom unpack a box of photos in our new living room, I came across a loose photo of your parents holding you as a baby with a banner behind them that said, "Happy Adoption Day!" I knew it had to be you in their arms but I didn't understand the banner. I showed it to my mom and she looked panicked. Finally, she said something about that being the day they adopted your cat Millie. At the time, I believed it, so I never said anything to you about it. My mom just stuffed it back in a box after that and I never saw it again.'

My shoulders relaxed and I unclenched my jaw. 'Andie you were a kid, if that's what your mom told you, then of course you'd believe her. Why would I be mad at that?' I softened, realizing Andie hadn't purposefully kept this secret from me the way my parents had. Relief washed over me. I didn't think I could cope with all of this if I lost trust in Andie, too. Then, another thought crept in. I narrowed my eyes at her. 'But that's not all of it, is it? You wouldn't feel so guilty if that was all this was. What else are you hiding, Andie?'

Andie puffed out her cheeks and looked off to the side, exhaling loudly. 'I did believe my mom in that moment. But something about the photo didn't feel right and it kept nagging at me. So, eventually I did the math. My mom's explanation didn't make sense, because if you were a baby on Millie's adoption day, then you and Millie

145

would be about the same age since your parents got her as a kitten. But I knew you weren't the same age, because we'd given Millie that lame third birthday party in your backyard when you were six and I was seven, remember?'

Andie and I had thrown together a makeshift party, with cupcakes formed from a mixture of wet and dry cat food. We'd stationed our stuffed animals around the plastic kids' table in the backyard and sprinkled confetti all over them. We even got Millie to wear a paper cone birthday hat. 'Okay, yeah, but why didn't you tell me then? You'd obviously figured it out.'

Andie reluctantly continued. 'I'm sorry, Liz. I knew what my mom told me about the photo was a lie, that you were three years older than Millie. You used to call her your little sister. I confronted my parents at dinner one night and told them that I knew Mom had lied about the photo. The conversation didn't go well. My mom came up with all these excuses and alternate explanations and I kept poking holes in everything she told me. Finally, my dad got angry and told me to stop questioning my mother. That I should stay out of it because it had nothing to do with me. It was one of the only times my dad ever yelled at me. It shook me to the core because you know my dad never gets angry. He told me not to say anything to anyone about the photo, that I didn't understand what I was talking about, and if I repeated it to you or Uncle Gary and Aunt C, there would be big trouble.'

My face hardened. 'You still should have told me, Andie. We tell each other everything. And you know how much it kills me to be in the dark about anything, especially something this major. Even if it would have upset me or our parents, I still deserved to know.'

Andie spread her hands out, trying to find the right

146

words to justify her betrayal. 'I point blank asked my parents if you were adopted and they vehemently said no. I'm not like you, Lizzie. I don't *need* to know everything. Especially if it might hurt people I love. And honestly, maybe I didn't want to know. If I accepted it, then I'd have to tell you something that would cause you pain and that was the last thing I wanted. My dad said the photo didn't mean what I thought it did, and as a kid I wouldn't be able to understand it so I should just let it go. I begged them to tell me what it meant. But Dad slammed his fist down on the table and told me to drop it. I'd never seen him that angry before.'

'Andie, you still should have told me! If not then, especially now when the DNA kit and everything came up over the last few weeks. You *were* awful quick to figure out how different our 23andMe results were. Why didn't you just tell me?' I jumped up and went to the kitchen. I yanked items out of the bags and threw the refrigerator door open, angrily putting my groceries away. Andie followed me and leaned against the butcher block table. 'How could you sit there pretending you were so surprised about my adoption? It was just another lie.'

'You're right, I should have told you then. When we were kids, I didn't want to make my dad angry and I was so young. I thought maybe they were right, that I was mistaken and that saying anything would just hurt everyone. I didn't want to believe you were adopted because I wanted desperately for you to be my cousin. The idea that you may not be terrified me. I was afraid of losing you. I know that sounds stupid but at eight years old, it really freaked me out. It was easier to believe them than to keep pushing. I was afraid of the truth, I guess. So, I just shoved it down and lived in denial about that moment for all these years. I felt like if I didn't say it out loud, then it wouldn't be true. Then after so much time passed, it almost felt like it never even happened, like I'd imagined it. When the adoption story came out, I just couldn't accept that I had known on some level all this time. I know that's not an excuse, I should have told you right away. But I was scared, Lizzie. I saw how upset you were with your parents, and I didn't want you to be angry with me too. It was wrong.'

I slammed the fridge door shut and pulled out the cutting board. Grabbing a knife and a few tomatoes, I rinsed them and began furiously chopping. Andie gave me a nervous look.

'I don't know what to say Andie,' I shook my head. It felt like steam was coming out of my ears like in the cartoons I'd watched as a child.

'Liz, please slow down. You're gonna chop a finger off. And then I'll have to rush you to the hospital and it'll be a huge ordeal. They'll have to give you a prosthetic finger and you won't be able to play piano ever again . . .' Andie said with a small, hopeful smile.

I dropped the knife. My hands were shaking. 'This isn't funny, Andie! First I find out my parents lied to me and now you.'

'I didn't lie to you Liz, I just didn't tell you about the photo.' She held up her hand as I opened my mouth. 'Yes, I know, a lie of omission is still a lie. But can you see it from my side for just a second? Please?'

Her eyebrows were furrowed, tears clinging to her lashes. Andie rarely cried. She looked so upset and worried that my icy exterior melted slightly. I put my hands on the counter and exhaled. Andie had perfected the sad, pitiful look over the years and it was incredibly effective.

She looked up at me with her big brown weepy eyes, chipping away at my anger.

'I guess I can see how something like that would scare you and you'd want to believe your parents and cling to that. I just . . . I'm still reeling from the fact that my parents *did* lie to me, and now I have this with you. You guys are the people I trusted to be completely honest with me. And now I feel alone in this.' Suddenly a thought hit me and my eyes flashed back to Andie. 'Is that why you gave me the 23andMe kit? Were you trying to make this all come out? You acted so surprised when you weren't one of my matches, but—'

'Oh Liz, no, that wasn't my intention at all. I just thought it was this cool thing that everyone was doing and I wanted to share it with you. Honestly, I'd pushed the memory of that photo down years ago and didn't even think about it again until the kit results came back and you found out you were adopted.'

She sniffled and shrugged one shoulder. I gave a small reluctant nod, doing my best to calm my anger and understand where Andie was coming from but my hands continued to shake as my heart pounded rapidly.

'I understand you're furious with me and I'm so sorry, Liz. I should have told you the minute your parents came clean. It's been killing me. I wish so badly that I'd told you way back then. Things would have been so different for you. Maybe you could have met more of your bio-family before it was too late. I can't help but feel like some of this is my fault.'

Exhaling long and slow, I finally replied, 'I'm not mad at you, really, I'm . . . sad, I guess.' I shook my head. I could tell Andie regretted keeping the secret and I didn't want to get wrapped up in a fight with my closest friend when I already wasn't speaking to my parents. But I wasn't quite ready to forgive her. Finally, I said, 'I think I need to take a walk. Get some fresh air and clear my head for a bit.'

Abandoning the half-chopped tomatoes on the counter, I wiped my hands on the kitchen towel and walked to the door.

'Lizzie, let me come with you. You shouldn't be alone right now. I'm still your cousin and I love you. Please don't shut me out.'

I paused with my hand on the doorknob. 'I think being alone is exactly what I need right now. I'll be okay Andie, I just need some space,' I said as I opened the door. 'I'll be back soon.'

Shoving my hands in my pockets in an effort to still them, I walked briskly around our block, absent-mindedly taking turns at random. I didn't know how to feel about this news. I wasn't lying when I'd said I could understand why Andie hadn't told me before. At the same time though, it felt like a betrayal, and she was the last person I thought would ever betray me. Over the years, we'd told each other our darkest secrets without judgement, always fessing up no matter how hard it was to admit some of our mistakes. Complete honesty had always been the code of our friendship. *How could she have kept this from me?*

After walking up and down nearby streets for another ten minutes, I circled back to my block and found myself at The Beast. I decided to go in and get a drink, hoping it would take the edge off. The bar had paintings of beasts from around the world lining its walls, with a scroll next to each painting detailing the monster's folklore. Sasquatch wandering through the trees, the Loch Ness Monster's head popping up from dark, murky waters, Medusa's snakes wavering around her head, their glowing eyes watching me as I walked past on my way to the bar. The dark paneled walls and dim lighting fit my mood perfectly. King Kong was playing on the TV above the bar, Jessica Lange clutched in the giant ape's hand. I pulled out an ornate, red velvet, high-backed stool at the bar and hopped up onto it.

'Hey Mickey,' I said to the bartender who was also our neighbor.

'Hey there, Liz. Usually don't see you in here on a weekday. Andie not with you?' He looked around, seemingly surprised that I was without my more social counterpart.

I grimaced. 'Nope, just me.'

'Alright, well what can I get for you then?'

'Whiskey. Neat.' Mickey widened his eyes in surprise but prepared the glass without comment, placing it in front of me. The sleeve of tattoos on his arm danced with each movement as the muscles bulged underneath.

I knocked it back, then quickly raised my finger in the air and ordered another. My throat burned but a warmth spread throughout my body, embracing me. Mickey whistled appreciatively as he poured my second drink before walking away to help another customer at the other end of the bar. I sipped the second one more slowly and as the whiskey scorched a hot path to my empty stomach and then up into my brain, I began to calm down. My shaky hands settled around the short glass.

Andie was still Andie. Deep down, I knew she would never intentionally hurt me, and she was just a kid when the incident happened. Logically, I knew I shouldn't be upset with her. I still was though. The fact that Andie could have told me the second I got the ancestry test results back, but didn't, was what really bugged me. That she had kept up the act of being surprised by my discovery when she had known all along, was something I couldn't easily let go.

'Have you ever been totally and completely betrayed, Mickey?' I asked before downing the rest of my drink.

Mickey paused where he was wiping down the bar in front of me with a black bar cloth and leaned forward on the polished wood surface. 'Haven't we all?'

A short, sarcastic laugh exploded from deep in my stomach. 'I hadn't, not until recently, anyway.'

'What about that sleazy ex of yours, the one you and Andie were always raggin' on?'

'Yeah, he was for sure a sleaze, but that doesn't even come close to finding out you're adopted and your family lied to you about it your entire life.'

'Oh,' he said, a little awkwardly but staring at me intensely, intrigued, running his fingers across the dark stubble lining his chin. 'Shit.'

'Yeah. Shit,' I said, swigging down the last of my drink.

Mickey grabbed the bottle and a second glass, pouring us both a drink. 'This one's on the house.'

'Thanks,' I mumbled into the amber liquid as we both took a sip. He placed a water on the bar next to me too, but I ignored it. 'I feel like I'm an overly forgiving, understanding person, Mickey. I try not to hold grudges, life's like, too short, you know? But this is HUGE. I mean, think about it. All the little lies that they told me along the way to prop up this enormous one. Like when my parents took me to the doctor as a kid, did they just lie on the family history section? Do I actually have high blood pressure and diabetes in my DNA that I should keep an eye on?' I splayed my hands out and shrugged. 'I may never know.' I took a sip, the resentment bubbling in the pit of my stomach. 'Or when I did that stupid family tree project in elementary school and they helped me cut and paste photos on poster board with stories of how our family came to this country. All of it was one big elaborate lie.' I took another sip and slammed the glass down onto the glossy wooden countertop. A splash of whiskey sloshed over the side. 'Sorry,' I said, sopping up the spill with my sleeve. My words were starting to slur; even I could hear it.

Mickey shook his head and gave a low whistle, 'That's a lot for anyone to handle.'

'I just can't believe they all kept this from me.'

Mickey gave me a soft, thoughtful look. 'You know, I can kind of relate.'

My eyes shot back to him. 'Really?' I said, taking another sip. 'Are you adopted, too?'

'Nah,' he said, 'But my mom did lie to me for most of my life. When I was a kid she told me that my dad had died in a car accident just after I was born. But I found out last year that she'd lied. Turns out he just wanted nothing to do with us and split before I was even born. Guess she was trying to protect me and didn't know how tell a little kid that.'

I leaned forward, placing my hands down on the bar. I couldn't pull my eyes away from his. They were a golden brown, with flecks of green sprinkled along the edges. I'd never noticed before.

'I'm so sorry, that's horrible,' I said, trying to keep my words steady. The whiskey was fighting to take control.

He shifted his weight, clearing his throat as he pulled his gaze away from mine and back down to his bar rag.

His shaggy brown hair momentarily covered his face like a curtain. We'd never spoken this openly to one other before. Usually Andie dominated the conversation, keeping things loud and light-hearted. Looking down, I noticed how close my hand rested next to his and I could feel electricity bouncing between our fingers. Or maybe it was the whiskey. I quickly pulled my hand back to my glass and took another sip. Mickey leaned in to wipe down the area in front of me and I caught a warm, woodsy scent wafting off him. I ran a hand through my hair, hoping it didn't look like a rat's nest after storming around the neighborhood. Suddenly, I became very self-conscious about how potent my whiskey-breath must smell and leaned away from him, nearly losing my balance. Thankfully, he didn't seem to notice.

Finally, he said, 'Yeah, it was rough. I was helping her clean out the basement and we found a dusty old box of his stuff. She finally cracked and told me the truth. Said it'd been eating away at her and she couldn't hide it from me any longer. Things have been a little tense since then.'

I was captivated by his story and although I knew it was wrong, I was glad Mickey had experienced something similar to my mess. It made me feel less alone. I had a missed call notification from my mom lingering from earlier that day. I pushed down the thought.

'So, what happened then? Did you find your dad?'

Mickey gave a crooked smile, 'Nah. He didn't want to know me as a kid, so I figured he doesn't have the right to know me now. I did alright without him, so what's the point?'

I nodded, my skin buzzing from a combination of the liquor and the excitement of this human connection. It was the first conversation I'd had with someone since my life got turned upside down that felt completely raw and honest. I needed that. Looking at Mickey again I saw him in a new light. Under his scruffy exterior was a deep, caring guy, and I was glad I'd finally come in without Andie and discovered that about him.

'Who knows, maybe you're the smart one,' I said, taking another sip. 'I couldn't resist trying to find out every detail about my bio-family and it's landed me in this web of chaos, but I just can't stop. I need to find my family and learn the truth about them.'

'Well, you're braver than me, Liz. It's great you're going after the answers you want. But if you ever need someone who understands how it feels for a parent not to want you, well, you know where to find me,' he replied, smiling softly. My stomach did a little flip but I chalked it up to the whiskey.

'I may just take you up on that,' I said with a half-smile as Mickey got called away to make an old-fashioned for a guy at the other end of the bar. While I was still upset, the conversation had calmed me, had pulled me back from the ledge ever so slightly.

By the time I finished the third drink and rose to go back to the apartment, throwing some cash on the bar for Mickey and thanking him for the talk, I realized I *was* angry at Andie and my parents. But that was only part of it. More so, I was hurt at being left in the dark about my own life by so many people, intentional or not. The only thing that would make me feel better, I decided, was to know everything. To take back control. I needed to know more about the circumstances of my adoption, more about my mother, and most importantly, I needed to know who in my family was a suspected killer. There was only one way to get those answers. I hurried out of the bar into the warm evening air, embracing the buzz from the whiskey, taking oversized steps to cover the short amount of sidewalk back to our apartment. When I got to our building, I hurried down the hall, anxious to call Rosie and set up another family get-together.

VICTIMS 10 & 11

Madison Frank & Samantha Kozac

1999

CHAPTER 14

He opened the door after her shower and led a terrified Sam back to the room, chaining her to the wall. She was wearing a similar dress to Madison's, which was pale blue with lavender starlings flying all over the fabric. Sam's was soft yellow with lemons and oranges. Both were buttoned all the way up their necks, nearly choking them. The man pulled out a thick permanent marker. It was the kind with the strong smell, like the one Madison had used to mark their boxes when she and Sam had moved out of the dorms at Montclair State University and into their new apartment just a few months ago. The two women had managed to save up enough for the security deposit by working all year at the campus bookstore.

The one-bedroom apartment they'd moved into was definitely cozy, but it was all they could afford so they'd put in two twin beds and made it work. As best friends, Sam and Madison didn't mind sharing a small space. If one of them had a date over, they simply took turns sleeping on the futon in the living room to allow some semblance of privacy. Their old box TV still worked fine, so they'd pooled their money together and bought a new stereo with a CD player. Between the two of them, their Case Logic CD wallet bulged with options. Excited to finally be on their own, they'd hardly noticed the tight quarters as long as they could blare Destiny's Child or TLC and sing at the top of their lungs in the living room.

Sam had been sitting next to Madison on their tattered thrift store futon, studying for their chemistry exam on the night they'd been abducted. It was one of the first nights in a while that they were both dateless and free of other obligations, so it was a treat to study together, even though they were dreading the exam. Sam made flash cards and they took turns quizzing each other. Every time Sam got a question right, Madison threw an M&M up in the air for her to catch as a reward, which made the process much less painful. When the clock struck one in the morning, they finally packed up their notes and fell into bed exhausted. Waking to a rustling sound, Sam opened her eyes to see a dark shape hovering over her just before the sharp pinch of a needle pierced her skin. In the moments before she'd passed out, she'd yelled out for Madison, looking over to her bed. Madison had been silent and motionless.

'Hold still,' the man's voice rang out, pulling Sam abruptly back to the present. He was crouched down in front of Madison, grabbing her chin, muscles bulging under his shirt sleeves with every movement.

He wrote something that Sam couldn't quite see on Madison's forehead, before walking over and writing something on her own. The stench of the marker was overbearing as it streaked ink onto her clammy skin.

He straightened and let out a long breath. 'I'd love to

spend more time with you girls but I must go; work tomorrow. I've left you enough food in the corner over there. You should be fine till I get back next weekend. In the meantime, make sure to keep yourselves clean. I'm sure you don't want me to take you back to the fish-kill room for another scrubbing. There's soap and toothpaste by the sink, and towels next to the food.' His thick arm gestured to the items. 'When I come back I expect every inch of you to be clean. We'll get started next weekend.'

He walked to the door, but before crossing the threshold he looked back at them with a soft, loving expression that was in stark contrast to his actions so far. He averted his eyes but hesitated, like he was reluctant to leave. Sam's body was painfully rigid as she tried not to move one muscle for fear he'd linger. She prayed he'd leave soon. Finally, he left with a loud click of the lock behind him. A few minutes passed before the girls heard the distant slam of the exterior cabin door. Once they were sure he wasn't coming back, they rushed to meet one another in the center of the room. Sam sobbed into Madison's shoulder, soaking the fabric of her dress with tears.

When they pulled away, Sam said in a wobbly voice, 'He wrote the number ten on your forehead.' She traced the black number with her fingertips. 'What did he write on mine?'

'Eleven,' Madison replied.

They stood in silence for a long moment before Sam asked, 'What do you think he meant by "get started next weekend"?'

Madison shook her head. 'I have no idea, but at least we have a week without him so we're safe, for now anyway. Come on, help me look for a way to escape. We have to get out of here before he comes back.' Sam nodded in agreement, taking a deep, steadying breath.

The women scoured the room as far as their chains would allow in every direction, looking under the boxes of food and the stack of towels. They ran their hands along the walls and floor, searching in every crack and crevice. Sam's fingers grazed something small and cool to the touch poking out of a crack in the cement. She picked it up and held it in Madison's direction.

'Look at this.'

Madison walked over and inspected the broken gold chain, taking it from Sam to hold up close to her face. She normally wore glasses but they had been left behind when the man abducted them. It was a gold nameplate necklace, like the one Carrie Bradshaw had made popular on *Sex and the City*. The name on the necklace read 'Sasha.'

'It belonged to one of the last two girls who were abducted,' Madison said, gesturing to the list of names etched into the wall next to the toilet. *Rachel and Sasha* were the last two names on the list. She clenched the necklace in her hand, a deep sadness washing over her as she felt a connection to the others who had never found an escape. The sharp corners of the letters dug into her palm but she barely noticed. They had seen a pattern of missing girls being connected on the news, but never in a million years thought she and Sam would end up here. 'Did you find anything to help us get out?' she finally asked, refocusing on the task at hand.

'Nothing,' Sam said, dejected. 'You?'

Madison shook her head. 'No. Maybe we should just start screaming. If someone's nearby, they might hear us. It could be our best shot.'

The women screamed for help until their throats were raw. They banged their shackles against every surface they could reach, trying to drum up as much noise as possible. The only response was the squawking of birds and the rustling of leaves on trees. Exhausted, they both retreated to their respective mattresses feeling defeated.

'Why do you think he numbered us?' Sam whispered, breathing heavily, rubbing her sore ankles that were bruising from the harsh metal digging in along the bone.

Madison looked at the names scratched into the wall. 'Not sure why he wrote them on us, but my guess is we're the tenth and eleventh women he's taken . . . Remember when they reported finding the bodies of those missing girls over the years on the news? I can't remember exactly how many they said there were but it was a lot. There are only eight names on the wall though, which doesn't add up unless one woman just didn't add hers. So who knows? He called me Ten in the other room, too. Maybe he can't face calling us by name, the bastard. Just another thing he's taking away from us.'

'Yeah, he called me by my number too.' Sam laid her chin on her knees and looked at the floor. 'We're going to end up dead just like the rest, aren't we? There's no one coming for us, is there?' Sam asked, her voice hoarse.

'I don't think so, Sam.' Madison sighed heavily, unbuttoning the top of her collar so she could breathe more easily now that he wasn't watching over them. 'Wherever we are, it's secluded and he's obviously gotten away with this before. He called the room next door where he washed us the "fish-kill" room, so I'm thinking this is some kind of fishing or hunting cabin. We drove for about three hours, which I guess would probably put us in the Catskills. My dad used to take us camping in upstate New York and it can get pretty remote. So yeah, it's not looking good.'

Sam began to cry again, sobbing with big heaves of her chest, snot dripping from her nose. 'What are we going to do?'

Madison dropped her head and thought, *There's nothing we can do.*

CHAPTER 15

I walked up the path to Cris and Rosie's door, fingering the locket around my neck. The package had come the day of Andie's admission about the adoption day photo and I hadn't noticed it in the drama that followed. But I'd found it when I came back from The Beast and quickly tore open the padded envelope and pulled out the jewelry box. Inside was a beautiful old silver locket with a cross etched onto the front and the words '2 Years Strong' on the back. Upon opening the locket, I found a tiny oval photo of Gloria squatting down next to a young Teresa, their arms around each other in an embrace as they smiled at the camera.

The note inside the box explained, 'Your grandmother, Gloria, gave this locket to your mother for her first communion but it was left behind when Teresa went away to prison. When Teresa came back to us and got clean, Gloria had the locket engraved on her second anniversary of sobriety and gifted it back to her to celebrate. Your mother cherished it and now, we hope you will too.'

I'd been wearing the locket ever since, feeling a closeness

to my mother who wore it before me. I dropped the locket and knocked on the door. The Uber that brought me from the train station backed out of their driveway and disappeared down the road. I didn't tell Andie I was coming up for a visit. Ever since I found out about the photo Andie had kept from me, I felt like I needed to take this journey alone. I also feared she would try to stop me from coming, afraid for my safety now that we knew a killer lurked somewhere in my family tree. But Andie would never really understand how I felt, no matter how hard she tried. How could she when *I* didn't even understand my feelings? I tried to push down the festering thoughts planted by the FBI agents. Even if Cris was a bit awkward, he and Rosie were perfectly lovely people and had given me no reason to think otherwise. I had a hard time believing I could be related to a serial killer but if I was, I felt deep in my heart it couldn't be him. I had already lost trust in my adopted family and discovered most of my biological family were dead; I couldn't lose Cris and Rosie as well.

I had called Rosie to set up another visit after I'd gotten back from The Beast and arranged to meet three days later when we were all free. I'd had several meetings at work that ran over that afternoon, so I'd called Rosie on the way to the station to let her know that I had missed the train I'd intended to take and would be later for dinner than anticipated. She was gracious and accommodating, promising to keep the food warm until I arrived. When we'd made these dinner plans, Rosie had also offered up their guest bedroom so I wouldn't have to go back to the city late at night or worry about the train schedule. I had politely declined. Partially because I didn't want to impose and partially because the FBI's belief that I was related to a killer hovered along the edges of my subconscious. However much I didn't want to believe it, I couldn't help feeling the need to proceed with some caution.

Instead, I'd opted to book a room at a nearby hotel with the promise that I would have breakfast with them in the morning before hopping on a train back to the city. My first meeting the next day wasn't until 11:45 a.m., so I had some time before I needed to be there. Rosie signed off on this plan with the caveat that I let them drive me to the hotel after dinner. While I was a little hesitant when she suggested Cris drive me to the hotel, I was touched by the level of care this woman I barely knew showed for me. To me, it was further evidence that Cris and Rosie were good people. Footsteps sounded on the other side of the door before it was enthusiastically swung open.

'Liz!' Rosie exclaimed, pulling me into a warm embrace. She had donned another brightly floral patterned dress and seemed just as immaculate and put together as the day we'd met. She put her hand to her chest and said, 'Oh would you look at that. Is that Teresa's locket?'

I smiled and nodded my head. 'Cris mailed it to me, didn't he tell you?'

Rosie's smile became strained for a second before she recovered. 'Oh yes, I'm sure he mentioned it. At my age it's easy for things to slip from my mind. Come on in, I'll pull dinner out of the oven and we can dive right in, you must be famished.'

The house smelled of tantalizing Latin spices, making my stomach grumble lightly. 'I'm starving,' I said with a smile. 'Thanks again for dinner and waiting for me to get here. Work got crazy today and it was impossible for me to sneak away,' I continued apologetically.

'Oh no problem at all. Cris has actually been upstairs going through some boxes that belonged to your mother and grandfather. I thought there may be some things in there that would interest you to see. But first, let's eat. Cris! Liz is here.'

I heard heavy footsteps moving above us. I looked around the space while we waited for him to come down and took notice of the living room off to the other side of the staircase. I hadn't paid much attention to it last time as we'd been shuffled right into the kitchen and dining room from the entryway.

'This room is beautiful,' I said, taking in the large bookshelves full of colorful leather bound books lining the wall of the living room. A fireplace with an oversized mantle sat across from a small leather couch with large velvet decorative pillows and a knit throw folded evenly over the back.

'Oh, thank you, Liz,' Rosie said, following my gaze. 'We don't spend as much time in there as we'd like, but it's lovely to cozy up and light the fire during the colder winter months.'

'I'm sure,' I said, taking a step further into the room. 'I'd love to have a functioning fireplace, but unfortunately the one in our living room is closed up so the best we can do is light some pillar candles for ambience.'

'Well that's not so bad either,' Rosie said.

On the end table next to the couch was a framed photo of two men. One was wearing navy shorts and a pale blue polo shirt but I didn't recognize him. The other looked like a much younger Cris, wearing a purple college football jersey with UAlbany emblazoned in gold lettering across the front.

Pointing to it, I asked, 'Is this Cris? He's so young.'

Rosie looked at the photo and smiled. 'Yes, that's Cris and Frank. Cris played in college and Frank was so proud when he made the team. Frank played as well and eventually became a college football coach, you see, so he spent hours training Cris for tryouts.' She paused, sadly looking at the photo for another second. Then she glanced over her shoulder and called out again, 'Cris!'

'I'm coming,' he said, the footsteps nearing the stairs now.

I took one last look around the room as my uncle came down the stairs to meet us. I loved to read and hoped one day they would let me go through their generous collection and borrow some titles. Maybe I would sit in front of the fireplace with them one cold, winter day. We could drink hot chocolate and watch the snow fall outside, maybe even play a board game. The thought of having a second family had taken hold of me, despite what the FBI claimed. On top of the mantle there was a vase of flowers and a small Praying Virgin Mary figurine next to a framed photo of Rosie, Cris, and three large dogs. It made me smile.

When my uncle reached us at the foot of the stairs, he again only made eye contact for a split second and gave me a partial smile as he passed us on his way to the dining room.

'Don't mind him,' Rosie said quietly, leaning in closer to me. 'He can be a little quiet at first but once you get to know him, he really opens up. He's had a bit of a stressful week, but well, I'm sure he'll talk with you more later.' She placed a comforting hand on my shoulder, and we followed him to the table.

I pushed my chair back from the table, folding my napkin and putting it on top of my plate. 'Rosie, that was delicious.'

We'd eaten a dish called Fideo, which Rosie described as Mexican spaghetti, along with rice and beans. Instead of forks we'd used tortillas to scoop up the food. Although, I'd noted how Cris used a butter knife to pile his tortilla with noodles, rice and beans, while I had followed Rosie's example of tearing off a piece and digging right in. I was quickly learning to love Mexican spices, which were slightly different from the Italian flavors I'd grown up with.

'So glad you enjoyed it, Liz,' Rosie said as she cleared the dishes from the table. 'Now, I bet you'd love to see some of your grandfather and mother's belongings that Cris found in Frank's things. Then we can all have some coffee before you head to your hotel,' she said, coming back to the table and standing next to Cris who still remained seated across from me.

'Sure, that sounds great,' I said with a slightly nervous look towards Cris. As Rosie had hinted, he started talking more openly at dinner about work. But I hadn't been alone with him and he didn't seem very forthcoming about showing me anything as he sat there quietly.

Rosie, likely noticing Cris's silence, spoke again to fill the void. 'Why don't I go ahead and take you up, since I know Cris has some work to check in on.'

Cris turned his head in her direction and gave her a look that I couldn't quite read. Rosie's smile faltered for the briefest second before she perked back up again. 'That would be fine, right dear?'

My eyes darted back and forth between them, still trying to figure out their dynamic. Rosie was so talkative and outgoing but every time Cris shot her a look, she quieted and checked for approval. It was very different from how my own family worked, where the women dictated the running of the household and rarely asked for permission. He seemed to be the dominant one in the relationship and I had to wonder how he treated Rosie when they were alone. Perhaps he toned his controlling nature down when company was present. But at the same time, he'd just lost his brother. The idea of going through his things was probably hard for him.

After a pause that made me shift uncomfortably in my seat, Cris gave a grunt and said, 'Yeah, okay.' He got up from the table. 'I'll be in my office.'

'Okay, let's head up to the storage room, then,' Rosie said, her bubby personality back at full peak as if the awkward moment had never happened. I got up to follow her as she exited and walked toward the stairs. 'Sorry about Cris,' she said over her shoulder while we ascended the staircase. 'I think he misses his brother. It's been so hard on him going through Frank's boxes. He's been at it for a while so he probably just needs a break from all the memories.'

'Oh no, that's okay,' I said, pushing down the mental image of the FBI sitting in my living room. 'I'm sure it's not easy but thank you for showing me.'

'Of course, dear.'

When we reached the top landing, we took a left and walked down a plush carpeted hallway. The walls were sprinkled with a mix of abstract paintings and intricately carved wooden art pieces. Rosie led me silently to a room two doors down on the right, pushing it open and walking in with a quick look over her shoulder as if to make sure I was still following her.

I gave her a small smile, entering the room in her wake. It appeared to be an extra bedroom turned storage room since they had no need for more than one guest room with no children of their own. It was the most organized storage room I'd ever been in. The walls were painted a light beige that blended with the beige carpet in a clean monotone blanket of neutral tones. It was sparsely decorated except for a vintage looking poster with rows of navy symbols on it, a large round mirror with gold trim, and a small wooden desk with a solitary lamp. In the corner next to the desk was a tall, wrought iron weight set, which explained Cris's impressive arms. A mix of storage containers and worn cardboard boxes were stacked in neat columns around the perimeter of the room. A few of them were open, their cardboard flaps yawning like jaws, sitting alone in the center with their contents exposed. She led me to one of the open boxes next to a padded desk chair and a vintage floral patterned armchair that reminded me of Gram's furniture. She gestured to the armchair for me to sit down, settling herself into the desk chair and pulling the box closer to her by its flap. I sat down and peered over to see what she was reaching for.

'I was talking with Cris,' she said, looking up from the box. 'We thought you may want to see some more about your mom when she was a kid. Frank, your grandfather, left all this to Cris when he passed,' she said, gesturing to all the boxes. 'He's slowly been going through it all but as you can see, hasn't made much progress yet. There's just so much stuff.'

'It does look like a lot to go through but I'd love to

see anything you've found so far.' I inched forward on the seat cushion to get closer to her. The scent of spices still clung to her clothing. Rosie reached into the box, pulling out a large leather bound book with sharp gold corners and brown stitching. She handed it over to me and I laid it down in my lap, feeling its weight.

'Cris came across this just yesterday,' she said. 'We thought you'd like to take a look.'

Opening its cover, I revealed pages of old family photos. Their corners were rounded, colors faded so that a light magenta hue washed over them, but I could still clearly make out moments from my mother's childhood. My breath caught in my chest as I ran my fingers delicately over the first page, taking in this missing piece of the puzzle from my mysterious past.

'That of course is your mother and your grandparents,' she said gently, leaning in and pointing at the photo at the top of the first page. I gazed at the people in the photo, taking in every detail.

I nodded. 'So, that's my grandfather? Cris's brother who passed away recently?' I asked, delicately, not taking my eyes off the photo.

'Sure is,' she said. 'That's Francisco, Frank to all of us, and his wife Gloria. I'm so sorry you missed your chance to meet them.'

'Me too,' I said, still studying the photo.

It was a family portrait, the studio's name engraved in delicate gold script on the bottom right corner. The three of them were impeccably dressed and I couldn't help but smile at the fashion. My grandfather wore a sharp double-breasted, three-piece suit and a matching black fedora. There was a red rose bud and a silky pocket square poking out of his front suit pocket and his dress shoes were polished so precisely that the shine was visible even in this old photo. He was smirking, his eyes twinkling under his bushy eyebrows that were quickly recognizable as our shared family trait.

His wife, my grandmother, Gloria, was standing next to him, their arms touching. She had a just a hint of a smile as she stood there in her floral dress. Although her style was much more severe than Rosie's, the women shared a few physical traits, like their heart-shaped faces, that made me think Cris and Frank had similar taste in women. Gloria's hair was parted down the middle and slicked back into a low bun, not one hair astray. Maybe it was my imagination but I felt like I had her eyes.

Standing in front of the couple was the person I really couldn't take my eyes off. My mother. Young Teresa was standing up close against her father's leg, wearing a floral dress that matched the one worn by her mother. It had a white lacy collar that paired well with the ruffled socks she wore under her black Mary Janes. Her dark brown curly hair was secured back with a large white bow. Her father's hand rested on her small shoulder, wrinkling the delicate fabric. Teresa's smile was so captivating it made me smile in return as I glanced up at Rosie, who was watching me closely.

'They used to love doing their family portraits,' she said.

'Yeah, I can see that. They look happy,' I replied, as I scanned a few similar photos. I pointed to one of Gloria and Teresa sitting on a couch, again wearing matching dresses, and said, 'Did they always wear matching outfits?'

'Yes, most of the time. Your great-grandmother Dorina was an excellent seamstress. After she died, Rodrigo gave her dress patterns to Cris's mom when they married, to carry on the tradition. She started making the dresses for herself and then years later when Frank and Gloria had Teresa, she made matching ones for them as well. Gloria never was very good with a sewing machine.'

'That's so cute that Cris's mom made the dresses for them,' I replied, my eyes still on tiny Teresa.

'It was,' Rosie said with a sad smile. Then she leaned forward and gave me a little wink like she was letting me in on a dirty family secret. 'When I married Cris, they'd all wanted me to continue the tradition and suggested I make the dresses for myself from Dorina's patterns too. But I refused. Behind closed doors, I used to call her patterns "chastity dresses".' She gave a quick laugh before looking thoughtful. 'There are very few things that I've stood up to Cris on but this was one of them. I already dress demurely, so I didn't see the need to push it *that* far. I have my own style.' She shrugged one shoulder and we smiled at each other.

'Yeah, those dresses are pretty, but *very* modest,' I said. 'I can see why you wouldn't want to wear them. Was the Dominio family always so conservative?'

Cris cleared his throat and I turned to see him standing in the doorway. With the carpeting, I hadn't heard him come up the stairs. He had his hands in his pockets as he reluctantly walked into the room to join us. *I wonder why he changed his mind?*

He picked up where Rosie left off, obviously over-hearing our conversation. 'Back then, Dominio women were more reserved and their only role was to take care of their children and their husband. Even if my mother had wanted to work, I don't think my dad would have allowed it because it would have cut into her duties at home. Besides cooking, cleaning and taking care of us kids, she would cut my dad's hair and lay out his clothes every morning, among other things.'

Rosie looked at me with a wry smile, 'Now sure, I enjoy cooking and taking care of Cris, but he's perfectly capable of picking out his own clothes and going to the barber.' She chuckled before saying, 'But that's nothing compared to some of the stories he's told me over the years.'

'Oh really?' I asked, intrigued. It felt so good to be finally getting some truths about where I came from. 'Like what?'

Rosie glanced at Cris, intimating he should take this question. He grabbed a folding chair and sat down next to the boxes with us.

'Well, when I was young, anytime my dad had friends over to watch football, us kids were told to go play in our rooms. After my mom laid out all the food she'd made for them, she would stay in her room as well. As a kid I assumed we were being punished, for what, I didn't know. It was like that old adage, "kids should be seen and not heard", except it seemed we weren't even allowed to be seen and neither was my mom.'

'Seriously? Well, I'm glad times have changed,' I replied before turning the page in the photo album still resting in my lap. The old paper pages crinkled as I flipped them.

'That next one there is your mother's First Communion,' Rosie said, not skipping a beat as she pointed to the photo at the top of the newly revealed page.

'Your grandmother loved to take photos. Frank bought her an expensive camera when Teresa was born and she was rarely without it. She took a lot of care in preserving these memories,' Cris chimed in, a rare softness taking over his features as he looked at the old photo.

I smiled at the lacy calf-length white dress with the puffy short sleeves that my mom had donned for this one. She wore the same ruffled socks and shiny dress shoes as in the last photo but had a small white floral crown perched atop her head. The locket that was now resting at the base of my throat was dangling down the front of Teresa's dress. Again, my mother was positioned close up against Frank's body, his hand placed on her shoulder. She had a proud smile on her face that mirrored Frank's. Gloria didn't match her daughter for this occasion but instead wore another floral dress with delicate lace trimmings. The three of them looked so happy. It was hard to believe things had turned out the way they did. Feeling a kinship, I touched a hand to my lips, remembering a similar photo of me at my own communion, that same smile lighting up my face while my mom and dad stood proudly on either side of me. In that moment, my anger toward my parents softened, the love and support they'd given me my whole life melting some of the resentment I'd been feeling.

'These photos are so great,' I said, giving them a grateful smile as I flipped through more pages. There were even a few old photos of Cris and Frank when they were kids, a much-appreciated glimpse into the life of the quiet man in front of me. I gave a laugh when I stopped on one of my mother with Cris and Rosie. Rosie smiled when she saw which photo I was looking at.

'She loved coming over here when we had foster animals running around the house.'

The laugh that little Teresa was giving off in the photo was infectious. She was crouched down in one of her summer dresses, her arms outstretched as a big fluffy brown dog enthusiastically licked her face. Rosie and Cris stood behind them, bent over and laughing. It was an affectionate photo, making me feel closer to my biological mother than I had since this journey started a few weeks back. Little by little, with each page, along with Rosie and Cris's stories, I was learning the history of their lives and was starting to feel like I was a part of it too. These were the kinds of gaps I'd been hoping to fill.

I flipped the page again and asked, 'Did she have any pets of her own growing up?'

'No,' Cris said, looking at the photo with me. 'Frank wasn't a big animal lover like me. He liked to keep things clean and orderly.' Cris glanced at me and shrugged a shoulder. 'Well, more so than me, I guess. He wouldn't have wanted to deal with all the pet hair and things that animals inevitably drag into your home,' he said with a knowing but curt laugh. 'Gloria tried to bring her over here or take her to the petting zoo when she could.'

I nodded, flipping the page over. A pleasant warmth was spreading through my belly as I listened to Cris talk about my mother. A loose photo slid forward and fell into my lap. Picking it up, I saw it was a much more recent photograph. My mother was older, probably closer to the age I was now. She and my grandmother were standing next to a hospital bed where Frank lay smiling, giving a goofy thumbs up. My mother was painfully thin, her bony arm reaching out to hold the bar of the hospital bed as if she couldn't stand up on her own. Her hair was thinner and messier, and she had dark circles under her eyes. She wore a baggy, stained Green Day t-shirt and a sad expression, hinting that she'd just been crying.

'When was this taken?' I asked, turning the photograph to show Rosie before staring at it again.

178

'Oh, that's from when Frank got sick with cancer the first time. Teresa came back into our lives and Gloria convinced her to get clean,' Rosie said wistfully. Her voice broke, a hint of sadness creeping through. 'You look so much like her, you know.'

'Yeah,' I said, staring at the photo. I ran my fingers over my mother's image. 'Man, we really did all get the same brow gene, huh?' I laughed, looking at the matching set on my mother.

Cris laughed. 'I'll have to see if we can dig up some photos of my grandfather. He had us all beat, they were about double that size and he had a matching mustache to boot!' he said, letting out a deep chuckle. It was nice to hear Cris laugh, something I hadn't witnessed much since I met him, and I couldn't help but join in. It changed his whole demeanor, his eyes crinkled in the corners, a dimple appeared in his left cheek, and a warmth filled his eyes. As we laughed together, I felt a tug toward my grand uncle, a connection being made.

Flipping the page again, I found a close-up photo of Teresa looking much healthier. She'd gained some weight and the dark eye circles were gone. Her hair had doubled in size, floating around her head in all its curly glory. Her eyes were bright and clear, and she was smiling as my grandmother kissed her cheek. The women clearly loved one another deeply. Besides the brows, I could see so much of myself in my mother. And even though her hair was much thicker and curlier than mine, she had cut it into a long bob that resembled the dark wavy lob I was wearing these days. A single tear slid down my face that I quickly wiped away.

I gently pulled the photo away from the gold corners holding it to the page. 'Do you have any more photos of

179

her that are more recent like this?' I said, holding it up for them to see.

'Hmm,' Cris said thoughtfully, looking around. 'Not that we've come across but there may be some in one of these boxes. If we come across anymore we'll put them aside for you. But if you want, you can hold onto that one.'

'Are you sure?' I said, my fingers gripping it tightly. 'Thank you both so much for the locket and the photos, and just . . . everything,' I said with a grateful smile.

I was filled simultaneously with happiness at getting to know my family and heartbreak at the hardships they went through. Could there really be a killer amongst this loving family who had suffered so much on their own? I hoped more than ever that the killer was from my biological father's side, or someone else distant to this immediate family that was finding its way into the corners of my heart.

'I know families can be complicated, but I never would've thought mine would have so many layers. It means a lot to get this insight into where I came from.'

'Of course, it's so nice revisiting these memories with you.' Rosie smiled at me sadly before clapping her hands together. 'Now, what do you say we go downstairs and have some coffee?' She smoothed out the wrinkles in her dress as she stood.

'Sure, that sounds great.' I kept the photograph of my mother and grandmother grasped tightly in my hand and followed her to the door, Cris trailing behind us.

'I've got to go check something in my office really quick,' Cris said as we reached the first floor.

'Okay dear, go right ahead, we'll get the coffee started,' Rosie replied cheerily.

I followed her into the kitchen. 'Can I help with

anything?' I asked as she gathered the supplies she needed to brew and serve the coffee.

'Oh, no, that's quite alright. You're our guest,' she said before facing the coffee maker again, filling it with water and piling in coffee grounds before hitting the start button. 'I'm glad Cris was more forthcoming with you upstairs. He really will open up as time goes by.'

'Yeah, he seemed more comfortable,' I smiled, setting the photo delicately on the table. 'I know this whole thing is unusual.' I helped lay out the coffee cups and saucers from Rosie as she took them down from a cabinet.

'He can be a little rough around the edges at first but he really does have a big heart, that man,' Rosie said, busying herself organizing vanilla crème cookies onto a serving platter. 'This week has just been so hard on him.'

I took the plate of cookies from her and set it in the middle of the table. 'What's been going on this week?' I asked, then quickly said, 'Sorry, I don't mean to pry, it's okay if you don't want to say.'

'Oh, it's just the craziest thing,' Rosie said, pulling out a chair and sitting down at the table while she waited for the coffee to brew. I mirrored her. 'The FBI showed up at the office this week.'

I froze, thoughts bubbling back to the surface from my own conversation with the FBI. 'Oh, really?' I asked quietly, unsure what to say.

'Yes, you'll just never believe this but these agents asked him for a DNA sample. Can you believe that?' she tutted. My palms were starting to sweat. I was sure they wouldn't appreciate that I was the reason the FBI had shown up.

I opted for, 'That's crazy. Did they say anything else?'

'Not really. He had a full room of furry patients so he

told them he didn't have time and to make an appointment. They certainly came on the wrong day. Cris was in a bad mood because I'd squeezed several appointments into his already tight schedule.' Rosie leaned in and whispered, 'Sometimes I have a hard time saying no, and it drives Cris crazy when I double book but he always finds a way to make it work.' She winked and chuckled quietly.

I nodded, grabbing a cookie and popping the whole thing into my mouth to give myself a moment to gather my thoughts. After I swallowed, I said, 'I can't believe they asked for his DNA. Did they say why they wanted his sample?' I was sure the FBI wouldn't have told them that he was under their microscope due to my own DNA profile but my nerves were getting the better of me.

'All they said was they had reason to believe someone in this family was linked to a case they were working on but wouldn't tell him why they thought that. It's unbelievable. It irritated Cris that they wouldn't give him any details yet expected him to drop everything for them. I'm not surprised he dismissed them.'

'Have you heard anything since? Did they call to make an appointment?'

'They left a message for Cris last night but I don't know if he's gotten back to them yet. Considering how many innocent people wrongly end up in jail these days, Cris isn't the most trusting of law enforcement, so I wouldn't be surprised if he's dragging his feet.'

At that moment, the sputtering coffee machine quieted and Rosie jumped up. Cris walked back into the kitchen. 'Oh, good, coffee ready?'

'Just about. Have a seat, dear.'

While I sipped my coffee, my brain went into overdrive

thinking about everything I'd learned that day. The fact that he hadn't given them a DNA sample made me pause. If he didn't have anything to hide, why not just give it? All I wanted was to enjoy this new relationship I was forming with him and Rosie but these questions were making it difficult. *Maybe he* was *just too busy,* I thought, trying to give him the benefit of the doubt. But I just wished he'd given the sample so he could be cleared and put my mind at ease. Realizing I'd zoned out, I snapped my attention back to the present and tried to make sense of the conversation buzzing in front of me.

Cris was explaining that he had popped into his office to see if he'd gotten a call back yet from Mrs. Lindel. He had been fielding calls from her all week about one of the medications their Goldendoodle, Charlie, was on. I tried to quiet my anxiety as I listened to Cris and Rosie talk about the dog. I only heard bits and pieces as my thoughts drifted, something in the back of my mind needling me. The FBI agents had seemed interested in the fact that Cris was a vet and now had shown up at his place of work to request DNA. Did they have other evidence that pointed to him? I couldn't stand to abandon my new family but I also couldn't get close to them until I knew the truth.

I looked across the table, watching Cris grip his coffee cup as he took a long sip, not making eye contact with Rosie as she spoke. Was it possible there was something sinister lurking beneath his socially awkward exterior? Or was he an innocent bystander getting roped into something he knew nothing about? I hadn't realized I was still staring at him until his eyes darted up, making me jump as they locked briefly with mine. I quickly looked away, taking a sip from the steaming cup in front of me. I thought I could feel his stare burning into me but when I looked back he was talking to Rosie as if nothing out of the ordinary had happened at all.

VICTIMS 12 & 13

Anna Morgan & Mary Klein

2002

Anna threw down the empty Cinna-Crunch Pebbles cereal box. All this pre-packaged food left a bad taste in her mouth and sat in her stomach like a solid ball of artificial colors and flavors. She'd been having vivid dreams about her mom's herbed roasted chicken and buttery mashed potatoes. Tears stung the corners of her eyes. She was getting sick of crackers and chips, beef jerky and granola; the alternating boredom and fear. She let out a deep breath and leaned back against the wall, looking over at Mary who was still sleeping. Anna tucked her bangs behind her ear, the bright red streaks she'd dyed into them now only tinging the tips. She had woken up just as the sun was rising outside their small window and couldn't get back to sleep. Pulling the metal barrette from her pocket, she rubbed her fingers against its cool surface. She'd taken it out of her hair when they were in the trunk of his car and quickly hidden it for safe keeping under the stack of towels in the corner of their room. She'd tried using it to pick the lock on her shackles but it was no use since the clasp was too big to fit into the keyhole. She scooted to the corner and continued scratching words into the wall with its edge. The front door to the cabin squeaked open, causing her to jump.

'Mare! Mare wake up, he's back.' Mary slowly rose from her mattress and rubbed her eyes. 'Hurry. You need to wash your face and brush your teeth before he comes in.'

Mary quickly shuffled to the sink, frantically scrubbing and brushing before settling back on her mattress, water dripping down her collar in her haste. Anna heard the man outside the door, moving things around. Their bodies stiffened at the sound of the lock clicking as he turned the key. The door opened and he stood in the doorway looking at them.

'Are you clean?'

Anna replied, 'Yes, we've washed every day like you said.'

'What did I tell you to call me?' he said, a steel edge to his voice.

'I'm sorry,' her voice cracked. 'We've washed every day, Master.'

The man smiled and pulled a syringe out. He walked over to Anna and injected her. Anna's stomach dropped, knowing what it meant to be chosen: she would be the one making his breakfast that morning. Their captor walked out the door but didn't lock it behind him like he usually did. She heard him jostling things around in the kitchen. Her eyelids drooped under their own weight and her body felt sluggish as the drug kicked in. It was just enough to make her too weak to fight or run but not quite strong enough to send her to sleep or numb her from the horror he was putting them through. He came back into the room and crouched next to her, his eyes darting inquisitively back and forth between each of her own eyes. It made her skin crawl and she desperately wanted to look away, to get some space between them, but she knew better by now.

After a second that felt like an hour, he said under his breath, 'Yep, that'll do.'

He detached her chains from the wall and led her to the kitchen. She waited as he locked the door behind them, separating her from Mary, then she shuffled to the stove where he'd laid out eggs, bacon and bread next to the toaster. Her stomach growled, her mouth watering at the sight. How she wished she could eat it herself.

He sat at the dining table while Anna lifted eggs out of the carton, preparing to fry them. She was so groggy that she dropped the first egg on the floor with a loud *splat*, the runny whites and bright yellow yolks spreading into the cracks in the floor. Her eyes widened at the mistake and then darted to him. The man walked over and slapped her hard across the face, leaving a painful stinging sensation in its wake. He grabbed her by the back of the neck and pulled her down to the floor, shoving her face near the puddle of egg.

'You'll eat that egg. You don't waste food.'

Anna started crying but she knew it was useless to argue with him. Once when she'd made his lunch, a glob of mayonnaise had dropped into the open trash can next to the stove. She'd begged him not to make her lick it up out of the trash, half-filled with the remnants of that morning's breakfast and wet coffee grounds. He'd slammed her head into the side of the stove and then shoved her face into the trash can. The memory of the painful lump on the side of her head reminded her not to disobey a direct order, no matter how disgusting. Anna's tongue darted out, lapping up the egg. She gagged several times but was careful not to throw up. She didn't want to find out what his punishment would be for defiling his space in that manner. His grip on her neck tightened every time she heaved. Finally, he let her straighten up and sat back down in his seat, staring at her intensely.

'What do you have to say for yourself?'

'Sorry, Master,' she choked out.

She continued making his breakfast, tears streaming down her face as she took more care, the raw egg churning in her stomach. When the food was done, the toast made to the exact color he'd shown her the first time she'd cooked for him, she plated his breakfast and set it down on the table, making sure the plastic knife and fork were lined up perfectly on the cloth napkin next to the plate. Anna knew she was supposed to wait until he inspected everything and deemed it worthy of eating, so she stood in obedient silence. She'd been through this routine many times before. Sometimes he approved what she prepared for him. Other times, he'd find one small thing wrong and throw the entire plate into the sink. On these instances, he'd make her cook the food all over again until it was right. Apparently only *he* was allowed to waste food. He looked up at her and smiled. She exhaled and lowered down to her knees, relief coursing through her. She was to kneel next to him and watch as he ate, just another form of torture after what little food they were given to survive on.

'Wipe those tears away, you should feel honored to spend your time with me.'

She couldn't believe she'd forgotten to show her forced gratitude. Anna quickly wiped her face and plastered on a contented smile. Not too wide, not too thin; the smile needed to be exactly as he expected. Her cheeks twitched at the effort it took to keep it in place but she did not falter. After he ate, she cleared his dishes and washed his plate, coffee mug, and pans. He only used plastic cutlery and disposed of them himself, she assumed out of fear they would be turned into weapons. When she was done, he inspected every dish before leading her back to the room. He chained her to the wall before he left, locking the door once more behind him.

Mary scooted over to Anna. 'You okay? You look sick.'

'Yeah, it wasn't that bad this time. Only got slapped once for dropping an egg,' Anna replied with a short laugh, her eyes still glistening with tears. Mary gasped. 'The worst part was he made me eat the raw egg off the floor.' She clutched a hand over her stomach. 'I'm so sorry if you have to witness me hurling it up, it took everything in me to keep it down.'

Mary ran a hand over Anna's hair and patted her shoulder. 'Oh my God, gross. If you need some privacy to throw up in peace, just let me know and I'll stare at the other wall.' Anna gave her a small smile. 'Guess I'll be making lunch then,' Mary continued, putting her hand in the pocket of her dress and pulling something out. 'But, look what I found.' She held up something curved, red and plastic.

'What is that?'

'It's an acrylic nail,' Mary replied matter-of-factly, and Anna looked at her for a long second, her face scrunched up in a morbid fascination.

Anna took the nail from Mary's fingers and inspected it. 'Ugh, that's so creepy. It's broken and looks like it has rust or something on it. Maybe she was trying to jimmy the lock with her nail?' Anna raised her eyebrows, thinking of the possibility. 'Not a bad idea really but I doubt it worked. Seems too large to fit in the lock.'

The man pounded his fist on the door. 'Keep it down in there.'

The women looked at each other, then Mary retreated to her mattress and lay down. Anna did the same, running her finger over the jagged edge of the broken nail, imagining the life of the girl before her that it must have belonged to. A girl who would never wear acrylic nails again.

CHAPTER 17

Andie actually let me DJ the playlist from my phone as she drove us in Travis's car over to Gram's house for Sunday dinner, which rarely happened. We were singing Taylor Swift's *ME!* at the top of our lungs when Andie glanced over and caught me scrolling through Mickey's Facebook page. He'd texted me last night, just checking in on how I was doing with all the family stuff. Seeing his caring words sent a little thrill through me and when I'd replied about being nervous about today's dinner, we'd ended up texting until two in the morning about our messy family histories. It was casual but I couldn't lie to myself. Unexpected feelings were developing, on my side at least, and the urge to stalk him on social media had taken over. I'd hoped Andie would be too distracted by driving and the music to notice. No such luck.

Andie lunged forward to turn the volume down, cutting our performance off mid-verse, and said, 'So you were at the bar with Mickey for a pretty long time the other day.' She had a mischievous grin on her face, her eyes darting between me and the road.

'Yeah, I guess,' I said, playing it off with a shrug and switching from Facebook to my email. If Andie knew I had any level of attraction to Mickey she'd never let it go. I could just picture her sticking her nose in and embarrassing me in front of him next time we went to The Beast. Subtlety was not her strong suit and I wanted to navigate it on my own. If there was even anything to navigate.

'So? Is there something going on there? I mean, he's not too hard on the eyes, now is he?' Andie pried with a playful nudge to my side with her elbow. 'I know he's not your normal type, but you can't deny he's a hottie.' I knew she was trying to heal any lingering tension between us after the adoption photo incident and I was trying my best to forgive Andie, to move forward and focus my energy on finding answers to my family mystery.

'He's great and all,' I said, deleting a few junk emails as I spoke. 'But I just have too much on my plate right now, Andie. I can't think about that too. He was cool though, we haven't spoken that much one-on-one before.' Even though I wanted to steer Andie away from my love life, I had to admit, Mickey had been popping into my mind at random times since our chat.

'Well maybe he's just the kind of fun distraction you need. You know you tend to get a bit serious when—'

'Andie! You'll never believe the email I just got,' I said loudly, cutting her off as I pulled the phone closer to my face in excitement, reading over the words again quickly in my head.

'Hey, don't try to change the subject here,' she said, smirking.

'No, seriously, I just got a reply from Adam's old employer with his phone number. I really didn't think that man was gonna give it to me.'

Andie bounced in her seat excitedly. 'Okay, you totally get a pass. Call him right now.'

'Wait, I want to do a reverse phone look up first,' I said as I navigated to the website.

Andie rolled her eyes. 'You and your sleuthing,' she said under her breath. 'We're almost at Gram's so speed it up.'

The results popped up instantly and my heart pounded faster in my chest. 'Okay, it looks like it's still owned by Adam and it's a Massachusetts area code.'

'Are you gonna call or what? We'll be at Gram's in like, a minute.'

Before I could talk myself out of it, I dialed. The phone rang several times before an answering machine clicked on.

A smooth, deep voice reverberated across the line, 'You've reached Adam. Can't come to the phone right now but leave a message and I'll get back to you as soon as I can. Talk soon.'

I wasn't sure what I was expecting but I felt a tinge of disappointment in my gut at how inviting his tone sounded. *Would a killer sound so normal and welcoming?* Then again, it was just a recording and I'm sure a killer would know how to mask their true intentions to the outside world. I decided to leave a message, unable to contain my curiosity.

'Hi Adam,' I said, trying to keep any obvious nerves out of my voice. 'My name is Liz Catalano and I'm Rodrigo Dominio's great-granddaughter, who I believe was your uncle. I'm trying to connect with my relatives, so I would love the chance to speak with you. If you could please call me back, I would greatly appreciate it.' I ended the message by leaving my cell phone number.

'Damn,' I said, disappointed that he didn't pick up.

Knowing that Adam was alive out there caused such a tangled web of emotions. On the one hand, I was intrigued and excited to have another relative to get to know. On the other, what if he was a murderer? It would be a relief if it were him instead of Cris. Though, there was still a chance the killer was hiding somewhere in my mysterious father's side of my family tree, so maybe I would just gain another relative. Massachusetts wasn't *too* far away.

Andie pulled the car up outside Gram's house and parked. She put a hand on my shoulder, pulling me out of my twisted train of thought, and said, 'We can try again when we get home tonight.' She smiled and said, 'Now, let's do this.'

I grimaced a little but exited the car with her. I closed the car door behind me very slowly, dragging out the moment for as long as I could. Before the truth of my history came to the surface, I would have been eagerly rushing in to see my family. Now my stomach churned with each step I took. I had been skillfully dodging calls from my parents, unsure how to talk to them since uncovering their deceit. I even tried getting out of the visit today but Andie convinced me to tag along, rightly pointing out that I'd have to face them eventually. The longer I avoided it, the harder it would become. At the same time, the nagging part of me always itching to know more wanted to confront them for more answers. I took a deep breath and picked up the pace to keep in step with Andie.

We walked up the familiar paved path that snaked through the grass in front of Gram's house in Paterson, New Jersey. The exterior of the mid-sized home was a mix of neutral siding panels and grey stone sections. We'd been coming here for family dinner on Sundays since we were kids, although in recent years, we'd missed more of them due to work and life across the river. Dinner was a very loose term as it actually took place in the late afternoon after Mass, but this was always what we called it and it was much too heavy a meal to be considered lunch anyway. Gram's was a warm home, decorated in her eclectic collection of religious relics and floral curtains that matched the antique couches and armchairs. Many of the rooms upstairs were small but the formal dining room was large and always busting at the seams with loud family members. As we got closer to the front door, I slowed my steps slightly as my nerves mounted.

'Come on Lizzie, you have to get it over with. Like ripping off a Band-Aid,' Andie said, grabbing my arm and dragging me forward faster. I pulled my arm out of her grip.

'I know, I just don't even know how to talk to them. And the whole family is going to be here, most of whom knew and kept this from me. It's embarrassing being the last one to know the truth about my own life.'

There was a brief awkward silence as we both remembered the recent tension between us over the adoption day photo. Andie put her hand on my arm. 'I get it. It sucks. But Gram is always a good buffer at least. If anyone tries talking she'll just shove an extra meatball in their face,' Andie said, laughing while we continued up the walkway. I snorted in response. 'I should warn you though, since you've been dodging your mom's calls she's been calling me to try to find out what's up with you.'

'What?' I exclaimed, stopping in my tracks and grabbing onto Andie's arm to bring her to a halt. 'Why didn't you tell me when she called? You didn't tell her about what's been going on with Cris and the FBI, did you?'

'What? No, of course not. Come on Lizzie. I didn't tell you because things have been a little weird between us and you've been obsessed with finding your bio-family and getting to know them, but I would never tell your mom anything behind your back,' Andie said.

'Obsessed?' I interjected, a mix of hurt and anger simmering dangerously close to the surface.

'You know what I mean,' Andie said quickly, shifting her weight uncomfortably. 'You didn't even tell me that that you were going to see Cris and Rosie again until after you got back from your last visit.' I could feel heat rising in my cheeks. 'I understand, Lizzie. I do,' Andie continued, talking faster. 'It's huge. And it's my fault things have been weird lately. I just meant I haven't really had a chance to tell you about her calling, and besides, there's not much to tell. All I told your mom was that you've been super busy.'

I relaxed a little, letting my shoulders slouch back down. I hadn't realized I'd tensed them up so high. 'That's all you said? Just that I was busy?'

'Yeah, I mumbled something about work and may have mentioned you had a date or two just to throw her a bone.' I rolled my eyes but Andie ignored me and continued, 'But hey, are *you* going to tell your parents about Cris or the FBI? Seems pretty major.'

I paused for a moment, thinking. 'I'll tell them about Cris and Rosie but I don't want to worry them with the FBI stuff. I mean, I really don't think it's him but if there's a chance it is, I don't know . . . you know my mom, she would freak out and probably try to make me move home.'

Andie smirked. 'Probably true. But Liz,' she adopted a more somber tone than I was used to hearing from her, 'you should be careful. I know I'm usually the one to throw caution to the wind but this time feels different. You could be spending time with a murderer. Your mom's overprotective concern may be warranted in this case.'

I raised my eyebrows at this sudden change in roles we were now playing. But I knew she was right. 'I know, I know. If anything concrete happens with the FBI investigation then I'll tell them. No reason to worry them when nothing has happened since that meeting. I'm sure Cris will be cleared soon anyway since they asked for his DNA.'

'Oh, that's good, Lizzie. Maybe you should wait till they get that back before you visit again, so we can all have peace of mind.'

'Yeah, maybe,' I said, not ready to commit to that plan. I looked at the house and took a deep breath, mentally preparing myself for the interaction to come.

'Now, are you ready?' Andie popped her elbow out in my direction, hand on her hip.

'Ready as I'll ever be,' I replied, resigning myself.

I linked my arm through Andie's and we walked the last few steps to the front door. I had barely pressed the doorbell when the door swung open, my mom standing there expectantly. It was strange how I had always thought I could see traces of my appearance in her face. Now it was clear that her eyes were a lighter shade of brown, the tip of her nose longer and more pronounced. I still wasn't sure what my biological father's heritage was but now that I knew I was at least half-Mexican, it made sense that my naturally bronzed skin had passed for Italian all these years. But looking at her now, we looked so different. The afternoon light illuminated my mom in the doorway, making it obvious that her skin was olive-toned, whereas I looked sun-kissed. *This must be what an identity crisis feels like,* I thought, my heart pounding in my chest.

'Lizzie, I'm so glad you could make it this weekend. We've missed you so much.' She pulled me into a big embrace, squeezing extra tight. 'And Andie, it's great to see you too.'

'Hey, Mom,' I said, pulling myself out of her grip.

Her face fell a little as I took a step back, not leaning into the hug like I normally would have. The smell of homemade pasta sauce, or gravy as Gram called it, wafted out and filled my nostrils, momentarily making me forget what a potentially awkward interaction I was about to have with my parents. My mouth watered at the thought of Gram's fettuccine al pomodoro and my favorite carbonara.

'Hey, Aunt C,' Andie said with a smile, breezing past her into the house toward the loud conversation taking place in the dining room off the entryway. 'Hey everyone,' she called out as she walked in.

There was a noticeable increase in volume as everyone hugged and talked over one another but I stayed glued to the foyer near my mom. I let my eyes wander for a moment, taking in the familiar home that I'd spent so much time in growing up. The same painting of Jesus Christ still hung in the entryway and the end tables straight ahead in the formal sitting room were still home to various trinket boxes and religious figurines. After a moment my dad rounded the corner from the dining room and came to join us, pulling my attention back to the impending conversation. His salt and pepper hair was greyer than I remembered, making me wonder if the stress of all this was aging him faster.

'There's my Lizard,' he said, pulling me into a hug.

'Ugh, Dad,' I said. We'd had countless debates on how much this childhood nickname needed to go.

'Alright, alright. My *Lizzie*,' he said, and I could tell he was happy to see me as well as extremely anxious from the way his brown eyes turned down ever so slightly at the corners.

Here we go, I thought to myself. The only saving grace was that this inevitable conversation had an expiration time, since I knew Gram would hustle us in for dinner at any moment. Feeding her loved ones was what gave her the greatest joy in life and we were more than happy to let her.

'Liz, are you still angry with us? We haven't really heard from you and I know you've been busy, but the way we left things when we spoke before, well, we've been so worried about you.' My mom wrung her hands together as she spoke.

My dad reached over and took one of her hands into his. I opened my mouth but before answering, I glanced in the direction of the busy dining room nervously. Making a decision, I directed my parents into the living room on the opposite side of the first floor to give us some privacy. I didn't speak until we were tucked into the tight space. It had a baby grand piano and two floral love seats, all situated close together.

'I know some of the family knows what's going on but I don't want to have this conversation in front of all of them. It's mortifying,' I said, my voice wavering with the underlying emotion that was creeping its way closer to the surface.

My mom looked at my dad and then said, 'Oh, sweetie. We're so sorry but no one thinks any less of you. They knew how much we wanted a baby and they've only kept it to themselves because we asked them to.'

I pursed my lips. It still stung that most of my family had known something so major about me when I'd had no idea. I thought about what Andie had told me about Uncle Vinnie pressuring her into not telling me about the photo. Even though I knew it was at my parents' urging, my face flushed hot with anger. I wasn't sure I'd be able to look Andie's parents in the eyes at dinner. But one glance at my parents' remorseful, fearful faces made me push down the resentment building in my chest. I didn't want to argue about this at Gram's house with the entire family just in the other room. While their decision to keep this from me for so long was highly questionable, the fact that they loved me was undeniable. They'd done their best to give me a good life, and possibly, kept me out of reach of a dangerous relative. I softened, letting the tension in my neck relax. I couldn't hold onto this anger forever, and what's more, I didn't want to.

'Well, you haven't heard from me much because I *have* been really busy,' I finally said after a long pause, hesitating on how much to say. 'But not so much with work. I've been trying to connect with my fam—, my biological family,' I said, catching myself. As frustrated as I was with their lie, I didn't want to be hurtful. 'I just wanted to know more about where I came from, try to get to know them.'

'Did you find anyone? Oh, sweetie, please tell us what's been going on with you,' my mom said. The tears that sparkled in her eyes were enough to cause my words to spill over.

'I found my grand uncle, Cris, and his wife, Rosie. They live in Connecticut and have been really kind, getting to know me and having me over for a few meals.'

'Grand uncle? On your mother's side?' my dad asked, his forehead wrinkled in concentration.

'Yeah,' I said, lowering myself onto one of the stiff loveseats that was practically pressed up against the back of my legs.

The wall behind my parents was almost completely covered in gilded framed photos of the family over the years and I felt the burn of their eyes all staring down at me. I squirmed, crossing then uncrossing my legs. My parents followed my lead and took a seat on the couch opposite me.

'He's my grandfather's half-brother. Unfortunately, my grandfather died just before I got in contact with Cris so I didn't get a chance to meet him. My mother, she died years ago.' I trailed off into a tense silence, staring down at my cream and navy striped espadrilles resting on the beige carpet so I didn't have to look them in the eyes. My dad reached over and put a warm, comforting hand on my knee. I looked up at him, finding myself holding back tears.

'Lizzie, I'm so sorry your mother and grandfather passed before you had the chance to meet them. That must be extremely hard for you. But we're glad you're getting answers and don't blame you for wanting to know more. Have you been able to find out much from them?'

'A little,' I responded. 'We're still getting to know each other. It seems like Teresa, my mother, was troubled like you said. They don't know anything about my father unfortunately, so he's still a mystery. But Cris, he's a vet, which is cool. They foster animals at their home all the time. And my aunt, she runs his office and is so sweet. You guys would like her.'

My mom nodded, giving me a smile. 'Maybe we could all get together one day.' She wiped a trail of tears off her rosy cheek. 'We never meant to hurt you or to keep you from them, Lizzie.'

When I saw my mom's tears, I knew I should probably drop it and move forward but I had to ask one more time. 'Why didn't you ever tell me? And don't say the timing was never right. There were plenty of opportunities over the years.'

My dad opened his mouth to speak but my mom put her hand on his arm. 'We had planned all along to tell you on your seventh birthday. We thought that was a good age for you to understand. But then you fell off the jungle gym at your party and broke your arm.' She paused and touched my arm. 'Remember? I just . . . I don't know, I took it as a sign that it wasn't the right time. It wasn't your dad's fault. He still wanted to tell you.' My dad put his arm around her while she cried. 'After that, we just kept putting it off until . . .' she glanced at my dad again, seeking comfort, 'well, we just buried it and convinced ourselves that it didn't really matter who gave birth to you since you felt so much like ours. The more time that passed, the easier it was to sink into our comfortable lives and avoid having that difficult conversation. It was wrong, Lizzie.' My mom's grip on my arm tightened. 'I'm so sorry, I know now it was a terrible mistake. Can you ever forgive us?'

I exhaled. 'Of course, I can forgive you.' I gave them a small, shaky smile. 'I've felt so lost and confused lately. I think I just need some space right now, to wrap my head around everything I'm learning and get used to this new life where I have these two very different families. I need to find out where I came from and get to know the relatives that I've been able to track down. I think that's the only thing that will really get me back to feeling comfortable about who I am.'

'You have our total support in seeking them out, just please, don't shut us out. We've always been close, the three of us, we're The Three Amigos!' my mom said, giving a nervous laugh. My dad nodded and smiled too. 'Just because you're meeting this new family, doesn't mean you don't still have the love of this one.'

I pursed my lips, nodding, a stream of tears flowing fully now. 'I'll talk to you more. Promise.' Thoughts of the FBI swirled around in the back of my head, making me feel guilty for not sharing this other piece of information with them. I convinced myself that if anything developed I would tell them. Now wasn't the time.

'That's my Lizard.'

'Dad,' I groaned but laughed and wiped my tears away just as Gram walked into the room.

'Elizabeth. Andie said you'd come with her but you're hiding from us.'

'Sorry, Gram,' I said, a big smile on my face as I got up and greeted the lively Italian woman in front of me.

I had to bend down to give her a hug and smelt the fresh garlic and basil clinging to her apron. Enveloped in Gram's arms, inhaling her scent that always felt like home, I was grateful this wonderful woman was a part of my life, even if we weren't related by blood. I realized in that moment that while I wanted to get closer to my biological family, I didn't want to lose this one in the process. Maybe I was lucky, getting to have both.

'Come on now, all three of you, the food's going to get cold,' Gram said, shaking her fist in the air.

'Coming, Mom,' my dad said, rising with my mom, and we all made our way to the dining room.

'Lizzie!' was shouted from every direction as I entered the room, greeting my aunts, uncles and cousins warmly. Now that the conversation with my parents was over, I felt like a weight had been lifted. A little bit of the guilt at discovering my new family ebbed away and I tucked down thoughts of Connecticut and the FBI as I sat down for a delicious home cooked meal with those I'd grown up with. Andie was deep in conversation with her own parents across the long wooden table from where my parents and I settled into our cherry wood-backed dining chairs.

'Mangia!' Gram shouted, scooping heaping piles of pasta onto everyone's plates in turn.

As we approached our apartment building back in Greenpoint, I dug through my purse for my keys since Andie's hands were full. One held a bag of Tupperware with leftovers from dinner that Gram had forced onto us, and the other held a bag from the liquor store on the corner. My fingers found the keys and I pulled them out, pushing past Andie to unlock the interior vestibule door near the buzzers. A warm night breeze whisked in, blowing a few strands of hair in front of my face. I fumbled with the key, unable to see for a second, before pushing the hair out of my eyes and continuing with the lock. It was an old building, so it was a roll of the dice whether the lock would stick or fly open as if it'd never been locked at all. It had been humid today, so of course, it stuck.

'You need me to get it?' Andie said loudly in the awkward silence. 'Not like my hands are full here or anything.' She lifted the bags, dramatically bumping them into my back. I bit back a retort and finally pushed the door open, holding it for her to walk through.

The two of us walked down the tiled hallway toward our apartment door in silence, the click of Andie's flats echoing along with the clinking of the bottles in the bag. Andie hummed along to the sounds like they were the percussion of a song. When we made it inside and Andie rushed to the kitchen to unload the bags, my phone buzzed in my purse and I glanced at it. Unknown number. I almost didn't answer it but I had an event the next day for work and didn't want to miss a potential work call. And what if it was Adam calling back?

'Hello?'

'Hi Liz, I'm so sorry to bother you but this is Agent Hannigan. Beck and I are near your neighborhood and wanted to see if you had a moment to speak with us again.'

A wave of nerves washed over me, my skin feeling flush. *Did they find more evidence about the killer in my family? Is it about Cris?* The thought made the two pieces of Tiramisu in my stomach turn to lead, but at the same time, I was intrigued to hear more.

'I just got home. Can it wait until later this week?' I asked, caught off guard by the surprise intrusion into my evening. While I did want to hear what they had to say, I felt like I needed to mentally prepare.

'We'd really like to have a quick chat right now if you can manage it. I promise it shouldn't take long.'

I let out a sigh but the more I thought about it, the more I knew my thoughts would run wild if I didn't find out what they had to say. What could be so big that it couldn't wait? I needed to know. 'Okay, sure. I'll see you soon.'

Just as I hung up, I heard a loud crash and glass breaking. I rushed into the kitchen to find Andie there yelling 'Dammit!' The bottle of wine we'd just bought was now a pile of glass shards and liquid pooling on our kitchen floor.

'I was really looking forward to trying that one,' Andie groaned, crouching down to pick up the glass pieces. I joined her, carefully picking up slivers and tossing them in the trash. Our buzzer sounded, causing both of us to whip our heads around and stare at the door. 'Who's that?' Andie asked as I ran over to the door and buzzed the agents in.

'You're never going to believe it,' I said before opening the door wide.

'Oh my God, are these the agents?' Andie asked excitedly, eying them up.

'My cousin, Andie,' I said, gesturing to her, wishing she would stop gaping.

'Nice to meet you, Andie,' Beck said before turning back to me. 'We just have a few things we'd like to discuss with you, Liz. Thank you for allowing us to intrude on your evening at such short notice. May we come in?'

'Yes, you can come in,' Andie replied with a huge smile on her face. I elbowed her and she gave me a *what did I do?* look.

'Make yourselves comfortable,' Andie said loudly as the agents entered and I closed the door behind them.

I walked into the living room, pointing them to the couch and pulling over one of the other chairs again to sit across from them.

'That's fine, you don't need to get me a chair too,' I heard Andie mutter under her breath.

'What can I do for you?' I asked, my curiosity mounting. Andie wandered back to the kitchen and busied herself making a drink. 'You already took my 23andMe log in information, I'm not sure how much more help I can really be.'

I looked Hannigan directly in the eyes as I spoke, trying to ignore the chinking of ice and splashing of vodka hitting the glass as Andie poured her cocktail. My thoughts began to swirl frantically. What if they'd found out I'd been continuing to spend time with Cris and had been trying to reach Adam? Would they be upset? Or had there been a major break in the case?

'Yes, again, we're sorry to bother you, Liz,' said Beck kindly.

'We've been diligently combing through your 23andMe and GEDMatch results and we know enough from your DNA data that we are still confident the suspect we're seeking is a familial match to you,' Hannigan started.

'Rosie told me that you asked Cris for a DNA sample,' I said, biting anxiously at the inside of my cheek. 'Do you really think he'll be a match?'

Hannigan looked at me thoughtfully for a moment. I realized I just outed myself about spending time with Cris despite their warning to be cautious, but he continued, 'The DNA evidence that we have for our case comes from the first murder, which took place in 1974.'

'1974? I thought you were investigating an active case? That's what, over forty years ago?'

Hannigan paused for a moment and then said, 'It is an active case but it goes back many years.' I frantically tried to remember the details of the serial killers I'd looked up. *Which ones have been operating for that long?* Hannigan interrupted my mental backtracking, 'Unfortunately, the sample was degraded, so even with current technology we won't be able to get a match with 100 percent certainty,' he explained.

'What? So why bother putting him through the harassment of showing up at his place of work and trying to test his DNA if it can't even clear him?' I asked, clenching my teeth at the sound of Andie dragging an extra chair over with one hand to situate herself next to me, her cocktail in her other hand.

Hannigan's eyes darted from Andie back to me. 'Even though testing your grand uncle would not tell us whether the sample conclusively matches him or not, it can tell us if the familial match comes from the Dominio side of your family. If none of the markers match up with Cristian, then we can conclude that the killer resides in another branch of your family tree, like your biological father's side. It helps narrow down our suspect pool immensely. Your uncle, however, did not give us a sample and has not returned any of our calls at this point,' Hannigan said pointedly.

I furrowed my brow and spun the ring on my finger, a delicate gold band with three small sapphires embedded in it. My dad had given it to my mom as a gift when they were dating to show his intentions were serious. My mom had passed it down to me on my eighteenth birthday, and ever since, it had become a habit of mine to fidget with it when I was nervous or uncomfortable, which I definitely was after hearing Cris had been dodging their calls. *Wouldn't an innocent man be eager to clear his name?*

'Liz, we have some information which leads us to believe Cristian is our prime suspect at this stage, based on our knowledge of your family tree.'

'What other information?' I said, taken aback that they considered him their official prime suspect. The beginnings of a headache prickled behind my right eye.

Hannigan looked at me intently with kind and sympathetic eyes. 'After Cristian denied our request for a DNA sample, we also tracked down Adam Dominio and requested a sample from him. He was more compliant and agreed to let us test his DNA.'

My breath caught in my chest, my thoughts racing. Andie sat silent and alert next to me.

'Due to markings matching up from Adam's DNA, the results show us conclusively that our suspect comes from the Dominio line. This means we can effectively rule out your biological father's family and focus our investigation more fully on Cristian and Adam, as there doesn't appear to be any other living male relatives on the Dominio side that fit the age and geographical characteristics of our suspect.'

I felt nauseated. I knew that Cris and Adam would be on their radar as male relatives but the danger didn't seem that close. There had still been a chance it was someone else I hadn't discovered yet. But now . . .

I took a deep breath, my desire to know more details wrestling with the fear churning in the pit of my stomach. Deciding it was worth a shot, I asked, 'But why do you think your suspect is Cris rather than Adam?'

Hannigan stared at me for a long moment before saying, 'Liz, unfortunately we can't share details of our evidence with you at this stage without risking hindering our investigation.'

'Please, you have to give me something,' I pleaded. 'I know you asked me to be cautious but I've been spending time with Cris, getting to know him. I need to know if there's a tangible reason why I shouldn't be.'

Hannigan took a deep breath, leaning forward. 'We aren't completely ruling Adam out at this time. You need

211

to be careful regarding both of them. But you told us that Cristian is a veterinarian. We've also confirmed that line of business.'

'Yes, but I don't see—'

'Liz,' Beck interrupted, leaning forward on her seat. 'You cannot repeat to others what we are about to share with you in regard to this case, as it could jeopardize bringing the perpetrator to justice.' She glanced at Andie and said, 'Actually, Andie, would you mind stepping out of the room for just a moment? There's a lot at stake with this case and we have to be really diligent about containing the flow of information.'

Andie looked at me anxiously, clearly not wanting to leave the room.

'Please, can she stay? We spend so much time together and if I'm related to someone dangerous that may put her at risk too. We both promise not to tell anyone what you share with us.' Andie nodded vigorously in response.

The agents stared at us for a beat before Hannigan gave Beck a short nod. 'Okay,' Beck said, looking back at us. 'But this really must not leave the room.'

'We promise,' I said, on the edge of my seat.

'I know that we were vague about which case we are working the last time we spoke, but it's time we bring you up to speed on who we are investigating.'

She paused, looking to Hannigan again. The suspense was killing me.

Hannigan crossed his hands in his lap, his expression hard to read. 'Liz, the criminal that we are investigating is The Tri-State Killer.'

Andie gasped, sloshing part of her drink out of the glass and onto her leg. I was frozen. A chill rushed over me, like a wave swelling and crashing down over my head so

I couldn't breathe or see which way was up or down. A confusing, all-encompassing darkness. The Tri-State Killer was the boogeyman. The monster who had evaded capture for decades, stealing lives in the darkness. Of all the possibilities of which killer I could be related to, he had seemed too far-fetched. I hadn't seen anything about him in the news for years, all signs pointing to him being dormant.

The last time I spoke with the FBI it had been a tenuous connection to a crime, something that had intrigued me as a person who needed to know every detail of the world around me. But now, there was no escape from the eerie truth at hand; a truth I didn't want to be a part of. I could no longer deny or make up excuses about the level of evil someone in my family possessed. Someone that shared DNA with me was capable of abducting and murdering women for over forty years. Women not all that different from Andie and me. It was a hard concept to grasp, and now, it was my reality.

I felt like I was on the verge of hyperventilating as panic took over. I leaned forward and tilted my head down. Pulling in deep, focused breaths, I closed my eyes and tried to calm the storm of emotions. There was no way around it, I was related to a psychopath. *What if I was already spending time with him?* I pulled my head back up sharply. It just couldn't be Cris. It had to be someone else. I *needed* it to be someone else.

I felt the weight of Andie's hand on my arm and her words brought the room back into sharp focus. 'Liz, are you okay?'

Trying to compose myself, I was suddenly very aware of all the eyes trained on me. I swallowed hard and muttered, 'Yes, sorry, I'm fine. It's just . . . a lot to take in. I just can't believe I'm related to TSK—'

Hannigan and Beck nodded sympathetically, giving me another moment to compose myself. As the initial shock began to wear off, the familiar itch deep inside me urging me to dissect, investigate, learn, reared its head. I had to know why they felt so strongly that it could be Cris.

'Please,' I said, with a calmness that surprised even myself. 'Explain to me why Cris and his career as a vet makes him a suspect. I saw you share a look in our first meeting when I mentioned what he does for a living and you've brought it up again today. Just tell me something concrete.'

Hannigan nodded, taking a second before he continued, 'Liz, hair strands from The Tri-State Killer's victims showed trace evidence of ketamine in their systems, which if you don't know, is an animal tranquilizer frequently used by veterinarians. Cristian would have and still does have access to it through his business. We know that TSK has been dormant, but we don't believe that makes him any less dangerous an individual. There's no guarantee he's done killing and we need to get justice for all the families he's already destroyed.'

I swallowed the lump in my throat, frustration and confusion mingling with panic, eager to come to Cris's defense despite how short a time I'd known him. 'Is that all? Couldn't someone else, like Adam, have figured out how to get ketamine, maybe illegally?' I countered.

'That's not all that we are basing our case on but I'm afraid that's all the evidence we can comfortably share with you at this time. We want you to understand why we have to continue to look into him,' Hannigan said. 'We need to ensure that there are certain things only ourselves and TSK know about the murders, so we know who is telling the truth if we get a confession. With big cases like these you get people coming out of the wood-work trying to claim they're the killer in order to fulfill some twisted desire for notoriety.' Like last time, Beck seemed to be studying my reactions carefully. Perhaps they were concerned about the relationship I'd been developing with Cris, especially after I fought to defend him. All of a sudden, I was very aware of every facial muscle and what they were each doing. 'We just want you to be aware of the potential danger so you can be observant and proceed with caution if you continue to spend time with Cristian. Until we conclude our investigation, you need to be careful.'

'But there's so many ways someone could get access to that drug,' I pressed, desperate.

'Yeah, I mean, I know some people—' Andie laughed, then abruptly stopped herself when she remembered who we were talking with. 'Never mind,' she said, taking a sip of her cocktail and averting her eyes.

My face flushed and I couldn't help but wish she would leave the room. Maybe I should have had her leave when they asked. Then I could have at least decided how much to tell her.

'When we questioned Cristian about ketamine use in his office,' Hannigan continued, thankfully ignoring Andie's outburst, 'he eventually admitted to us that a large stash of ketamine went missing from his storage room years ago, around the time when we think the paired abductions began. He never reported it, suspecting it was someone he knew and preferring to handle it personally rather than get them into trouble. But because he didn't report it, we have no way to confirm his story.'

My head was spinning and the headache bloomed

stronger behind both eyes now. I rubbed my temples with my fingers. None of this proved anything but I could tell they were confident in their assumptions. I didn't know what to say.

I shook my head, trying to clear out my conflicting emotions and gather my thoughts. 'Why are you telling me this?'

'Well, first of all, we want you to be safe,' Hannigan said. 'We know you're actively trying to establish relationships with your biological family and because of this situation with the familial DNA there is a level of danger inherent for you. You need to be careful regarding both Cristian and Adam until we are able to clear them conclusively.'

I tensed up as the full reality of those words sunk in. Even if it wasn't Cris, I could still walk unwittingly into the den of a monster if I continued my quest to know Adam.

'And secondly,' he continued, 'Liz, while we want you to prioritize your safety and stay out of their paths as we investigate, please do let us know of any contact made. You're in a unique position to observe truths about your biological family that may be hidden from us because of our badges.'

'What exactly am I supposed to be looking for?'

'We're not asking you to do anything out of the ordinary,' Hannigan continued. 'We certainly don't want you to put yourself in further danger, but we have formulated a profile of the killer using behavioral analysis. We aren't able to divulge it all with you but you should note that both Cris and Adam fit the age range, 60–70, and have both lived near where victims have gone missing over the years. TSK would also be extremely intelligent

216

and manipulative, especially towards young women. He's so good at hiding in plain sight that you may not even realize you're talking to a killer.'

I felt like I was on an episode of *Criminal Minds* but tried to force down the fascination and disbelief that this was really happening inside my living room, and instead focus on the words he was saying. This wasn't a show, this was very real. And more importantly, the danger was real.

'He also likely owns at least one remote additional property that allows him to hold the young women captive before killing them and dumping their bodies. If we can locate that property, it will likely hold extremely valuable evidence.'

While this didn't concretely tie Cris to the crimes, my hesitation toward my uncle was growing, the seed they planted fighting to take root in my subconscious. Part of me, however, was determined to stand by the only biological family I knew.

'Is that all? I haven't heard Cris or Rosie talk about any other properties,' I said, clearing my throat. Andie was sipping her drink, looking back and forth between me and the agents like she was watching a tennis match.

The agents rose from the couch at the same time so I stood as well. 'Yes, well, that's all we can tell you right now but please show caution concerning Cristian and Adam. And keep what we've shared of the killer's profile in mind if you continue to be in contact. Something unexpected may jump out at you that could assist us in our investigation. You have my business card, yes?'

'Yes, but I'm not sure I'll have anything to report back,' I said.

'Well, all the same, if you think of anything at all that may help us bring the person responsible for the murders of all those young women to justice, please give me a call. I know this is overwhelming but even the smallest things that seem insignificant may be of help. So many victims and their families have been terrorized by TSK, and this match to your family's DNA is the first real lead we've had in years,' Hannigan said.

I nodded, frozen by the severity of that implication, fear overtaking my desire to protect my new family. This didn't just affect my life, but the lives of everyone hurt by TSK. I couldn't brush off their request no matter how much I wanted to. It wasn't their fault I was related to a serial killer. If I didn't help them and other women were killed by TSK in the future, I would never forgive myself. I had to keep digging.

'You're not just looking into Cris, though, right? I know as of now you think he's a better fit than Adam but is there a chance it could be someone else who we don't know about yet?' I asked urgently.

'Our team is working hard to develop your family tree. Based on the information you've given us access to, as of now, Cristian and Adam are the only males that match the profile, but we are exploring all avenues,' Hannigan said. 'We can't share further details with you at this stage but rest assured, we will thoroughly vet all possibilities. We just want to get to the truth, Liz.'

'Have you looked into Adam beyond just getting his DNA?' I asked, trying to pull more details out of them before they left.

'Ah,' Hannigan said, looking thoughtful, as if trying to decide how much to share. 'We have conducted a brief interview with him and are continuing to assess his background. As you can imagine, there's a lot to track down as far as potential alibis and evidence over such a long span of time, but we haven't stopped vetting either Adam or Cristian.'

I nodded, taking some comfort in his words.

'We'll show ourselves out,' Beck said, giving me a small but grim smile.

They exited the room followed by the sound of the apartment door slamming shut. I stood silently next to my chair, staring after them. Even though they were looking at Adam and remaining open to other possible avenues, the conversation had me second-guessing everything about Cris.

'Damn,' Andie said, breaking the tension. 'You need this?' she said, reaching her drink out in my direction.

I grabbed Andie's glass and took a swig, my mind firing rapidly, trying to take in everything I'd just heard. Sure, it made sense that they were looking at Cris after the ketamine discovery, but I knew nothing about Adam. Could he fit the killer's profile too? The sliver of hope that someone may be able to replace Cris as the main suspect gave me a renewed sense of energy. Adam was the only other male relative I could look into. I grabbed my phone and started scrolling.

'Ooh, what are we doing?'

'I'm calling Adam again,' I said, just as I found his number in my call history.

Andie sat back in her seat and when I stole a sideways glance at her, she looked hesitant.

'What?' I asked, my eyes already back on the screen.

'Do you really think that's a good idea, Lizzie? I mean, you know I'm always down for taking risks, but after that meeting this seems like it may actually be dangerous.

This is TSK we're talking about. The FBI are looking into it, so why don't you just let them handle it? Come on, let's have a drink and watch some TV.'

'Andie, I can't let it go. You know me, I'm not good at being in the dark and I have no guarantee that the FBI will share what they find with me. How could they in a case this big? You saw how evasive they were about giving more details. I'm lucky they've even told me as much as they have, and that was only because they think I can help in some way. Besides, I'm not putting myself in danger by just calling him.'

'You may already be putting yourself in danger by spending time with Cris, you heard what they said about him being their prime suspect.'

'That's why I need to find out more, Andie. If there's someone it could be instead of Cris, then I have to know, and Adam seems like a good possibility,' I said, refocusing on my phone screen.

Giving up the fight, Andie sighed and clicked on the TV, the voices from *Below Deck* filtering through the speakers. I dialed Adam's number but got the answering machine again. I tried to distract myself by watching the show but an hour later the lack of response was making me edgy. I felt like a needy high school girl in a relationship, calling every ten minutes and hanging up when he didn't answer. I willed my phone to ring but it remained silent. *What is taking him so long? Was the friendly outgoing message on his answering machine just an act and he's avoiding me?* Realizing it was getting late, I resigned myself to the fact that I had to stop trying him for the night. Not ready to fall asleep quite yet with my thoughts spiraling, I grabbed my laptop and began searching for everything I could find on TSK. I squinted

220

my eyes at the sketch of his general appearance given by the two almost-victims who had escaped his abduction attempt. I desperately searched for shared characteristics but the drawing was too vague to be helpful. As I went down a dark rabbit hole, I noticed most of the articles surrounding TSK were written by the same investigative journalist, Beccah Williams. I looked up her bio and read:

'Beccah Williams is an American journalist, best known for her award-winning series interviewing family members of The Tri-State Killer's victims. She graduated with an MFA in Writing from Columbia University, where she now leads workshops on creative non-fiction and investigative journalism. Williams also serves on the Board of Directors for the National Association of Black Journalists.'

Scrolling through the list of awards and accomplishments Beccah had to her name, I knew I had to speak to her. After a few furious minutes of searching I was able to find an email address and fired off a message asking if she'd be willing to connect and discuss the case with me. Perhaps she would have more details than the FBI were willing to share. I closed my laptop and poured myself a nightcap, hoping I could mask the dark images filling my mind enough to fall asleep.

VICTIMS 14 & 15

Miranda Grey & Laura Harrington

2004

CHAPTER 18

Miranda stirred the soup with a wooden spoon in the saucepan, making sure not to burn it. When Laura had accidentally burned one side of his chicken last week, he'd pressed her palm to the hot stove top, scarring the inside of her hand badly. She'd whimpered all night long, clutching her hand to her chest. It still hadn't healed. Miranda turned on the burner under the cast iron skillet to make his grilled cheese. He was reading the newspaper rather than watching her, which was rare.

Miranda stole a look over his shoulder at the article he was reading, eager to get some glimpse of the outside world. A photo of Janet Jackson, sweaty and looking down at her chest, standing next to Justin Timberlake accompanied the headline *CONTINUED CONTROVERSY OVER SUPPOSED WARDROBE MALFUNCTION DURING SUPERBOWL HALFTIME SHOW.* The man grunted disapprovingly and her eyes darted frantically in his direction. His dark eyes were still scanning the page. *Oh, thank God!* she thought. *That grunt was about Janet, not me.* Maybe after all this time of dutiful obedience he was getting comfortable with them, letting his guard down. This was her chance; she was really going to do it this time. That morning she'd found the words, 'You can't beat the person who won't give up' scratched into the wall in the corner of their room. She'd had to stretch her chain as far as it would go to make out what it said but the words had stuck with her, replaying over and over in her mind. She'd thought about this cast iron skillet for weeks, the only thing he let them handle that could be used as a weapon. He kept his keys on the table when she made his food, so that part would be easy. As the pan heated on top of the flame, she tested it with her finger until it was just right, then quietly turned off the burner.

'The burner won't light,' she said looking back at him.

He pulled the corner of the paper aside and looked at her over the top of the pages. His thick eyebrows pulled together. He exhaled, annoyed, and rose from the chair. She gripped the handle so tight her knuckles turned white, and when he was within striking distance she swung the pan through the air and slammed it into his face with a loud *thwak*. She'd underestimated the weight of the pan and overestimated the strength in her groggy arms. It didn't hit him as hard as she'd hoped but his head snapped back. Stunned, he grabbed his cheek and stumbled a few steps away from her. She dropped the pan and lunged for the keys. He screamed out, pain and anger reverberating through the air. Tripping over his chair, he landed heavily on the ground. Miranda took the opportunity to make a break for the front door, yanking it open. The sunlight blinded her and she pulled her arm up to shield her face. She could barely make out the outline of his car and a gravelly path next to it. Knowing she didn't have much time she shuffled in that direction, the shackles around her ankles making it difficult to run. He was still screaming from the kitchen. As her eyes adjusted to the outside world she saw the dense forest surrounding her.

'I'm coming for you, Fourteen!' erupted not far behind her.

Miranda did not dare look back. She knew that she didn't have time to figure out if one of the keys on the ring fit the car; he may have kept those separate. Instead she scrambled forward faster, the drugs in her system making her vision waver slightly. She made it past the clearing and hobbled down a path.

'You'll regret this!' the man called out again, closer than before.

She jumped at the sound of his fury. Miranda darted into the woods and found a bank of large boulders with a deep crevice on the other side. She ducked behind it and crouched down low. She gripped the keys, frantically flipping through them until she found one small enough to fit the keyhole in her shackles. Her hands were shaking so badly, it took her three tries to unlock them. His footsteps were louder now on the path, getting closer every second. Miranda clamped a hand over her mouth to muffle her rapid breathing. *I can do this, I'm almost free. Just keep quiet.* The thumping of her heartbeat banged so loudly in her ears she could barely hear anything else, afraid he too would hear it and find her.

'Where are you, Fourteen? It's no use, you can't beat me. And if you do manage to escape, I'll torture your friend. Is that what you want? They'll hear her screams for miles.'

Miranda's heart jumped into her throat. *Oh no, I can't*

let him do that to Laura. But this could be our only shot to get out of here. She heard some nearby bushes rustle in front of her, and she froze, her panic ratcheting up a notch. *Maybe it was an animal,* she tried to convince herself. Doing a quick visual search of the area, she tried to come up with a plan. Miranda knew she would have to leave Laura behind and go get help. Surely there was a house somewhere nearby? Feeling bolstered by her decision, Miranda inched forward and peeked around the rocks. Her eyes scanned left to right. The coast was clear. She straightened and broke into a run, dodging around trees. She looked all around her. *Where is he?* Her arms pumped as her feet plowed through the underbrush. Rocks and twigs tore up the bottoms of her feet, a stabbing pain bearing down on her chest, her lungs not used to working so hard. She barely felt any of it with the adrenaline coursing through her veins, clearing the haze from the drugs.

Miranda saw a break in the trees. There was a road just beyond. *I'm gonna make it!* A road meant cars. It meant people. She couldn't believe it. *I'm gonna escape!* She ducked her head under a low branch. Just as she came out of the trees and her feet hit pavement, a large hand grabbed her by the scruff of her neck. He had found her. Yanking her back into the thicket of trees, away from freedom, her legs flew up into the air as he clamped his beefy arm around her throat in a choke hold. Miranda fought like hell, kicking and jabbing, but it was no use. His grip was tightening, her airway getting smaller and smaller. She struggled to pull in air and remain conscious.

Just before she passed out, he growled into her ear, 'That was a dumb mistake, Fourteen. You're gonna pay for this.'

Miranda vaguely felt her body being dragged through the underbrush. Quick glimpses of trees and cloudy skies fluttered through her consciousness. Her feet trailed along the gravelly path back to the cabin and then through the front door. He dropped her body carelessly onto a cold tiled floor. She could hear the familiar hum of the refrigerator and somewhere in her mind, she registered she was back in the kitchen. Miranda was jolted fully back to consciousness when he pressed the hot pan against her cheek. She screamed as the pan seared her flesh, a horrible burning smell filling her nostrils. The pain was so intense she thought she might throw up but then everything went black. She woke on the floor, her cheek burning so badly tears sprang to her eyes the moment she opened them. He yanked her up from the ground like she weighed nothing and dragged her across the room where a layer of pebbles was arranged on the floor next to the far wall.

'No, not the rocks. Please! I'm so sorry. Please don't make me do it.'

'Kneel.'

Miranda cried and reluctantly laid a knee down on the pebbles.

'Lift the dress!' he yelled out, hovering close behind her.

She forced in a deep breath, shifting her weight to lift the hem of her dress above her knees so that her bare skin rested upon the rocks. She gently lowered her other knee, and then cringing, let her full weight rest upon the cold, harsh pebbles below. She cried out as tears streamed down her face, stinging the burned flesh on her cheek. She gritted her teeth and stared at the wall, listening to the taunting ticks of his old white kitchen timer. The timer went off twenty minutes later but to Miranda it felt like an eternity.

'Come over here,' he said, slow and even. She rose with difficulty, flexing out her tender knees, the skin on them aching with each movement. She could see angry red indents from where the rocks pressed into her flesh before dropping her hemline down to cover her legs. 'You'll attend to my cheek now,' he said sternly, his voice low and ominous. This sudden calmness worried Miranda.

His cheek bore a bright red burn in the round shape of the pan and she had to stop herself from smiling at the sight. She sat down next to him and applied the burn cream to his cheek, desperately wishing she could apply it to her own as well. Smiling at the obvious pain she was in and the look of longing she was giving the tube, he ripped it from her shaking hand when she was done and told her to continue making his lunch. He'd taken the skillet away and laid out lunch-meat in lieu of grilled cheese. She heard him rearranging the pebbles behind her. Her knees were still throbbing, she wasn't sure she could handle kneeling on them again.

When she set the plate in front of him, he didn't smile, but grunted and said, 'Kneel.'

Miranda looked at the ground next to him where he'd spread out another thin layer of pebbles. She tried to stop the tears but they slipped out anyway, stinging mercilessly as the warm salty liquid traveled over her cheek. Lifting the bottom of her dress once more, she lowered herself slowly to the ground. When her knees hit the rocks she bit the inside of her cheek in an effort not to scream, the copper taste of blood filling her mouth. She tried not to yell out again for fear that he'd hit her. She watched him eat with the obligatory smile on her face, her cheeks trembling with the effort. As awful as the pebbles were, if this and the burn were her only punishments for her actions, then she could push through.

After she washed all the dishes and he approved her work, he led Miranda back to their room. She waited behind him, anxious to put distance between herself and him even if it meant being chained to a wall. But before he unlocked the door he turned around, startling her. He hauled his arm back and punched her in the face. Blinding starbursts filled her eyes as she fought to remain conscious. He held her body upright when it sagged toward the floor. He grabbed her by the throat, making it difficult to breathe. She felt a warm trail of blood trickling down her left cheek.

'You try something like that again, and I'll kill you. You hear me?' he growled, his spit landing on her forehead. 'Do you understand, Fourteen?'

She tried to say yes but couldn't get the words out with his hand around her throat. Instead she mustered every bit of her strength to give him a small nod. He let go, opened the door and shoved her into the room. She stumbled and landed roughly onto the cement, catching herself with her hands just before her sore knees could smash into the hard surface. Her wrists stung from the impact. Coughing and sputtering, she tried to catch her breath. She heard Laura gasp at the sight. He chained Miranda back to the wall and left, slamming the door and clicking the lock behind him.

'Are you okay?' Laura asked, worried, scrambling to get closer to her.

'I hit him with a hot pan,' she replied and then began laughing despite the pain it caused her injured face.

'Are you crazy? Miranda, he could have killed you.'

'He's gonna kill us anyway, Laura. Don't you get that? I had to try.'

Laura's face relaxed and she sat back on her heels. 'Besides your blistering cheek, your eye is swollen and there's a cut up by your eyebrow. At least let me help you clean it.'

'Yeah, I can feel it swelling.' Blood dripped from her face and fell onto the blanket. Miranda wiped it away but it left a stain.

Laura looked at her and said, 'I'm sorry.'

Miranda let the tears fall. 'Yeah, me too. I may have just blown our only chance of getting out of here. I was so close, Laura. I made it outside and ran all the way to the road before he caught me.'

'You were outside? What was it like?' Laura whispered, her eyes wide.

'It was amazing. The fresh air, the sun on my skin . . .' She could still smell the damp leaves, could feel the wind whipping across her face. Her heart ached at the feeling of elation she had when she'd thought she'd reached freedom, only for it to be ripped away again.

As Laura cleaned the cut near Miranda's eyebrow with a cool, damp washcloth, Miranda pressed another to her burned cheek. Biting her lip at the stinging sensation, she pushed away the despair at her failed escape and instead thought about the pan she'd held in her hand. She could feel its weight, the rough texture of the iron under her fingertips, the *whoosh* it made when it sailed through the air, the hum it made when it hit his face. Miranda smiled. If they couldn't beat him, she sure as hell was going to go down swinging.

made for maturity. The wolf and raven watched it race
through the . . . the ha . . . I made was a bright hot
. . . orange red. How? coolant. . . but the . . . saw me as
I . . . the . . . running . . . down . . . my . . .

CHAPTER 19

Travis ordered a round of beers while Andie and I racked up the balls on the faded green pool table. When Travis had suggested hot wings, beer and pool at our favorite local spot, The Royal Brooklyn, me and Andie had jumped at the idea. I needed to get out of the house to try to take my mind off all this serial killer business and the fact that Adam still hadn't answered my calls, and Andie had finally finished a hellish week at work. We'd gorged ourselves on spicy buffalo wings, fish tacos and french fries, chasing them down with a round of Brooklyn Brewery Pilsners. The Beatles blared through the jukebox and various sports played silently on the many TVs positioned strategically throughout the bar. I hummed along absentmindedly to *Don't Let Me Down*, swaying my hips to the beat. Andie squinted as she determinedly lined up her pool cue with the neat triangle of balls, getting ready to break. After she released her shot, her force a little too weak to send any balls soaring into the pockets, she swore under her breath and glanced up at me. I'd been fairly quiet through dinner, barely commenting on Andie's story about the guy she'd dealt with at work that day who had so many piercings he'd spent twenty minutes carefully removing earrings from his nipples and genitalia before Andie could take his X-rays.

'Still thinking about what the FBI agents told you?' she said with a sigh.

I glanced up at her. 'Yeah, sorry, I'm trying not to think about it but it keeps creeping back in, you know? The FBI made some pretty good points and I see why they're looking at Cris. But you've met him, Andie. Sure, he's a bit awkward but there's no way he could be a serial killer, right?'

Andie came around to my side of the table, forcefully slamming the bottom of the pool cue into the ground, leaning on it like a staff and said, 'Honestly? Yeah, he seemed nice. But I'm sure Ted Bundy seemed like a good guy too.'

I arched my eyebrows in surprise, sure that she would have been on my side. 'So are you saying you think it could be him?'

Andie avoided my eyes, grabbing the blue chalk cube and rubbing it over the tip of her cue stick. 'I'm not saying anything definitively. Is it possible? Yes. Is it likely? I don't know, Liz. I don't know him well enough.' She sighed and looked back at me.

I chewed on my lip as I reached over and grabbed the first cue stick my hand came into contact with from the holder on the wall near our table. My phone dinged and I paused, pulling it out of my pocket. While I scrolled through my alerts, Travis came back with the next round of beers, handing one to Andie and then to me.

'Thanks,' I mumbled, barely looking up from my phone screen.

Travis grabbed a cue stick and said in a caveman voice, 'The big strong man against the little women.' He flexed his muscles and kissed his forearms. Then, seeing the pathetic spread of balls on the table, he said, 'Looks like you needed these bad boys to get a good first break.'

'Oh, you mean the big strong man who was huddled up on the toilet this morning because he saw a mouse? *That* big strong man?' Andie said, punching him in the ribs softly.

Travis feigned clutching his side. 'That was no ordinary mouse. It was huge.' They both laughed but I was hardly paying attention to what they were saying.

'Oh my God. I signed up for news alerts about The Tri-State Killer when I was looking into him, and I just got a notification – look.' I held up my phone to show the article I was reading.

MISSING BOSTON UNIVERSITY STUDENTS POSSIBLY LINKED TO THE TRI-STATE KILLER

'Those two women who disappeared from Boston last year, Zoey Wilson and Addie Davis, are now suspected to be his latest victims. The FBI assumed he was dead or dormant because it'd been six years since another pair went missing but now that's all out the window.'

Travis and Andie quickly scanned the article. 'Lizzie, that's not good,' Andie replied before grabbing her beer and taking a swig.

I was lost in thought, disturbing images racing around my brain, taking in this new development.

'Liz?' Travis snapped his fingers in front of my face. I tore my gaze from my screen to look up at him. 'You're playing too, right?'

'Yes. Sorry, I just can't stop thinking about the fact that the FBI thinks it could be my uncle. And now knowing that two women are in danger . . . it's just a lot.'

'Well if they know it's a familial match, there's still a chance it's someone else, right?' Travis asked.

'They've been combing through my 23andMe matches who I haven't connected with yet but it seems like they still think it's either Cris or Adam. They said Cris is the best fit based on what they know at this point. I've been trying to connect with Adam, even if it's just to talk to him and see what he's like, figure out if he's a viable alternative and give me at least *some* peace of mind about seeing Cris and Rosie. But he still hasn't returned any of my messages.'

Andie leaned down to take a shot, ignoring that it was actually Travis's turn. Before she pushed the stick forward, she looked up at me. 'I know you think Cris seems too nice to be TSK but he could be manipulating you. They did say TSK was good at that.' She hit the ball with gusto, having better success than her first attempt and sending a striped ball zooming into the far corner pocket. Andie's arm shot into the air and she danced around in a circle in celebration.

Travis whistled and said, 'Nice shot, babe.'

As Andie moved to the other side of the table to line up another shot, she said, 'You shouldn't go back up there, especially not alone. With these new abductions, TSK is clearly making a comeback. It's not a good idea to see Cris again until you're sure it's not him.' She took the shot and then straightened up. 'I'm worried about you. This is really dangerous, Liz. Last time you didn't even tell me you were going. What if something had happened to you?'

'But maybe I'll find out more by spending time with him that'll sway me one way or the other. I really don't think he'd hurt me.'

'Said the cat to the mouse,' Andie said under her breath.

I frowned. I trusted my instincts but I trusted Andie's too. If Andie was worried, maybe I should take her concerns a little more seriously. While Travis took his shot I looked back at my phone, the article still on the screen. The pool balls clanged and the sound of a ball sinking into a pocket seeped into my ears but I kept reading.

Andie was biting Travis's ear playfully when I interrupted them, holding my phone out to her. 'Andie, look.' She regretfully pulled away and squinted at the screen while I rambled on. 'This article says the girls were taken from their homes at night while they slept. The police confirmed there were signs of a break-in found at Zoey and Addie's apartment. It matches similar evidence of break-ins found in the more recent victims' homes. The screen over a window had been cut and the lock broken. There were scratch marks on the metal window trim on the outside. You really think my uncle could be capable of something like that?'

Suddenly, a chill ran up my spine as I thought about our own apartment, its back window lock never quite latching from the way the old building had shifted over the years. I'd been a bit nervous when we'd decided to take a first floor apartment but we'd been so excited about the large space with the low price tag, we just thought we were lucky to find it. But now I couldn't help but see the similarities between the TSK cases and us. Two women, around my and Andie's ages, roommates, stolen away in the middle of the night, never to be seen alive again. Was it already too late for Addie and Zoey? A bead of sweat formed along my hairline and I hastily wiped it away with the back of my hand.

Andie's face scrunched into a frown. 'Liz, you see how scary this is, right? He's not dormant. He's still actively hurting women and you're purposefully putting yourself into his path. Hell, you're putting both of us in his path. We kinda seem like his type.'

I swallowed hard, a small piece of guilt nudging at me that I was also putting Andie at risk by continuing my quest for information. Clicking the button on the side of my phone to put the screen to sleep, I stared at the green felt on the table while Travis took his turn. *Is she right?* Maybe this *was* too dangerous. But as I thought about Rosie and Cris, I knew I couldn't let this newfound family go unless I had concrete proof of his guilt.

'I have to go to Connecticut anyway for that exhibit I'm covering tomorrow and I already told them that I'd visit. I just can't shake this fear that if the FBI couldn't solve it after forty-five years, this could go on forever without me ever knowing the truth. I can't just freeze Cris and Rosie out indefinitely. He just doesn't seem violent to me but I promise, I'll be careful. I'm going during daylight and Rosie will be there.'

Then another thought hit me, when I mentioned Rosie. If it *was* Cris, how much did she know? Was she complicit? Or was she another victim, blissfully unaware of his actions? Or maybe aware but too afraid to say anything? I thought back to my last visit and the way Cris had given her a stern look when she'd initially suggested showing me Frank's belongings upstairs. At first, I thought it was simply a difficult moment due his brother's passing. But now I wondered whether it was more ominous than

240

that. More controlling. But what about Adam? What if he fit the bill even more than Cris? I still hadn't even gotten him on the phone.

'Wait,' I said, interrupting as Travis tried to show Andie how to line up a certain play on the pool table. 'I just thought of something. Adam's phone number is a Massachusetts number and these new women were taken from Boston. The original article I found with him in it was from when he worked a job in Boston.'

Andie walked over and grabbed me by the shoulders. 'Take a deep breath for a sec, okay? Can we please just enjoy our time out tonight? This whole thing is crazy and dangerous and I'm worried about you. But also . . . damn, I don't know, Liz. I just want to play pool and have fun with my cousin. Not rehash your obsession with The Tri-State Killer when you should be leaving the investigation up to the professionals.'

I shrank back. 'That's the second time you've called me obsessed. Tell me Andie, how would you feel if you found out at the age of twenty-seven that you're adopted and that, quite possibly, the only person you knew from your biological family is a serial killer?' I realized my voice had risen but I didn't care. Several guys from the neighboring table looked at me.

Andie inhaled and dropped her gaze to the ground. When she looked back at me she shook her head. 'You're right. I have no idea what this feels like. I'm sorry that I don't want to talk about this right now but it's all we've talked about for weeks. This isn't some movie or distant news article anymore, Liz. This is real life. You could be inserting yourself into the life of someone who kills women like us. I've tried my best to be supportive through all of this but now that we know TSK is active, this is

241

really scary, okay? I just want to have one normal night out without a cloud of danger hovering over us. Is that too much to ask?' Andie's eyes pleaded with me.

But I couldn't drop it. As much as I wanted to put it out of my head, it wasn't happening. Maybe I *was* obsessed. But maybe that was natural given the circumstances.

I smiled thinly at Andie and grasped her shoulders, looking her directly in the eyes. 'I'm sorry, Andie. I know you're trying to look out for me but I can't stop thinking about it. I'm just gonna go home and let you and Travis have the night to yourselves. You'll have more fun without me.' I dropped my arms to my side and looked around for my purse which had been stashed on a bar stool next to our table.

Andie bowed her head and rubbed her eyes, smearing her smoky eye a little, and said, 'That's not what I meant.'

'Come on, Liz, don't go. You guys are winning,' Travis said.

I gave him a weary smile. 'I'm sure Andie will kick your ass with or without me.'

I placed my cue stick back on the rack, grabbed my purse off the stool and threw a twenty down for the beers I'd drunk.

Before I walked toward the exit, Andie grabbed my arm. 'Liz please don't go. You know that's not how I meant it.'

I placed my hand over Andie's and squeezed. 'I know. It's okay, really. I'm just gonna go home and try calling Adam again. I wouldn't be much fun now anyway.'

Andie's face fell. 'Liz, it's really scares me that you're trying to hunt down a serial killer. I don't think you should be calling Adam anymore. Please, leave this to the FBI.'

I looked at her for a long minute and then said, 'Sorry, Andie. I just can't.'

242

She nodded and said, sounding resigned, 'Alright, well I'll see you back at the apartment then.' She turned to walk back to the pool table but then spun back around and added, 'And be careful, Liz.'

I gave her a reassuring hug and waved at Travis, turning to leave. I felt Andie's eyes on my retreating back for a moment as I walked to the exit. Before I moved through the door, I heard Andie say, 'Are you ready to lose worse than that time Gram killed you at Five-Card Stud, Travis Baker?' I smiled and exited the bar.

After rushing home, I dialed Adam's number and felt like throwing my phone at the wall when his answering machine picked up yet again. *Did this guy ever answer his phone?* I kept waiting and pacing the apartment, then I called him again. The Massachusetts connection to Adam was bolstering my feeling that it could be him instead of Cris. But without definitive proof, I was a ball of anxious energy.

Staring at my silent phone screen was driving me crazy so I picked up the remote control and clicked on the TV to distract myself. Chevy Chase, Steve Martin and Martin Short glammed up in black embroidered Mexican suits and sombreros danced across the screen. Growing up, my parents and I used to regularly watch my dad's favorite movie, *Three Amigos!*, which had inspired our nickname. And even though I'd forgiven them, the images that popped into my head of us piled on the sofa with a big bowl of buttery popcorn, me tucked in between the two of them, still needled at me. Every memory seemed tainted and I wasn't sure how to get past that. This reminder of happier times just brought up all the lies along with it and I felt saddened by the actors' antics instead of amused.

Groaning loudly, I quickly pulled up the channel guide to find something else to watch. Before I could make up my mind on what to select my phone rang, causing my heart to stop. *Adam?*

I picked it up so frantically I almost dropped it. It wasn't Adam's number but it also wasn't a number I recognized. Puzzled, I answered the phone, my hand shaking slightly from the adrenaline.

'Hello?'

'Hi, I'm sorry to call so late but is this Liz Catalano?' A woman's crisp voice filtered through the line.

'Yes, this is Liz,' I replied, both confused and intrigued by the mystery caller.

'Oh, great. Hi Liz, this is Beccah Williams, I received your email inquiring about my work investigating The Tri-State Killer. Apologies again about the time but as you can imagine I've been a bit busy since the news broke on the possible link to the women from Boston.'

My heart raced. 'Oh, no apologies necessary. Thanks so much for calling me.'

'Yes, of course. Well, I could tell from your email you were really passionate about finding out some answers about TSK. To be honest, it reminded me of a few dogged emails I sent around in my early writing days hunting for information.'

Heat flushed my cheeks. I guessed that was a compliment but suddenly I was a bit self-conscious. Beccah was a true investigative journalist, something I always imagined being. 'I know I didn't go into a lot of detail in my email beyond saying I was personally connected to TSK but I'm so grateful you've got in touch.'

'Yes, well that certainly caught my interest. Would you mind telling me a bit now about how you're connected?'

I could hear a familiar need-to-know tone in her voice. I took a deep, steadying breath. Every time I spoke about it out loud the danger felt a step closer.

'I guess I should probably start by asking for this to be off the record. I'm not sure if I'm supposed to be sharing any details about what I'm going through but I need some answers and I think you may be able to help.'

'Sure, Liz. We're off the record.'

A mix of nerves and thrill coursed through me. 'Well, after doing a DNA-ancestry kit recently that uncovered I was adopted, I uploaded my DNA to GEDmatch in the hopes of finding more biological family members.' I took a long pause and I could sense an excited tension hanging on the line between us. 'The FBI got a familial hit on my DNA that connects me to TSK. And even crazier, they think it's one of two relatives I've been trying to get to know. One of which, I've already spent time with.'

Beccah gave a long, low whistle. 'Wow. Liz, that's huge. I mean I've been investigating this case for a very long time and that's the biggest break in the case that I'm aware of.'

'I know. Which is why I'm hoping I can trust you to keep this between us. I don't want to mess up the investigation. But at the same time I really need answers. The FBI isn't exactly being forthcoming with me and if I'm walking into the den of a serial killer, I need to know.'

'I'm not surprised they're keeping their evidence close to the chest,' Beccah said. 'But I can't blame you for wanting to know the truth about your family history. How can I be of help?'

Relief bloomed inside me at her willingness to speak with me. It was nice having someone who understood the dark ins and outs of TSK and who wouldn't shy away from discussing his horrible crimes.

'I'm just hoping there may be some details on him, his profile, evidence he may have left behind. I don't know really, anything that the FBI isn't sharing with me. I know I'm asking for a lot but I just feel like I'm swimming blind here. All they would really tell me was his age, that he's lived predominately in the Tri-State Area, and that he is manipulative and good at hiding in plain sight.' I thought back for a moment. 'Oh. And that he may have additional properties. Is there *anything* else you know that you could share with me?' I knew it was wrong to share the information the FBI had given me in confidence, but I was so grateful to finally speak to someone who might actually help me. At last, here was someone who knew the case intimately and could connect some of the missing pieces of this dangerous puzzle.

'Ah,' Beccah said, pausing for a beat before replying. I was nervous I'd pushed too far, but then she continued, 'I can see how that would be frustrating for you. To basically be told your life could be in danger but then only be told those vague characteristics.'

'Yes, exactly,' I said, thankful she understood me.

'So, here's the thing,' Beccah said. 'The reason I'm able to cover this case so extensively is that I've developed a close bond with one of the retired detectives. We'd bounce ideas off each other, he'd give me quick peeks at cold case files, and in return I wouldn't break his trust and publish details that could jeopardize the investigation. It's been a relationship that I truly prioritize and value.'

My heart sunk. Was she about to tell me she, too, couldn't help me? Her experience with the investigation was fascinating. I was envious of her access.

'Wow,' I said, clearing my throat. 'It must be so interesting seeing case files and talking openly with someone so close to the investigation.'

'Yes, it's been both incredibly interesting and heartbreaking.' She sighed, seemingly running through her options. 'I'm not sure I feel comfortable telling you everything I know at this point but I don't think there'd be much harm in sharing a few more profile details with you, to help you keep an eye out for your own safety. Us women have to stick together.'

A smile bloomed across my face, my blood pumping. 'I totally understand and that would be incredible. Anything you could give me would be a big help. And I promise I won't share what you tell me.' At that moment, I decided having Beccah's trust and access to her information was more important than filling Andie in on this call. She was already worried and getting burnt out on my determination for answers, so this was something I would keep to myself.

'Great, I appreciate that. Well, in addition to what the FBI shared with you, I can tell you that we believe him to be college educated and have strong religious beliefs. Additionally, we believe he's held a job that involves travel, particularly on the weekends, as that's when he seems to hunt and abduct his victims.'

'Because that would make it possible for him to cover such a wide geographic territory?' I asked, hanging on to her every word.

'Exactly,' Beccah replied. 'It's even possible he visited these areas multiple times to stalk his victims before abducting them. His ability to abduct two women at a time and leave so little evidence and no witnesses behind points to his intelligence and methodical advance planning. And it's likely he's remained physically fit even as he ages. He's extremely organized and skilled at what he does. Perhaps even to a level of OCD.'

'I just can't believe I'm related to this monster,' I said, my head spinning. 'And now, knowing there's a possibility that he's resurfaced . . .'

'I know it goes without saying, Liz, but do please be careful. For years, I've looked at the photos, autopsy reports and details of what TSK has done and it's truly a nightmare. If the FBI are warning you to keep your distance, you should listen. But I also know what it feels like to need answers to a mystery that's haunting you.'

'I know it's dangerous,' I conceded, 'but he's gone this long without the FBI catching him, what's to say they'll actually get him this time? What if I never learn who in my family is too dangerous to get close to?'

'I see your point,' she said after a brief pause. 'I'm not sure I feel comfortable sharing much more at this stage until we see how things play out with these new developments but I'll give you one more point from the profile.'

I was on the edge of my seat, eager for more details. 'Beyond his intelligence,' she continued, 'we also believe TSK to be good with technology. He's left so little evidence behind in both his abductions and his disposal of the bodies that he must have some understanding of surveillance and how to avoid detection, especially with all the recent advancements in technology. He would've had to adapt efficiently to the changing times in order to continue murdering. I know that's not a lot more to go on but I hope I've been able to shed a bit more light.'

A vague image of the man in the shadows was starting to form in my mind. 'You did, and I can't thank you enough. I know I need to be careful but any little bit

248

of information is a huge help. Would it be okay if I reached out again if I have a question or anything major progresses in the case?'

'Absolutely,' Beccah replied kindly. 'This number is my cell, so feel free to shoot me a text anytime and if I can help out, I will.'

'I really can't thank you enough,' I said, grateful to have a kindred spirit on my side who understood my need for the truth.

'Thank you for sharing your story with me too, Liz. Have a great rest of your night and stay safe.'

'Thanks, Beccah. Goodnight.'

I ended the call and stared blankly at the dark screen. Slowly, I was starting to get a fuller picture of the monster that was TSK. He was sixty to seventy years old, intelligent, extremely organized, religious, had or has a job that involves travel, and probably owns other properties. He was likely good with technology and physically fit. And then of course, there's the ketamine usage that I didn't share with Beccah. *Did she know about it and just didn't say?* It wasn't a lot to go on but it was something. At least I had a few more characteristics to keep in mind moving forward. And hopefully the next time I spoke with Beccah, if I could gain her trust, perhaps I could learn more from her. She was clearly hanging onto some details that might be important.

I heard the front door swing open and then shut again, the ding of Andie's keys hitting the bowl in the entryway. 'Lizzie?'

'Yeah, I'm on the couch,' I called back.

'Oh, good,' she said, turning on a light as she entered the room with Travis on her heels. I hadn't even realized how dark it had gotten during my talk with Beccah.

'Oh hey, Trav,' I said, giving them a small smile.

Andie sat down on the cushion next to me while Travis headed to the kitchen. I could smell the lingering scent of beer on her warm breath as she leaned in.

'I'm sorry if I was insensitive back at the bar, Lizzie. I know you're going through a lot. This whole thing just has me so spooked. I mean, his victims are so much like us. And we live in this apartment, where we sacrificed security for budget. Now that we know he's still active, I'm worried.'

'I know. I'm sorry, too. I wish I could turn off this need to know but it's my family. It's like there's this huge gaping hole in my life that won't feel complete until I fill it in. But I know it's dangerous. I'll try to be careful and I'm sorry you've been dragged into this.'

I fingered the locket dangling around my neck, thinking about my twisted family history.

'Oh my God, Liz. The locket!' she exclaimed, pointing at my neck.

'What?'

'Cris mailed you the locket.'

It took a moment before the weight of her words sunk in. I had given Cris our address. It had seemed harmless at the time but now in light of TSK's recent activity, I couldn't help but wonder whether it had been a ruse to learn where we live. I felt sick. If it was Cris, I'd inadvertently put Andie and I right in TSK's crosshairs.

'Oh, Andie, I'm sorry. I didn't know at the time that things would escalate to this level.'

'Of course you didn't. But I hope you don't mind,' Andie said as Travis walked into the room with two glasses of water and a bag of Andie's favorite chips. 'I asked Travis if he would stay with us for a while. He sleeps over a lot anyway and I would feel so much safer if he were here with everything going on.'

Travis gave me a small smile as he rested on the arm of the couch near Andie.

'Oh, yeah absolutely. Honestly, I think that's a great idea, especially now that one of the prime suspects has our address,' I said, feeling guilty.

Andie looked relieved that I'd accepted her proposal so quickly but it was the least I could do and it did make me feel safer. 'Trav,' she said looking up at him. 'Would you mind starting out by making sure the front door is locked and checking all the windows? Especially that back one that never latches. Maybe we can put something up against it to hold it in place. That seems like prime real estate for TSK.'

'On it,' he said, jumping up and rushing around to check all our entry points.

Andie got up to go change out of her bar clothes and I looked down at my phone to see what time it was. My heart sank when I saw I still had no call notifications from Adam. After the call with Beccah, I was more determined than ever to get ahold of him. I wasn't sure I could cope with the guilt if I'd unwittingly invited TSK to our doorstep. It was too late to call Adam. Reaching out again would have to wait till tomorrow. I took a deep breath, getting up to search for something to wedge into the top of the window frame and make it more secure. I tried desperately to push away the images fighting for attention in my mind: a man with my eyebrows, prying open our back window while we slept.

VICTIMS 16 & 17

Rosa Ramirez & Rowan Morrison

2006

CHAPTER 20

When he was done eating his dinner, Rosa stood from her kneeling position on the floor and cleared the table. She washed the dishes and stacked them on the towel covering the counter. Grabbing the sponge, she wiped down the cast iron skillet and then the saucepan. Both were chained to the counter next to the stove with only enough slack for them to sit on the burner or to be lifted a few inches to clean. It was clunky and awkward but Rosa guessed it was so they couldn't be used as weapons. That's what she dreamed of using them for, anyway. When she was done cleaning, the man inspected all the dishes. He found a single small spot on the edge of his plate and he made her rewash them all. After checking everything again, he thankfully found them satisfactory. Rosa heaved a sigh of relief that she'd avoided punishment this time, but she quickly became disgusted when she remembered what was coming next. He sat down in his chair and removed his socks, rolling up his pants to expose his calves and feet. Rosa groaned inwardly. She hated what he was about to make her do.

Obediently, she picked up the large plastic bowl that was always next to the sink and filled it with warm water, grabbing the scrub brush from the counter before returning to him at the table. She shuffled forward slowly, focusing intently on not spilling any of the water on his clean floor. Rosa set it down carefully on the ground, then dutifully took the soft towel waiting on the table and spread it on the floor next to the water.

'Let me test it first.' The man dipped a finger in the water and frowned. 'It's a bit hot but I guess it'll do.'

She sat down on the ground in front of him, guided his large calloused feet into the bowl, and began scrubbing them. Rosa hated feet. It took everything in her not to gag as she ran her fingers between each toe like he'd demanded the first time he gave her this task. She tried to zone out when she did his feet. She daydreamed about search efforts to find them; posters plastered everywhere with their smiling faces peering out. She wondered if her Myspace page was filled with hopeful messages from friends or if they'd already been forgotten. It'd been over six months. Would they still be posting and hoping?

He grunted, breaking her out of her trance, and said, 'That's good,' lifted his feet out of the water and placed them on the towel to the side, where Rosa dried them off.

She poured the dirty water into the sink, placing the bowl back in its spot on the counter, and then sank back down to the floor next to him. She knew the drill. She held her hands out and he squirted lotion into them. At least they were clean now, she thought as she worked on his left foot. For the next half hour Rosa massaged the man's rough, ugly feet, until he pulled them away and rolled down the cuffs of his jeans. He took her back to her room, attached her shackles to the wall, and locked the door behind him when he exited. Rowan, unsurprisingly, was still sleeping on her mattress. She wasn't handling their captivity well. When she wasn't crying, she was sleeping. Rowan wasn't eating much either, causing her to lose a significant amount of weight. She barely even talked to Rosa.

Rosa tried to be understanding but she found herself feeling resentful. She and Rowan weren't exactly friends before the man abducted them and brought them here. Rowan had answered Rosa's ad for a roommate to share her small two-bedroom cottage that was within walking distance to the university. They'd only lived together for a few months before the man snatched them from their beds in the middle of the night. Rowan had her own circle of friends and a fairly opposite class schedule, so they didn't hang out much. In fact, they mostly only saw each other in passing when they were getting ready to go to sleep. It didn't bother Rosa because most of her time was consumed by studying anyway. She'd also just beaten out several of her male counterparts for a highly coveted government internship, so she would've been spending even less time at their cottage.

But now she felt like she was being held captive alone, which made this whole mess even worse. She wouldn't want to impose this torture on someone she loved but she wished desperately for any companionship to help her get through the darkness. Rowan's inability to be her friend in this time of need made Rosa feel cold and bitter. In the beginning, she had tried to connect with Rowan and help protect her from the man's wrath. But now, Rosa practically forgot Rowan was even there. Sometimes when she heard Rowan crying in the night, she couldn't decide if it was real or if it was in her own head as she slowly descended into insanity.

Rosa pulled the blanket flat in front of her and ran her fingers over the dried drops of blood there. When she'd first received the blanket and saw the stains, she had tried frantically to wash it out at the sink, disturbed by its implications, but the spots had remained. Now, it made her feel less alone, connected to someone, even if the blood did belong to a dead woman. Rosa assumed the man had killed her. After all, he had to be the one they'd been referring to on the news. She and Rowan weren't the first two women to go missing and bodies had been turning up across the Tri-State area for years. It was probably only a matter of time till their own bodies were discovered abandoned in plastic bins out there somewhere, just like the rest of them.

She sighed and pulled the wrappers out from under her pillow. She'd been using the wrappers from the granola bars to make an origami bracelet. It helped pass the time and sometimes she hummed songs under her breath as she folded the delicate creases, trying to fill the quiet void that Rowan left. She'd already made one bracelet but the man had snatched it away when he saw it on her wrist. He'd said a proper lady should not be decorated. She decided she would hide this one under her pillow instead of wearing it when he was here, to protect the one thing she had control over.

Rowan woke and sat up, groggy. 'Did he come for his dinner?' Her voice barely existed, scratchy and quiet from its lack of use.

'Yeah, you were sleeping so I took care of it, even

though I did lunch, too.' She tried to keep the resentment out of her voice but it trickled in regardless.

'Thanks.' Rowan rubbed her eyes, stared off into the distance for a minute and then began sobbing again.

CHAPTER 21

I unplugged the curling wand, placed it on the bathroom counter and reached for my hairspray for one final coat. I ran my fingers through the large sectioned curls, loosening them just enough so the waves looked sleek and purposeful, rather than their natural limp state. I wished I had inherited my mother's natural curls, I thought, as I remembered all the photos I'd seen at Cris and Rosie's. Hers was so thick and bouncy, and looked like it didn't require nearly the same amount of effort mine did just to leave the house. I ran my hand over my black silk jumpsuit, smoothing out some wrinkles. The exhibit I was covering for work didn't require me to look fancy, nor did lunch with my uncle and aunt, but looking put together made me feel more in control. The visits from the FBI and the search for TSK had me on edge and I was having trouble feeling grounded.

I had always considered myself a good judge of character but now I felt like I couldn't be sure of anything. Despite all the uncertainty part of me was still looking forward to seeing Cris and Rosie again. Taking a deep breath, I exited the bathroom and grabbed my purse and cell phone off the desk.

Looking around to make sure I hadn't forgotten anything, I looked down at the time on the phone in my hand. Biting my lip, I calculated how much time it was going to take me to get to Connecticut. Unable to resist, I opened up the recent call log on my phone and selected Adam's phone number. I had time to try him one more time before I left.

'Hello?' rolled across the line, low and smooth.

My heartrate jumped. 'Hello? Is this Adam Dominio?'

'It is, who's calling?'

'This is Liz Catalano. I'm sorry to bother you, but I've left you a few messages—'

'Ahh, yes,' he said, drawing out a long, low whistle. 'Not a bother, not a bother.' There was another brief pause. 'I'm sorry, I got your messages, I just don't talk much about that side of my family these days. I'm not sure I can be much help to you, honey.' His voice was almost melodic when he talked. A low, even cadence stringing each syllable together.

'Please don't hang up,' I pleaded, hoping I didn't sound too desperate. 'I'm pretty sure you're my grand-father's cousin and I haven't been able to get in touch with many relatives from my biological family. You're my last hope.'

He exhaled loudly but stayed on the line. A balloon of hope swelled in the pit of my stomach. Maybe I would get some information from him after all.

'Your last hope? Well, then what can I help you with, Lizzie?' The way he adjusted my name into a familiar nickname as if he'd known me for years took me aback a little. I wasn't sure why, but it made me uncomfortable.

262

'I just want to connect with some family members and learn more about where I came from. I recently found out I'm adopted and—'

'Adopted, huh?' He gave another low whistle. 'I can see how that would be tough for a girl such as yourself. How old are you, 23? 24?'

A chill ran up my spine and sprawled down my arms, all the way to my fingertips gripping the phone. Something about the way he asked my age in those calm, measured tones made my skin crawl as I thought about how all of TSK's victims were around that age, not far off from myself and Andie. I shook my head and took a deep breath. *He could just be curious to know more about me?*

'Twenty-seven,' I replied, injecting a false calmness into my voice.

'Ahh, twenty-seven,' he said, drawing out his syllables. 'A young woman then. You must have a boyfriend or a husband, I'm sure.'

I swallowed hard, trying to quiet the unsettling feeling that was growing in me the longer we stayed on the line. 'No, no boyfriend or husband quite yet,' I said. Then, trying to get the conversation off me and back on track, 'So you're Cristian and Frank Dominio's cousin, right?'

After a beat he said, 'Yes, yes. I am. But I've had no contact with the Dominio family in a long time. My own family is a bit of a handful themselves, you see.'

My hopes soared. 'Is there other family? Someone else you could put me in contact with as well?'

'Oh, no Lizzie. There's not.' I cringed again at the way the nickname rolled off his tongue. When he spoke, he was somehow simultaneously intriguing and eerie. 'The only family I have left is from my mother's side and they've got no relation to you, so I'm afraid it wouldn't be much help at all.'

'I'm not sure if you heard but your cousin Frank passed away.' It exploded from my mouth before I could stop myself. I was torn between my desperation to get to know another biological relative and my desire to uncover if he could be The Tri-State Killer. Either way, I knew I had to keep him talking as long as I could.

He paused before saying, 'No, I hadn't heard but I haven't spoken to Frank since we were kids.'

Chewing on my lip, I scoured my brain for some way to keep the conversation going in a helpful direction. 'I just want to know who my family is. Is there anything you can tell me? Please.'

For a few agonizing seconds all that came through the phone was the sound of his deep, measured breathing. 'Well let's see, my dad passed away from prostate cancer when I was young.' He gave a large, exaggerated sad sigh. I couldn't tell if he was being authentic or acting. 'My mom never really liked his brother, Rodrigo. She said he was a jerk who talked down to her and was always trying to control every situation. He and Aunt Dorina fought constantly and my mom always suspected he was cheating. I think it worried her that he might encourage my dad to do the same. So, after my dad died, we moved to the West Coast near her family.'

'What about Frank? Can you tell me anything else about him?' I asked, curious for his take on the only other male relative I knew about.

'Frank? Not sure how much I can tell you. I was pretty young when we moved away. I haven't seen him since his birthday party when I was a kid. Frank teased me the entire time and I told my mom and dad I didn't want to go back there after that. We were never close and I didn't like him, to be honest. He was a bully.'

I wondered if I could trust this opinion since it was in direct contrast to the image Cris and Rosie had painted of Frank. Thinking back though, Cris did say that Frank wasn't happy that Adam came to the birthday party. But kids could be unkind and still grow up to be better adults. Maybe it was just a misguided childhood rivalry.

'Oh dear, would you look at that?' he said. 'I have plans and I'm running late. I'm afraid I have to go.'

One last try couldn't hurt. 'Oh sure, I'm sorry to keep you. Would you be willing to meet up on a day when you have more time? I could come to you, if it's easier. I promise it won't take long, I just—'

'Oh sure, sure, Lizzie. Look, I'm on my way out of town for the weekend so why don't you call around next week and we'll figure it out.'

'Oh okay, where are you headed? I'm traveling to Connecticut for a work event and may have some downtime, if you're not too far away maybe our paths could cross?'

'Connecticut? Oh, um, well I'm going to this boat show in Rhode Island but my schedule is very tight. I'm afraid I wouldn't have the time. Just give me a call next week and we'll work it out.'

'Do you know a day that may—'

'I really have to go, honey, but call me next week. We'll talk soon. Bye now.'

The click as he ended the call resounded in my ear, followed by silence. I pulled the phone away and looked at its blank screen, cringing at the *honey*. I was torn after that call. On the one hand, he was fairly forthcoming and agreed to meet up. On the other, he had given me sleazy, used car salesman-type vibes in how he addressed me and needled for personal information before giving up any of his own. And why was he rushing me off the phone so quickly? Something told me that I should look up that boat show he mentioned to see if it was really happening.

A text from one of my coworkers brought my attention back to my phone as the notification lit up my screen, and I noticed the time. I was going to be cutting it close. I grabbed the car keys and ran for the door. I'd have to do a deeper dive into my loaded conversation with Adam later.

I sat in the driver's seat of Travis's air-conditioned car that he'd generously offered up again for this trip to Connecticut. The flexibility of having the car would make it so much easier to pop over to the art exhibit I was covering after lunch as well, rather than having to rely on Uber to get around. I kept thinking back on the call with Adam as I drove and it filled me with frustration. While he'd vaguely said he would meet up, the way he'd brushed me off made me feel like he really didn't want to. But if I could get him to schedule a meeting I'd need to find out more before I committed to visiting him. Racking my brain for an idea on how to do that, a snippet of something Travis said to me and Andie a few months ago after he'd won a really complicated case came to mind. Eagerly, I glanced down just enough to grab my cell phone. Eyes darting between road and screen, I navigated to Travis's number and hit call, putting it on speaker so I could focus on driving.

'Hey, Liz, what's up? Everything okay with the car?'

'Yeah, everything's fine. Thanks again, Trav. I just have a quick question for you,' I said.

'Sure, what do you need?'

'Remember a few months ago you told me and Andie how your firm won some really complicated case by using a background check company to investigate the defendant? Sorry, I don't remember all the specifics—' I said, grasping at the hazy pieces of the conversation floating around in my memory.

'Oh yeah, sure, the Hicks case I think it was. What about it?'

'Well, I got ahold of Adam on the phone this morning. It was pretty brief but he said I could call him next week to plan an in-person meeting. I can't decide if he was creepy or if I'm just totally overthinking everything he said, so I'm trying to figure out how I can find out more about him.'

'Oh man,' he said, sighing. 'This must be so hard. I'm sorry, Liz.'

'Yeah, it's been a lot to take in. And I really need to know more about him, to figure out how dangerous it is to visit him. I had this idea that if you could help me run a background check on him, I may be able to find out if he fits the suspect profile. I know it's a lot to ask; I'm just desperate, Trav. I'm on the way to see Cris as we speak and I need to know if I'm putting myself in danger or if there's a better chance it could be Adam.'

'I wish I could, Liz,' he said after a long pause. 'But it would be highly unethical for me to use the firm's resources for a personal matter like that. I could lose my job. I'm so sorry.'

My heart sank but I knew what I was asking was unreasonable.

'No, I'm sorry, I shouldn't have asked. I just thought—'

'Actually,' Travis interrupted, 'I heard about a free background check website from a coworker. A buddy of his used it to make sure an old expunged drug charge was definitely off his record when he was job hunting. Apparently, it gave some pretty detailed information from searching public records. If you want, I can ask him what it was called and shoot you a text with the info, and you can look Adam up yourself.'

'Oh my God, that would be great. Thanks so much, Travis. You're a lifesaver, yet again.'

He laughed. 'No problem. Be careful though, okay, Liz? Andie would kill me if I helped you walk into a dangerous situation.'

'I will, promise. And thanks again.'

I clicked off the phone, another surge of excitement coursing through me. Maybe the background check would give me the information I needed. I'd just pulled up in front of my uncle's house when my phone buzzed, indicating a text message. Looking down, I saw it was from Travis.

'Hey, the name of the service is IntelliFind. He said if you just google it, the website will pop up and the instructions are pretty straightforward.'

'THANK YOU!' I typed back, a smile on my face. A tapping sound startled me, making me drop my phone in my lap. I looked up to find Cris's face in the window. I gasped and clutched my chest before giving an awkward laugh and rolling down the window. He was wearing a t-shirt drenched in sweat and workout shorts.

'What are you doing out here? Did Rosie not answer the door?'

'Oh, no I was just answering a text really quick.' I

picked my phone back up and waved it around. 'I'm done now, though,' I said as I unclicked the seatbelt. I rolled the window back up and turned off the ignition, grabbing my bag from the passenger seat and taking a deep breath.

After exiting the car, I immediately crouched down when I saw Cris was holding the leash of what I assumed was their new foster, a small panting dog that looked like a cross between a rat terrier and a cocker spaniel. His curly white fur brushed against my cheeks as he licked my face, his puppy breath hot against my skin.

'Who's this?' I asked, smiling and laughing.

'His name is Harley. We just went for a run. He's got a lot of energy to burn so he's been joining me. He was rescued from a breeder. Loves people, hates other dogs. He wasn't doing well in the shelter so we volunteered to take him until he finds his forever home. If you know of anyone . . .'

I scratched Harley behind the ears and he pushed his head into my hand. 'I wish I could take him but our apartment building only allows cats. I'll keep my ears open though, our neighborhood is very dog friendly.'

I rose to a standing position and looked at Cris. He looked uncomfortable and I realized this was the first time we had been alone together. He quickly said, 'Rosie's made a casserole, are you hungry?'

'That sounds great, I could eat.'

We started walking but Cris veered away from the front door. 'Let's go through the garage. I need to close it behind me.'

I followed Cris, nerves mounting at being in a confined space with him, even if only for a moment. I knew Rosie was just inside but maybe something like that wouldn't matter to a serial killer, especially if she was aware of his actions. Looking around, I took in our surroundings, but was careful to keep Cris in my line of sight at all times. The right side of the garage was taken up by a car covered with a beige canvas cover. I pulled the corner of the cover up slightly and trailed my fingers under the cover along the slick green surface, my fingers coming up clean. The car had clearly been well taken care of. I was about to ask Cris about it when I spotted his tools organized on hooks along the wall opposite the car. Everything was in its proper place. Shelving under the tools carried rows of small plastic containers with labels like '1/2" washers' and '3/4" bolts.' Next to the door that presumably led to the house were stacks and stacks of clear plastic bins carefully marked describing what was inside. I read 'PILLOWS', 'ORNAMENTS', and 'KITCHEN' among them. A workbench ran down the side of the garage and on top of it sat a microwave with the back panel opened up and wires sticking out everywhere.

'What's going on here?' I asked as I walked over to the workbench, trying to keep things casual and not give away the growing uncertainty I was feeling toward him.

Cris followed me over and gave a light chuckle. 'My hobby, I guess you could call it. Our microwave died a few days ago and I wanted to try and fix it before buying a new one. It drives Rosie crazy, me constantly fixing old appliances instead of just replacing them.' He paused, putting his hands in his pockets and looking around the space. This was the most naturally he'd spoken to me since we met. Maybe he was finally getting comfortable enough to open up. I softened a little, his demeanor putting me more at ease. 'It takes me a bit longer these days, my hands get a little stiff in my old age. But she's given me a week to fix it, otherwise she's heading to the store.'

'I think it's awesome that you can do this. I'm useless when it comes to this kind of stuff.'

'I've been taking things apart my whole life.' He rocked back and forth on his feet a little, looking at the microwave in front of us. 'When I was growing up, I even cracked open my little transistor radio, just to see if I could figure out how it worked. Unfortunately, I couldn't get that one back together, but I'm a bit more skilled now,' Cris said with a light laugh before turning abruptly and heading toward the door. 'I remember Frank and a friend of his from down the street making fun of me for that failed attempt.' Cris gave a quick grin before looking away again.

While it might have seemed insignificant to others, hearing Cris laugh and tell me more about his life made me really happy. It helped disperse the cloud of suspicion planted in my mind about him. The more relaxed he became around me, the more it seemed impossible he was a killer. Or maybe, it was me becoming more desperate for it to not be him. Either way, I smiled at the mental image of my young grand uncle fiddling with his radio, his face lit up with glee and determination. These little tidbits of Cris's life were helping me round out who he was and who my family really was aside from all the accusations and speculations. After Cris pressed the button to close the garage, he held the door open for me and unclipped Harley's leash. Harley dashed into the house, then came back and sniffed my leg before walking forward a few steps, as if he were beckoning me inside. I laughed and followed him into the dining room. Rosie was setting the table.

'Oh, you're here!' She rushed over and gave me a warm embrace. I inhaled her sweet floral perfume and squeezed my aunt in return.

'Hi Rosie,' I said as we pulled apart. 'Thank you so much for having me again.'

'Oh, it's nothing. You're welcome any time. Come in, come in.'

I wandered over to the kitchen sink and washed the dog smell off my hands.

'What can I do to help?' I asked. She gave a warm smile and handed me a fistful of silverware which I laid out alongside the napkins at each place setting, while Cris ran upstairs for a quick shower. Rosie kept up a steady stream of chatter, telling me about the charity dinner they'd just had for Pause for Paws and how much money they'd raised.

'Cris's mobile spay/neuter van needs repairs and we're hoping to buy a few more since we were able to sign several other vets up for the weekend pet drives. The money will come in real handy. But to tell you the truth,' she lowered her voice to a whisper, 'I wasn't upset when he said the van had to go in for its repairs right away. It's not often I get to have him home on the weekends and it timed so nicely with your visit.'

I was only half-listening, my mind still going over the garage in all its organized glory. Cris padded down the stairs, his hair still wet from the shower, just as Rosie placed the casserole dish and salad bowl on the table. As usual, Rosie served up Cris before serving herself. I filled my own plate and then reached across the table to clasp my aunt's hand, now accustomed to saying grace before each meal when at their house.

'Bless us, oh Lord, and these thy gifts which we are

about to receive from thy bounty, through Christ, our Lord, Amen.'

'Amen,' I said in harmony with them as Rosie ended the prayer and we all dug into the food. Cris and Rosie kept up the conversation and I absentmindedly gave yeses and noes when the conversation seemed to point to me. I was having trouble staying in the moment. While I was happy to be enjoying this family meal, I felt a growing unease rise within me.

'Liz?'

I snapped back to the present. 'Yes?'

'Did you enjoy the casserole? I can give you the recipe if you'd like, it's quite easy to make.'

'Yes, it was delicious. Thanks, I'd like that. I'm sure Andie would love if I made it. Here, let me help clear the dishes,' I said, rising to grab some of the plates.

'Oh, you don't have to do that,' Rosie said.

My phone buzzed in my pocket and I pulled it out quickly. The photographer I'd hired to shoot the Global Citizen Festival in Central Park that day was calling me. Rob never called unless there was a problem. 'Sorry, this is a work call. Is there somewhere private I can take it?'

'Sure. You can just go into Cris's office, it's right over . . .' she trailed off when Cris gave her a sharp look.

I sensed some tension between them, like when Rosie had suggested going through the boxes on my last visit. 'It's okay, I can just go outside.'

Before I turned toward the front door, I noticed my uncle hesitate and then he said, 'It's too hot outside. You can use my office. Head out the kitchen and take a left down the hallway and you'll see a set of glass French doors on the right.'

I gave him a close lipped smile and said it wouldn't take long. Cris stood and opened the sliding door to the backyard for Harley while I walked to his office. The call had already ended since I hadn't picked it up in time, so I called Rob back after closing the doors behind me. Pacing around the room, I listened to him complain about not getting the access he needed for some of the photos I had requested. I promised I would contact the organizer and work it out. After two calls to my various contacts I was able to get ahold of the right person and work out the issue, ensuring he would be permitted to take photographs backstage in addition to the press section in front of the stage and crowd shots.

Normally I would have gone to the festival in person to resolve these issues on the spot, but it was hotter than usual in Manhattan for the end of September, and I wasn't as into the bands selected this year as I usually was. Getting scorched by the sun while thousands of people crammed together on the lawn didn't seem very appealing this time around. Instead, I'd opted to cover the art exhibit in Connecticut so I could see Cris and Rosie, especially once I found out that Cris would be home on the weekend. I knew my photographer would get good enough coverage without me hovering over his shoulder and I was glad I could resolve the access issue by phone.

I dropped into Cris's office chair with a sigh of relief and looked around. His desk was so spotless it shone like it'd been dusted that morning, a faint hint of Lemon Pledge lingering in the air. His computer keyboard was lined up precisely in the center of his monitor. On the desk were not one but three pen holders. Each one had a handful of pens in matching tones. One cup had red pens, another had blue and the third had all black.

As I scanned the rest of the small room, I noticed the bookshelf on the wall. I rose and ran my fingers over the books' exposed spines. Most were practical veterinarian books. The shelf below held books on religion and others on the art of gardening. When I stepped back, a pattern emerged. The books, while clearly organized by subject, were also organized by color. On the wall next to the bookshelf was a faded, framed print of the Virgin Mary. She was draped in white and her hands were placed together in prayer, angels circling her veiled head.

'Liz, would you like some dessert?' I heard Rosie call out from the kitchen.

I ran a finger over the gilded gold frame, feeling the deep grooves under my fingertips. Pieces of information in my brain shifted and slid into place but I wasn't sure what they were telling me. Everything seemed out of focus. It was like my brain was working independently from my conscious mind and I had no control over it. I shook my head and smiled at a photo on the wall of my aunt and uncle at some event, both dressed to the nines. Rosie was beaming into the camera, while Cris clutched Rosie's shoulder with one arm, his lips slightly raised at the corners. It was clear how much they loved one another. But my smile fell when I looked at Cris's face more closely and I wondered yet again if this man could be TSK, and if so, how much Rosie knew. I hated that these thoughts constantly threatened the connection I was making with my bio-family.

'Liz?' Rosie called out again.

I dragged my eyes away from the photo and yelled out, 'Yes, coming!'

VICTIMS 18 & 19

Kristen McKay & Sarah Scarangella

2008

CHAPTER 22

Sarah's back was killing her. She sat back on her heels and stretched her arms overhead, flexing her achy fingers. She'd been gripping the toothbrush for almost an hour and it felt like her fingers would be permanently bent in that position. They'd finished cleaning the toilet and sink and were now working on scrubbing the grout between the tiles on the floor. He'd already interrupted them twice to use the toilet, making them face the wall in the bathroom until he was finished and then demanding they re-scrub it. Sarah wasn't sure she knew anyone who peed so frequently. Every Saturday sometime between lunch and dinner, the man led them to his private bathroom and ordered them to clean it, tossing them a bucket with frayed toothbrushes, old rags and a box of baking soda. On Sundays they cleaned the kitchen.

'Come on, we're almost done,' Kristen said under her breath, tucking a few stray strands of auburn hair behind her ear.

Sarah sighed and got back to work. He popped his

head in sometime later. 'Are you ladies done yet? What's taking so long?'

Sarah and Kristen pulled themselves into a kneeling position and nodded their heads. He didn't like them to talk unless absolutely necessary, especially when a nod or shake of the head would suffice. He pulled on white cloth gloves, ready to give his inspection. Only once had they cleaned the bathroom perfectly on the first try, and he had rewarded them with two fresh apples. The apples were so decadent after eating only packaged food for months that Sarah had spent over an hour eating hers, taking small bites and savoring the flesh for minutes before swallowing, not wanting it to end. Kristen, on the other hand, had been ravenous, eating it so quickly she almost choked, unable to control herself.

The man leaned down and inspected the sink and then the toilet. He ran his finger along the baseboard and pulled it up to his face. He frowned and shoved his finger in Sarah's face.

'Do you see that? That's dirt. Why can't women do anything right?' He shook his head. 'How lucky you are to have me teach you the proper way to clean. You know what this dirt on my finger means. Now I have to watch you do it all over again. Properly.'

Sarah clenched her jaw and started recleaning the toilet with the toothbrush and baking soda mixture, wiping the surfaces down with the rag afterwards. She whispered, 'asshole' under her breath.

'What did you just say?' he growled as he towered over her.

Kristen gave her a panicked look and ever so slightly shook her head.

'Nothing, Master.'

He grunted and leaned against the wall. 'Get back to work.'

The women continued to scrub and wipe. When Sarah was in the corner, running the toothbrush back and forth in the crevice between the baseboard and the floor, the man crouched down and put his hand over hers, startling her. She hadn't heard him creep up so close.

He gripped her hand painfully tight and with his mouth right up against her ear, said, 'I know you're a weak woman but try to use *some* muscle, Eighteen.' The bones in her hand crunched under his grip. Sarah gritted her teeth and tears sprang to her eyes but she did not complain or yell out.

After they had recleaned the entire bathroom the man deemed it acceptable and led them back to their room. When they entered the space that had become their personal prison, they went to their respective walls. They placed their foreheads and palms up flat against them like one would if being searched by the police. It was how he'd shown them to stand the first time he'd taken them both out at the same time, a way to easily watch and control them. Behind her Sarah could hear him chaining Kristen to the wall. He then came up behind Sarah and attached her shackles to the wall as well.

'Turn around, Eighteen.'

Fear shot up her spine and down into her fingertips. They were supposed to remain facing the wall until he left. The one time that Kristen had turned her head to look at him he'd backhanded her across the face hard enough to leave a welt. He'd never asked them to turn around before. Slowly, Sarah turned but kept her eyes to the floor. He didn't like them to look him directly in his eyes except when he was checking their pupils to see if the drugs had kicked in. Just as her body came around to face him he landed a punch directly on her jaw. Sarah's head whipped to the side from the force. She felt a tooth dislodge and fly out of her mouth. White bursts filled her vision and she fell to the cement floor, metallic blood filling her mouth. She coughed, spraying blood across the floor. Kristen gasped from across the room. The pain in Sarah's mouth was unbearable, bringing a wave of nausea hard and fast. She felt her lip swelling in front of the newly formed gap in her top row of teeth.

The man crouched down next to her and said, 'I hear everything. A proper lady doesn't curse. A proper lady doesn't disrespect her master. You do that again and I'll kill you. Do you understand, Eighteen?'

Sarah was still on the ground, her face turned sideways, her cheek against the cold concrete. The man's face wavered in front of her eyes as he looked at her expectantly. Between the drugs and the blow to her mouth Sarah could barely nod her head. The man rose and sighed loudly.

'After everything I've done for you girls, you spite me. You ungrateful bitch.'

He turned and stormed out of the room, locking the door behind him. Kristen rushed over and helped Sarah to her feet, leading her over to the sink and running water from the faucet. Sarah leaned down into the basin and opened her mouth under the stream, wincing when the water hit her raw gums. She swished the water around her mouth and spit several times, dark pink circling the drain. The inside of her mouth stung and her lip throbbed like it had a heartbeat of its own.

'Here, let me see.' Kristen pulled her face up by her chin and Sarah opened her mouth. 'Oh my God!'

'Yeah, I felt the tooth come flying out when he hit me. I'm sure it looks just *great*,' she groaned, trying not to touch the raw open pocket with her tongue.

Kristen dropped her hand and looked her in the eye. 'You have to be more careful, Sarah. You might lose more than a tooth next time. Why'd you do it?'

'I don't know, Kristen,' Sarah lisped. 'I just couldn't take it anymore. I can't take it!'

She began crying and Kristen gathered her into her arms. As Kristen stroked her hair Sarah gazed up at the small barred window, harsh sunset light filtering through. A small blackbird with a bright orange beak landed on the window ledge outside. It peered inside at Sarah and then flew away. Oh, how she wished she was that bird. Her eyes fell to the floor. She spotted the colorful paper folded carefully into a braided bracelet sticking out slightly from under the thin mattress. She'd found the origami bracelet wedged in between the wall and the stack of towels the first day, left behind by one of the girls before her. Once they were each given a mattress she'd stashed it under hers for safe keeping. She took it out from time to time, rubbing her fingers over the ridges whenever she felt desperate and hopeless. She pulled herself from Kristen's grip and reached for it, clutching it to her chest as she lay down on her bed.

She heard Kristen shift onto her own mattress across the room and the two of them lay in silence. Sarah undid the buttons going up her throat, exhaling loudly now that she could breathe better. She was so sick of these restrictive dresses that offered little in the way of warmth. She'd give anything to have her comfy hot pink velour Ed Hardy tracksuit back. She hadn't seen it since he took it from her that first night after her cleansing.

She wondered what he'd done with it. *Thrown it in the trash, probably*.

Sarah thought about the person who had made the origami bracelet now gripped in her fist. She wasn't stupid, she knew where this was all headed. They would meet the same fate as the rest and losing a tooth was the least of her problems. From the moment they got here she understood they would probably never get out. Sure, she'd held onto a sliver of hope in the beginning that someone would save them. But as time carried on her hope drifted away like the blackbird and was replaced with sad acceptance.

This man had to have been the one on the news: the one they called The Tri-State Killer. The reports said that TSK was likely very controlling and misogynistic, which fit this guy perfectly. She was sure the world couldn't be so ugly that there would be more than one monster murdering in this way. He had gotten away with his crimes for so many years and they were just two more pawns in his sick game. A game he was outsmarting everyone in, continuously winning. Sarah squeezed the bracelet tighter, internally thanking the girl before her for leaving it. She hoped the man would be caught and punished but if he wasn't, then she hoped that something from her own spirit would grant comfort to the next girl who found herself on this tattered mattress. They were like a sisterhood, this group of stolen girls. Dead but not forgotten.

CHAPTER 23

On the drive home after we'd finished lunch and I had gotten all the content I needed from the art exhibit, I replayed my entire visit with Cris and Rosie. Something was bugging me but I couldn't quite put my finger on it. Too many opposing thoughts rolled around in my head. I pulled up to a toll booth and handed the attendant a twenty. She pulled out a stack of bills and thumbed through them. They were sorted by denomination and I noticed how she removed a misplaced bill and expertly inserted it back into the stack in the proper place. After pulling out two bills and handing them to me, the attendant carefully placed the stack into a plastic Tupperware that was the exact right size and snapped the lid shut tightly.

Staring at the container something shifted to the forefront in my mind. The car behind me honked and I snapped back to reality, putting my foot on the gas and pulling forward. Billie Eilish's *Bad Guy* was playing softly in the background through Travis's state of the art sound system like the soundtrack to my thoughts. Then it hit me, it wasn't *one* thing that was bugging me, it was everything. The preciseness of Cris's office, the organized patterns in the books, the print of the Virgin Mary, the wall full of tools and containers labeled in neat rows in the garage, the plastic storage bins that reminded me of the ones full of bodies on the news, the age range and geographic location of TSK, and of course, the ketamine. A shiver of panic spread through my body and jabbed at my fingertips. Taken one by one, they were harmless little facts. But put all together at once, they fit the profile of the killer to a T. No wonder the FBI were lasering in on him. I shook my head. *Am I really saying I think he's the killer?* I needed to talk this out with Andie. I sped up and weaved in and out of traffic, not caring if I got a ticket.

After parking the car a block away from our apartment next to the smoke shop and a café that exclusively sold gluten-free pastries, I grabbed my purse and jumped out of the car. I pulled out my cell phone and texted Andie.

'Hey, are you still at work? I really need to talk to you. I don't want to be alone right now, I'm freaking out!!!' I added extra exclamation points for emphasis, something Andie did in her own texts quite frequently.

As I rounded the corner onto our street, I saw the three dots indicating Andie was replying. 'Ugh! The tech who was supposed to relieve me for the late shift called in sick and there's no one to cover. I'll try to get out earlier but I can't promise anything. Hang tight, I'll be home ASAP!!!'

I read the text while I walked down the dim hallway to our apartment. After opening the door and dropping my keys in the bowl and my bag by the entrance, I paced the space between the living room and dining room. I'd been so happy to have this connection to my biological family that I'd been dismissing all the clues. *But are they clues? Or am I just reading into everything because the FBI agents, Beccah, and all the news articles have gotten into my head?* I grabbed my phone and dialed Beccah's number but it went straight to voicemail. I needed to talk this through with someone. I had a few friends in the city besides Andie that knew the broad strokes of what was going on but I wasn't ready to have *this* conversation with any of them. Then I thought about my mom who, before this, would have been the obvious choice if I needed a sounding board. As much as I didn't want to worry her, the guilt that was building at keeping this massive secret from her was chipping away at my resolve to keep her and my dad in the dark. She was my best option and now that things had escalated, she needed to know. It was time I told my parents what was going on. I picked up my phone and after a few rings my mom's smiling face appeared on the screen.

'Hi, sweetie. I'm so glad you called. Your Uncle Vinnie is planning a family trip to . . . Lizzie, what's wrong?'

My mom could always tell when something was troubling me even when I tried to hide it, which I wasn't even bothering to attempt right now. 'Mom, I have something I have to tell you.'

My mom's smile dropped. 'What is it?'

'Remember I told you about meeting up with my grand uncle?' My mom nodded. 'Well, there's something I didn't tell you. I uploaded my DNA from the genealogy kit into this database called GEDMatch in the hopes of finding more family members. There's an option to make your DNA available to law enforcement and I decided to opt into that since you said my mom had spent time in jail. I just wanted to cover my bases.' I bit my lip, nervous about how my mom would react.

'Liz, just tell me.'

'About two weeks after I uploaded to GEDMatch, I was contacted by the FBI. They came to our apartment.'

'The FBI? Oh Liz, what have you gotten yourself mixed up in?'

I rushed past the concern on my mom's face, trying not to lose my resolve to fill her in. 'They told me that my DNA profile got a familial hit to a DNA sample they have from The Tri-State Killer case.'

My mom drew in a sharp breath and her eyes grew wide. 'Lizzie, oh my God, are you serious? I don't like the sound of this at all. That man is a maniac. And I can't believe you didn't tell me or your father right away.'

I arched an eyebrow at the irony of her words. 'Really, Mom?'

She pursed her lips and nodded. 'You're right, I'm sorry. Okay, so what did they tell you? Are you in danger? Do you need to move home until he's caught?'

I exhaled loudly and leaned back into the couch. Her reaction was exactly as I'd predicted. 'It's scary but I don't need to move home right now Mom, really. What they've told me was that they are confident someone from my biological mother's side of the family is The Tri-State Killer.' My mom was about to say something but I cut her off. 'I know Mom, I know. It's freaking me out too. They gave me a few details about the case and said they think my uncle is a prime suspect. At this time Cris fits the profile better than anyone else. Mom, I've been going out there and visiting him and my aunt and . . . it just couldn't be him. They've been so nice to me. He takes care of sick animals for Christ's sake.'

'If you're so sure it's not him, then why are you worried?' I wanted to hug my mom for prioritizing being supportive rather than voicing her motherly concerns. I could tell she was working hard to keep the panic from exploding out of her.

'I don't know, Mom. Between the things the FBI told me and some additional details I got from this journalist who's covered a lot of the case, I'm questioning everything. They got into my head and now I can't stop thinking about it. When I went up there today it was like I could hear them in my ear and I started seeing suspicious things everywhere. I hate that I'm thinking these awful things about him when he hasn't done anything bad to me. I don't know what to do.'

'What makes you think it could be him? What exactly did you see?'

'The FBI said he fits the geographic location and age range of the killer, and DNA proves the killer is definitely from the Dominio family line. There aren't many men still alive who fit those characteristics but the real kicker is,' I paused, figuring out how to best word what I had to say next, 'Mom, one of the reasons I haven't said anything is because I've gotten some details that are not public. So you can't say anything to anyone, otherwise you might ruin the investigation. You can't tell anyone, you have to promise. I'm not supposed to say anything but I really need to talk this out.'

My mom looked to the side and then nodded her head. 'Lizzie, I can't keep this from your dad. He's not home right now, or I'd have him come hop on and hear it from you himself, but I have to tell him.'

'Well, I kind of figured that but neither of you can tell anyone else.' My mom nodded her head. 'The murdered women all had traces of ketamine in their system. It's a drug heavily used by veterinarians, and obviously with Cris being a vet that's a big red flag. But today when I went out there, I started noticing all this other stuff. The profile says the killer is extremely meticulous and methodical. Mom, you should have seen his office. Everything was aligned with such precision and his pens were organized by color. He also had the same plastic bins in the garage that they've described in the paper that the women's bodies were discovered in. And the journalist told me the killer would have a job that has him traveling a lot on weekends, and Cris does that too.' Suddenly another clue popped into my head, my body tensing. 'Mom, the journalist also said the killer would probably be good with technology. There was a microwave with all its wires exposed in Cris's garage and he said he was fixing it. I know that isn't the same but he is clearly savvy with electronics so who knows what other technology he's good with, you know?'

My mom's face went white. 'Have you told any of this to the FBI, Liz? This is not something you should be investigating yourself, it's too dangerous.'

I felt guilty that I'd chosen to tell all this to my mom rather than updating the FBI with what I'd seen at the house. I never used to brazenly keep secrets or flout authority but ever since I found out this messy truth about my family history, it was like I'd become someone else completely. After a long, tense pause, I said, 'No, not yet. It's all pretty fresh and I'm still processing it but I'm not sure I have anything concrete to really give them.' I didn't quite make eye contact with her until I was done speaking.

She pursed her lips. 'I don't want you going out there

anymore, Lizzie. I don't know if anything you saw means he's the killer but you shouldn't take that chance. Promise me you won't go up there again. Especially not alone.'

I understood my mom's concerns but I didn't know if I could keep that promise. That would mean I may not ever get the answers I was so desperately looking for. It may mean the end of any contact with my biological family. But as I looked at my mom's worried expression I knew I couldn't put her through that stress. We'd already been through so much in the past month, it was unfair to pile onto that.

'I promise, Mom. I don't have any other trips planned right now anyway but what do you think? Am I crazy for reading into all this supposed evidence? I'm so worried that if I help them point the finger at Cris and it's not him, I'll have played a role in ruining an innocent man's life. He's already suffered enough with losing so much of his family. And what if the real killer gets away? There's two innocent women missing who could die and we may never know the truth. Which would mean I may never know if it's safe to get to know my biological family.' I stopped my tangent, taking a few big breaths to stop myself from completely spiraling out of control.

My mom clenched her lips together and then exhaled loudly. 'You're not crazy for seeing potential evidence around you, sweetheart, but it is possible that these are all just coincidences. Most people have those bins for storage, we even have a few to store our old stuff. And a lot of people are really organized, including yourself, but that doesn't necessarily mean anything sinister. All that aside, you can't blame yourself if the crimes remain unsolved. I know that would be a devastating outcome but it's not your job to sleuth clues for the FBI, although you *should* tell them if you know something already that may help. Is there anyone else in your biological family that it could be?'

Suddenly I remembered Adam and what Travis said about the background check website. I'd been so focused on Cris and everything I'd seen at their house that day, that I'd somehow forgotten about Adam.

'Yes. Cris's cousin Adam is their other top suspect, although he willingly gave a DNA sample to them. I'm not sure if that's from confidence of being innocent or some level of twisted arrogance. I called him and he kinda gave me the creeps. I don't know a whole lot about him, so Travis gave me information on how to do a background check. I'm going to see if there's anything in his history that may also match up with the killer's profile and make him a more viable suspect.'

'Honey, I don't think that's a good idea. You should leave this to the FBI and stay out of it.'

'But Mom, I need to know if it's Cris. And besides, doing an anonymous background check from the safety of my living room won't put me in any danger. I can't go on not knowing the truth.'

She paused for a long second. 'I know you want to believe in your grand uncle and are building a relationship with him but at the end of the day, there's a chance it could be him, Lizzie. I know that's not what you want to hear and I'm sorry, but this does worry me. I want to support you in learning where you came from but this is too dangerous. You need to be really careful.' She watched as I rubbed my lips together like I'd just put on lipstick, something I did when I was trying to work something out. 'Honey, are you sure you don't want to come home? Even just for the night? I know it's getting late but you can sleep here and tomorrow we can have a girls' day. We could see a movie and get our nails done. What do you say? We'd love to see you.'

'No, that's okay. Thanks anyway, Mom. I'm just worked up. I'll be fine. Andie will be home later to keep me company, so I won't be alone all night. And Travis is staying with us right now just to be on the safe side, so he should be getting home soon too. I'll call you tomorrow if I need anything, promise.'

My mom inhaled and exhaled through her nose, clearly upset that I was choosing to stay in Brooklyn. 'Okay, well if you need anything at all, let me know. We're here for you no matter what.'

I smiled for the first time since I left Cris's place. 'Thanks, Mom. I'll keep you in the loop now, I swear.'

'Love you, sweetie. Please be careful,' she said, her eyes watery.

'I love you too,' I said back.

I hung up the phone and fell back onto the couch. My nerves felt like needles poking through my flesh. I understood my mom's concern and was grateful we were speaking more again but I also needed answers and the FBI certainly weren't giving me enough of them. Against my mom's wishes I grabbed my laptop and navigated to IntelliFind, the website Travis had told me about. After inputting everything I knew about Adam – his age and current location – the website was able to find him. While I waited for the report to be generated, I jumped up and poured a glass of wine. By the time I came back to the couch I had an email with a link to view the report. The page came up and gave several known addresses for Adam Dominio and my hopes spiked. While Adam and his mother had moved to California like Cris and Rosie had mentioned, Adam had moved back to the East Coast in the late eighties. Since then, he'd lived all across the Tri-State area, including New Jersey, upstate New York and Connecticut in addition to several Massachusetts addresses. He wasn't on the sex offender database but when I clicked the criminal search button, I gasped. Adam had two records. One for assault in New Jersey and another for drug possession. Both items could point to him being a viable suspect. Assault: clearly, he was violent. Drugs: the killer had access to ketamine. A wave of relief washed over me as I mentally thanked Travis for the suggestion. While it didn't prove anything, it meant he was still a feasible option. I didn't have to give up on Cris quite yet.

Still yearning for something else to ease my worries over Cris and since I had a blueprint of towns where Adam had lived, I searched online yearbook photos from the high schools in those towns during the span of years Adam would have been a student. I barely noticed the clock tick over to another hour as I stretched my achy arms and flexed my stiff fingers. I kept scrolling until suddenly, I found something. A grainy black and white high school yearbook photo of the Franklin High School AV Club, that listed Adam Dominio on the bottom row. From his address history and his age it seemed likely that this was the same Adam. *So, he's good with technology too.*

Thinking back to my call with him, I returned to Google and tried searching for boat shows this weekend in Rhode Island since Adam claimed he was attending one. Even though he said he would be too busy to see me, Rhode Island was accessible by train. Despite it being a four-hour trip, I could still just show up and surprise him, make him talk to me more. Running into him in a public place full of people seemed safer than meeting him on his home turf. I tried several combinations of search terms with no success. I couldn't find any event postings for the current weekend. With one last attempt, I removed my dates on the search and finally stumbled onto an article highlighting the Newport International Boat Show, but it had occurred two weekends ago. Biting my lip, I snatched up my phone and decided to try calling him again. It rang several times before clicking over to the answering machine.

Grunting in frustration, I threw the phone back down on the couch. I'd have to try him again later. Either there was another boat show this weekend that I somehow hadn't found in my search or he had lied to me. Considering my research skills, it seemed the latter was more likely.

I turned on the TV to take my mind off the case until Andie came home. NY1 came on and two photos of the missing women took up most of the screen. The photos minimized to the bottom right corner and the brunette newscaster looked gravely into the camera.

'The search intensifies for the latest suspected victims of The Tri-State Killer, Addie Wilson and Zoey Davis . . .'

I groaned loudly, hit the power off button and downed my glass of wine. I was just getting up to pour another when my phone rang. When I saw Beccah's name appear, I quickly pulled it up to answer, almost smacking myself in the face with it in my haste.

'Hi, Liz. It's Beccah. I saw a missed call from you.'

'Beccah, thank you for calling me back.'

'Oh, it's no problem. What's on your mind? Has something major happened in the investigation?'

'Are we off the record again?' I asked, nerves and adrenaline pumping through me in harmony.

'Sure,' she replied.

'Thank you,' I said, looking for the right words to say. 'I got back earlier today from my grand uncle's house, one of the FBI's main suspects. And I felt like all the profile points were lurking in the back of my head and I was seeing signs of his guilt everywhere. But then there's this other relative who I've only spoken to on the phone, their other main suspect, and he gave me the creeps. I think I've caught him in a lie too, about a boat show he claimed he was going to. But maybe he made that up just to get off the phone with me quicker. I don't know what to think anymore. I feel like I'm going crazy. Can you talk me off the ledge here?' I said, a pleading in my voice. Any hesitation about asking for information was long gone. I figured I didn't have a whole lot to lose at this point.

'Oh Liz, I'm so sorry you're going through that. It must be so frightening, wondering each day if you're talking to a killer. Once again, I feel I need to emphasize that you should look out for your safety here, but I know if it were me, I wouldn't be able to stop searching either. Hell, I haven't been able to stop searching for TSK after all these years and I'm not even related to him.'

I smiled a bit at this. Everyone else in my life seemed to be telling me to stop. But Beccah got it. She understood my need to know despite the danger, and for that I was grateful. Maybe if I shared a new detail with her it would gain enough of her trust that she'd spill the beans on everything else she knew about TSK. It was worth a shot.

'One of the reasons they think it's my grand uncle I've been spending time with,' I said, preparing the bait, 'is that he's a veterinarian. I'm not sure if you've seen the details of the coroner reports in the cold case files but the FBI told me that ketamine was found in the victims' bodies.'

Beccah was quiet for a second. Then she said, very carefully, 'And they think that connects to your grand uncle because of his profession?'

'Yes, well that, and when he was just getting started at his own practice a large supply of ketamine went missing. He never reported it.'

I felt like I could hear the wheels turning as Beccah took a moment to process this. 'Wow, Liz. I know that's not a smoking gun but it's certainly a red flag.'

'I know,' I said. 'But I looked into the other relative I mentioned, and he had an arrest record, one of which was drug related. I feel like I'm spinning my wheels here, trying to figure out who is the better fit. Is there anything else you can share with me? I promise I won't tell anyone.'

'Hmmm,' Beccah said. 'I suppose I could tell you a bit more about the profile and what the FBI believe his motives to be. I'm not sure I can divulge much evidence but maybe I can round out your understanding of him further.'

'I'll take anything you can give me.'

'Okay,' she began, 'first of all, we believe TSK to be a mission-oriented killer. Do you know what that means?'

'I'm a bit new to the world of serial killers,' I said, 'but I've seen that in passing in some of my research.'

'Basically, it means that he justifies his murders as a solution to a problem. He sees them as a necessary means to an end, to remove a certain type of person from the world who he views as harmful to society. It can relate to a lot of different groups of people, like the homeless population or prostitutes, maybe someone that is just plain different from the killer by race or sexual orientation. Anything that the killer sees as a detriment to society. And they can't stop because they feel as though they are providing a necessary service. In the case of TSK, we believe his rage is centered around women and cleansing them of, what he deems, their evil deeds. He seeks control and power over them, hoping to wash away what he judges to be their mortal sins.'

I was simultaneously fascinated and disgusted by this mentality. How could I be related to someone who felt this way about women? 'Is there something that leads you to believe that? Besides the fact that it's young women he's abducting and murdering in such a repetitive pattern?'

'Well,' Beccah replied, 'he rigorously cleaned the bodies before dumping them. Now, this could partially be related to eliminating evidence but we believe it goes beyond that and connects more to ritual and a desire to cleanse them of their sins.'

'Wow,' I said, his personality coming to life as she spoke. I felt like he was closer to me, the hairs on the back of my neck rising. I quickly looked over at the door, just to make sure it was locked.

'I actually interviewed the two victims recently who escaped his abduction attempt.'

'You did?' I said, intrigued. 'How are they? What were they like?' I hoped desperately that they'd moved on to find happiness so I could cross their names off the list of people whose lives had been ruined by my murderous relative.

'They're about as you can imagine,' Beccah said sadly. 'Still very traumatized by this experience, especially now that it's suspected he's still out there. They left the Tri-State

298

area a few years back but still sleep with their lights on, can't stand to be home alone. I desperately hope, as you do I'm sure, that we find answers for them soon. I think they'll sleep a lot better at night once they know he's behind bars.'

My heart broke at this and my desire to find the truth strengthened even more. I couldn't bear the thought of any more lives being stolen.

'I think we'll all sleep better when that happens,' I replied. 'Well, I can't thank you enough for sharing all this with me,' I said, taking another sip of my wine. 'I know you can't share everything so I won't take up more of your time right now. But it means a lot to just have someone who doesn't shy away from talking to me about this. It's been very lonely, this journey.'

'I can imagine,' she said softly. 'I'm happy to lend an ear. As you know, TSK has taken up a large part of my professional career. If you see anything else of interest, I'd love to hear about it. You never know what could be a vital piece of evidence. But hopefully with the new lead from your DNA, he'll be caught soon.'

'Let's hope so.'

VICTIMS 20 & 21

Elise Rainer & Nina Sayer

2010

CHAPTER 24

'A woman's highest calling is to be obedient and respect the rules and traditions set forth by her man, her master. His success and desires will dictate her own. The man is the true head of the household and it is the woman's job to serve and follow direction without question. The woman must always greet her master with a warm but not overtly attention-seeking smile. She must not only satisfy her master, but also show her appreciation for his leadership. A proper woman is clean, groomed, and standing tall in eager anticipation when the man returns home. It is a woman's duty to ensure a clean house for the man out of respect for him and his domain.

'The man's ideas are more important, therefore he should always be the first to speak and will dictate when it is your turn. An obedient woman should never raise her voice and should ensure all she says is in line with her duty to comfort and support, never complaining. A wanting woman is not a right woman. The woman should feel honored to be in her master's presence and should show this with gracious words when permitted to speak. Should the master be in a bad mood, it is the sole responsibility of the woman to manage his morale. A happy master is a happy home,' Nina read aloud, kneeling on the cold floor in front of her mattress.

'That'll do, Twenty,' the man said.

Nina closed the book, the spine cracking as the light blue linen cover met the pages. The book was easily sixty years old, maybe more. The cover had no images, just the title *How to Be an Obedient Woman*. She placed the book down gently at the end of the mattress as he'd instructed her so many times before, and then she lay back. The man stood hovering nearby and watched them. Nina kept her eyes straight ahead, staring at the ceiling. One time she'd glanced at him after he'd watched them for almost ten minutes and he'd slapped her across the face, splitting her lip wide open. After several agonizing minutes, he said goodnight and left.

Nina exhaled and looked over at Elise lying on her own mattress, still staring at the ceiling. 'That shit is disgusting,' Elise said.

'I know, but out of all the things he makes us do, it's the easiest. At least we don't have to kneel on the pebbles when we do it,' Nina replied, cringing at the thought of the rocks.

Elise rolled onto her side, facing Nina, and propped herself up on her elbow. 'Yeah but if you mess up one word, he makes you start all over again. That crap is from like, the fifties or something. "A woman's highest calling is to be obedient. A wanting woman is not a right woman." I mean, what the hell is that? When he makes me read it, I wanna throw up. Last time he made me reread it three times. I'm starting to hear it in my sleep. God! How can you stand it?'

Nina sighed. She'd heard this complaint from Elise before. 'I have it pretty much memorized at this point. I just zone out while I'm reading and try not to pay attention to what the words are actually saying.'

Elise sat up and shuffled to the area near the sink where their food was stored. She opened a box of granola bars and threw one to Nina. 'You deserve a reward for that. Thanks for volunteering to read again. I was worried he was going to make me do it since it was so obvious that I didn't want to. I really need to work on my poker face.'

Elise sat down on the ground next to the food and ripped open her own granola bar wrapper. As she was eating she absentmindedly ran her hand over the uneven cement floor, something she did frequently. She'd said she liked the feel of the grooves and bumps under her fingers. It reminded her of the old wooden swing set she had when she was little. There'd been a little cove at the top of the slide where she spent hours reading and running her fingers along the wood. Her hand traveled along the cold, cracked surface over to where the box sat that housed their soap and toothpaste next to her mattress. Suddenly, she whipped her hand back to her side like she'd been burned.

'What is that?' Elise exclaimed.

'What?'

Elise leaned closer to the wall and pulled something from behind the box. It was small and white with a few dark stains on it. From where Nina sat it looked like a piece of dirty Chicklet gum. Elise inspected it for a second before gasping and throwing it across the room, where it landed near Nina's mattress, giving a gentle *ping* as it bounced along the floor. Nina reached for the object, not sure what all the fuss was about.

'It's a fucking tooth, Nina!'

'Oh my God.' Nina could see the remnants of blood and gum tissue, now dried and hardened, rimming the root. Squeezing her eyes shut, she let it fall back to the floor, nauseated. She quickly kicked it away with her foot, not wanting it near where she slept.

Elise jumped up and began pacing the space in front of her mattress as far as her chains would allow. She unbuttoned the tight floral collar, giving her space to breathe.

'We've gotta get out of here, Nina. I can't do this anymore. This asshole has kept us here long enough. I don't want it to be my tooth that the next girl finds. I'm sick of beef jerky and crackers.' She kicked the snack box, sending it spinning across the floor toward Nina, where it tipped over. 'I'm sick of being his slave and calling him fucking Master. I'm sick of being chained to a damned wall. And you've seen in the news what he's done to those other women, because come on, he's obviously the same guy from those articles that were going around on Facebook about The Tri-State Killer. We can't end up like them. We have to get out of here!'

'And how do you propose we do that?' Nina asked, unbuttoning her own collar and righting the snack box, tossing in the small bag of Doritos that had fallen out, before shoving it back across the cement. Elise would have to put it back in its proper place before he came in again.

Elise sighed and stopped pacing. She dropped down to her mattress. 'Look, there's two of us and only one of him. When he comes in tomorrow morning and he goes to give you the shot, his back will be to me. I'll rush him when he's within striking distance of my chains. When I do that, you grab the needle from his hand and inject him with it.' She paused, clearly expecting Nina to meet her enthusiasm on this new plan. 'Well, what do you think?' she asked after she was greeted with silence.

Nina looked at the hope on Elise's face, something she herself had none of left. She wanted hope to fill her heart so badly, like it had for Elise. But as much as she tried, it wouldn't come. She was sure it was a lost cause.

Lying back onto her bed, Nina said, 'I think you're going to get us killed.'

CHAPTER 25

I crossed my legs underneath me on the couch, pulling my warm silver laptop closer in my lap. I couldn't believe it was already Thursday. This week had been a blur after the emotional exhaustion of the week before, so I was grateful to have a day working from home. I'd tried calling Adam countless times since discovering he'd lied about the boat show on Saturday but was met with his suave outgoing message every time. It was hard to focus on work when all I could think about was the identity of TSK. I constantly grappled back and forth, one moment thinking it had to be smooth-talking Adam, and the next worrying about just how meticulous Cris was and how little I actually knew about him. Even if it wasn't Cris, the fact was, I still shared genes with a sociopath and it was very likely the killer was one of the two relatives I'd come in contact with. Cris or Adam. I felt doomed either way but was desperate to know the truth.

Opening up a blank Word document on my laptop screen, I started typing out some points from the killer's profile. Next to the profile points I made two columns: one for Cris and one for Adam. I could check off a tally mark for each trait they fit and maybe once I laid it out, it would be clearer who was a stronger match.

First, TSK had to be in his sixties or seventies and have lived in the Tri-State Area. A mark for each of them. Second, TSK likely had a job where he travelled weekends. A definite mark in the Cris column but Adam's was more ambiguous. A question mark in his column. Third: TSK would probably appear normal, maybe even charming. Cris was socially awkward and even though our bond was deepening the more time we spent together, I wouldn't necessarily call him charming. But Adam, well, he definitely fit the charming aspect, even if it did come across as a little creepy. He was calm, confident, and skilled at being disarming enough to get personal information, like when he'd asked about my age and relationship status and given me a nickname in our brief call. Sure, that could have been innocent, but I could see him being able to manipulate young women into trusting him. Definite check mark. They both had some sort of tie to drugs so that one wasn't a helpful distinction. A check for both. Good with technology: well, Cris was tinkering with things in his garage and Adam was in the AV Club. Check and Check. *Ugh!* I caught sight of the time on the top right-hand corner of my laptop screen and I realized how behind schedule I was. I minimized the document comparing my two relatives and rubbed my eyes. I'd have to continue that debate later.

Pushing the internal battle aside, I forced myself to focus on the blast I had to post on Facebook for work in the next hour. I wished I hadn't procrastinated all morning. My mind was everywhere except on the food festival I was supposed to be encouraging our followers to attend. Just as I was searching through the folder of image assets to pair with my commentary, the loud apartment buzzer went off, breaking my fragile concentration and making me jump in my seat. My heart raced from the surprise intrusion.

'Who could that be?' I mumbled to myself, noting the time on my phone said 12:32PM.

There was a missed call and voicemail notification I hadn't seen until now. I would check the message after I was done with this post. Realizing I hadn't turned the volume back on my phone after waking up this morning, I switched it back on. Normally I ignored random buzzers, as living in New York, especially in a first-floor unit, I had grown cautious of granting unexpected strangers access to our building. But after a few moments, the buzzer impatiently rang out again. I moved the laptop to the cushion next to me and rose from the couch, walking to the intercom box by my front door.

'Who is it?' I asked.

'Special Agents Hannigan and Beck,' Hannigan's familiar voice reverberated over the crackling speaker.

'Really? Right now?' I said into the empty room. Had there been a development? I hadn't seen anything public on my news alerts.

Then a surge of fear danced around in my belly. After the last trip to Connecticut and the talk with my mom, I wasn't so sure about Cris anymore. The background check on Adam had given me a potential alternative suspect to hold onto, but what if they'd found more incriminating evidence against Cris, closing the door on that part of my family forever? Or what if they knew I'd

311

been investigating on my own despite their warnings and were here to scold me?

I ran a hand through my hair, flipping a section of it over to the other side of my face. I paused for a moment, nerves and curiosity wrestling in the pit of my stomach. Steadying myself for whatever was about to be revealed, I clicked the button to unlock the exterior door. As I waited by my door, I looked down at what I was wearing. 'Great,' I mumbled, taking in my green yoga pants, favorite oversized black t-shirt with a hole near the collarbone, and fuzzy socks. I wasn't sure my work from home attire was appropriate for a meeting with the FBI but they'd caught me off guard. After a moment I heard the knock signifying their arrival. Taking a deep breath to calm my nerves, I unlocked both the deadbolt and door handle locks, opening the door.

'Thank you for seeing us Liz. We're sorry to bother you again. We tried calling and left a message to warn you that we were going to be stopping by,' Beck said with a warm smile.

The ticking deadline on my post for work was going off in the back of my mind but I shoved it aside. If I cut right to the point, maybe I could find out what they knew and still get my work done on time.

'What can I do for you today?' I said with a forced calmness, trying not to betray the adrenaline buzzing just under my skin. 'I'm afraid I don't have a lot of time, I'm on deadline for work so . . .'

'We'll try not to take up your whole afternoon,' Hannigan said.

His eyes looked tired, extra wrinkles framing them today, and his normally well-kempt hair was astray. His jacket and pants were slightly wrinkled and I noticed he'd missed a belt loop on his pants. Beck's clothes were a bit tidier but her bun was loose, a few strands falling rogue at the bottom. I imagined the case was taking a toll on them. While I was frustrated that the DNA and missing ketamine had caused them to home in on Cris, I tried to remind myself that these were the good guys. They were trying to stop a killer and rescue a pair of missing women. Somehow, I'd gotten roped into that process and it wasn't their fault who I shared genes with. I unclenched the tension I was holding in my jaw and gestured them back toward the living room, eager to learn why they'd shown up on my doorstep.

'Can I get you some water? Or coffee? We have a Nespresso so I can whip you up a cup pretty quick,' I asked, noticing how tired they both looked. I moved the laptop off the couch so they could sit down and pulled up the desk chair for myself, sitting across from them like in our previous meetings.

'No, no, thank you,' Beck said. 'We'll try to make this as efficient as possible.'

'I'd appreciate that,' I replied, grabbing my own cold coffee off the table and taking a sip. I scrunched up my face and set it back down. I'd have to make a fresh cup after they left. 'So, what brings you here today? Has there been a break in the case?' I tried, but I couldn't quite keep an anxious tone completely out of my voice.

Hannigan cleared his throat, leaning forward and clasping his hands in front of him. 'Liz, we know we've intruded into your life but we really need to bring this killer to justice. As I'm sure you've probably seen on the news by now, we're fairly confident we have connected the two missing young women from Boston to TSK. They

313

weren't initially identified as his most recent victims due to the fact that they didn't fit in his established pattern. Not only had they gone missing from outside the Tri-State Area but there was a six-year gap since he abducted the pair before them, rather than his usual two-year pattern. We'd initially assumed he was dead or possibly dormant. But after getting your DNA match, which was the first new connection we've had in a long time, more agents were added to our task force and resources were increased in order to trace all the branches of your family tree. We also widened the search parameters outside his normal hunting grounds in case he'd moved and actually hadn't been dormant for the past six years. That's when one of our investigators discovered the similarities in TSK's abduction tactics within the Boston case file.'

'I did see that in the news, but besides the same break-in method, what other similarities are there that make you so sure Addie and Zoey are his latest victims?' I asked, my stomach turning at the thought of the two girls being held captive right now by someone who shared my genes.

'When we examined their case file, we found that a needle was recovered from under Zoey's bed with traces of ketamine inside. There were signs of a struggle, so our guess is, it fell and in the chaos the killer left it behind. While we can't prove with 100 percent certainty that it's the work of TSK without the bodies or further evidence, we certainly can't dismiss the coincidences.'

I gulped, agreeing with their assessment. If I'd never uploaded my DNA to GEDMatch would that connection ever have been made? Would those women have been lost forever?

'With the knowledge that we may have missing victims that need to be rescued, we have to accelerate our efforts. We've decided it's time we shared more about the case with you to see if it connects with anything you've seen or heard. Normally, we wouldn't be so open but we fear we are running out of time to save those two women and you and your family are the only solid lead we have.'

'I know but I don't believe my grand uncle could have done this. He hasn't said or done anything to me since the last time we spoke that seemed dangerous.'

I stood up for Cris with a level of confidence that I didn't fully believe. *Am I trying to convince them, or myself?* I pushed down the nagging doubt that had been creeping in since our last meeting, all the things I'd seen that matched up with their profile. But they didn't know I'd been getting additional information from Beccah and I was terrified of telling them any circumstantial evidence that they may use to further villainize Cris. But the investigative part of my brain yearned to hear more details on the case, even if it pointed to him. I couldn't imagine living in the dark now that I knew I was connected. There was also a lingering trail of guilt that if I didn't help them, two innocent women could die. And maybe future victims after them. Hannigan stared at me thoughtfully for a second and then continued on. He could probably sense that I was wavering.

'Liz, we understand you haven't wanted to give up seeing your grand uncle before we had further proof but you have to understand the potential severity of the consequences if you repeat anything we tell you to him or his wife. If it is Cristian, we can't risk tipping him off.'

'I understand,' I replied with a nod.

'TSK's pattern up to this point has been to keep the women captive for about nine months, murder them, and then discard the bodies one to two weeks later. But Addie and Zoey have passed that deadline by over a month. We aren't sure whether that's because the bodies haven't been found yet or if it's because he's deviated from his routine. But it stands to reason that if the women are still alive, we have very little time left to rescue them.'

He paused, flipping open his notebook and retrieving two loose photos from it. He put them down on the table in front of me. Smiling back at me were two headshots of attractive women around my age. One with long brown hair, the other blonde. I recognized them from the news. I quickly averted my eyes back to Hannigan.

'I still don't understand how I can—'

'We know you don't want to believe that your grand uncle is capable of this. We've been working our way through your genetic connections, exploring your other male relatives. This has been difficult because of the complications of your family tree but based on the information at hand, Cristian is still the best fit for TSK. There just aren't many living males on the Dominio side that fit the characteristics. As we've mentioned, we have been looking into Adam Dominio as well, but he's been more compliant in our investigation and it's appearing that most of the evidence is pointing toward Cristian at this stage.'

My hands shook slightly. *Should I tell them I've looked into Adam, too? Found out things about him that keep him in the running?* Instead I asked, 'Have you found any other relatives? Cleared anyone from the suspect pool that I could potentially connect with? That was part of our deal when I gave you my account information, remember?' I said, my eyes darting back and forth between them.

Beck replied, 'Until we have irrefutable proof of who TSK is, we need to keep this circle pretty tight, I'm afraid. Once we conclude our case, we'll be happy to let anyone we've contacted know that you'd like to be in touch.' She gave me a sympathetic smile, then asked, 'Have you been in contact with any other relatives since we last spoke?'

A confession about speaking to Adam was on the tip of my tongue. But Hannigan was looking at me sternly, as if he was ready to reprimand me, so I bit back the truth. 'No, I haven't. But can you tell me more about Adam? Why do you think he doesn't fit the profile as well as Cris?'

'Well, Adam has lived across the Tri-State area and seemed to fit some aspects of the profile at first but we are gaining confidence that we can soon rule him out.'

'What? Why?' A shot of dread dropped into my stomach and a wave of nausea rolled over me. How could they be close to clearing him when the things I'd discovered seemed to line up so perfectly?

Beck looked at Hannigan who nodded, giving her silent permission to continue.

'We've been combing through cell phone records and conducting interviews with potential alibi witnesses. Adam was very forthcoming with access to items such as old calendars, emails, event tickets, etc. Those pieces of information combined with the cell phone records we've gained, have led us to say with a level of certainty that there are several abductions he would not have been in the local vicinity for. We have more to confirm but we have not yet been able to rule out any of those dates for Cristian.'

The air pushed out of my lungs like I'd been punched in the gut. After everything I'd found, deep down I'd convinced myself that the killer was Adam, that I would be cleared to have a relationship with Cris. With that hope dashed, I struggled to grasp at any straw that pointed away from him. It just couldn't be the man I'd been getting to know. Was I really that naïve? Was Cris so manipulative that he'd effortlessly pulled a blanket over my eyes to obscure the true horror inside him? For some reason, I felt angry at the agents for clearing Adam, as irrational as I knew that was. The logical side of my brain struggled to take over, to see this as a definitive piece of the puzzle. I replayed what Beck said in my head, looking for any loopholes but came up empty.

'The profile points you've shared with me previously were pretty vague and you said you'd share more with me today. Can you tell me anything that specifically points to Cris?'

'Yes, that's what we want to go over with you, Liz,' Beck replied. 'The information we are going to share with you is highly confidential, and if leaked, it could drastically hinder the capture and prosecution of The Tri-State Killer. We need you to assure us that you'll keep these details private. As we've mentioned, we normally wouldn't share this much with anyone during an open investigation, however, your relation to the killer may be our best chance at catching him.'

'Okay,' I conceded, nerves bubbling to the surface. I was suddenly very aware of how dry my mouth felt so

I reached forward and grabbed my glass of water off the coffee table, taking a large sip and clinging to it as Hannigan spoke. Nervously, I tapped my ring against the glass, making light pinging noises. I saw Beck's eyes focus on my hand and I stopped immediately. My cheeks flushed.

'We know we can't stop you from seeing your grand uncle but we urge you to be careful. If you're going to spend time with him, we want you to be aware of what to keep an eye out for. Even if you don't think you've seen or overheard anything yet, you may at some point. I know it's difficult to imagine a relative being capable of these heinous crimes and to feel like you're betraying their trust but we just ask you keep an open mind. Not only for the case but for your safety as well,' Beck said, gentle but with an edge to her words that conveyed the seriousness of the conversation.

I nodded and took another sip of water for lack of knowing what else to say or do.

'Okay,' Hannigan said, taking charge again. 'We've already shared with you part of the general profile based on his age and personality traits.'

'None of it felt very specific though,' I said, inching forward on my seat.

'Yes, on its own it can feel very broad. But when we line these traits up with the evidence and compare everything to our suspect pool, that's when we can really narrow our focus. The profile is just one of our tools for determining which suspects fit the mold.'

'Besides his age and where he lives, what can you tell me?' I asked.

'Something that we haven't released to the media,' Hannigan said, 'is that all the young women that were

319

found had their hands tied with a specific type of nautical knot, called a bowline knot, into a prayer position in the bins where they were discovered.'

I cringed, feeling sick. This was not a visual I wanted in my head.

'The type of knot is one thing we are looking into. Have your grand aunt or grand uncle mentioned anything about sailing?' Beck asked, trying to pull me back from the dark images swirling around my mind.

'Um, no,' I shook my head. 'No, they're not sailors. They haven't mentioned any family boats or anything like that.' After saying I hadn't been in contact with Adam, I couldn't admit to them that he had mentioned a boat show. It didn't matter anyway now that he'd essentially been cleared from the investigation. A small sliver of relief flitted through me that one of the clues at least pointed away from Cris. I tried to hold onto that little bit of hope.

Hannigan made a note in his notepad. 'The positioning of their hands is also significant,' he said, making eye contact with me again. 'The praying hand position could be reflective of strong religious beliefs. Have they spoken about your family's religious background at all? Maybe they have religious art or have mentioned religion in some other way?'

Unconsciously, my hand rose to the locket hanging from my neck and I began rubbing my fingers on its tarnished surface with the engraved cross. I sat in silence for a long moment, reflecting on my time in Cris and Rosie's home and the conversations we'd had, how we had said Grace at each meal. An image of the painting in Cris's office slid into the forefront of my mind. The

320

praying Virgin Mary. And then, like rapid fire, another memory of a small Virgin Mary statue resting on the mantle in the living room. I squinted, furrowing my distinctive family brows, trying to see more clearly into my mental picture. Yes, it was a Praying Mary statue that had rested there, too.

The Special Agents picked up on my long pause and leaned in toward me expectantly. 'Do you remember something, Liz?' Beck asked softly, treading carefully.

'I mean, it's probably nothing,' I hesitated, still fingering the locket hanging from my neck. Hannigan's observant eyes zeroed in on it, so I dropped my hand back to my lap quickly.

'Why don't you go ahead and tell us anyway, just in case,' Beck prompted. Hannigan was still staring at my necklace.

'Is that a cross on your locket?' Hannigan interrupted, gesturing to the locket. 'I don't remember you wearing it during our previous conversations.'

'Oh,' I said. 'Yeah, Cris sent it to me. It belonged to my mother.'

'So, they are a religious family then, yes?' Hannigan asked.

'Um, I guess so,' I said hesitantly. I swallowed, trying to force down the lump in my throat. 'They are religious but I'm not sure to what extent. There are a few praying Virgin Mary relics in their home. A painting and a figurine.' I looked nervously between the two of them, but their stoic expressions gave away nothing. Hannigan took down another note before flipping to the next blank page.

'That's really good,' Beck said, encouraging.

321

'It might not mean anything,' I said hurriedly. The walls felt like they were closing in on Cris and panic was creeping in. 'My adoptive family is religious too and my grandma has tons of religious art around her house,' I added.

'Sometimes you have to fit all the pieces together in a complex investigation like this before you can tell what's important,' Beck said. 'But that's why it's crucial you share anything with us that you think of, even if it may seem insignificant. Remember, just as you're afraid it may point the finger at your uncle, it may also help clear him if he's innocent. It's our job to interpret all the data available so that the correct person is brought in for these crimes. It wouldn't help anyone to go after the wrong guy.'

I tried to believe her. I remained quiet for another long moment, waiting for someone to break the tension.

Hannigan rubbed his chin, looking at me thoughtfully as if debating what he should tell me. 'Okay Liz, I want to share something else with you about TSK.'

I nodded, shifting uncomfortably in my seat. The responsibility of knowing private information about the crimes weighed heavily on my shoulders but at the same time, I needed any detail they would give me.

'Remember how we talked about the young women being found in the storage bins?' I nodded again, trying to keep the visual of the bodies at bay. I wondered if I should tell them about the storage containers that I saw in Cris's garage but kept quiet. Like my mom said, most people had those. 'A detail that we've kept private is that there was a layer of small pebbles at the bottom of the containers that their legs were pressing on.'

I bit my lip, looking out the window across the room.

A pigeon on the ledge was cooing, its sounds softly crossing the threshold of the old poorly sealed window.

'When we drove past your grand uncle's home,' Hannigan said, 'we noticed an elaborate rock garden in his yard that had a variety of pebbles in it. I'm sure you've noticed it during your time there.' Their ability to read me was making this difficult. I glanced at the clock above the dining table, realizing how close I was to missing my work deadline.

'What kind of pebbles were in the containers?' I asked, buying myself some time to think.

'Grey rocks, about the size of pennies and smaller,' Hannigan said, closing his notebook and slipping it into his inside pocket.

'I don't know a whole lot about pebbles,' I said with a feeble, unconvincing laugh. 'But yeah, I guess maybe there were some filler rocks like that in his garden.' My fear was growing with each new piece of evidence stacking against Cris. It was getting to be too much to explain away.

'We know this is a lot to digest, Liz,' Beck said, 'but can you see that a lot of what we know has possible connections to your grand uncle and that's why we have to continue our line of inquiry?'

I nodded, worried and conflicted. I couldn't deny the level of coincidence it would take for this all to match with one person who also happens to share DNA markers with the killer. Suspicion was seeping into my veins like ice water, chilling me more with each new sliver of information.

'I guess I can see how there are a lot of similarities between the profile and him,' I said, hesitant to give way to these new feelings of fear and familial betrayal. But I

323

was also angry. Angry that he had manipulated *me* too. Angry that I'd found a family member willing to let me in, only for that connection to be ripped away from me. 'Have you found *anyone* else on the Dominio side that could fit the bill? You said you were investigating my 23andMe results, right?'

'We've ruled out most relatives by age, location, and alibies,' Beck replied.

'With the information we have available,' Hannigan said, 'Cristian checks all the boxes. I'm sorry, Liz. Since we now know TSK comes from the Dominio side of the family, there aren't really any other male Dominios that meet the specifications of TSK. We aren't quite ready to bring him in for questioning yet, as we don't want to spook him before we are sure there's enough concrete evidence to hold him. But we're getting closer.'

I looked down and gripped the edges of my chair tightly. I understood there was a level of danger inherent in my situation that wasn't normal for seeking out long lost relatives, but I was so tired of feeling like I was spinning my wheels, clawing to get information, only for something to get in the way. I felt guilty for lying to the FBI about speaking to Adam but it didn't seem as terrible now that I knew I hadn't talked to a killer behind their backs. My conversation with him would have no effect on their investigation now anyway.

'Liz, it's important that you don't share any of this information with Cristian. Even if it turns out that he is not the killer. If he's in contact with the killer in any way, we don't want them to be tipped off and rush the timeline in regard to Zoey and Addie; if they're still alive.'

I nodded in disbelief at the situation I found myself

in, all from doing an ancestry test for fun. I looked down at the photos of Zoey and Addie again, feeling the burn of their frozen stares.

'Good,' Hannigan said, standing. 'Thank you for speaking with us Liz. It's been very helpful. And please be cautious. We encourage you to stay away from Cristian. But if you do have any contact with him please call us right away should you happen to see or hear anything else that may assist us.'

He made a big show of scooping the two photos off the coffee table, as if I needed another reminder of what was at stake. Beck reached out to shake my hand again as she stood. I was numb, leading them to the door and saying goodbye. Paranoid thoughts chased each other around my head, stringing together the new clues that now all seemed to point to Cris. I was out of alternative suspects. My brain kept envisioning the sad ending all these girls had met. Now I couldn't get the image out of my head of my uncle standing over them as they lay folded up in storage bins on a bed of rocks like discarded trash. I felt a bit dirty. Knowing I shared genes with such an evil human being felt like a stain I could never wash off. The memory of his victims would cling to me no matter where life took me. He had ripped away the joy I'd felt at finding biological relatives and instead dropped me into a nightmare I could never awake from.

I locked the door behind the agents and quickly rushed to my computer to finish the Facebook post for work, trying to forget the visit from the FBI. I succeeded in posting just a few minutes after the deadline but I knew it wasn't my best work. Hopefully my boss wouldn't notice. I reopened the document I had minimized earlier, comparing Cris and Adam to the TSK profile, and with sadness and frustration, grunted as I closed out of it without saving. It didn't matter anymore.

I walked to the kitchen to make a fresh cup of coffee. While I selected my coffee pod, I mentally scoured every inch of Cris and Rosie's house that I could remember, trolling for any clues I might have missed. I opened the utensil drawer for a spoon to mix cream into my coffee. As I thought back to the storage room upstairs where we had gone over the old family photo album, I stopped in my tracks. There, clear as day now in my memory, was a framed poster hanging on the wall. On the antiqued white poster, were neat lines of anchors, compasses, and *nautical knots*. I sucked in a breath and shut the drawer, slamming my finger in it.

'Dammit!' I screamed, hopping around clutching my bruised finger.

I opened the freezer door and grabbed a handful of ice, quickly shoving it in a Ziplock bag. I buried my finger in it, waiting for the cold to overtake the pain with numbness. After a few minutes when the throbbing subsided, I discarded the bag of ice and returned to the task at hand, wishing it had numbed my internal pain too. I grabbed the cup of freshly brewed coffee and returned to the living room. But as I turned on the TV, my mind wandered back to that poster. There was too much mounting evidence to ignore. *Am I really saying it's Cris? Should I call Hannigan and update him about the poster?* And then, with a sinking feeling in the pit of my stomach, I thought about Rosie again. Was she in danger? Or was that sweet, loving woman capable of enabling a killer? I was sick of being in the dark. I deserved answers and the only way I was going to get them was by finding them myself. Telling Hannigan about the poster wouldn't be the fastest way to get results. I picked up my phone and dialed. I knew it was reckless but I didn't care.

VICTIMS 22 & 23

Elizabeth Benton & Kelly Davidson

2012

CHAPTER 26

Beth was confused. Normally the man came around midday to have one of them make his lunch but today he hadn't. They'd heard him out there cooking his own meal about half an hour ago. This change to his pattern was unsettling.

'What do you think this means?' she asked.

'I don't know but it makes me nervous,' said Kelly. 'He's had the same routine every weekend the whole time we've been here. I mean, he's obviously The Tri-State Killer. All the names of the women listed in the news articles as his victims are engraved right there,' Kelly said, pointing to the names etched down the wall next to the toilet. 'And we know from the news that he keeps the women alive for what, about nine months, right? I've been trying to keep track of time passing by counting each weekend he's come to spend with us and I think we're pretty close to that now.'

'Maybe he'll let us go! I know it hasn't ended well for the others but maybe there's a chance. We've been so good, following along with everything he says. It's been so long since we've been punished. What if he killed the others because they didn't obey him like we have?' Beth said, clinging to the thought, no matter how unlikely it was.

A look of skepticism took over Kelly's face. 'Or maybe it's time to add our names to the next news article.'

The key scraped into the lock and the doorknob turned. Both women bolted upright to stand next to their mattresses. When the door opened the man stepped into the room. He wasn't wearing his usual jeans but instead had on dark pants and a white button-down shirt. It seemed odd paired with hiking boots. His grey hair was combed neatly to the side and glistened with hair product. Beth could smell a pungent cologne wafting off his skin, filling their small space, making her feel sick. The lines etched deeply into his face seemed more pronounced than usual.

'Today is a very special day. You've both been so good that I've decided to reward you with a walk outside.' Beth looked at Kelly and both women smiled. 'I knew you'd be pleased. See? I'm a reasonable man. Now face the wall.'

He pulled out the syringes from his pocket, popping the covers off the needles while the women got into their stance. Beth was so used to the pinpricks now that she barely even flinched at his rough technique. He left the room, leaving the door ajar.

'We're going outside,' Beth whispered excitedly. 'See? I was right!' Kelly smiled and nodded but the enthusiasm didn't reach her eyes. 'What's wrong?' Beth asked. 'Aren't you excited? Kelly, we're going to breathe fresh air and smell the trees we've only seen glimpses of through that window.'

332

Kelly just nodded, looking out the window at the hint of green. Her eyes had started to droop. Beth recognized the signs and quickly felt the drugs hit her as well. It dulled her edges but the sensation was not enough to dampen her excitement at leaving the cabin.

Kelly opened her mouth but quickly snapped it shut again when the man came back in. He glanced at his watch then walked over to Beth. He unlocked her ankle chains and then released Kelly as well. He motioned for both women to walk through the door first, like he always did, following behind. When they got to the door of the cabin, they stopped.

'Go ahead, open the door,' he prompted.

Kelly didn't move. Beth glanced at her. After all these months in such close proximity, she could read Kelly like a book. She sensed Kelly was frozen by the fear that this was all a test, or some sick joke. Kelly had always been the less trusting of the two. Beth, however, could hardly contain herself, sure that their obedient behavior over the last month was indeed being rewarded. They hadn't slipped up once, hadn't been hit or asked to reclean the toilet or the sink. The joy of stepping outside, something so simple, something people took for granted every day, filled her up and she couldn't keep the smile off her face as she reached out with a trembling hand and turned the knob. She felt a rush at how the cool brass felt in her hand and pulled the door open quickly, before he could change his mind. The sunlight hit her face and she was temporarily blinded, reaching up to shield her eyes with the palm of her hand. When she finally adjusted to the foreign brightness, she looked around. As they had suspected, they were in a forest.

The man's green Camaro, the one they'd ridden in the

333

trunk of when he'd brought them here all those months ago, was parked off to the right. To the left was a path that went further into the thicket of trees. Taking full advantage of their treat, Beth stepped forward and turned down the path, only able to shuffle short steps with the shackles still binding her ankles together. She inhaled deeply and the fresh scent of pine filled her nostrils. She wanted to absorb every bit of nature that she could. Beth turned and looked happily at Kelly who was gazing up into a tree. Beth followed her eyes to a large hawk peering down at them.

As Beth walked slowly down the path ahead of him and Kelly, she heard him name all the birds they saw, pointing out different species of plants, but she wasn't listening. Her senses, dulled from months in that room, were waking up, taking in everything around her. She felt herself coming alive again, even under the sedation of the drugs. It was like the world was blossoming and glistening, just for her. They walked in silence for a while, the sounds from the wind in the trees and animals scurrying under bushes the only noises, until she heard a loud crack behind her. She turned back looking for the source of the disruption. The man was standing above Kelly's body, a large rock gripped in his hand, now covered in a white latex glove like a doctor would wear. Kelly was crumpled on the ground, her eyes closed, her hair matted with blood where it pooled on the side. Beth froze. The smile fell from her face. He hunched over and slammed the rock into Kelly's head again. And again. Then his eyes shot to Beth, a disturbing twinkle sending a cold stab of fear rushing down her spine. She screamed and shuffled away from him as fast as she could. He laughed, loud and deep. Beth stole a quick glance behind her. He was following her at his normal pace, seemingly unconcerned by her attempt to flee. Beth screamed again.

The man said in a taunting voice, 'There's no one around to hear you, darlin'.'

His legs were much longer than hers. He was gaining on her with minimal effort, only a few feet away. The crunch of leaves and branches beneath his boots echoed around her as he closed the distance. She frantically shuffled faster. The shackles dug painfully into the skin around her ankles but she didn't stop. Her foot caught on a small branch littering the path. She stumbled and felt a stab of pain shoot up her right leg, her twisted ankle pulling her to the ground. She scrambled back up. When she tried to put weight on her right foot, she yelled out in pain. Frantically, Beth hopped on one foot, dragging her useless foot along behind her. The man was so close she could hear his excited breathing.

Suddenly, he grabbed her by the neck and slammed her body against a tree. The blow forced all of the air out of her lungs. Beth coughed, desperately gasping for air. She tried jabbing a finger into his eye, anything to gain some space from the monster squeezing the life from her. But he dodged her attempt easily. He brought his other hand up to her neck, tightening his grip. He had an evil grin on his face as his eyes bore into hers. The pressure on her neck was so intense Beth felt as though her head would pop. Her arms were weak from the drugs pumping through her veins. She grabbed at his arms, flailing and slapping him in the face. But her feeble blows were useless against him. Beth tried pulling his hands off her throat but her fingers slipped off the gloves' slick exterior. Blackness crept into the edges of her vision. She felt like she was floating away from the man. The circle of her vision grew smaller and smaller. She looked to the right of his head. The hawk landed on a nearby branch to watch them. She smiled at the bird until her heavy eyes closed of their own accord. The hawk squawked loudly as she felt life draining out of her. She took comfort in the fact that another living creature bore witness to her final moments. She wasn't alone.

CHAPTER 27

Standing on Cris and Rosie's front porch, I rethought my decision to come back here. This was the most Andie-esque thing I'd ever done, impulsively coming out alone against everyone's wishes. I'd called Rosie and casually asked if they'd be around today as I might have time to stop by. I didn't want to risk running into Cris, it felt too dangerous at this point, but I needed to get into their house again. When Rosie mentioned Cris would be at work most of the day I knew it was the best chance I had to look around for more clues without him hovering nearby. I would hope that Andie, at least, would understand my bold decision and appreciate that I did it at a time when it was only Rosie at home. I pulled out my phone and tapped out a message to let Andie know where I was. Before I hit send, I thought about what her reaction would be. No matter how much I wanted her to be on my side, I knew Andie would be upset. She'd tell me I was crazy and that I should have waited until she could come with me or not have gone at all. She'd want me to get back in the car and go home.

Maybe I *was* crazy but no one in my life really understood what all this secrecy had done to me. I felt like a different person than who I was just weeks ago. Having your whole life turned upside down could do that to a person. I was finally taking control of my situation and it felt good. I was going to find the answers no matter what anyone else thought. I hit send, then turned the ringer off and put my phone back in my pocket. Surely Travis mentioned to her by now that I'd borrowed his car again but since I told him I was just running errands, she would now know that I'd lied. I couldn't bring myself to read her reply when it inevitably came through. There was no turning back now.

I raised my hand and knocked on the door, the bright afternoon sun blasting my back and making me sweat. My other hand was in my jacket pocket, fingering the pepper spray I'd decided to bring, just in case. I knew I probably didn't need it since I was just going to be seeing Rosie, but it was reassuring to feel it in my hand. On the ride up, I'd mentally gone over all the moves Andie and I had learned at the self-defense class we'd taken last year after increasing reports of muggings in our neighborhood. I'd done it for safety, while Andie had spouted on about becoming a badass. Hannigan's words still rang in my ear, feeding my concern about what lay ahead. There were too many coincidences to ignore: everything pointed to Cris and I couldn't deny it any longer. I had to keep digging and find proof to stop him. Visiting their home was my only option to find that proof. I smiled as the door creaked open but it quickly fell from my face.

Standing in front of me was not Rosie, but Cris. 'Liz, how are you?' he said calmly. I wasn't sure if I was imagining it but it felt like the small smile he gave me didn't quite meet his eyes. I felt nauseated, really second guessing my decision to rush up here now.

'Hi, Cris,' I said, clearing my throat after it came out hoarse from my surprise. 'I didn't realize you'd be home today.'

'Oh, well my afternoon appointments were rescheduled so I ended up having the rest of the day off. Rosie had to run an errand but she shouldn't be gone long. It's a nice surprise that you were able to take a half-day off work and make an impromptu visit. Come on in.' He opened the door wider, ushering me through.

The fact that Rosie wasn't here and I'd be alone with him gave me major pause. I wished she had mentioned earlier that she may be out. It would have changed my mind about running up here alone. But there was no way I was turning back now. At least it sounded like she would be back soon. I followed him inside where he led me to sit in the living room I'd admired on my last visit. I felt like the Virgin Mary statue was staring at me now, mocking me, as if saying, 'How'd you not catch on to what he was up to?' I remained quiet, unsure how I felt about being alone with the potential Tri-State Killer. I sat there for a long moment, battling internally with what to say, wondering if I should just confront him and gauge his reaction. But how do you tell someone you think they may be a murderer? *Hi newfound uncle, are you by chance a serial killer?*

I shook my head, spinning the ring on my finger as I looked at him sitting next to me, only one cushion's length between us. *This is a huge mistake. What if he catches on that I know he's TSK?* I'd never been good at lying. My confidence waned. I wasn't sure if I was capable of acting casual, when just under the surface I was terrified.

339

Especially in front of a serial killer who was known for manipulation. I bounced my leg anxiously, the urge to bolt creeping up on me. Maybe I should have just left all this to the FBI, like my mom and Andie both told me to. The fear spreading like wildfire down my limbs forced me to make a decision. This was definitely a mistake. If I confronted him and I was correct in my assumptions, then I'd just offered myself up on a silver platter. He'd probably kill me too. But there were two women missing. I couldn't turn back now. He needed to be unmasked and there was still a chance I could save them. I rubbed my lips together, thinking about how to get out safely without turning this whole trip into a complete waste of time. If I could distract him somehow then I could look through his office drawers and maybe see if we could sort through more of the boxes upstairs. I also wanted another look at that nautical poster.

'So, what brings you up here today?' Cris said, snapping me out of my scheming.

'Well . . . Um . . . I had an event cancel unexpectedly and I just thought it was a beautiful day for a drive and a quick visit,' I finished lamely. I knew it sounded weak but I couldn't come up with anything else on the fly. In my rush this morning on the phone, I hadn't gone much beyond asking Rosie if she'd be around today.

'Well, luckily I have some free time last-minute today too. I was about to make a sandwich; care to join me?'

'I already ate but don't let me stop you. Actually, I do need to make a quick call. Do you mind if I use your office again?'

After a brief pause, he nodded and said, 'Go ahead. I'll eat my lunch and then after we can sit together and wait for Rosie to get home.'

I smiled appreciatively, trying not to let my nerves sneak onto my face. Cris walked to the kitchen and I darted into his office. The doors were glass so I had to be careful but he couldn't see the office directly from the kitchen or dining room. I quietly closed the double doors and glanced around. Everything appeared the same, still impeccably organized and clean. I pulled open the first drawer in his desk and moved some pens and a box of paper clips around. My hand hit the back of the drawer and found nothing. The large drawer underneath held hanging file folders. I glanced through all of them: bills, medical records, taxes. They all seemed legitimate and nothing pointed to Cris being a killer. In between pulling out papers and inspecting them quickly, I kept glancing at the door, listening for any sign that Cris was coming this way. The room felt hot. After I closed the large drawer I unzipped my jacket and wiped a bead of sweat from my forehead.

Reaching down, I pulled the handle on the smaller drawer at the bottom but it didn't open. It was locked. *Why would he have a locked drawer? Only Rosie lives with him so what would he need to keep from her?* I found a letter opener on top of the desk and tried jimmying the lock but it wouldn't budge. The sound of footsteps approaching cut through my racing thoughts, sending a sharp chill up my spine. I quickly threw the opener back on the desk and straightened, pulling my phone from my pocket and holding it up to my ear as if I was still on a call. Out of the corner of my eye, I noticed the letter opener was crooked. He'd surely spot that. I lunged forward, straightening the opener to the position I thought it'd been in before I messed with it. Cris came into view just a second later. I held a finger up to say one minute and then pretended to end the call.

'Sorry to interrupt but I let Rosie know you'd arrived and she asked if you would stay for dinner?'

'Oh, thanks for the invite. Maybe next time? I promised Andie I'd make her and Travis dinner later tonight for their anniversary and I don't want to keep his car too long in case he needs it.' The lie slipped easily out of my mouth. I wasn't sure where that had come from. 'Travis loves my lasagna, so . . .'

Cris nodded. 'Rose will be disappointed but there's always next time. Why don't I make some coffee? We can have a cup while we wait for Rosie, before you have to head off again.'

'Actually, I was wondering if you've found anything else of my mother's in Frank's boxes? The photos and the locket are so great but they've just made me want to know even more about her life.'

'I haven't really had a chance to go through more of the boxes since your last visit but we can head up there now and take a gander.'

I smiled politely and followed him over to the stairs, wondering how I was going to search effectively with him in the room. It would have been so much easier to fly under the radar if it had been Rosie. Just as he was about to step up, his cell phone rang. He pulled it out and answered, nodding at the frantic voice on the other end of the line before turning to me. He covered the phone speaker with his other hand.

'Sorry, I have to take this. The Fleschers' cat just had a seizure and Mrs. Flescher is upset. Go on up and I'll join you when I'm done here.'

I couldn't believe my luck! I nodded, trying to contain

my relief at the chance to dig through the storage room without him looking over my shoulder. He walked toward his office and I rushed up the stairs, eager to get as much time alone as possible. Taking a beat, I studied the poster. It was exactly as I'd remembered it. A row of different nautical knots and the last one had 'BOWLINE' printed underneath it. Feeling encouraged that I was on the right track, I grabbed a box from the wall and started pulling out its contents, a flurry of papers going every which way after I scanned them. When I got to the bottom and found nothing of interest, I haphazardly piled the pages back in and yanked out another. The first thing I spotted when I opened the second box was a small faded black and white photograph. Pulling it close to inspect it carefully, the photo showed a young boy standing next to a tall man wearing overalls and galoshes. They were both holding fishing poles with fish dangling from the ends. Squinting, I noticed a small cabin out of focus in the background behind them, faded from the passage of time. The boy could be Frank or Cris, or it could be someone else entirely, I had no idea.

My mind was playing a game of ping pong, the side wanting to trust Cris battling with the other side that was being pushed by each new clue to believe he was TSK. I tucked the photo into my jacket pocket and grabbed some papers that ended up being old utility bills for Frank's house in Connecticut. *Who keeps old utility bills?* Dropping them back in the box, I quickly grabbed another. In my haste to search it, I accidentally knocked another box off the stack next to the desk, causing its contents to spill everywhere. Cris would surely notice if I left everything a mess, so I frantically scooped everything back inside. Out of the corner of my eye I saw something metallic lying on the carpet between the stack and the desk. I leaned forward and picked up a keyring with a jumble of keys in various shapes and sizes. *Did these fall out of the box I'd tipped over, or are these Cris's keys? Maybe they'd fallen off the desk during my frenzied search?* Unsure what they belonged to, I had no way of knowing if they were important or not. But the FBI did say that they suspected the killer had additional properties. Maybe the key to that murder hideout was on this keyring. I took a chance and tossed the keys into my purse, just in case. If they were Cris's keys, hopefully he wouldn't notice right away.

I went back to the box I'd originally pulled aside and continued searching. A tense few minutes passed, my hands shaking from adrenaline. Soon I was at the bottom of the box and no closer to identifying the cabin in the photo or the keys. I pushed the box aside, getting up to grab another. Cris's phone conversation floated up the stairs, instructions on what to watch for in Mitsy, the cat. The call seemed to be wrapping up. Panicking, I combed through the contents of the box in front of me, the pounding in my chest making it hard to breathe. The box was full of old tax returns, mortgage papers and several folders that held strategies for football plays. Finally, I stopped rummaging and sat back on my heels, holding what looked like a certificate with large Old English typeface headlining the top.

'Mrs. Flescher why don't you bring Mitsy by tomorrow morning. I'll have Rosie squeeze you in first thing.'

I only had a few more seconds to myself. I refocused on the document. At the top it read 'NEW YORK DEED WITH FULL COVENANTS'. The grantee name on the document was Rodrigo Dominio. So, Rodrigo owned a property when he died. And as far as I knew, unless the property was given to a specific party by means of a will, the property would automatically be passed down to the next of kin. In this case, Cris and Frank. I couldn't be sure but I felt a jolt of electricity flow through me, convinced I was onto something. The address was listed below in Shandaken, NY. I had no idea where that was.

'How's 8:30? I can see you before my first appointment of the day.'

His voice came from just down the hall. Quickly, I pulled out my phone with shaky hands and managed to snap a photo of the deed.

'Great, I'll see you then.' He was just outside the door now.

Right before he walked into the room, I straightened and dropped the deed back in the box. When he appeared in the doorway, his eyes darted down and I followed his gaze. The deed hadn't landed in the box but instead, had brushed against it and fallen onto the carpet. My heart pounded painfully in my chest, making me feel like I'd just run a marathon. My fingers itched to snatch the deed up and return it to the box but I'd just be calling more attention to it. I didn't know what to do.

'Did you get everything figured out with Mrs. Flescher?' I asked, awkwardly shifting my feet in a pathetic attempt to block the deed from his view. This property could be the killer's secret hiding place and if Cris knew I'd found it, who knew what he might do. I shivered.

'Yes, sorry about that. She was a wreck. But I understand. When your pet has a seizure and there's nothing you can do, you feel helpless. Find anything?' Cris said as he walked into the room, peering around where I stood.

Trying to act casual, I shoved my hands in the pockets

of my jacket to hide the trembling, my fingers bumping against the pepper spray in one pocket, the photo in the other.

'No, not really. Just this old black and white photo from a fishing trip somewhere.' I pulled the photo out and handed it to him, willing my hand not to shake. 'Did you and your dad go fishing a lot?'

He took the photo and looked at it closely. 'Oh no, not me. I wasn't much into that sort of thing. That's Frank there with Rodrigo. He used to take him on weekend trips, showed him how to fish and hunt. This must be from one of those times. My dad took me and Frank fishing once at a lake near our house that we could walk to when I was old enough. But it didn't go so well. My dad got impatient with me when I kept asking questions. After a bit, I gave up and just sat there bored, watching them fish.'

'You never went up to this cabin with them then?' I asked, inching closer to the door now that he'd moved further into the room.

Cris looked again at the photo and narrowed his eyes. 'I'm not too sure.' Then looking back at me with a furrowed brow he said, 'Why do you ask?'

I felt frozen with fear but tried not to let my face show it and shrugged my shoulders with a smile, 'Just curious. Never mind,' I replied, trying to figure out how to get out of here without raising any suspicion. It took all my strength to keep calm and act like everything was normal, but my heart raced along with my mind as I tried to think of an exit route.

'Uh, I have some bad news,' I said, taking my phone out of my purse and faking reading the blank screen. 'Unfortunately, I have to head out. I got a text from my boss and she needs me to post an article about a book launch for a coworker who just called in sick, so I need to squeeze that in before making dinner. I'm going to be cutting it close if I don't leave right now. I'm so sorry we didn't have more time and I'll miss Rosie.' I slipped the phone back into my bag.

Cris scrunched up his nose, looking at me intently. 'Oh, well that's too bad. You came all the way out here for nothing.' He took a step closer to me.

I smiled nervously. 'That's the nature of my job, I just have to roll with it sometimes,' I said as I crept closer to the door and farther away from Cris. 'Hopefully I can make another trip up soon when Rosie is around too.'

As I walked down the stairs, my thoughts firing rapidly on what I'd found in the boxes, I vaguely registered Cris saying I should come by next week and he and Rosie could take me to their favorite local restaurant that made a delicious jambalaya.

'Sure, that'd be great. I'll give you a call when I know my schedule better,' I said quickly, holding my purse tight to the side of my body as I stood near the front door.

Cris looked at me for a beat, his eyes squinting like he was sizing me up. 'Are you sure you can't stay for dinner? You could use my office to do your work before Rosie gets home,' he said slowly.

His tone had an edge, as though he suspected I was acting off. *Oh no, is he on to me? Is this just a ploy to keep me here so I can't raise the alarm?* I tried to look at him and not the bag, afraid my eyes would give away the stolen keys within.

'Sorry but I really do have to get back,' I replied as I turned the knob and opened the door. 'But I'll be sure to call later and set up that jambalaya date.' Cris pursed his lips and rocked on his heels but remained quiet.

After I made it to my car, I exhaled the breath I'd been holding. Pulling out my phone, I entered the address from the deed into my Google Maps app. When the map loaded, Shandaken appeared to be in the Catskill Mountains in upstate New York. I switched to directions and the app estimated about a two-hour drive. I glanced out the window to the house; Cris was standing in the living room window watching me. A shiver ran through my body as he raised his hand in a wave. There, clutched in his other hand hanging at his side, was a piece of paper. It had to be the deed. He must have seen my fumble to get it back into the box and gone back to check what I'd been so eager to conceal. Ignoring my pounding heart, I waved back and started the car. Before I released the parking brake, I hit the start button on my GPS. As I backed out of the driveway into the street and shifted the car into drive, I spotted Cris's garage door slowly opening. I felt panic rise up through my chest and into my throat as my foot hit the gas. As I drove away, I looked in the rearview mirror and could have sworn I saw smoke from a tailpipe coming from the garage.

The bumpy road the navigation led me down after exiting the highway some ten miles back jostled me in my seat. From the directions on the screen, I should come upon the cabin soon. I felt sick the entire drive and I had gripped the steering wheel so hard I was sure when I prized my fingers away they would leave an imprint. I'd anxiously watched my rearview mirror the entire trip, certain Cris had followed me. At one point I was convinced I saw a car following me, taking all the same exits and turns that I did. But I'd since lost sight of it. I couldn't tell if I was being cautious or paranoid but all I knew was that I had to get to the cabin. When I was forced to wait at a train crossing, I locked my car doors and texted Andie, letting her know that I'd come up to the cabin and was now certain the killer was Cris. I sent her the address of the cabin and told her if she didn't hear back from me within an hour to call Hannigan and tell him where I'd gone. I felt better that someone knew where I was and that I had gotten out of Cris's home safely. I was scared about what I might find at the cabin, but determined to find out the truth, once and for all.

I wondered if Hannigan and Beck knew about this cabin? It would be the perfect place for the killer to use since it was so remote, I thought as I scanned the untamed forest surrounding me. The sun had dipped down past the tree line but bright streaks filtered through the evergreens, casting long shadows. If they'd already discovered the cabin then my trip up here may be futile. But with this new piece of information, something told me I'd find the women at the cabin. If I was right, I had to save them before Cris got to them. Despite my new conviction, there was still a small part of me that was worried I was completely wrong. I didn't want to waste the FBI's time if I had totally missed the mark on this. If I found anything that might be helpful, I would call Hannigan and Beck immediately, I said to myself, trying to rationalize my reckless decision to drive all the way up here behind their backs. I just hoped my fears about Cris following me were unfounded.

'Turn left,' projected the voice from my phone.

At the next break in the trees, the only indication of a

road nestled in the forest, I turned left and drove through a dense thicket of trees that clearly hadn't been trimmed for a long time. Branches and leaves swatted at the windshield like an automated car wash. Suddenly, I came to a clearing with a small wooden cabin. I stopped the car and squinted out the windshield. It looked like the cabin from the photograph. It appeared to have been kept up, the windows were intact, the roof looked relatively new, and the area around the cabin was clear of major debris. Just a sprinkling of leaves and small twigs littered the walkway.

My nerves prickled just under the surface of my skin like electricity rolling over me. *What would I find here? An empty cabin? Two dead women?* Shaking off the ominous feeling, I pulled the key ring out of my purse and opened the car door. When I stepped out into the crisp mountain air, I zipped up my thin jacket, the fall temperatures significantly cooler than back home even though it was only a few hours away. A breeze ruffled my hair, the smell of trees and chirping of birds feeling foreign to me after waking up that morning in the concrete and steel framework of New York City. Had I been here under different circumstances, I would have enjoyed its natural beauty. I slammed the car door shut and waited for a minute, listening for the sounds of a car. If Cris had followed me, surely he wouldn't be too far behind. Since I was in the middle of nowhere, I could hear every little sound coming from the trees and wind but no engine.

I turned and ran up the short path to the doorway, turning the keys over in my hand. My palms were slick with nervous sweat. I rubbed them quickly on my jeans. I pulled one key out from the ring and inserted it into the lock but it didn't turn. Frustration and worry simultaneously ballooned in my stomach. *What if I just drove all this way and the keys weren't even for this cabin?* I looked over my shoulder but there was still no other car. Then I glanced at the window next to the door, contemplating if I'd be able to jimmy it open and crawl through if none of the keys fit. The window looked pretty secure and I wasn't keen on breaking it. I turned back to the door and tried a few more keys. On the fourth key the lock turned. Excitement and dread mingled in my mind. Warily, I inched into a rustic kitchen, the air stale and dead. To the left was a small, dark living room, bare except for an old recliner and a single end table set up facing a vintage boxy television.

'Hello?' I called out timidly. But I was met with complete silence. I exhaled. For now, it seemed I was alone.

I beelined through a door right off the kitchen and found a small room with just two wooden chairs, a cot and an end table. Dust covered all the surfaces. It appeared to be an unused room, maybe a den or guest room, but too small to be considered a true bedroom. I rushed out and checked a door on the other side of the living room. I pushed it open, bracing myself for some important reveal. It was a bedroom, the bed neatly made with tightly tucked corners, an off-white crocheted blanket folded over at the bottom. When I ran my finger along the dresser, dust came up on my fingertip. I couldn't imagine Cris letting dust collect on any surface but maybe he'd spent less time here now that the FBI was closing in. On the nightstand was a newspaper dated from almost two months ago. Underneath the paper were several sports magazines. The address labels read *Frank Dominio* and carried a different Connecticut address than

Cris and Rosie's house. *Were Frank and Cris in on it together? The women were taken in pairs after that first victim. Cris must have been his partner, carrying on alone now that Frank was gone.*

After frantically looking around the nightstand and dresser and finding nothing else of interest, I turned and just before I was about to exit the room, I noticed that there was a small, dust-free square on top of the dresser. Crouching down, I looked under the dresser and found nothing. I reached around the side and felt around blindly. My hand came into contact with a small piece of slick paper. It was a photograph. When I pulled it up I froze. A wave of nausea rolled over me, the hair standing on the back of my neck as goosebumps spread along my arms. *Oh God, Cris really was manipulating me this whole time! Finally, concrete proof of his deception.* There in the photo was my great grandfather, Rodrigo, several years older than in the black and white photo I'd seen in the box. He was again in front of the cabin with his arm around Frank at about age ten or eleven. His other hand was placed on the shoulder of a smaller boy, about age five or six. That had to be Cris. Having my suspicions confirmed heightened my anxiety about Cris following me up here. My hand shook as I shoved the photo in the back pocket of my jeans.

I quickly checked a small door next to the bedroom that ended up being a bathroom. The toilet paper was stacked evenly in rows alongside the toilet. I opened the cabinet above the sink and found prescription bottles, over the counter medications for headaches and acid reflux, and a small bottle of mouthwash. All the bottles were lined up next to one another, their labels all pointing precisely outward. On the bottom shelf was a neat row of identical small bottles. I picked one up and inhaled sharply when I read the label. This was definitely The Tri-State Killer's cabin. All the bottles were ketamine.

With my heart pounding I fumbled the bottle, almost dropping it, but managed to catch it and place it back in the cabinet. Backing out of the bathroom, I spotted another door near it that wasn't closed all the way, so I pushed it open a few inches wider, making a face at the sight in front of me. The room looked like a large shower, tiled all around with a drain in the middle. If I wasn't looking for a serial killer the room would seem innocuous, like a room you would find in any hunting cabin where you'd clean fish or store any game you'd shot. But considering my mission the room became menacing, like a good place to rinse off blood or destroy evidence.

A loud pulsing filled my ears, keeping in time with my heart threatening to burst from my chest. I was so close to finding answers, I could feel it in my bones. I ran back to the kitchen and looked around. Something sticking out from the wall caught my eye. A doorknob. I'd walked right past it because the other doors in the cabin were stark white. But not this one. This door was the same wood as the walls, camouflaging it, but with a small brass doorknob that matched its earthy tones. I tried turning the knob but it was locked. I knocked on the door. When there was no response, I pulled the keys out of my pocket and tried a smaller key on the keyring. It slid in but didn't turn.

Suddenly, I heard a car engine outside and my blood ran cold. I rushed to the kitchen window and looked out. Cris was getting out of a bright green Camaro that he'd parked next to Travis's car. He stopped and stared at Travis's car for a second and then glanced at the cabin.

I quickly crouched down. Looking around frantically, I ran back to the newly discovered door. I flipped the keychain around and tried another key that hadn't worked on the front door. It fit and the knob turned smoothly. I rushed into the dark room and snapped the door shut behind me, stashing the keys in my pocket. My eyes hadn't adjusted from the light of the kitchen and I could only just make out a small window near the ceiling. My heart thumped in my ears and I jumped when I heard Cris enter the cabin.

'Liz?' he called out and I clamped my hand over my mouth so I didn't scream.

I listened as he walked around the cabin from room to room. I pulled the pepper spray from my pocket, turned the safety latch to the off position and stood behind the door, ready to pounce. With my free hand, I searched my pocket for my phone to call 911, trying not to make a sound as my fingers brushed against the keys. It wasn't there. *Shit! It's still in the car hooked up to the charger.*

'Liz, are you here?' came Cris's voice again, fading as he walked away from the room I was hiding in.

In the quiet, I suddenly heard something in the room with me. Breathing, heavy breathing, and then a whisper. 'Did he take you too?'

VICTIMS 24 & 25

Addie Wilson & Zoey Davis

2019

CHAPTER 28

Addie licked the inside of the granola bar wrapper again, desperately searching for any crumb that might be hiding in the crevices. She dropped the wrapper on the ground with the rest of them. Zoey watched her with vacant eyes.

'Get anything?' Zoey asked.

'I don't think so.'

She turned back toward her mattress. Every movement ached. Addie hadn't gotten up from her mattress all day until now because of how much it hurt to lift herself. Zoey began laughing hysterically from the other side of the room. When Addie laid back down on the bed, she winced as her body met the rough fabric of the mattress and her vision blurred, the axis of the room tilting behind her closed eyelids. Addie forced her eyes open again and looked at Zoey, still laughing on her own bed. She was fingering her ribs that were jutting out from her sunken stomach. Her lips were dried and cracked, her eyes sunken into dark circles and her skin, an ashy grey. Addie grimaced, figuring she probably looked about the same. There was no mirror in the room but neither of them had eaten anything in four days and starvation was settling in. The man hadn't come back one weekend. They'd assumed he'd be back the next, so they continued to eat the food he'd left for them. But by the following weekend he still hadn't appeared. Sure that he would check on them soon, they kept eating to keep the hunger pains at bay. When they hit weekend number three with still no visit by the man, they began to ration the remaining food. Between the two of them, they'd only had one bag of trail mix and one sleeve of crackers left. For each meal over the next two weeks they'd each had one peanut, one almond, two raisins and a cracker. By the end of the week they were out of food completely.

Addie had been drinking water directly from the faucet to try and trick her stomach into thinking it was full, but she couldn't remember if she'd drunk any today. The thought of getting back up was too painful, so instead she turned her attention to Zoey.

'What are you laughing at?' Addie croaked.

Zoey moved her head slowly back and forth. 'I have no idea, but isn't it funny?'

Addie felt like she'd never want to laugh at anything ever again. Part of her wished the man had just killed them before he disappeared, ending their misery swiftly, instead of leaving them here to watch each other slowly waste away. She turned her back to Zoey and faced the wall. She started to cry but no tears fell, her body shaking with each dry gasp. She supposed she was dehydrated and knew she should force herself to get up and drink some water, but she couldn't muster the energy. Instead, she ran her finger over the hatch marks on the wall. At this point she couldn't really say how long it'd been since the man had come for them. Her thoughts were a jumble most of the time, each day blurring into the next. It could have been a month. It could have been two. It felt like a lifetime. She kept thinking about Elizabeth Warren on the Senate floor refusing to back down, the men spouting what would later become a battle cry, 'Nevertheless, she persisted.' Addie had been repeating those words in her head for weeks, clinging to them like a mantra. But the words disintegrated under the fog that now took over her thoughts. She wasn't sure how much longer she could persist.

A car door slammed outside. Addie rolled over onto her back and looked at Zoey who had stopped laughing. 'Did you hear that?'

'It probably wasn't real, Addie. Maybe we imagined it.'

'Both of us?' Addie waited for other noises, and for a minute there was nothing. She closed her eyes, straining her ears to listen intensely. Then they heard the front door to the cabin scrape open. She looked at Zoey, her eyes wide.

'He came back, Zoey. He came back!'

Both girls pulled themselves painfully up into a seated position. The effort left Addie panting. It felt odd to be happy that this monster had come back for them but she felt intense relief that he hadn't abandoned them. Maybe that's what he wanted, for them to see him as their savior. They waited in silence, hearing footsteps on the other side running from room to room. She hoped he'd come soon and give them more food. She knew they should wash up, be clean like he demanded, but she didn't have the strength.

'I know I said I never wanted to see beef jerky again but I really hope he brought some,' Zoey whispered.

'And Doritos,' Addie replied with a small, weak laugh. She was almost euphoric at the thought of food. After another few minutes, the handle to the door finally jiggled, followed by a knock on their door. *Why is he knocking?* Addie thought. Keys jangled and then it sounded as though he was trying several keys. *Has it been so long that he forgot what key it is?* Another car door slammed. Addie's eyebrows knitted together. Finally, the right key went into the lock and the doorknob turned. A woman rushed into the room, quickly closing the door behind her. She seemed scared. She squinted at them but didn't seem to see them. She was too busy pulling some kind of cylinder out of her pocket and flattening her body against the wall behind the door, as if anyone could hide from him. *Did he kidnap someone else to join them?* He'd already gone off his normal routine, maybe he was adding someone new to the mix.

'Did he take you too?' Addie asked the woman, causing her eyes to dart in Addie's direction and widen, finally seeing her sitting on the mattress. The woman put her finger up to her mouth and quietly hissed, 'Shhh! He's still out there.'

Addie was confused. *What did this mean? Had the woman escaped from his clutches?* If so, she'd certainly picked the wrong room to hide in. Suddenly the doorknob turned and when the door inched open, a man stood in the doorway. The mystery woman tensed, looking ready to pounce and attack the man from behind as he stepped in.

Addie slowly stood, and clearing her throat, she asked, 'Are you our new Master?'

Perhaps their captor had passed them along like hand-me-down dolls to his next of kin. They shared several physical features, most notably their eyebrows. Addie would never forget the way those caterpillars hovered over his cold eyes as he stared down at her.

The new man stood still with his mouth open. A few seconds passed before he answered, 'What? No. Are you . . . Are you Addie Wilson and Zoey Davis?'

The woman's hand flew to her mouth as the keys in her hand fell to the floor and she gasped. 'Oh my God.'

The man opened the door wider and peered behind it. 'Liz?'

The woman still had the cylinder poised in her shaky hand. 'You're not TSK?'

The man seemed to deflate like a balloon. 'Liz, no. How could you ever think that?'

'I don't know . . . I'm so sorry,' she cried, tears starting to pour down her cheeks.

The man looked at the woman for a long moment. Addie coughed, her throat dry, and it seemed to bring his attention back to her and Zoey. He turned and abruptly walked out into the kitchen where Addie heard him saying, 'We found the two missing women from the news. Please, send help right away. They need medical attention.'

The woman – Liz, he'd called her – walked a few steps toward Addie. '*Are* you Addie and Zoey?'

'Yes. I'm Addie and that's Zoey,' Addie lifted her hand in Zoey's direction. But it dropped halfway up, too weak.

Liz closed the gap to Addie and gently touched her arm, 'I'm Liz, I'm here to help. Are you hurt?'

Addie fell into Liz's embrace and sobbed. When she opened her eyes, she saw Zoey behind them, a smile on her face.

'Are you real?' Zoey asked. Liz turned her head in Zoey's direction and nodded vigorously in response.

'Addie, we're rescued. We're rescued,' Zoey repeated, her voice cracking. 'We did it.' The words seemed to take everything out of her.

Addie released Liz and pulled Zoey into a triumphant hug. Behind them Liz picked up the keys and tried them in the locks on their shackles, starting with Addie's. When the smallest key slid in and turned, the shackles released, and Addie felt them fall away from her ankles. Then Liz scooched closer to Zoey's feet. Addie heaved with dry sobs, trembling as the weight of her imprisonment was lifted. A world of possibilities lay ahead of her that just moments ago had seemed out of reach forever. The click of Liz unlocking Zoey's shackles brought her back to reality and she eagerly clasped Zoey's bony hand. The two women walked toward the front door, away from the dark shadows of certain death and toward the last rays of fading sunlight.

CHAPTER 29

I propped myself up on the bed, pushing away the morning haze as I scrolled mindlessly through emails on my phone. After the enormity of what I had experienced just four days ago, I was relieved my boss understood that I needed some time off. I couldn't imagine going straight back to work after seeing firsthand what those poor women were subjected to by my own grandfather. It seemed likely, since the women hadn't recognized Cris, that Frank was the sole perpetrator, but it was hard to completely shift my thinking once again. Had Cris known what Frank was up to? Could he have been working behind the scenes to help in some way? I didn't know.

After the police and EMTs had arrived, Zoey and Addie were taken away on stretchers and I'd been questioned by an officer about what had brought me to the cabin of horrors. I told them everything through a curtain of tears, including my meetings with Hannigan and Beck. They walked me back to my car and told me they'd be in touch. Cris had been led away somewhere else, I assumed to be questioned, so I wasn't able to talk to him myself. When I climbed into the driver's seat, I picked up my phone from the charger, forgotten in my rush to enter the cabin. I had several missed calls and text messages, which wasn't surprising given the last text I'd sent Andie. I navigated to her most recent voicemail first.

'Liz! Answer your phone. Okay you know what, this is crazy! I can't believe you went up there alone. I'm not waiting an hour to notify someone if you might be in trouble! I'm calling Hannigan and Beck right now.'

I looked at the next voicemail above hers, an unsaved number. I had a pretty good idea of who that was from but I hit play anyway. As I suspected it was Hannigan, saying they were on their way and urging me not to go inside the cabin.

Oops, I'd thought wryly, *too late.* Knowing they were probably fairly close at that point, I waited in my car until they got to the scene. The first thing I said, at a loss of how to even begin to justify my actions, was, 'I kinda went inside.'

I gave them the photo I'd found in the cabin and they admonished me for my risky behavior, but in the end, were grateful I was okay and that Zoey and Addie had been rescued. It took some time before my hands stopped shaking enough to drive back to the city, the sky darkening around me. I called my parents on the way, who met me back in Brooklyn and took me home to New Jersey the second I returned Travis's car. All I had time to do was quickly drop his keys off at our apartment and shove a few of my things into a duffel bag. I'd shot off a text to Andie, asking her to FaceTime me when she got home from her shift, promising I was alright and apologizing for the anxiety I'd caused her. But I was relieved to be back with my parents now, far away from everything that had happened.

So far, it'd been radio silence from the cops. I hadn't heard anything from Hannigan either, even after leaving a couple of messages, and I wasn't sure if I would. They were likely still sorting through the evidence while I sat there wondering if my uncle was a part of Frank's twisted web of lies and murder. They'd been more forthcoming with me during the investigation than I would have thought the FBI would be, but at the time, they'd needed something from me. Now that they didn't need me, would they share the full truth? The image of the women emaciated and shackled in that tiny barren room was seared into my brain and the fact that I got any sleep since Thursday felt like a true miracle.

I faintly heard the sizzling of a frying pan and smelled the tantalizing scent of bacon wafting up the stairs towards my childhood bedroom. I was grateful I'd listened when my parents insisted I spend some time at home recovering. Despite all the difficulty over the truth behind my adoption, they had given me a better life than I would have had otherwise, and their loving embrace comforted me like a safety blanket now. I shivered at the idea of being raised in a household connected to someone like Frank, capable of hurting so many young women.

Andie had been horrified when I'd recounted my adventures at the cabin and had been texting and calling nonstop to make sure I was okay. I appreciated her concern but it was also nice to have some space from her to process. Andie would be the one to help distract me and hype me up when I was ready to get back to everyday life. But right now, I needed a break from it all. I needed my mom and dad.

A soft knock on the door pulled me from my contemplation, and I gave a tired 'Come in' that came out mangled by its accompanying yawn.

'Hi sweetie,' my mom said, popping her head into the gap as she opened the door. 'Breakfast is ready whenever you want to come down and join us.'

'Okay, I'll be there in a sec,' I replied, giving her a half smile.

Getting to the bottom of my unread emails, I saw one from 23andMe notifying me of a message from another user. I paused, almost afraid to click on it after the emotional rabbit hole I'd just been down. Reminding myself that my whole family couldn't be that bad, and at the end of the day, I had helped save two women because of my search, I pushed my nerves aside and navigated to the inbox. After all, maybe this person would help balance out the black spot in my family tree with some light.

I opened the message and began to read.

Dear Elizabeth,

I just received my 23andMe results and noted that we had a fairly high percentage match as relatives, 25%. I showed it to my dad since I thought it was strange that I'd never heard of you before. My dad took one look at the photo on your profile and nearly dropped the laptop on the floor, he was so taken aback by how much you resemble his high school girlfriend, Teresa. Please don't take offense, but he said he would remember those eyebrows anywhere! After some prodding he finally opened up to me that he had gotten her pregnant and since they were both young and caught up in a string of drug usage, they had discussed her getting an abortion, which he had assumed she had gone through with. Once she was arrested, he took off and got out of the city so he could focus on getting his own life back on track. After seeing your photo and the amount of DNA we have in common, we suspect that she didn't have the abortion after all, and that you may be my half-sister. He says had he known, he would have tried to find you years ago. But we'd like the chance to get to know you now. We live just north of New York City in New Rochelle, if you'd like to connect and maybe meet up. We both hope to hear from you soon.

Best,

Connor Daniels

I sat still for a moment, unable to believe it as I read over the message for a second time. My father was alive. I had a brother. They wanted to know me. Tears gushed out of my eyes as every emotion from the past month exploded out of me. My phone buzzed in my hand and I looked down to see a text from my mom.

'Food's getting cold! Coming soon?'

'Be there in a few, just need to respond to an email really quick,' I tapped out.

With trembling fingers, I typed back a response.

Dear Connor,

It is so good to hear from you. It's been quite the emotional rollercoaster over the last month, trying to find my biological family and learn more about where I come from. I was adopted as a baby and just recently found out after getting my own 23andMe results. I'm so glad you reached out to me and I would be thrilled to get to know you and your father. Who, I guess if we are siblings, is my father. I live in Brooklyn so I can meet in the city or travel up to you, if that's easier. If you'd like to connect by phone first, I'm including my cell number below. Please feel free to text or call me anytime. I look forward to hearing from you both.

All my best,

Liz

Before I hit send, I added my phone number underneath my signature. I wiped my eyes and took a deep breath. I was still having trouble processing everything I'd been through but now I had this silver lining of a brother and father. If someone had told me when I first sent in the 23andMe kit that this is where I would have ended up, I would have thought they were insane. I laughed and rose to go downstairs. But before I made it through the door my phone rang. *Well that was fast,* I thought as I fumbled to answer the call. It was an unknown number and my excitement spiked.

'Hello?'

'Hi Liz, this is Agent Hannigan.'

I tried to tamp down my disappointment that it wasn't Connor. Hopefully, this call would confirm whether or not Cris was involved so that I could have some level of closure. If he was completely innocent, I didn't want to lose him and Rosie.

'Oh hi. Thanks for getting back to me. Are there any updates on the case?'

'Well, we've had a couple of days to go through the

evidence we gathered from the cabin and have interviewed Addie and Zoey at length, so we've learned a lot. We were hoping you could meet with me and Agent Beck today? We'd like to give you an update in person and thank you for your role in saving Zoey and Addie. I have to say though, Liz, it was extremely dangerous, what you did going up there. I wish you had called us first so we could do a proper search rather than jeopardizing your safety.'

He took a deep breath, during which I felt the heat of shame flow across me. He was right, what I did *was* dangerous and I was lucky it hadn't turned out worse.

'But Beck and I are glad you made it out safely,' he continued. 'The cabin had not turned up in our investigation of Cris or Frank. We'd done a thorough property search on all our suspects but the cabin was never uncovered. When Rodrigo died, ownership was never officially transferred over to Frank and Cris, who technically inherited the cabin by default. It also appears that when Rodrigo bought the cabin back in the sixties some papers were never properly filed. Because of this error, the cabin never showed up in the Dominio family records when we did our initial search. I'm not sure we would have found it without your help.' I relaxed a little as his tone turned from reprehensive to grateful. 'Our office is in Westchester, if you don't mind traveling here. It shouldn't take long but since you were so involved in this case, and per the agreement we had about sharing information with you before it hits the media, we'd like to go over some details on what we've found.'

I shivered despite the flush of heat burning my cheeks. While I wanted to know more about the case that had weaved its way through every aspect of my life over the past month and a half, it would mean hearing more awful details about my grandfather and what had been done to those women. It would mean more vivid images in my head, haunting me and keeping me up at night. The idea of hearing the truth I'd wanted so badly suddenly scared me, and I hesitated. But I knew the details would come out in the news anyway, so there was no point hiding from it. After a long pause I decided it would be best to hear it from them directly. It was better to be prepared and be able to ask them questions. But first, I needed to know if Cris was involved; I was too anxious to wait.

'Sure, I can do that. But I have to know, was Cris involved? Did he know what Frank was up to?'

'It's probably best if we discuss everything in person when you come in.'

'No, I need to know, please just tell me. It's been eating me up that the person I've been getting to know could have been even remotely involved in what was done to those women. I know he and Frank were close.'

I heard Hannigan sigh. 'From everything we've found in the cabin and after interviewing Cris, we are certain he was not involved in Frank's crimes.'

I exhaled loudly. 'You're sure?'

'Yes, we're sure. We recovered no physical evidence that placed him at the cabin prior to the rescue, and it was very difficult for him to accept what his brother had done even after seeing Addie and Zoey chained up in that room. Once we show you the evidence, I'm sure you'll be as confident as we are that he was unaware of Frank's actions.'

I looked down at my hand and picked at my cuticles. With the information that Cris wasn't involved, I was consumed by guilt that I'd ever thought it was him. 'Okay, what time should I meet you?'

'Can you be here by 1 p.m.? I'll text you the address.'

'1 p.m. it is. I'll see you then.'

I hung up and after Hannigan texted me the address, I figured it would take me about an hour to get there by car. My parents would probably let me borrow my mom's car; after all, they were still working tirelessly to earn my forgiveness after the adoption reveal. I'd told them several times that I loved and forgave them but their guilt ran deep, and I knew they wouldn't deny me a request like this one. Thinking about the emotional journey this experience had been for all of us, I decided I would also tell them about Connor and my biological father. It was time for the family secrets to end; they'd done enough damage. Having them in my corner as I opened this new door would help to comfort the nervousness simmering inside me. It wasn't likely that Connor or my father were dark and dangerous like Frank, but there was still a mystery about them. What were they like? What if we didn't get along? I was grateful I didn't have to face this next chapter alone. I ran downstairs to fill my parents in. Back together again, The Three Amigos.

I pulled my mom's cream-colored Lexus up to the building and rechecked the address. The office exterior was nondescript, steel with dark tinted glass. As I got out of the car and walked up to the building, I rethought my decision to come alone. My parents had wanted to join me, eager to keep me close after all that had happened. I'd insisted I wanted to do this on my own to get much needed closure. I'd thought about calling Cris on the drive to apologize but was unsure of what to say. 'Sorry I thought you were a serial killer,' just seemed insufficient. When I opened the doors to the building, a woman sitting at a desk in the center of the lobby smiled warmly and asked for my ID.

'Everyone's already in the conference room. I'll take you back,' she said and handed me a paper badge to clip to the lapel of my blazer.

She led me down a hallway and then turned a few times. It was a maze of offices and long hallways, so much so that I wasn't sure I'd be able to find my way back to reception without a guide. Finally, the woman opened a door and I spotted Cris sitting in a chair. I was shocked into silence. I wasn't aware he'd be here too and I didn't feel prepared to see him again just yet. My whole body tensed as we eyed each other nervously. He stood slowly and took a hesitant step forward.

'How are you?' he asked.

'I'm okay,' I said softly, clearing my throat. 'Still reeling from everything. But I'm doing as well as can be expected. What about you? How are you holding up? I never even knew Frank but you grew up with him, so I know this must be even harder on you.'

He puffed his cheeks out and exhaled. 'It still hasn't fully sunk in, to be honest. It's hard to imagine the brother who taught me how to ride a bike and change the oil in my car could have done these things. But at the same time, I keep remembering other odd times when his behavior didn't really track. Times he was too forceful with your mom and grandma, trying to control their actions. I always brushed it off because he was my brother and I blamed it on his inability to cope with Teresa's rebellions. I didn't want to believe it was true but it seems the evidence doesn't lie,' Cris said, rubbing his chin, his eyes tired. I was sure he hadn't been sleeping well either. 'Anyway, it's nice to see you're doing well, all things considered. I know you didn't know Frank but finding the women in that cabin wasn't easy,' he said, his voice heavy.

Suddenly my emotions overwhelmed me and I blurted out, 'I'm so sorry that I thought you might be involved in this.' Frantically, I tried to come up with reasoning that would explain my suspicions. 'The FBI came to my house just after we met,' I said, shooting a quick glance at the agents. 'The reason they found you in the first place is because after I did the 23andMe kit and found out I was adopted, I wanted to find my biological family. I wasn't getting any responses from my matches, so I uploaded my DNA into GEDMatch, which is searchable by law enforcement if you opt in. When I did that, my DNA came up with a familial match to The Tri-State Killer. I'm so sorry.'

Cris's eyes widened. Quietly, he asked, 'You were talking to them the whole time? About me? Were you just spending time with us so you could report back to them?'

'No! It wasn't like that,' I said quickly, my cheeks feeling hot. 'They did come to see me a few times but they did most of the talking, trying to figure out what male relatives I had that could fit the killer's profile and warning me to be careful. I told them that I'd just met you and didn't believe you could have done this. But then they told me about the ketamine that went missing that you didn't report and gave me some details that seemed to match up with you, and I didn't know what to think. You had that nautical print in the storage room and you and Rosie have religious relics all around the house. They told me the killer used a specific nautical

373

knot and that he was likely very religious. It started piling up and I couldn't help but think . . .' I trailed off, not wanting to say it again. I felt out of breath, exhausted. 'I'm so sorry,' I repeated, dropping my head and letting the tears fall freely.

Cris rocked on his heels and looked at the ground. 'The nautical print was a gift from Frank.' He barked a short, hard laugh. My eyes shot back to him. 'And I didn't report the ketamine because I thought it was your mother who had stolen it.' He looked back up at me. 'You know about her drug problems. She came to visit me all the time and when I noticed it was missing, I confronted her. She wouldn't give me a straight answer and stopped coming around after that. I didn't want to get her in trouble with the police since she'd already had a few run ins with the law. I figured if I said anything it would just make things worse and I wanted desperately for her to get on the right path. At the same time, I was new to owning my own practice. I was afraid admitting I'd already lost a controlled substance could potentially tank my business too.'

The guilt I felt at having read into all of these clues in the wrong way was growing with each word Cris said. I gulped before saying, 'God, you must hate me. I'm really sorry.' Tears slowly slid down my cheeks.

Surprisingly, Cris didn't seem angry, just sad. 'I wish you had come and talked to me about this. But we haven't known each other that long. Anyone might have thought the same in your situation. I understand, Liz. And I don't hate you. You're family. I know I was a little hesitant to open up to you at first, which I'm sure didn't help your suspicions, but I was afraid to let you in.'

'Afraid?' I sniffled. 'But why?'

'It seems silly now but you're Teresa's daughter. We loved that girl so much, like she was our own, but everything went so wrong. When she got mixed up in drugs, the sweet child we knew turned into someone uncontrollable who constantly caused drama within the family. Part of me was afraid you'd take after her.' He paused and looked at me, tears glistening in the corners of his eyes. 'Then, just as we thought we were getting our kind and bright-spirited Teresa back, she was ripped away from us. I was afraid if I got to know you, even if you didn't have her rebellious streak, that you too might get ripped away.' He shook his head and looked down.

I threw my arms around him. His body stiffened for a second before he relaxed and squeezed me back. I clenched him tight and inhaled his woodsy scent mixed with the smell of dog fur. I thought this whole case and my suspicions about him would have torn us apart and separated me from my biological family forever. I hoped, instead, that it would bring us closer. Hannigan cleared his throat, interrupting our moment. I quickly stepped back and wiped my face with the back of my hand until Cris handed me a cloth handkerchief from his pocket.

'Liz, Cris, thank you so much for coming all the way out here,' Hannigan said, putting out a hand which I clasped in a shake. 'I know this is a difficult time for both of you.'

Beck reached out next and shook my hand with both of her own, smiling warmly at me in greeting. Both agents looked more relaxed than they had at any of our previous encounters. Cris and I took a seat across the long white conference table from them. I gratefully reached for the glass in front of me and took a swig of water.

'Thank you both for coming to speak with us. I know

375

this hasn't been easy for either of you.' He nodded at us, opening a manila folder in front of him and shuffling through his stack of papers. 'Now that we've had a few days to process the evidence, we have a more complete picture of Frank's routine. As family who were directly impacted by his actions and who played such an integral role in rescuing Addie and Zoey, we felt it was right to share with you some of what we found before anything is released to the press.'

He took an enlarged photo out of his pile of documents and placed it on the table in front of us, turning it around so we could get a clear look. It was a photo of an ordinary box, a little dirty and worn with age. It was sitting in some sort of crevice, engulfed in shadows, with a small folded yellow evidence card denoting the number 30 in large block black letters sitting next to it. They had probably documented every inch of that cabin.

Hannigan continued, 'In a crawlspace under the floorboards in the bedroom, we found a very helpful box. It held about eight years' worth of journals, detailing his routine. His college football schedule basically dictated his timeline, which was always something that confused us. Why were the pairs taken around the same time of year? Why were they murdered nine months later each time? We came up with a lot of theories but nothing concrete. Now, knowing more about him, it makes sense. Three months of the year he was in football season and unable to dedicate his time to the young women. He'd kill them right before the season started back up. We're guessing he skipped a year after each set of abductions because those murders kept him satiated during that time, until the urge returned.'

I was stunned, disgusted that he had planned his horrors

around a football schedule, interacting with his team and community in-between murders as if nothing had ever happened. Each detail I learned about him seemed to be more horrible than the last.

'His progression is unique once you look into it further,' Hannigan continued. 'Most serial killers who continue to kill for a long period of time, while they may stick to a pattern, they usually show some level of escalation. For example, maybe they start out simply burglarizing homes or killing animals. Once they get a taste, they escalate to rape – if sexually motivated – or torture. Then one day, the urge to kill becomes too much and they murder. Eventually, a routine will develop in order to experience that rush again and again. But not with TSK. Frank had no criminal history nor any signs indicating he'd become violent someday.'

Cris nodded. 'I think that's why it was so hard to accept that he'd done this. Frank never showed any sign of violence or broke the law growing up. And while he didn't love animals like me, he never hurt them.'

Hannigan was nodding too. 'TSK is a unique case in that way. Out of nowhere, he went straight to murdering. He did escalate initially after his first singular victim, changing to paired abductions. But after that he knew exactly what he liked and stuck to it. He likely also used his travel for games, camps, and scouting, as a cover for selecting potential victims, using that time to stalk his next target. After he retired, well, he'd already established a pattern that worked for him and he maintained it for the most part.'

'Did you find out anything else from the journals?' I asked, turning my attention back to the agents.

Beck took over, flipping her long dark hair over her

shoulder. I was so used to seeing her in a severe bun I hadn't realized how long and shiny her hair actually was. It changed her whole persona; she wasn't as intimidating and seemed like someone I might be friends with if I met her under different circumstances.

'Frank kept a diary of the movements of the young women he was stalking for potential victims, up until the botched attempt. He logged what times they came home at night, if they were alone, together or with other people. He even kept track of any dates they had, following them to bars and restaurants. From the journals, he tracked multiple pairs of women at any given time. Then, over the span of a few weeks, he would narrow it down to one pair.'

I shook my head, 'Wow. I can't even wrap my brain around that. You said eight years, though. Weren't the women taken over a span of like, forty-five years?'

'Technically, yes,' Beck replied. 'However, the first singular murder was in 1974. We believe that to be a crime of circumstance, rather than a planned killing. But it seems to have whet his appetite. The next abduction, the first pair of young women, didn't occur until 1991.'

'That's a seventeen-year gap. That seems odd, doesn't it?' I asked.

'We aren't sure what caused a renewed interest in taking women in 1991, but he married just a year after the first murder in 1975 and had a child, your mother, shortly after. Our guess is, the gap can be attributed to his family life. Why that changed, we don't know.'

'1991?' Cris asked. The agents nodded. 'In '91 Teresa turned sixteen years old and started dating that boy Frank didn't like. Teresa was a very obedient child up until her teenage years hit. Things went downhill pretty rapidly after she started dating that boy. They fought all the time. Then she got into trouble with the law and started doing drugs. I remember Frank saying he couldn't control her anymore, that she wouldn't listen to him. He felt helpless.'

Hannigan and Beck shared a look. 'Well that could certainly explain it,' Hannigan replied. 'His motivation to abduct and kill seems to have been to control and dominate. He wrote extensively about a woman's role, the superiority of the male gender, and how women had begun to challenge the natural order. He believed he was doing these women a great service, helping them atone for their sins, so to speak. There was a mission statement about showing women their proper role and fulfilling their duties here on earth as subservient to men. If his daughter, who'd previously obeyed his every word, began to rebel against that, he may have felt out of control. The abductions could have been his way of regaining that control. We think he escalated to abducting pairs to heighten that level of dominance. With more risk comes more reward.'

'It makes sense,' Cris replied, glancing at me. 'His mother, Dorina, was incredibly strict, and from what my dad and Frank told me, she pretty much controlled our father. Frank hated that. He told me that his mother had gone against God's will, that she should have served our father rather than the other way around. Instead of bending to his mother's will, it sparked a rage in him. I felt it every time he talked about her but I just assumed she must have been abusive. He told me once that his mother had forced him to kneel on a bed of pebbles in a dark corner of the basement as punishment whenever he misbehaved.'

He shook his head, looking down at the table. I

stiffened, remembering the way the women's bodies had been found folded over on pebbles in the bins when Frank had discarded them. The dots all started to connect. I looked up at the agents and saw them sharing a meaningful look as well, as if to say, 'Aha. Another answer to the twisted puzzle.' Hannigan made a note on the pad in front of him but remained silent. I turned my attention back to Cris, hungry to know more now that the veil had been lifted.

'From what you've told me about Rodrigo and your mom's relationship, it seems like Frank must have gotten the idea from him that men should control women. Because it doesn't sound like Dorina believed that,' I said, shaking the disturbing visual of the bodies from my head.

Cris nodded, thinking. 'The Dominio side *was* very strict about gender roles. The women were the caregivers and the men were head of the household.'

'But that was pretty standard during that time, no?' I asked.

'Yes and no. My mom, while more compliant to Rodrigo's will than it seemed Dorina was, still stuck up for me and pushed back when she saw fit. So, it wasn't the complete domination that Frank seemed to idolize.' Cris shrugged. 'But I know my dad was raised in a very different environment. The men dictated when and what the family ate, how the children were raised, and if punishment was doled out, it was always given by them, not the women. Once Dorina passed away, Frank and our dad developed an incredibly close relationship, like a club that I never quite became a part of. I overheard him say to Frank one time that a wife's role should be as a servant to her husband, rather than a partner.'

'Servant? That seems extreme,' I replied, hanging onto his every word.

'When I was growing up I didn't think much about it, but now looking back in this day and age, I guess it was quite extreme.'

He paused, taking a sip of water from the glass in front of him before setting it back down, adjusting its position so that it was lined up perfectly with the glasses on either side. Now that I knew my uncle wasn't the killer, his quirks seemed less ominous, although I couldn't help but mentally relate it to Frank's dark obsessive behaviors. I hoped that in time, I wouldn't think of Frank when I looked at him.

Suddenly, the family photos I'd seen of my mother with Frank and Gloria popped into my mind. The studio portrait and Teresa's communion. Through the new lens of who Frank really was, what I'd interpreted as a loving, fatherly gesture, resting his hand on her shoulder, now seemed menacing and controlling. Keeping her and Gloria close and obedient.

Cris continued, 'To be honest, Frank always seemed angry when my mother served our father. At first, I thought it was jealousy, but now I don't think so.'

'Angry? Wouldn't your mother serving your father fit into his ideology?' Beck asked.

'I think he was angry that his own mother hadn't been subservient to our father, and my mother's loving relationship with me and my dad probably just emphasized that difference to him.' Cris looked over at me. 'He hated Dorina for her punishments most of all. Not only because of how harsh they were but also because he didn't believe she had any right to punish him in the first place. He even told me he believed the reason she'd died so young at age thirty-two was because God had punished her for being an unholy woman.'

I listened with wide eyes, shocked that I was actually related to such a man. 'That's insane.' It was difficult hearing about this outdated ideology my grandfather clearly believed in.

'Everything you said fits with what we've found in the journals. They've been a big help in determining method and motive,' Beck replied.

'But still, if the journals started in 1991 and spanned eight years, that only takes us to 1999?' I countered, my own investigative brain spinning rapidly.

'Yes, as you know, there was a botched attempt in October of 1999. The one time someone got a firsthand look at TSK and gave us a vague description. From his journal that year, he spoke of the failed attempt and wrote about needing to update his methods. Watching them only on weekends when his travel schedule allowed, he theorized, hadn't given him enough information and that is what he believed had caused the failure. This is where it gets interesting,' Hannigan said, a smile on his face.

I glanced at Cris and then back at Hannigan, 'I'm not sure interesting is the right word.'

Hannigan pursed his lips. 'Sorry. Interesting to us from an investigative standpoint,' he replied giving me a wry smile. 'In the box alongside the journals were a number of video tapes and, in later years, DVDs. The videos chronicled the movements inside the homes of all his victims and several other pairs he was contemplating abducting, starting after the failed kidnapping attempt. He kept the same pattern, following two to three pairs of women, then narrowing down to the pair he eventually abducted. But he started using technology so that he could watch them, even when he wasn't in town, and track their whereabouts more precisely.'

'So, he installed cameras in their houses? How was he not caught doing that over so many years?' I asked in disbelief.

'The videos appeared to be shot from somewhere near the television,' Hannigan explained. 'It took us a while to figure it out but after interviewing Zoey and Addie and looking back at the crime scene inventory, we now know that he was sending the pairs fake invitations to become Nielsen households. You know, the Nielsen ratings for television? Well, the normal protocol in most cases, would be a technician coming to set the box up in your house but our victims didn't know that. They were sent a letter with a fifty-dollar bill inside, requesting that they fill out the survey and if accepted, a box would be mailed to them with instructions on how to set it up and they'd receive a monthly stipend for their participation.'

'Wait, are you saying he installed cameras in these boxes and the women set them up themselves? They unknowingly put the cameras in their own living rooms?' Cris's eyes were wide.

'Ingenious actually,' Beck replied. 'The instructions were essentially plugging the box into a power outlet and then connecting the box with the camera to the internet. He could remotely track their movements without them being any the wiser, and no one ever thought to take the box apart and look inside as they looked like standard cable boxes. He wrote all about it in his last journal. He'd taken immense pleasure in the fact that he was able to lure these women into doing his bidding by their own greed, that a measly fifty dollars a month was enough to allow him into their lives.'

'Jesus,' I said under my breath. 'Honestly, these women were college students and they were probably broke. I can't say if Andie and I got that offer that we wouldn't take it too, even now that we're out of college. I know it doesn't seem like much but when you're just barely able to make rent and bills, fifty dollars would seem like a Godsend for doing nothing.'

'Well, that was what he was banking on. And it worked,' Hannigan concluded.

'Wait, there's one thing that doesn't track here. Frank was never good with electronics. I was always better at that and he'd call me over to his house to fix things all the time. I just can't see him having the knowledge to accomplish something like this.'

Hannigan looked long and hard at Cris, and then glanced at Beck. 'There's no way to know since the journals ended after he switched methods but maybe he read a book or looked it up online. It's possible he learned how to do this one thing that he needed to carry out his mission. When a killer like Frank is motivated, they'll go to any length to make sure they're able to keep killing.'

Cris looked unconvinced but didn't say anything. I didn't know Frank to form an opinion on the matter but it seemed possible he had taught himself what to do. He was obviously intelligent if he'd gotten away with murdering women for over forty years.

'What about the photo from the cabin? Do we know who that other young boy is then, since it isn't Cris?' I asked, looking at Hannigan. He pulled the photo out of the file that I had handed over at the scene and placed it on the table.

Cris picked up the photo and squinted at it. 'That's definitely Frank and our father, Rodrigo. Sorry, I don't recognize this other boy. We're talking what? Fifty some odd years ago?' He shrugged. 'My memory isn't that great these days. Maybe one of his friends from the neighborhood. I have no idea.' He looked at the photo again, pulling it closer to his face. 'They're a bit out of focus, and my eyesight isn't too great either. I'm sorry, I really can't make out the boy's features,' he said, before placing the photo back on the table.

Hannigan picked it up. 'Since no one else is mentioned in Frank's manifesto or represented in evidence at the cabin, we are confident that Frank acted alone. Other than the women, only Frank's DNA was found at the scene and Addie and Zoey never saw anyone other than Frank until you rescued them. We'll hold onto this photo in our file but we have no reason to believe the boy in this photo is relevant to the case.'

I nodded, a little bothered that I didn't have the answer to the mysterious boy, even if he wasn't relevant. It seemed I could never turn off my curious brain. Loose ends were my pet peeve.

'Anyway, that's about all we've got so far on his methods,' Hannigan continued, placing the photo back into a folder. 'It's a bit more than what we are releasing to the press but we thought after everything you've both been through, you deserve the whole picture. And Liz, from the entire task force, we want to extend our gratitude for your help in this case. But please, if you ever find yourself in a similar situation again, call law enforcement instead of investigating yourself. Not only do crime scenes need to be preserved to be used in court but you must put your safety first. You were lucky the killer had passed away and you weren't in danger at the cabin.'

'Well, hopefully this is the last evil relative lurking in my family but thank you for holding up your end of the bargain,' I said with an apologetic smile.

We all rose and shook hands. Hannigan promised to let us know of any other major developments. Before I left the room, I turned to face them one more time.

'Wait,' I said. 'What about Addie and Zoey? You said you interviewed them. Are they okay?'

Hannigan gave me a smile, warmer than any I'd received from him since we first met. 'I can't release any medical information to you but physically, they're going to be just fine. It'll take time to heal but they have their whole lives ahead of them, thanks to you.'

I gave him a tearful smile.

'Oh, which reminds me,' Beck said, scrambling to grab a piece of paper and a pen off the table. 'They actually did mention that they'd like to see you, if you feel up to visiting them. Now that they're getting their strength back they want to officially meet the person responsible for saving them. Here.' She scribbled something down on the paper. 'This is the hospital and room number where they're located.'

I nodded, wiping a tear from my cheek as I took the paper, placing it in my purse for safe keeping. 'Thank you, both.'

I walked outside with Cris, both of us silent, trying to process the horrific details we'd heard. When I got to my mom's car, I turned to Cris. He took my hands in his and made direct eye contact, his gaze no longer darting around uncomfortably when he addressed me.

'I hope this doesn't turn you off to our family. Rosie and I would love to continue having you in our lives. Despite Frank, we are good people, I promise.'

Tears sprang to my eyes again. I couldn't remember ever crying as much in my life as I had in the past week. I squeezed his hands back. 'I would love to keep in contact. In fact, my parents would really like to meet you. Maybe you and Rosie could come for dinner at my parents' house next week in New Jersey?' Cris smiled and nodded, tears in his eyes reflecting my own. 'I also wanted to tell you, I was just contacted on 23andMe from someone who I think might be my half-brother on my father's side. It seems like my father may be alive and well, that he got out of the drug scene he and my mother were in all those years ago. So yes, believe it or not, I'm still going to search for family, even after all this,' I said with a short laugh.

'That's great Liz. Really, I'm happy you're finding what you've been looking for.'

'You and Rosie are a big part of that, you know. So, my grandfather was a serial killer,' I winced as I said it and then shrugged, 'but you guys are amazing. I'm lucky to have found you.'

CHAPTER 30

I'd visited Zoey and Addie in the hospital yesterday. The women were doing better, the color had come back to their faces and their eyes were now bright and clear. It was an emotional meeting. They'd asked if they could reach out to me from time to time, feeling an indescribable bond, and I'd agreed that they could before parting ways to let them rest.

A tinkling bell raced down the hallway, bringing me back to the present. I looked down and spotted my new cat. Someone had left a carrier with a young female black and white tuxedo cat outside the front door to Cris's veterinary practice. They had been fostering her when Andie, Travis and I had gone up this past weekend. After telling Travis about Cris's adorable foster dog, Harley, he had requested with gusto to go and meet him. Travis was interested in adopting him since he was allowed dogs in his apartment building, especially now that we didn't need him to stay with us twenty-four-seven for safety.

When we'd all got to Cris and Rosie's, I'd never

expected we'd also be leaving with a cat. I hadn't even thought about having a pet since both Andie and I were so busy, but the cat had taken an immediate liking to me. She'd rubbed up against my leg and planted herself in my lap for over an hour. Andie had been captivated and begged me to take her home. Between Andie's relentless pleading and the cat's cuteness, I couldn't resist. Harley won Travis over within the first hour of our visit and he brought him home, too, so I still got to snuggle Harley whenever we all hung out.

I picked up my cat and rubbed my finger over the name tag that was engraved with her new name: Teresa. I wasn't entirely sure why I'd named her after my biological mother but it had felt right, it had felt like a connection to this new part of my life. While Teresa snuggled into my lap, my phone dinged with a text from Andie. 'OMG yaaaas, check this out!' Underneath was a link to an article in *The New York Times*. Andie had been a whirlwind of support since I'd returned home. She listened with wide eyes as I told her everything we'd learned from the FBI agents, then in true Andie fashion, she dragged me to The Beast and bought me drinks to take my mind off it all. The weirdness over the adoption day photo was long forgotten.

I clicked on the link and started reading. The article was about a bill that was making its way through New York State legislature. The bill, if passed into law in 2020, which seemed likely, would allow adopted adults unrestricted access to their original birth certificates. I knew it wouldn't tell me anything that I didn't already know but I still wanted my original birth certificate. It was a part of me, a part of my journey. Relief and joy simultaneously washed over me that soon myself and others like me would have access to this important piece of our history, our existence.

My phone went off again with another text, but this time, from Mickey. 'Hey Liz, the bar's pretty dead right now, are you still coming over?'

I smiled, tapping out my reply. 'On my way!'

Gently putting Teresa on the floor, I packed up my laptop and notebook and made a dash for the door. As I walked the short distance to The Beast, I thought back to the drastic turn my life had taken over the last few weeks. Beyond finding out the truth about the dark spot in my family tree and rescuing Addie and Zoey, my personal life had morphed into something I wouldn't have expected just a few months ago.

When Andie had first dragged me to The Beast upon my return, I couldn't take my eyes off Mickey. Sure, we'd bonded over our family dramas recently, but now, with the weight of my family secret lifted from my shoulders, I noticed the way his eyes crinkled as he laughed. The way he truly listened to every word I spoke. The way the room felt electric every time I got close to him. At first, I'd chalked it up to a crush on the guy who I'd opened up to, figuring he didn't feel the same. As a skilled bartender, being attentive to anyone who walked in the door was a part of the trade. But then I went back to the bar a few times while Andie was at work, and before I knew it, I leaned across the bar and kissed him. I still don't know what came over me that night. The old Liz would never have been so bold. But this new Liz? *I guess she is*. And that was that. I'd somehow stumbled into a relationship. Of course, my mother was ecstatic.

I entered the empty bar, a smile lighting up my face when I saw him standing there, polishing a glass.

Butterflies still fluttered around my stomach when I saw him. He returned my smile, coming out from around the bar to greet me with a kiss.

'Hey, you,' he said, enveloping me in a warm embrace. 'Bring your article to work on today?'

'Yes,' I replied as I pulled back, patting my bag with my hand. 'I'm close to finishing, just double checking some things before I send it to Beccah.'

'Here, grab a seat and I'll make you a drink. What are you feeling today?'

'Something smokey,' I said, and he laughed. Whenever I came to the bar now, he would ask what kind of mood I was in and then concoct a craft cocktail to match it.

Settling myself into my usual seat at the bar, I set up my laptop and grabbed my notebook. I pulled the taped photo off the inside front cover, attaching it to the top corner of my laptop screen. My extra motivation.

'Did you find anything out about him yet?' Mickey asked as he gathered my drink ingredients.

'No, not yet,' I said, looking at the photo staring back at me.

Once the dust settled, I'd reached out to Hannigan and asked him for a copy of the photo I'd found in the cabin with the mystery boy. While they'd said it meant nothing, something inside me couldn't rest until I knew who that boy was. Maybe he was just a friend but he'd known Frank before Frank turned into the monster he later became. I had to know his story.

'You'll find him,' Mickey said. 'If there's one thing I know about you by now, babe, it's that you don't stop till you find what you're looking for.'

I laughed at this understatement and opened up the Word document still minimized on my screen. Beccah had reached out to me when the news of rescuing Addie and Zoey broke, eager to get some color for her newest investigative piece she was writing on the truth behind TSK's identity. Promising to leave me unnamed for the time being, we met up for coffee. She was beautiful, with her black braided hair and warm, radiant skin. She exuded power and confidence.

Our conversation had taken a turn that I could only have dreamed of. She told me I should write my own story and kick off the journalistic career I'd always hoped for. At first, I wasn't sure I wanted the notoriety that would come from being named as the infamous relative whose DNA helped capture TSK. But Beccah made me see the side of the story that his crimes had overshadowed: the human side. Never mind the fact that my story, she'd said, would sell itself if I wanted to break into a career like hers. After that, things happened fast. She became my writing mentor, connecting me with a friend of hers at *New York Times Magazine*. I'd been barely two sentences into my pitch when they'd made me an offer to publish my story.

The gentle tap of glass on wood pulled me from my thoughts as Mickey set the drink down in front of me. I'd been so distracted, I hadn't even noticed him torching the wood, my favorite part. I reached forward and gave his hand a quick squeeze before turning my attention back to my screen. I scrolled down to the end of my piece, wanting to read over it one last time before I sent it off to Beccah for feedback. My deadline to turn it in was just a few days away. The focus of my article had been the impact my innocent venture into 23andMe had on my life, and how my journey to discover TSK's identity had changed my path forever. It was the most personal writing I'd ever done. As I got to the end, a swell of pride washed over me.

'All the women my grandfather had taken and killed were a part of me now. They came to me in dreams, they whispered their names in my ear, their faces passed through my mind every day. I felt them around me and sometimes I even felt my mother with them, keeping them safe, keeping Frank Dominio's spirit at bay. I was connected to these women by a tragic web woven by a man I'd never met, all because I'd done a DNA kit. They were part of my story now. The 25 and me.'

EPILOGUE

The wooden walls were rotted in spots and the cement floor of the basement had a river of cracks flowing across it. None of that really bothered Jack though. It was still his special space. He kept it locked, away from the prying eyes of his wife who was never permitted to enter. She thought of it as his mancave, a place he tinkered with tools and cleared his mind after a long day; somewhere she had no purpose or desire in being. She also knew that if he told her to stay out, she must obey. On the wall in front of him, a framed black and white photo of Rodrigo, Frank and himself standing in front of the cabin holding fishing poles stared back at him. How he missed Rodrigo, and now Frank. Jack reached out, delicately dragging his arthritic fingers across its shiny, faded surface.

Rodrigo had shown him how to fish when his own father drank himself into oblivion every day. Rodrigo had been there to comfort him when he'd accidentally seen his parents having sex one night and had been left lost and confused at the complicated barrage of emotions it whipped up in him. He'd felt great shame until Rodrigo told him it was natural, that he had nothing to feel guilty about in witnessing the act or in the way it made him feel. It was then, at age seven, that Rodrigo told him the truth of his secret birth. It was the best day of his life, the day he learned who he really was. Rodrigo had had an affair with his mom that lasted less than a year and ended when his first wife, Dorina, died. Shortly after, his mother realized that not only was she pregnant, but that the baby was Rodrigo's, not the man she'd married who drank so heavily each night he'd never remember that they hadn't slept together in months.

Rodrigo told him it was best that no one knew his real father lived just down the street, and Jack should go on living as he always had. And since Jack and Frank were already such good friends from their fishing trips, Rodrigo had brought Frank in on their secret. They had always made Jack feel like a Dominio. Cris, however, had been left in the dark. Rodrigo said he wasn't like them and wouldn't understand. Jack didn't mind, he had never gotten close with Cris anyway. But he'd been so excited to have Frank as his new half-brother, even if no one knew but them. And since he'd inherited his mom's aquiline features and lighter skin tone, no one ever suspected. Having a secret this big with people he looked up to made him feel special. But what he'd loved most was that the drunk who had raised him, who was listed on his birth certificate, was not his real father. Rodrigo treated him as a real son for the most part, having him over on a regular basis to hang out with Frank, even if he did have to sleep in the house down the block every night. But Rodrigo had taken him under his wing. He and Rodrigo, along with Frank, became close and were together more often than not.

Rodrigo had also told him, at age eleven, that it was normal curiosity when he'd been caught peeping through windows. He'd watched his neighbor shower and a classmate change her clothing; nothing too depraved. Someone eventually called the police on him and his dad had given him a black eye for his actions. The shame he'd felt had been overwhelming. But Rodrigo had convinced him that his desire to watch was something he was entitled to, that women were there solely to serve and arouse. He'd also been lucky to have Frank, an older brother he could share deviant thoughts with. Frank's intensity had scared him at times, but it had also comforted him. He'd felt a kinship from the very beginning. Even if their desires were different, their objective was the same: ridding the world of women who didn't fulfill their proper role in society. Frank always wanted to be hands-on, whereas Jack preferred to watch from the sidelines. This, of course, made them the perfect match.

Jack scanned over the rest of the photos lining the wall, spanning the years. His favorite one was of him and Frank after the first abduction he'd helped with. Frank had come to him and confessed what he'd been doing. He'd opened up about his failed kidnapping attempt and asked for help. Frank knew that he was smart, good with technology and that times were changing. His methods also needed to change. So, like a good brother, he'd done his part, coming up with and facilitating an idea that even he had to admit, was so clever they probably never would have figured it out if Frank hadn't kept all those damned tapes and DVDs. The excitement they'd both felt when the women actually plugged in the fake Neilson boxes and transmitted images into his basement was clear on their faces in the photo. They'd been so triumphant that day. Frank hadn't been interested in watching beyond tracking the women's movements, but for him, being able to watch the pairs, even those who weren't selected, gave him a continued source of exhilaration.

The rest of the photos on the wall showed each new celebration, each new accomplishment, every step of progress in their mission. The last photo was of them just days after number 22 and 23's bodies were discovered, and the police still had no leads. Frank's huge smile tugged at Jack's heart. He missed his brother. He was sad he wouldn't be adding more photos of the two of them to the wall. Next to the photos, in a large gilded frame, was their mission statement – their manifesto – printed on the best paper he could find. He read the words every day, words passed down to them from Rodrigo like a mantra.

'Emmy, I just heard about a party tonight at the Kappa Sigma house. Wanna go? I think Mason is going to be there.'

The conversation coming from the large monitor mounted on the wall alongside the framed manifesto drew his attention back to the screen. Allie, the blonde who had spoken, pulled her sweatshirt over her head. He glimpsed the bottom curve of her bra for a split second, the shirt came up so high. His breath quickened. But she pulled it down before he saw much of anything. He could watch these women for hours, the anticipation of what he might see next surging his desire.

The day Frank told him about the abductions had been the second-best day of his life. It hadn't just been *him* indulging in deviant behavior, Frank had been too. As an adult, Jack had only been caught peeping into women's bedrooms once. But even then, he'd escaped arrest by darting into an alleyway and sprinting home before the police arrived. He'd since found other ways to watch. He was too smart to be caught. Frank had thought so too. But he'd been wrong. The FBI figured out that it was Frank because he'd used too many things that could be traced back to him. The pebbles in the bins, for instance. Frank had told him and Cris about Dorina making him kneel on pebbles as punishment. And he'd shown both of them how to tie the bowline knot. Who knew how many other people he told about those things? Frank had always been a popular guy.

He'd warned Frank not to use that knot and to stop using the pebbles. But Frank had been adamant that they'd never find him, that he couldn't change his technique. It gave him too much satisfaction. And then, Frank had been stupid enough to detail everything in his journals, giving it all away. He was lucky Frank had not continued the journals after they started filming the girls. It saved *him* from being outed in the process. The rush of getting away with this for so long had blinded Frank to his mistakes. Which was why Frank had ignored Jack's warning and taken the last two girls anyway. Frank had wanted to carry out their mission one final time before he died. Jack had been right to be concerned about Frank making a blunder in his diminished state. He'd dropped that damn needle, ruining the protection that going outside their normal hunting ground had granted them. Of course, they'd been able to pin it on Frank. He'd been too arrogant. But they still didn't know about *him*. Because he'd left no traces, he'd made no mistakes. He was a ghost; he didn't exist in their minds.

In the early days, he'd only spoken with Frank in

person, usually in this basement. But in later years, they'd both had burner phones. Frank had hidden his behind a loose brick in his basement. Jack had gone there the day after he heard about Frank's passing, sneaking in after midnight, and taking the phone so no one could find it. He'd given it to his grandson, Tyler. It felt right to carry on the tradition this way for Frank. His own phone was in his locked safe in this room, where only he knew the combination.

All the same, he'd needed to update his methods. The Neilsen box would no longer work. Women would be on guard now. But he'd encouraged his grandson to follow in the footsteps of his most useful hobby. Technology. Tyler had started his career as a cable engineer six months ago. It was the perfect ruse to continue installing Jack's precious cameras. Tyler had been successful in installing not one, but three cameras in Emmy and Allie's apartment.

He watched as the women discussed their plans for that night with his arm around his grandson next to him. When Tyler was twelve and was caught stealing panties from houses in the neighborhood, the whole family had been shocked and disappointed. But not him. He'd been excited and intrigued. *Had his own desires filtered down the line?* Jack had shown Tyler that his desires were not wrong, not something to be suppressed, but something to be nourished. When he'd shown him one of the live feeds, he'd recognized the hunger on Tyler's face, the excitement that trembled through his fingers. And now that Frank was gone, Tyler would continue for them.

Jack rose and walked over to his work desk with wires and knobs littering the surface. Picking up the letter that

Frank had mailed him right before he died, he traced his wrinkled fingertips across the shaky black ink that was etched into the page by Frank's own hand.

Here's the key. You know what to do.

It'd been a year since they'd found 24 & 25 in the cabin. All the hubbub had died down, the papers had moved onto other crimes, other murders. Soon it would be time to use the key. He'd come up with a new process, something the police would never be able to connect to The Tri-State Killer. And why would they? The Tri-State Killer was dead. Emmy and Allie were the ones, he and Tyler had decided. They had watched them both go on dates with various men over the past three months; they were clearly not chaste or demure. Definitely not obedient. He and Tyler would soon show them how to repent. It would be their final life lesson.

He turned to Tyler and smiled. 'Let's get started.'

Acknowledgements

From Steph and Nicole:

We are so thankful that our editor at Avon Books, Tilda McDonald, found us on Twitter during #PitMad. Sorting through the seemingly endless number of elevator pitch tweets, she managed to find our book and it has been nothing but a wonderful partnership ever since. From the first meeting, Tilda not only shared our love for true crime, but also the vision for our book and our careers. We can't thank you enough for all the time and dedication you've given to us and our novel. Everyone at Avon and HarperCollins have been supportive and encouraging as we've waded through this process. We couldn't ask for a better publishing team.

We'd also like to thank Ania Skurczynska, our amazing contract lawyer who negotiated our contract on our behalf, and always kept our best interests at heart. We couldn't have done this without you and are grateful for your encouragement.

Lastly, there are several experts who were generous with

their time and knowledge who've helped make this book possible. Jessica Battaglia, as always, you are a wealth of information on the scientific side. Every question we've thrown at you was answered thoroughly and quickly, even if you didn't know the answer, you made it a priority to find out through your network of experts. We especially want to thank FBI agent Jeffrey Heinze. Your insight was invaluable in rounding out our characters and our serial killer investigation. We are forever indebted to you for taking the time to answer all our questions. And finally, Kim Cairelle Perilloux, Genealogist extraordinaire, we messaged several Genealogists and you were the only one willing to share your knowledge and help us through the tangled web that is genealogy. You were incredibly generous with your time and we can't thank you enough.

From Steph:

To my fearless co-author, mentor, and friend, Nicole. To say this book wouldn't have been possible without you is an understatement. Thank you for your unwavering support of my dreams, for continuously throwing plot ideas at me, and for always having an open mind when we have to make decisions. I am forever grateful for your encouragement of my writing and for your trust in me to help bring our ideas to life. I never could have imagined that getting hired on the same day as photo editors in 2012, would lead to a life-long friendship and partnership as a crime fiction writing duo. Thank you for always answering my FaceTime even when it's about an insignificant plot point or word that I'm overanalyzing, and for consistently spending over 5 hours straight staring at my face on Zoom calls. Your dedication to brainstorming, research, and always squeezing in one more read-through, has been invaluable to our success. From sitting across from you on a couch for an entire day outlining this story, to the following year spent bringing it to life through our long-distance relationship, I couldn't have asked for a better partner. I can't wait to see what other twisty stories we come up with together.

I want to thank my wonderful, selfless beta readers and friends who made this book better with each comment. Lauren Totten, Megan Hilbert, and Jessie Kerr, thank you for your honest feedback and your support. The evolvement of our characters and all the twists and turns would not have been possible without your honesty, ideas, and encouragement. Megan, I'm so especially grateful for your friendship of over a decade, continuing to be my biggest cheerleader through the ups and downs.

To my Tbooz: Lilli Winn, Darí Brooks Ahye, Amanda Mulligan, Lauren Totten, and Elisabeth Barker. I am so lucky to be surrounded by a squad of such intelligent and loving women. Thank you for your enthusiastic support on this journey and for your friendship. And to Sara McCarthy, who has continuously showed up to celebrate the wins and help navigate the losses, I am so grateful for your continued love and for your friendship that has always felt more like being family.

To my husband Danny Mullin. Thank you for loving me and believing in me as I navigated taking on a second career as an author. The long days, nights, and weekends spent glued to a computer screen were made so much easier by your continued affection, bringing me food, cleaning up around the house, and cheering me on. You've continued to be my best friend and other half, and I'm so grateful to have you by my side on this journey.

And last but not least, thank you to my family. To my mom and dad, Ann and Dave Durso, for the unwavering love and support you've given me since day one. You have always encouraged me to go after my dreams and pursue my passions, and for that I can never fully repay you. Where I am today would not have been possible without your selflessness and the opportunities you've given me. To Katie and William Bagdorf, and Chris and Kim Durso, thank you for being such supportive and loving siblings. I know I can always count on you to cheer me on in the good times and cheer me up when things get hard. And thank you to the Mullins, my second family, who welcomed me with open arms when I married Danny and have continued to help celebrate me and my successes. I am so appreciative of your love and enthusiasm.

From Nicole:

To my amazing co-author, Steph. From the moment I called you that one fateful night in 2019 and said, 'Something about 23andMe. Go!' you were completely on board. Even though we both had solo projects we were working on, thank you for seeing the potential in this idea, putting your own project aside and becoming just as engrossed as I was. We put our collective foot on the gas and did not let up until we had a finished manuscript two months later. I can't thank you enough for running with the idea and working tirelessly alongside me. This book would not exist if it weren't for you hopping on a call every hour and talking through plot points and character profiles. Thank you for listening to all my crazy ideas, jumping on the ones that actually worked, and delicately letting me know which ones didn't. Thank you for working from morning till night, side by side on our couches and later on Zoom calls. When we met at Travelzoo in 2012 as co-workers, I never would have imagined that our shared passion for true crime would lead to us collaborating on crime novels, but I am so happy that it did. I am grateful every day that we found our way to becoming co-authors. I couldn't ask for a better partner in this journey. I look forward to a long career with you by my side.

I want to thank my amazing and selfless beta readers, Deborah Kriger, Sarah Sanchez and Karen Chesley. Your insight has helped in so many ways. I appreciate you taking the time to give detailed notes, chapter by chapter, and letting us bounce ideas off you. The courses our characters took were heavily influenced by your feedback and I am so grateful to have such willing and shrewd readers.

To my dog park cohorts, Min Chen, Lori Janowski, Melissa Raymond, Bill McDonald, The Genriches, and The Powells, thank you for all the support and encouragement. From the minute I started writing my debut novel years ago, you have been nothing but amazing. You all have become my New York family. I appreciate you celebrating every step of my writing journey with me and I cannot imagine going through this without such an incredible support group.

To the photography department at my day job, thank you for always being supportive and celebrating each win with me. Our group is so unique and is really more like a family. I'm grateful to be surrounded by creative people who inspire me every day.

And finally, to my family. Mom and Dad, not only do I thank you for giving me a wonderful childhood, but also for your full support along this journey. Never once did you doubt I could do it. You've pushed me and celebrated my successes as though they were your own. I feel lucky to have you as parents. To my niece Julia, thank you for listening to my ideas, watching countless horror movies with me and picking up the slack with our animals when my eyes were glued to my computer screen. To my nephew Johnny, thank you for sharing my awards and reviews constantly on your own social media pages and for your words of excitement and support. I am so grateful to be surrounded by a loving and encouraging family.